A Novel

Elwood Reid

DOUBLEDAY

New York London Toronto Sydney Auckland

PUBLISHED BY DOUBLEDAY

a division of Random House, Inc.

DOUBLEDAY and the portrayal of an anchor with a dolphin are registered
trademarks of Random House, Inc.

Yes, a man calling himself Dan Cooper jumped out of a plane with $200,000
after holding the crew hostage. That much is true. The rest is purely fictional,
including depictions of the flight crew and FBI agents who worked the Cooper
case. As for Cooper's imagined escape and subsequent odyssey, that too is fiction,
but open to correction should Cooper want to contact the author.

Book design by Chris Welch

Library of Congress Cataloging-in-Publication Data

Reid, Elwood.

D.B. : a novel / Elwood Reid.—1st ed.

p. cm.

1. Cooper, D. B.—Fiction. 2. Hijacking of aircraft—Fiction. 3. Fugitives from
justice—Fiction. 4. Americans—Mexico—Fiction. 5. Detectives—Fiction.
6. Retirees—Fiction. 7. Mexico—Fiction. I. Title.

PS3568.E47637D3 2004

813'.54—dc21

2003055180

ISBN 0-385-49738-5

PRINTED IN THE UNITED STATES OF AMERICA

June 2004

First Edition

1 3 5 7 9 10 8 6 4 2

For the ladies, Nina, Sophia, and Lilliya. And for
Bill Thomas, editorial son of a bitch,
whose input made this a better book.

Maintain character. . . . If you whore, all ideas change.

—from James Boswell's journals

What Happened

November 24, 1971

A s the 727 taxied down the rain-damp runway of Portland International, the man in 18C stubbed out his third unfiltered Raleigh and passed a note to the stewardess, a honey blonde named Susan who'd strapped herself into the vacant seat across the aisle.

Anticipating another clumsy come-on, she quickly covered her name tag and took the note, flashing him a polite drop-dead-creep smile. Phone numbers scribbled on the back of business cards, inappropriate comments about her legs, and men ordering Dewar's, splash of soda, without once looking up from her breasts were occupational hazards she'd long since learned to fend off with a diverse arsenal of bitchy half smiles, beverage choice queries, and requests to buckle up and take seats during turbulence. She figured that as soon as the plane hit cruising altitude and she went to roll the drink cart down the aisle she'd just toss the unread note into the trash. But when she examined the intricately folded note and felt its moist edges she knew she had to open it and see what was inside, maybe share the contents with her fellow stewardesses.

It read: I have a bomb in my briefcase and I am prepared to use it.

Her hands shook. She read it again, the words popping inside her brain like tiny mushroom clouds: *I have a bomb in my briefcase and I am prepared to use it.*

She took another look at the man, sitting cool like Robert Mitchum under a haze of cigarette smoke, Ray-Ban Wayfarers parked on his narrow face. He had on a dark suit and a skinny black tie he'd wrestled into a full Windsor and jabbed with a pearl stickpin. His hair was perfect and for the moment his name was Cooper, Dan Cooper, to be exact.

Susan gathered up the gold cross that hung around her neck on a chain and pressed the cool metal to her chapped lips to stop her hands from shaking. For a brief moment her thoughts drifted to her fiancé, a pipe fitter from Tacoma who'd been after her to quit the airline.

"Do you understand?" Cooper asked, giving her twin reflections of her own terrified eyes in his mirror shades.

She nodded and, like Dorothy in some terrible Oz, tapped gold to enamel three times, hoping for some magic to pull her out of this bad dream. Only nothing happened and she let the cross drop.

"Good," he said, sitting back and stroking the briefcase on his lap. It occurred to him that there would be no going back, that this aluminum tube with wings slicing through the clouds and mist might be the last thing he saw. And so he sucked in the stale cabin air and lamped the neat rows of seats through the twilight of his shades, taking in the dozens of heads G-forced back and tenderly exposed above the seat cushions like eggs in a carton. The cabin filled with the mindless chatter of people on their way to Seattle anxiously putting words and smoke into the stale air in the hope that it would somehow negate the nagging possibility of a crash or some other disaster—say a duck sucked into the engine or pilot error. He sat, watching and listening to the nervous fraternity of lonely passengers filling the empty space with the ordinary laundry of their lives—the kids away at college, Maytags, the new lettuce diet, the lonely guy at the office who finally got his ashes hauled, Vietnam, breast cancer, Nixon and China, how the new Buicks don't hold a candle against the old Buicks, Muhammad Ali, orthodontia, coffee stains on the stove top, church bake sales, that *Jonathan Livingston Seagull* book, tax deductions, beer cans left to ring end tables in familiar patterns, heart disease, tax shelters, cheap weekend getaways, Idi Amin, college tuition, gas bills, Evonne Goolagong, UFOs, electric crockpots, lumbago, the wife and kids, and what exactly that song "American Pie" was all about.

As the strange swoon of gravity denied sent a hush through the cabin, Cooper decided to twist the fear blade a little deeper and so he tapped the stewardess on the arm and opened the briefcase. "See," he said, holding two stripped wires. "I touch these and the shit hits the fan, honey." The plane skipped and his hands swayed inside the briefcase, the wires almost touching as he eased the lid down.

"I understand," she mumbled.

"Now I want you to write down what I say and trot it up to the captain so we can get this thing started."

Her hands trembled as she pulled a pen and drink napkin from her apron and readied herself.

"Okay," he said. "Now here's what I want. Two hundred thousand in used bills and I want 'em in a knapsack. Two back parachutes, two chest parachutes. After we refuel, passengers go free. No police. Oh, and say takeoff from Seattle by five. You got all that? Good. Now nod that pretty little head of yours and gimme some smile."

When she'd finished scribbling the message down she nodded, unbuckled, and stood unsteadily, quickly looking around to see if any nearby passengers had heard them. They had not. She was all alone, with the blooming dread of what the man had just so calmly dictated to her. And then there was the note, *I have a bomb in my briefcase and I am prepared to use it.*

"Go on," he said. "Hustle up there and bring the note back. I need it for my archives. But first I want you to bring me a highball, plenty of ice."

She lingered a minute, gawking at him, waiting for some cruel punch line or smile. But none came. He wanted a drink. He had a bomb.

Cooper stared right back, thinking: Boom motherfuckin' boom! He'd always been good at tough thoughts and it worked, because she brought him a highball and then made her way toward the cockpit, rushing past the unsuspecting passengers as the plane punctured the clouds on its way to Seattle.

From his smoky perch in the back of the plane Cooper sipped his drink and got into character, trying to imagine them all dead and scattered into the air, bits and pieces of them seeding clouds, raining down like fertilizer.

BEFORE: THE NAME he'd given at the ticket counter was Dan Cooper. It was not his real name, nor was it his first choice. He'd briefly toyed with Rip or Quint but ruled them out as too memorable, settling finally on Dan Cooper; a name with just the right amount of generic menace. Dan Cooper sounded like the sort of guy who might hijack a plane the day before Thanksgiving and Dan Cooper would have a bomb and he would ask for money and they would give it to him, because on this gray day the man seated in seat 18C calling himself Dan Cooper did not give a shit if he lived or died. He was tired of mediocrity and the long flat road that his life seemed to be speeding down and he had arrived at this plan, as a drowning man flails for a towrope across riptide and chop. The plan was pure, a thing to hone and polish and stick to if deliverance was to be granted, and the minute he'd stepped onto the plane and spotted the unoccupied backseat, he'd steeled himself for the worst that could happen, be it crash or cowardice on his part. That there would be no future for him or anybody else on the plane—no Thanksgiving Day turkey, creamed peas, oyster stew, or ginned-up relatives sleeping in recliners—was of no consequence. Dan Cooper was getting the hell out. End of story or maybe the beginning, depending on how things sorted out.

In the cockpit Susan relayed the message, her voice cracking with every bump and bang of the fuselage as Captain Yount instructed her to look for a gun and note the hijacker's demeanor. "Can you do that for me, Susan? I need you to be my eyes and ears, size him up. We need to know what kind of maniac we're dealing with here." She nodded, taking comfort in Captain Yount's square-jawed calm as he said, "Be brave, Susan."

She exited the cockpit and noticed that her knees had stopped quivering and that she was able to meet the passengers' curious stares. But as she neared the back of the plane and saw Cooper waiting for her, hands resting on the briefcase, she felt her heart surge into her throat.

"Are we on?" he asked.

"Yes."

He plucked the note from her fingers and dropped it into the watery remains of his highball, stirring until it became mush. "No funny stuff this way," he said, lighting another cigarette.

He knew he had to scare her and so he opened the case and gave her another brief snatch of the coiled wires and batteries and dynamite-looking cylinders strapped inside. "Hell in a box," he said, still with the crooked grin. He pointed at the seat next to him, motioning her to sit as the engines strained, blanketing the cabin with their drone.

She sat.

And Cooper knew he had her and that his plan would work—it would all work. He would get the money and parachutes and he would disappear. It would be his grand gesture, the last great thing. He pushed up his shirtsleeve and read the rules he'd ballpointed across his wrist.

Be cool.

No guns.

Don't take any shit.

So far so good. The plane continued to climb momentarily over the storm clouds, the cabin filling with bright bars of light. A silver-haired man three rows up turned to have a look around. His face was toppled with sun, maybe too much booze, and he was sweating, his tie jerked down, generous thighs squeezed into navy slacks. Cooper nodded and the man rolled his eyes and shrugged as if to say he was just getting by and that it was enough that he rose every day to answer the bell, kick back the stool, and tap gloves with what he called his life.

Susan rose and Cooper turned on her. "Where do you think you're going?" he said.

She pointed at his glass. "You want another drink, right?"

"Exactly."

A minute later she returned with another highball and tried to see if he had a gun in his coat or a wedding band on his finger—some telling detail she could report back to Captain Yount about—but her eyes kept returning to the briefcase.

"Tell you what," he said, lowering his shades. "Trot back up there and tell Captain America I'm not foolin' around here. Tell him we're not landing until the money and chutes are ready. And remember, any funny stuff and we all go to pieces together."

She nodded and again made the trip to the cockpit, pausing every other aisle to stare into the pool of each passenger's lap as she tried to get a handle on the situation and the possibility that they might all be blown and scattered in the wind. Instead she focused on the little things—pilled seat arms, magazines sliding under seats, and the incredible dandruff of the man in 7B.

Captain Yount was on the radio when she entered the cockpit, his brow now damp with sweat, the copilot too focused on the controls and gauges. Captain Yount told Susan to stay calm, they were doing everything they could to meet the hijacker's demands.

She hurried back and approached Cooper, mustering all her poise only to see it crumble when he looked up at her.

"Well?" Cooper said. "Did they say how long?"

"He wants you to know that we're doing all we can to make this happen," she said. "He doesn't want anybody to get hurt."

"That dog don't hunt, sweetcakes. I want my demands met sooner rather than later." He pinched the Raleigh dead, dropped it into the ashtray, and pulled another from the pack. He motioned for her to light it, saying, "Now, how about giving me some fire."

She did. Their fingers brushed as she whipped the match away, snapping it with a practiced snap of the wrist.

He took a long pull, let his face leak fresh smoke, and said, "I sure hope we don't have a hero behind the controls."

Susan told him Captain Yount was a good man who was just trying to do his job.

He pointed for her to sit again.

Two hours later, after circling in a holding pattern, the plane landed in Seattle and taxied down a runway lined with waiting vans, fuel trucks, and luggage tractors. He saw sharpshooters crouched along the terminal roof like bland gargoyles, breathing in between heartbeats, and inside the terminal stood men Cooper figured to be FBI agents, their faces pressed against the aluminum-frame windows, fogging the glass.

After a delay a courier car containing the requested chutes and cash approached the aircraft. As instructed, Susan met the car and transferred the chutes and bag of money, dragging them past the rows of nervous passengers to the back of the plane, where the man in the black suit and Wayfarer shades sat holding his wires, waiting.

"Good work," Cooper said as Susan dropped the chutes and sack of money. He inspected the chutes quickly and then snapped open the sack and allowed himself a moment of pure gloat as he fingered a brick of twenty-dollar bills. "Okay," he said, pointing at his fellow passengers. "Get them out of here."

Susan nodded and went to the cockpit. Minutes later Captain Yount came on the PA system and instructed the passengers to begin deplaning, his voice cool and reassuring.

They rose like churchgoers popping up from pews at the first organ blast of the doxology, clutching at coats, purses, and attaché cases, a few glancing at the man in the back with puzzled expressions and the dim awareness that something bad had happened or was still happening or was about to happen. But as the people in the front of the plane began draining out the door, down the steps, and onto the tarmac, squinting into the lights, even the rubberneckers were pulled out into the damp night as a stewardess wished each of them a happy Thanksgiving. And like that they were gone, leaving the cabin and crew to Cooper and the next phase of his plan.

When the hatch closed and the fuel truck backed away, Cooper gave Susan instructions to relay to the pilot, telling him to chart a course for Mexico City. She looked up and down the empty rows of seats and the small litter of departed passengers before pulling her eyes back to Cooper. "Mexico City's nice," she said. "It's warm and . . ."

"Goddamn right it's warm," he said. "And it's not here." He pointed out the window.

"But why?"

He grinned. "I like that," he said, tapping the briefcase. "Not too scared to ask questions."

She frowned, her chin no longer shaking, eyes dim and red. She gave him a tiny nod and he went on. "Now here's how we're gonna do this. I wanna go low—ten thousand feet, no more, no less. I want the flaps at fifteen degrees—fifteen degrees or, hell, I don't need to tell you what's gonna happen." He pointed at the briefcase, made a little boom sound. "Then I want you back here with me for takeoff. Okay?"

She whispered okay and trotted toward the cockpit, stopping to whisper to the dark-haired flight attendant before parting the first-class curtain and disappearing.

Cooper turned his attention to the chutes, spotting the bad one right away. "Fucking amateurs," he said, tearing it out and snipping the cords to bind the money sack to him. The others looked good and the money felt nice and heavy—if not two hundred, then close.

Ten minutes later the jet circled back onto the runway, engines firing. Cooper waved good-bye to the rigidly silhouetted John Q. Law types watching him from inside the bright terminal, their hands on radios, just itching to give shoot orders, the very same men who would be looking for him, scouring the land, crawling through the plane dusting for prints, spitballing possible motives, and interviewing oblivious hostages, sifting for that criminal needle in the haystack. He wished them lots of luck.

When he turned around Susan was standing a couple of yards away, broken and awaiting further instruction.

He pointed. She sat. Then the plane muscled off the ground and began its steep climb as Cooper stared out at the smudgy dark blur of lights.

When they had stopped climbing at ten thousand feet he told Susan that he wanted her to clear out of the cabin and go up front with the other gals. She hesitated, pointing at the briefcase containing the bomb.

"You wanna know how it's going to end?"

She nodded.

"I'm about to find out," Cooper said. "Now trot up there and pull the curtain."

For a moment he considered letting her in on the joke and telling her that the dynamite was really a couple of old road flares strung together with some colorful phone cable and a radio tube he'd pirated from a twenty-inch RCA he'd found abandoned behind his trailer. But he decided not to. It was best to leave her scared and sure of her own heroism as she vanished behind the first-class curtain like a magician's assistant, trembling with anticipation.

For a few long moments he just looked out the window, enjoying the plane minus the passengers as he replayed the dozens of jumps he'd taken over the humid jungles of Vietnam, a world away from the ocean of fir trees, brush-tangled hills, and twisted creeks of Washington that waited, cold, dark, and wet below. Here it was, he thought, one of those moments in life at which you arrive totally unprepared. But his demands had been met and there was the money and all his tough talk and months of planning. Certainly no going back.

It was time to jump.

When he rose and checked the chutes a second time he felt that dead, sapped-out feeling creep into his legs—the one that had enabled him to jump despite the presence of snipers waiting for him under vine-ridden blinds, ready to shoot his heart out expertly. He would be the dangling man all over again, a piece of meat on a string caught between earth and sky, waiting for the kiss of earth or tree. But this time there would be no gunfire, just the long run to the border, where some new life awaited him.

When he went to snap rubber bands over his pant legs and shirt-sleeves he discovered that he'd somehow forgotten to wear the jungle boots he'd bought from the Army surplus store. Instead he had on his house shoes, a thin pair of oxblood penny loafers with bad stitching. He kicked at seat backs, cursing his stupidity, until his toes hurt and he realized that there was no option but to suck it up and soldier on, boots or no boots. So he said fuck it and inventoried his pockets, feeling the reassuring lumps and bulges of the waterproof matches, barlow knife, Hershey bars, compass, waxed twine, aspirin, leather gloves, wool watch cap, and the tin flask of bourbon he'd carried during the war. He went to examine the rear hatch and pressed his face to the tiny window, hoping to see the lights of Merwin Dam or the dull glow of snow on Mount Saint Helens. But there was only gray-black sky—an eternity of it.

He took hold of the red hatch handles and pulled down. A blast of cold air quickly filled the cabin and sent alarms buzzing, lights flashing. His ears popped and the plane bucked as the captain's voice came over the PA system. "Is everything okay back there? Anything we can do for you?"

Cooper let go of the hatch, rushed over, and grabbed the interphone and said, "No!" He waited, eyeing the curtain, half expecting the copilot or one of the stewardesses to rush back and stop him. But they left him alone and so he charged the hatch again, shoving with every fiber in his body until it cracked open a few feet and another wave of cold air swept through the cabin, launching stray cocktail napkins and sending discarded newspapers flapping around like trapped birds. He kept pushing until the stairs snapped into place, the wind punching him against the door frame, tearing at his chest and legs.

He took a moment to steady himself, his hands tugging and checking the chute, pulling on the cord that held the money sack as he looked down and forced his legs to move, sure that at any moment he would be blown off into the night, sucked through the engine turbines and transformed into bloody ribbons. The first step was going to be a bitch, he thought, no retreat.

He placed one foot on the tread and much to his surprise his grip held even as he ventured another cautious step and then another until there was nowhere else to go except down into the howling void.

And so he pushed off and fell, tumbling past the roar of the 727's engines into the rip of wind and rain that whipped his hair back and snatched the half-empty pack of Raleigh unfiltereds from his jacket pocket and instantly numbed his face and fingers and straightened the narrow black necktie until it stood behind him like a noose that would jerk him away into the nothing as he spun through clouds and sheets of hard rain toward the green rolling hills of the Columbia River valley far below.

But there was the money, an enormous encouraging hand slapping his back as he pumped his hips into the cushion of air, screaming until his lungs fell empty and his body felt as if it had been sprung from some dark cage into the roar of a waiting coliseum.

Down he went, hurtling toward the sprawl of lights and trees and interstates lit with lonely taillights of tractor trailers and cars full of families traveling to Thanksgiving celebrations the following day where they would wake to the smell of risen bread and roast turkey and to the newspapers announcing his deed and the $200,000 he'd run off with or died trying to.

So he pulled the rip cord. The chute fluttered and then popped open, jerking him back and jumpstarting his dead heart with a snap. The easy part was over, he thought, time to take the money, get lost, and slip down the rabbit hole and vanish.

CHAPTER ONE

1984

On the Saturday before his retirement party Frank Marshall's wife, Clare, told him he looked tired and urged him to take a nap instead of going fishing. He decided to ignore her and waited until she went to show a three-bedroom ranch to a couple from Spokane before leaving a note and changing into his fishing shirt, a tattered chamois button-up with torn pockets and fish scales fused to the fabric. It had rained for three straight days and as Frank loaded his rod and tackle box into the car the sun warmed the damp pavement and the air filled with the rich smell of earthworms soft boiling in shallow sidewalk puddles.

He drove out of town until he came to the abandoned haul road that led down to the small mountain lake where he kept an aluminum johnboat and a lawn chair chained around a tree trunk. A few other men fished the lake and sometimes he'd run into one of them coming or going and they'd exchange words in the glib and crafty manner of all fishermen—a bit of misinformation about what the fish were biting on, followed by a quick exit wink and tip of the cap. He fished to get away and so the truly good days were the ones

when he had the lake all to himself and he could fish and drift without any of the petty competition that arose from the sight of another
man hauling in fish left and right.

Frank had reached mandatory retirement after twenty years as an
FBI agent and six before that as a deputy in the sheriff's department,
a make-do job he'd taken after an abortive stab at grad school. Although happy with the retirement package offered by the Bureau, he
found himself increasingly bothered by the fact that the Bureau and
its massive bureaucracy had done nothing to prepare him for what
came next—the end of his career, or what the other agents referred
to as being put out to pasture with the civies.

During his career he'd traveled to Quantico dozens of times for
training seminars on hostage negotiating, crime-scene photography,
defensive tactics, skip tracing, rudimentary forensics, drug purity determination, criminal profiling, wiretapping, and the Bureau's code
of conduct. He'd seen bodies rotting in fields and men in lab coats
hovering over them with instruments, measuring and marveling at
the embarrassing riches of the dead. He'd always assumed that there
would be one last call to Quantico or perhaps a closed-door sit-down
with a special agent in charge to discuss retirement—the real purpose of which would be to strongly discourage him about talking to
the press concerning any ongoing investigations or writing a tell-all
book in the hope of making the talk-show circuit when people
wanted answers as to why some normal, well-liked man from the
Midwest had started stuffing little boys under his floorboards or feeding old folks ant poison and doing strange things with severed body
parts and dog skulls. But there had been nothing and as he approached his last day, the retirement party looming like some wake,
he found that all he wanted to do was pick up one last case and feel
that electric thrum of fresh information, the swirl of events coming
together as he built the file, sought suspects, weighed theories in anticipation of that moment when he would enter gun-first through a
splintered door, his blood ripping around his veins, eyes beating with
adrenaline as he drew a bead on the accused or maybe just tricked
him into cuffs with his nice-guy act. Instead he'd been put to shuf-

fling paper and answering tip hot lines. It was, he supposed, an undignified but necessary way to wind things up, meant to painlessly transition him to humdrum civilian life. But none of it seemed to help the impending sense of internal collapse Frank Marshall felt pressing down on him as his days dwindled. In fact, the more phones he answered and reports he filed the worse he felt because, now that he had time to look around, he'd noticed how much the Bureau had changed.

During these last few months he found himself seeking refuge on the quiet lap of the lake. He'd boiled the whole thing down to a sacred ritual, packing his gear the exact same way and always parking under the same crooked pine and then walking out to stretch and take a look at the water before dragging the boat out and setting it in the shallows.

Today was no different. He parked and unloaded, stopping every so often to watch the mist dance and curl through the cattails and trees that ringed the lake. Fish dimpled the surface, delicately sipping at caddis flies as swallows swooped from the trees and a deer bucked away through the heavy undergrowth, its shocking white tail triggering several other deer he'd not detected.

At the water's edge his own reflection startled him, in particular the bloom of gray in his dark curly hair that had grown wider and deeper these last few months. He examined the blunt topography of his face, pleased that his chin had not softened into the well-fed wattle of other men his age. He noted his crooked nose, courtesy of a bank robber named Pierce Hyde whose m.o. was to walk into a bank and blast away with a semiautomatic before demanding money from the terrified tellers. Hyde was quick and on a roll, and he'd gone interstate.

Frank and several other agents worked the case hard after the last jolt, a bank in Spokane where Hyde had critically injured a guard and walked with $29,000 before heading south into Oregon, where he quickly hit three more banks.

A week later they received a tip that Hyde was holed up in a Howard Johnson ordering shrimp salad, leaving trash in the hallway, and demanding that fresh bars of soap be delivered to his room. Frank had been the first one through the door, his revolver drawn, shouting, "FBI! FBI!" the room thick with dope smoke, shower steam, and some kind of piney cologne.

When Hyde saw what was happening he dived off the bed and be-gan pelting Frank and the other agents with full cans of beer, the last one snagging Frank square in the face. Frank heard the crunch of tiny bones and tasted blood but kept charging, the pain causing his finger to tense around the trigger until he was on Hyde, mashing him into the dingy shag carpeting, the gun buried in the guy's throat like a sword. For a moment he'd wanted to pull the trigger and watch the man's neck explode, but when he looked into Hyde's eyes he saw his own fear coming right back at him tenfold until agents Jeffers and Stillman dragged him away and cuffed Hyde, giving Frank the easy-buddy eye.

In the weeks following the arrest he tired of telling the story and took to staring at the younger agents, many of whom underesti-mated Frank because of his size but at the same time feared him. Yes, he was large and had trouble finding clothes to fit his broad shoul-ders and he was, by his own admission, baffled by computers, his un-willingness to rely on them to help solve crimes a mark of his age and another small sign among many that the Bureau was passing him by. Because of this some of the newer agents made the mistake of assuming that Frank was somehow less discerning or perceptive when it came to casework. In fact, he did everything to encourage this prejudice, moving filing cabinets for the secretaries and hauling boxes of tractor feed paper, two at a time, from the dank basement. Part of the job was knowing when to pull out the smoke and mir-rors. The rest was cop work—twenty years and that was all he knew.

HE POKED AT the reflection and waited for the water to reassemble his face, minnows twirling through the muddy shadows like bullets. Then he unchained the boat and loaded his gear into the hull. The boat bobbed and accepted his weight as he pushed off and rowed out into the middle of the clear blue water. After ten minutes of steady rowing he felt the warm hum of exertion radiate up his shoulders and down his lower back. He knew there would come a time when he'd be forced to break down and buy one of those tiny electric trolling motors, but for now he relished the honest burn of rowing, the ache and creak of muscles being called upon once again.

A slight wind luffed off the water, rattling a band of cattails at the south end of the lake, where he rarely fished. He found his spot and locked the oars before picking up a rod and dropping his line, enjoying the flutter of monofilament as it sped to the bottom. When the lead sinker hit the soft muddy lake floor he cranked it up a few turns and set the pole against the gunwale. He picked up his casting rod and flipped out a long smooth cast, watching the Panther Martin crash silver and chartreuse against the pond surface. He waited and then retrieved it, jerking the rod tip left and then right, thinking, Hit it, hit it now.

As the boat drifted he kept up a steady rhythm, casting and retrieving, waiting for that first smack of a fish. He rarely caught much although when he did he'd slide the gasping fish back into the water and watch it disappear through the blue to the black bottom of the lake. Sometimes he'd gill one and be forced to keep the fish or else watch it roll belly up and float around the boat, its white stomach taunting him and ruining the rest of the day.

Lately, being out on the lake brought back the woman he'd found all those years ago on a cold and rainy Thanksgiving Day during the hunt for the man identified as D. B. Cooper.

How her bones had ended up in the millpond, shoved down between two rotten pilings, remained a stubborn mystery. Officially she was Jane Doe and the file on her, now a zero file, had gone cold and dead, buried along with the thousands of other unidentified bodies. The file consisted of a few scant entries—phone calls logged, searches run on the missing persons' data bank, random tips from concerned citizens, a letter from a local psychic who said the killer was now happily married and had children and was living in Tacoma, fiber analysis of the purse, and a list of stores (too many) that sold such models. The coroner's report noted little more than her approximate age and position of the bones and the fact that she'd broken her leg, perhaps in childhood. There were grainy photographs of the pond and surrounding woods and a disappointing forensic facial reconstruction. The clay-and-wax rendering reminded him of the Neanderthal women in *National Geographic*, who were always shown hunched around small fires clutching bones, waiting for their heavy-browed men to drag some fresh mastodon home, and not of some young woman snatched away and murdered too young. The rest of the file was blank and waiting.

He had long since ceased wondering why, of all the thousands of cases he'd handled, she should be the one to haunt him. The victim had been found and then lost in the wake of the Cooper skyjacking, a small pile of bones and nothing more, her death made special and brought to his attention only because a man had hijacked an airplane and disappeared near where the Jane Doe had spent what Frank imagined to be the last long minutes of her life. She came back to him especially when he was out on the lake staring down into its sunless bottom, wondering if there were bodies waiting to be discovered everywhere—an army of the dead and gone, the vanished.

THE DAY AFTER the skyjacking Frank had been one of hundreds of agents combing the tangled underbrush for any sign of the man they were now calling D. B. Cooper. It was one of those cases that he knew was white-hot by the way the higher-ups were jockeying for position and scrambling to affix motives and theories that would shape the search protocol. Already there were agents following the skyjacker's back trail, interviewing witnesses, dusting the plane for prints, canvassing the airport as they built a profile of the sort of man it took to hijack a plane and then parachute out the day before Thanksgiving. It smacked of protest and un-American sentiment, and although there'd recently been an alarming surge in hijackings, Cooper had pulled off his crime with a minimal amount of complication, a truckload of cool, no discernible political agenda, and zero violence.

Even though the weather had turned to shit over the search area—rolling, heavily timbered hills and soggy bottomland—there was hope among the searchers that his body would be found wrapped shroudlike in his failed parachute, dangling from one of the towering Douglas firs, the money fanned out below on the forest floor. But as the rain and snow worsened and the light started to fade over the mountain tops, Frank Marshall began to entertain the idea that perhaps the guy had gotten away with it and that maybe this time the FBI would not get its man, and he was surprised to find himself privately rooting for Cooper to remain at large. While resting against a wind-downed tree he allowed himself to imagine what it would feel like to take that jump with $200,000 strapped to his back and hit the ground ready to run away from everything in his life that seemed less than perfect. The fantasy kept him plodding over hill and valley until he was soaked to the bone, tired and hungry, thinking only occasionally of the roast turkey and candied yams being passed around the dining room table without him.

He walked under the thwock of helicopters and small planes buzzing back and forth in search grids, and from time to time he caught glimpses of other agents moving through the woods. He heard them cursing as they struggled over deadfall, plucking prickers and raking burrs and sticktights from their pant legs.

At the top of a low rise Frank scanned first the canopy above and then the thick ground cover for a telltale flash of white or some sudden movement. It had been twenty minutes since he'd stepped off his assigned search path and veered south toward a stand of tall fir trees where he hoped the walking would be easier. Out of some macho nod to his late father, a timber scout for Georgia Pacific, he'd left his gloves in the car and now regretted the decision as he struggled to keep his hands warm and dry. The rain gave way to large snowflakes that landed on his face, melting into his hair and neck, mixing with sweat. He could have easily marked off his spot and made his way back to the logging road, where idling vans waited and inside there would be ham sandwiches and hot coffee. But the idea that he was breaking new ground propelled him forward. It wasn't that he was eager to find and arrest Cooper but more that he wanted to know why a man would resort to such a reckless act. The radicals he could understand, but this Cooper? Of course there was the money, but it still didn't seem to Frank reason enough to leap out of a jet.

As he pushed through a stand of saplings and low branches he imagined a brief chase through the woods—perhaps he'd have to shoot the man, wing him a little and then call in the boys. But the woods gave nothing away and as he pounded down another slope he went back to rooting for this D. B. Cooper to escape, hoping he was well on his way to some tropical island with the bagful of cash and enough brains to avoid foolish capture at a routine traffic stop. It would be tough to blame a fellow for wanting something like that and having the stones to jump out of a plane to get it.

He followed a shallow creek down the hill to a murky pond banded by a heavy skirt of neat pine trees and curled cedar, where he scanned the dim watery perimeter. His boots sank into the muck and made deep sucking sounds as he neared the edge. Even though he knew the choppers had already hovered over the pond searching for a floater or the ghostly white of a sunken parachute, he decided to have a look before heading back.

Halfway around the pond he discovered a partially collapsed mill house perched on tumbled stilts near the water's edge. What was left of the roof hung off three rotten walls, tangled with frozen weeds and vines. The north-facing wall had fallen inward and was now a jumble of moss-covered timbers, tar paper hanging like brittle skin. Frank pushed forward and saw that there had been a fire some time ago and it had been hot enough to cripple the massive fir tree that loomed over the mill house into a limbless sickle.

Inside, two large millstones lay in the center of the ruined building like gears sprung from some ancient machine. Beer cans decorated the dim interior, their labels poached white from rain and snow. He reached out and touched a section of wall, shoving a thumb into the rotten timber until he saw the pale segmented body of a grub rear up at him, its pincers working like tiny steel traps.

He pulled his thumb away and rested a minute, huddling against the wall and out of the rain as the wind suddenly stopped and he entertained the idea of setting a crude camp under the collapsed mill, maybe even building a fire. It would enhance his image among his fellow agents, most of whom were made uncomfortable by the woods and preferred to limit their contact with the wild to the weekly lawn mowing or occasional golf outing. But then he heard the lonesome bays of the search dogs and the steady chop of helicopters and he drifted back to Cooper, remembering the hasty sketch he'd been shown of the hijacker and the scant details of his crime and how he hadn't rattled or mentioned some left-wing cause as reason for his actions. All the more reason to suspect they were dealing not with some amateur but with a man who'd planned and executed his crime with precision—a man who knew what he wanted and was not afraid to die chasing after it.

On the other side of the mill house the creek exited the pond over a slip of cracked concrete, the wooden sluice gate long since crumbled. He turned his attention back to the millpond, his gaze tracing the remains of a wooden stairway that led down the bank and to the water's edge where a sunken dock fingered its way past the support stilts before disappearing under the murky surface.

Just as he was about to turn and go, something caught his eyes on the bank below, a flash of red amid the wintry gray brown of dead leaves and washed-up branches. The red didn't fit, it was too vivid and fresh and looked like blood or perhaps a small animal turned inside out and eaten by another.

So he slid down the embankment to investigate, slowing himself by grabbing at stunted trees and old exposed roots as snowflakes twirled clumsily around him, forming a flickering and delicate pattern along the still edges of the pond. As he neared the object he saw that it had been there a long time and that it was not blood but a red purse handle buried under the sand and rocks. He pulled it free and rinsed the muck away in the pond. The vinyl was stiff and brittle, its corners disintegrating as Frank opened it to find a stew of rotten leaves, caddis larvae, and small pebbles. He dumped the mess onto a large stone, where it landed with a satisfying glop, and hunkered down to stir his finger through it. He found a pitted metal lipstick tube and two Mercury-head dimes, and after brushing the dimes clean against his sleeve he dropped them into his pocket, wondering how the purse had ended up buried in the pond bank—not just any purse but a red vinyl purse, not the sort of thing carried by folks in this neck of the woods. He looked around for other errant trash but saw only a crushed oil drum, a half-buried tractor tire, and a garbage bag snagged in the cattails.

He dropped the purse, and as he turned to go, a large fish rose just off the edge of the sunken dock, its dorsal fin disturbing the knit of snowy slush. Frank figured it was some old pike or a trout grown fat in its splendid isolation. Curious, he walked over to where the ruined dock met the bank and saw that only ten feet of it appeared steady enough to risk walking. He decided to step out onto it anyway, hoping that the fish would rise again and he could get a better look at it. The wood groaned and shifted, the tip of the dock sinking deeper. He waited but there was only the sound of water slapping against the timbers as the fading light bathed the pond in a woozy rain-socked glow. It would be dark soon, and Frank knew that it would take a half hour or maybe more to find his way back to the road and every moment spent lingering over the water looking for a fish he'd never have the chance to catch only added to the time he'd spend batting his way through the darkening woods. He thought of his wife and daughter waiting for him to return and eat what remained of Thanksgiving dinner. Clare would be smiling and trying to make the best of it, asking Lucy, their nine-year-old daughter, to help with the dishes while his in-laws, Walt and Mary, sat handing out advice and bickering with each other. He should have wanted to get back, but standing there on the dock, he felt no great urge to get back to any-thing. Thanksgiving had come and gone without him, all because a man had jumped from a 727 with $200,000 and vanished without a trace. He was on the job.

He crept out as far as the dock would allow without totally sinking and hunkered down, putting his face to the water, hoping to spot the fish or perhaps an even larger one threading its way through the dock structure below. His breath rippled the water as he cupped his hands over his eyes and peered into the quiet underworld of the pond.

Just as he was about to pull away he saw something white twirl and wave past the algae-covered piling. It rose and sank from view before he could make out what it was and so he waited, letting the rain slip down his shirt collar, running thin and cold along his spine before soaking into his already wet shirt. He hoped that whatever small current or spring that had first pushed the object up out of the depths would circle back and do so again before it got too dark.

Several long minutes passed before he saw it again, shimmering in the shifting gray-green water just long enough for his brain to catch up to his eyes and his breath to unhitch itself from his lungs.

It was a hand or the bones of a hand. He was sure of it, but the why and how of its sudden appearance were slow to dawn on him.

"Christ," he muttered, sitting up to remove his coat and roll his shirtsleeves back.

He plunged his arm down into the water and groped along the piling. He felt the bones brush against his hand for a second; then they were gone again. Despite the icy water wicking up into his shirt he reached deeper through the tangled algae that clung to the piling until he managed to feel the bones again. He grabbed them and tugged and felt a soft click as they came away free in his hands. He slowly raised them out of the water. Several small bones dropped away and disappeared back into the pond. He cradled the rest and set them gently on the dock to examine. Most of the phalanxes were gone, as were other bones he couldn't name, and only one of the arm bones had made it to the surface—the radius, he thought. They were whiter than he imagined and seemed to hungrily absorb the last of the milky light leaking through the cloud cover and treetops. He reached out to touch them again and found them not only cold but covered with an invisible film, as if in their underwater tenure they'd developed a fragile skin.

One of the bones fell away from the rest and rolled toward him. It was narrow and gently tapered to a knob where it would have met the next bone. He picked it up and dried the bone against his pants, rubbing the slimy film away before sniffing it. It smelled clean, just like the black beach stones he'd collected as a child, the ones his father called "lucky stones" because they had a stripe of white quartz in them. He set it back next to the others but it slipped between the dock timbers. Carefully prying it out with his knife, he dropped it into his pocket, where it clinked in strange reunion alongside the two Mercury-head dimes he'd taken from the purse.

He bent over the piling again with the calm certainty that there were more bones, perhaps even a whole body, bits of hair, teeth, and scraps of half-dissolved clothes hiding below the water. This was no accident—the bones were a part of something vastly larger that seemed to confirm a primal suspicion he'd always harbored about water. As a child he'd feared water, sure that at any moment some unknown creature would rise and suck him into the chilly depths. All those old fears came back to him as he stared at the bones drying on the rotten dock wood. There was something down there and it had come for him.

Two hours later the place was crawling with agents and men from the local sheriff's office, who'd set up a noisy generator. Spotlights revealed that the rest of the skeleton had been lashed to the piling with rope and chain. A clump of long hair was tangled in the chain and other "items" on the pond bottom. Forensics had been called in and there was talk of bringing in a diver in the morning as well as a few boats to drag the rest of the pond with chains and grappling hooks.

"Lonely place to die," said the sheriff, offering Frank a thermos top of coffee. Frank knew the man vaguely from his days as a deputy sheriff. He wore a string tie and burned Old Golds, one after another.

"Odd thing for you to notice way out here," he said. "Only way in here's a logging road, but I think it's pretty much gone wild. Herman Kweller used to fish up here and was pretty cagey about it. Used to be I'd see him pretty regular on the road with his lantern and tackle box. He's living over in Washougal now after that thing with his wife. I suppose he'd be one to talk to. And there's Raynal, he might know something. These are just names to you and I'm not saying these men would have anything to do with this. Tell me, how did you end up looking down off that dock?"

"It was a mistake," said Frank. "Hell, I was just looking for this fish I saw rise."

"No shit?"

Frank nodded. "Instead I saw the bones. I'm not going to tell you I had a hunch because I don't believe in them."

The sheriff rocked back on his boot heels as if he'd just been gob-smacked by some bit of wisdom. "Well, that's police work for you—happy accidents, death, and bad coffee." He clamped Frank on the shoulder and leaned in close, his breath stale with tobacco. "I think we can safely rule out this Cooper fellow's involvement." It was meant as a joke, but the sheriff's poached cowboy face gave it a rue-ful spin. "But then again we might never have found her if it weren't for that crazy son of a buck."

"She's been there a while," Frank said, trying hard to ignore the criminal math that put flesh on the bones, a voice, and a life cut vi-olently short.

The sheriff fixed him with his tired eyes and said, "Anything else?"

Frank let his hand drop to his pocket and felt the stray finger bone there. Now was the time to set it alongside the others and tell the others how he'd inadvertently slipped it inside his pocket without thinking. Instead he shook his head and said nothing, letting silence and cold rain fill the moment.

He went down to the pond, where a few agents were talking, sip-ping coffee, and tossing stones into the water while they waited for the forensics team to arrive. Frank accepted another cup of coffee and listened as a field agent from Seattle theorized about how

Cooper had probably bought it on the way down. Cooper was what they all wanted and not some pile of bones—a cold-dead catch of a case that would ultimately be passed off to the sheriff, whose only chance to solve it would be a lucky break. No, Frank thought, he'd keep the bone and try to find out how she'd ended up out here in the middle of nowhere.

He never told anybody about the bone he'd put in his pocket that day or how he kept it with him years after or how the small knobbed bone was part of the daily jumble of half-eaten Rolaids, spare change, pocketknife, and bandless watch he loaded into his pants before heading off to work. It had become a memento mori of the unidentified woman and Cooper still out there somewhere.

■

BEFORE THE LEAP he was just Phil Fitch from Portland, Tulsa, and parts Midwest—ex-military and ex-husband of one Geena Rae Pitt, who'd packed her things and left after getting off shift early from the diner one night only to arrive home and find him in front of the television watching *I Dream of Jeannie* and stroking off into a gym sock. She accused him of all sorts of misdeeds. The worst—the camel breaker—being that he'd lied to her when he'd said he had plans for their future, that they'd be well off and quite possibly extravagantly wealthy because he'd known since childhood that he'd been marked for greatness, destined for big deeds. But so far a rented trailer and the occasional steak dinner at Ringside (no drinks or flaming desserts) did not, in her small book of the world, even hint at better things. What scared her was that she could see things getting a whole lot worse. She figured that the best-case scenario were she to cast her lot with Fitch till death did them part would be a garage apartment complete with cat-crazed landlady, late-model used cars, secondhand furniture, rent-to-own appliances, home perms, the occasional payroll loan to make the electric bill, one or both of them in a bowling

league, good postargument sex, and just maybe a kid or two somewhere down the line. She'd shop at JCPenney and Sears, clip
coupons, and frequent rummage sales. Vacations would be whittled
down to cheap weekend getaways to the ocean, where they'd stay in
one of those tiny motels with rust-stained sinks, dusty burlap curtains, bug-clogged screens, and an aluminum-framed oil print of a
harbor at dusk hanging over the bed, the seagulls little more than
hasty checkmarks canting over the cheated and blurred horizon. It
would be a predictably marginal ride with Fitch. But what could she
expect from a man who urinated off the back deck so often that the
grass had died and the boards had begun to rot? Or a man who
dipped his fries in mayonnaise? Whatever love she'd had for him
had been nickeled-and-dimed right out of her. The dashing war vet
she'd married in a beery backyard ceremony had become what she
could only charitably call a scofflaw. There were dozens just like
him—men who sat at her lunch counter gabbing, scheming, and
bitching tersely about their shake in things as they shoveled down
pie and left her tiny tips after dozens of free coffee refills. They talked
a good game and had complicated theories about how they'd found
themselves a day late and a dollar short in life. Half of them lived
with their mothers and the rest were celibate divorcés who could no
longer conceal their hatred of women or their growing paranoia that
people were out to get them.

As for Fitch, he had reason to expect greatness. He often found
quarters and half-dollars winking at him from sidewalks or rolling
toward him as they fell from the pocket of a passerby. Dogs liked him
and came when he called; even the strays that skulked around
knocking over trash cans and pursuing bitches in heat fell into fawn-
ing tail-slashing dances when they saw him. Babies returned his
smiles and bees followed him around for days, hovering over his
shoulder until they dropped dead far from the hive, to be eaten by
passing crows. Also, he'd survived not one but two tours of duty in
Vietnam, where he'd watched friends die ordinary wet jungle deaths
while he'd been allowed to slip out of that beautiful bug-filled green
hell unscathed back to an America full of people in vans looking for

peace, sex, drugs, and rock 'n' roll moments. He did not fit in, because he kept his hair in a stiff brush cut and still called men his senior sir. He opened doors for women and said please and thanks and sometimes dreamed of going back to college, but couldn't bring himself to say "Peace" or "Groovy, man" without feeling like a phony. Worse, he'd killed gooks, taken orders from the Man, pledged loyalty to God and country, named his rifle, marched, and sworn all kinds of sacred duty and honor oaths. But he'd survived the war with the knowledge that it took all types to die—the rich bled like the poor, and Bible toters and atheists swallowed lead in equal numbers, and the slick black dude from Detroit fell shoulder to shoulder with the goober from Texas who called him a spearchucker and watched his pack closely when bunking down next to him. They were all dead boys, one and all, and that was war for you. Fitch got by because during his first weeks in country he knew that there were things he would see and do that would be beyond his or anybody else's comprehension and that any attempt at order was folly, especially when you had to tuck your buddy's pancreas back into his stomach, look him in the face, and tell the necessary lie that he was going to be okay. Or maybe it was watching snipers shoot oxen, meticulously blowing out their knees and watching them topple and then doing the same to the old straw-hatted ladies who ran screaming to their defense. Then weeks later when wading through the same rice paddy you'd stumble across the bloated remains of one of these women and realize as you noted the dark fan of her hair floating in the water that she was not old but say nineteen—somebody's sister—and then imagine despite what the heat, wasps, blowflies, leeches, and rats had done to her that she'd been not only ten times stronger and more beautiful than your average American homecoming queen but crazy brave to die defending a stupid ox. The only thing to do was to avoid the swollen ox carcass and make sick jokes with your fellow grunts. Survival, Fitch learned, depended on basic human ignorance and the ability to sum up the crazy twists and turns with a simple "Fuck it." He had that in spades.

Fitch's only mistake upon coming home was in figuring that after enduring the jungle and its eight million ways to die that America would be a cakewalk—the land of milk and honey for a man marked for great things.

Besides Geena Rae, all that luck got him was a one-bedroom trailer and a string of crap jobs—cog degreaser, brush hogger, fence poster, insulator, shingle lurch, and all-around odd-jobbing step and fetchit. One by one the jobs had taken the spit and polish out of him, wearing him down into another lunchbox working-class joe who was beginning to realize that maybe the American Dream was just a big shit sandwich stacked with empty promises. He began to suspect that even the guys he met with tidy houses, families, and nice nine-to-five jobs were faking it, hiding some deep urge to run away and never again clip the hedge or replace another storm window or pay another gas bill. Fitch saw them on weekends standing outside in their short-sleeved oxford cloth shirts, preparing to mow the lawn or pick up dog crap with this blank look of bliss pasted across their average faces as noisy kids hung upside down from monkey bars and the wives stood peeking out from behind lace curtains with vaguely worried expressions. Although Fitch took note of this hidden despair, he kept trying to stay the course and work his way up into something even though his resolve to advance his cause was sporadic at best and constantly undermined by the great unanswerable questions that flocked his every move: So what? Who cares?

To make ends meet he took a side job hauling trash and dragging dead water heaters out of dank basements for twenty extra scoots a week. Later he tried the door-to-door bit, Fuller Brush, Electrolux vacuums, but never got past the training—all that snappy flesh-pressing etiquette was lost on him. It wasn't that he hadn't given the real workaday world a spin. There had been plenty of false starts, jobs with "promise" and "opportunity for advancement." But then he'd fuck the dog—forget to show and that would be it and he'd return to the trailer and watch Geena get ready for her night shift at the diner and he'd tell her how he'd been unfairly fired or let go due to lack of work.

"What I need," he'd say, "what I need is a good lawyer to sue their ass. Like Sam Cisco." He knew Sam from the bar and they'd spent many drunken hours scheming.

"Sam Cisco's not a real lawyer, hon. He got his degree from the back of a magazine. He runs around calling himself Esquire. Us girls call him Assquire. And that hair . . ."

"What's wrong with his hair?"

"Toupee city—rug-o-rama."

"I'd watch it," Fitch said. "You don't want him drawing up slander papers with that silver pen of his."

She held out her hand and made it quiver. "Sam Cisco can't even make change. And what kind of man leaves his business card instead of a tip?"

Fitch squinted at her, trying to discern whether or not she was telling the truth. It was just like her to put him off a good idea. He suspected that part of her enjoyed seeing him squirm under her ruthless logic—it had teeth and often sent him out into the night puzzling where he'd gone wrong as she took a small event, say a ketchup stain on the carpet or forgetting to shut the screen door and letting a few mosquitoes in, and whipped it up into high crimes and misdemeanors. Her mother, a razor-thin widow who worked at a beauty parlor, was ten times worse and had no problem listing Fitch's many faults in her nicotined rasp of a voice. She also left news clippings for him. The articles were usually hard-luck stories or cautionary tales of fallen men who'd resorted to crime, repented, and now worked happily as mail carriers or bus drivers, aware that things could have been better, that they'd defeated themselves, dug too deep a hole, or else just didn't catch enough breaks and would get old and die, gumming about their squandered opportunities. Some of the men had found Jesus or the love of a good woman, for which they seemed to be a little too thankful.

"Well, Sam got Fred a fair settlement," Fitch reminded Geena. "Four figures, medical, and apology from the company."

"Didn't Fred stick his hand in a band saw?" He looked across the counter at her. "On purpose," she snapped. "What kind of fool sticks his hand in a band saw on purpose?"

"I'm not sayin' what Fred did was right, all I'm sayin' is that Sam Cisco made the company pay. He's the defender of little people, shield for the workingman."

"I know, Phil," Geena said impatiently. "I've got an apron full of his cards."

"Well, in my case it's just plain and simple discrimination is what it is. Picking on the little guy. Trickle-down meanness. Less fortune for the less fortunate."

Of course, he didn't tell her how it was entirely his fault—how his heart wasn't in it or how they'd caught him sleeping on a pallet in the back room or slipping tools into his lunch pail or sticking hairpins into the punch clock to steal time.

"Give me a break, Phil," she said, squinching her hard brown eyes at him. "Eladio, the guy Nick pays a dollar twenty-five an hour to scrape dirty dishes is a little guy."

"Eladio is an illegal and . . ."

"And . . ."

"Come on, baby, I'm tryin' real hard here to do us some good."

"Good?"

"That's what I'm all about." He cut her with that smile of his, a crooked little thing he'd practiced in the mirror, as he reached out and tried to rub her shoulders, but she pushed him away and lit another Kool.

"Put the charm away, Phil," she said. "I gotta go to work. And fix your fly, you're open for business."

"Whoa," he said, looking down and zipping up. "Almost let the livestock out. See, I'm all warmed up."

She leaned over and sniffed his hair. "It wouldn't hurt you to shower once in a while." She took a drag and passed him the rest of the Kool. "Now move out of my way. I'm ovulating."

"So?"

"So we used the last of the condoms, plus I'm not in the mood."

"Come on, Geena, I've got disabled sperm, you don't have nothin' to worry about."

"Very funny. Now move."

"Where you going?"

"Work—you know what work is, don't you?"

It was one of those questions with no right answers. It instantly melted the smile off his face and snatched his mind away from the dirty little scenarios pinballing around his brain as she quickly gathered up her apron. After slipping on her shoes she gave him a peck on the cheek and was gone.

Geena worked at Nick's America #1 diner, owned by a large Greek named Nick who everybody called Cyclops because he'd lost an eye in a grease fire and wore a black felt eye patch to cover the curdled orb. As if to compensate for his accent and unpronounceable last name, Cyclops had become an overzealous American-history nut, his bible Hendrik van Loon's *The Story of America,* a rambling, highly opinionated view of American history written with real drama and sweep. The diner's menu featured an American flag on the cover and had specials named after chapters in the van Loon book. There was the Uncle Tom and Puffing Billy (chili and cornbread), the President Santa Ana and the Vacuum (cheddar cheese omelet with hot peppers), and for dessert the New Zion at Twenty Below (hot sundae with a submerged brownie). Every plate came with small paper flags attached to toothpicks and a placemat on which Cyclops had mimeographed a page from van Loon, usually something about the French and Indian Wars or Ben Franklin and his bathtub.

When things were bad between them, Geena would come back from the diner smelling of fryer grease and dried ketchup and demand that Fitch massage her feet, slapping his hand away when he tried to creep it between her legs to the magic kingdom. But when things were good between them, all he had to do was stare at her box for a couple of hours—keep the heat lamps on her, basically put her on notice that his sap was rising and that he was full of love and compliments and wanted some reward. If she went into the kitchen to make some ice tea and linger over the dishes, Fitch followed her, giving her his best Brando stare, mumbling, "You look good, Geena. In fact, you look pretty close to fine. How about we have ourselves some love practice?" He watched her dress and undress, fold laundry, file her nails, all the while keeping that thousand-watt stare on her until she gave in and led him to the small, hot bedroom and let him go to work on her while she watched *My Three Sons* on the black and white, going on about her late father's uncanny resemblance to William Demarest. Later, after he'd laced into her several different ways and he was lying there picking at his moles and smoking, she'd start in on him about the rickety TV trays and how they needed some furniture that didn't come from scratch and dent sales, some new drapes, a hi-fi system, and one of those refrigerators with an ice-maker to replace the leaky and rattling Frigidaire they'd bought sec-ondhand. It had become increasingly clear to her that if Fitch wasn't going to do anything about it, she'd just have to work more double shifts at the diner or start moonlighting as a cocktail waitress.

So Geena started pulling doubles at the diner and Fitch responded by landing a job sweeping floors at the Georgia-Pacific warehouse. He knew he was losing her because she no longer demanded foot rubs or laughed when he did his Dean Martin impression. Instead she arrived home too exhausted to even yell at him for leaving ap-ple cores out on the windowsill or for hanging his dirty socks over the shower stall.

He started looking for shortcuts.

Sam Cisco counseled him to do a slip-and-fall number on Georgia-Pacific. "Nothing too dramatic," Sam said, handing Fitch another of his cards. "Remember the word *lumbar*—it's a very painful region. Tell them you can't feel your toes and then go see this man." Sam passed him a slip of paper with a number on it. "That's Doc Spun-gin's number—a good man who I guarantee will arrive at a favorable diagnosis. And if it goes to trial he'll heave the *Merck Manual* at them and woo the jury with his mastery of medical lingo and Latin."

Fitch hesitated and Sam sent him on his way with a hearty slap and a wink. "Trust me, they'll pay through their corporate noses if they want to protect their reputation."

He quickly scrapped the slip-and-fall scheme when on Friday he found a job-safety pamphlet stapled to his punch card. The pamphlet depicted two men cheerfully lifting wooden crates with their legs, spotting each other on ladders, and painlessly enduring assaults on their toes—Hi-Lo tires and dropped lumber—all because they were wearing their steel-toed safety boots. On the back someone had written "FYI" in black grease crayon. They were on to his plan to bleed the company dry with fraudulent lawsuits. So Fitch held on to the job and learned to shut his brain off and drive the dust mop across the cement floor, chasing dust bunnies and mouse turds into neat little piles. And after his probationary month was up he began to experience tiny and unexpected bouts of job pride. He talked pension with the old-timers and discussed making the jump to shipping and receiving, where it was possible to get promoted, or "bumped up" as the guys called it.

But then Geena left in August, calling him pathetic, sick, and twisted as she slammed the trailer door in his face and went to blubber and stew in her mother's knickknack-laden den. He tried calling her but got an earful from her mom, who seemed to Fitch to be a little too pleased with the situation. She informed him blithely that her daughter planned to D-I-V-O-R-C-E him ASAP. He hung up on her, figuring Geena would cool off and return to extract a list of promises from him. All he'd have to do is toe the line for a couple of months and convince her that he was a changed man. But after a few days it became clear to Fitch that she wasn't going to call, that she'd pretty much given up on their future and the more he thought about it the more he figured it was for the best.

A week later, her brother Gary, a barrel-chested linoleum installer, arrived in his pickup truck and began loading up her clothes. When Fitch offered to help, Gary pushed him into a busted recliner. "Take a load off and watch some television," he said, smirking. "Maybe *I Dream of Jeannie*'s on."

For a minute he thought about taking a swing at Gary. Instead he went out back and shot Blatz bottles with an air pistol.

ON AN UNUSUALLY muggy September evening Sam Cisco dropped by to serve Fitch with divorce papers. He signed them while Sam ad-

vised him in complicated legalese that not only would he do well to
avoid the diner but he should give up any hope of a reconciliation.

"It's over, Fitch," Sam said. "Get on with your life. Living well is
the best revenge."

Fitch told him he'd keep that in mind as he studied the papers. In
return for assuming several thousand dollars in joint debt, he got to
keep the lime-green Dodge Dart, two aluminum kitchen chairs, the
vinyl sofa, two braided rugs, all dry goods and condiments, the clock
radio, the wandering Jew and scraggly ficus, a mismatched set of
plates and saucers they'd picked up at a garage sale, the eight-track
tape player, the television, and a pair of oven mitts shaped like trout.
Fitch had fond memories of chasing Geena around the trailer with
the mitts on, telling her the fish were biting as he grabbed her ass.

Geena's departure became the talk of the trailer park. The old
women he met at the mailboxes avoided his gaze; jailbait rode by
snapping their gum at Fitch, making sure he got an eyeful of their
training bras when they came by asking him to buy beer for them. A
gangly long-haul trucker who lived two trailers over offered Fitch
the advice "If it flies, floats, or fucks, it's cheaper to rent, budro." Several of the local widows and unmarrieds took turns dropping by the
trailer bearing crumb cakes and pitchers of friendship tea with orange slices floating in it. They were mostly chubby women with bad
complexions, severely tweezed eyebrows, and frazzled hair from too
many home dye jobs who thought Fitch somewhat desirable because
he kept to himself, had straight teeth, and possessed the dirty charm
of all skinny men.

One night Pam Tarantino brought him a pan of scalloped potatoes
topped with crushed Fritos and burnt Velveeta and tried to give him
a back rub with some Wesson she'd scented with rose petals and
Jean Naté afterbath oil. He ate the totally good potatoes but took a
rain check on the back rub when he saw that Pam was wearing a pair
of French cuts and had an open sore on her calf that looked like a
tiny red mouth. She started crying and Fitch felt obliged to comfort
her with an awkward hug but she turned on him, suddenly angry.

"Can't you see I'm trying to be a better person?" she said. "I've lost weight, waxed my bikini line. I've even swore off bikers and dry-wallers."

"How do I fit into that equation?"

She socked him in the arm and stormed out of the trailer calling him a faggot loud enough for his ever-curious neighbors to hear.

The next day at work he got called into the office by the shift supervisor, a pale, schlubby guy whom everybody called Tits behind his back.

"Have a seat," Tits said.

Fitch sat and Tits proceeded to hem and haw about mandatory cutbacks due to the piss-poor price of lumber and about Fitch's lack of seniority on the job totem pole as he slid a pink slip across the cluttered gray desk, licked his lips, and asked him to sign it. "Just a little release signature is all we need to prevent any unpleasant and frivolous legal thumb wrestling."

The flickerings of job pride Fitch had felt just hours ago gave way to a sudden blast of soon-to-be-jobless fury as he stared at the pink slip and Tits, who was perched in his swivel chair examining his uncallused hands and tapping his loafers against the desk. Deep down Fitch knew he hadn't exactly given body and soul to the company but he'd put in his eights, worked weekends when asked, and taken orders from knuckle draggers who fervently toed the company line. He'd taken the job to get Geena off his back. But she was gone and here he was getting his job nuts handed to him by a man who hid in his office all day listening to the radio and reading *Popular Science*.

Fitch briefly entertained the idea of trashing the office but changed his mind when he saw a piece of rebar easily within the man's reach. Not wanting to catch some steel to the skull, he signed the pink slip and checked the box indicating that he was accepting a voluntary dismissal, or more accurately, Fitch thought, the unlubed I'm-just-doing-my-job-middle-management dildo.

"Here you go," Tits said, sliding Fitch's paycheck across the desk. "Feel free to use me as a reference." He tucked the signed pink slip into a manila folder stuffed with them. Apparently the bottom of the totem pole was a crowded place.

"That's it?"

"Unless you have any questions."

Fitch shook his head.

"Okay then," Tits said, pointing at the door. "Thanks for taking the time. Good luck. It's a jungle out there."

"Sure thing, Tits," he said, watching as the man's face turned red and he quickly folded his arms across his chest.

"Get out," he snapped.

He didn't bother to shut the door behind him because a squat-shouldered guy who worked as a loader stood waiting outside the office, smoking his last cigarette and gnashing his jaw in anticipation of his dismissal.

"I can't catch a break," said the man.

"Me either," Fitch said.

On the way out to his car Fitch snapped his broom in half and pummeled the time clock with a chunk of two-by-four. Outside he found Tits's Impala, let the air out of the tires, and bent the antenna.

A week later Fitch hit the road in his lime-green Dodge Dart. He'd paid two hundred dollars for the car and found that a two-hundred-dollar Dodge Dart didn't get you very far or for that matter score many points with the plentiful hippie chicks who he'd heard were crazy for free love with strangers. The only thing that looked good behind the wheel of a Dodge Dart, he decided, was an old blue-haired lady on her way to church or some social gathering. Fitch recalled his departed mother and tried to imagine her behind the wheel of the Dart, riding the brake pad, muttering about the reck-lessness of teen drivers and bakery deliverymen.

His recollection was ruined when the Dart thumped over a swollen jackrabbit carcass, and as he surveyed the dramatic plume of old blood and rotten gore sprayed across the road like an exclama-tion point, the excitement he'd felt was replaced with a gnawing sense of dread. But a mile later the open-road joy returned and he looked out through the Dart's bug-spattered windshield, admiring the deep pool-liner blue of sky that stretched forever into the distant mountains. He rolled down the windows and let the wind suck through his hair. Getting out of town was exactly what he needed. It was the closest he'd felt to being free in a long time, even though he was out of work and at the moment had no plans of ever working again. And women? Fuck them. He would stick and move. From now on he was gonna be open-road Fitch, duke of the two-lane blacktop, the stars for a roof, a woman in every state or something like that. But after he'd filled up the tank twice and mashed his knuckles replacing a fan belt, his drifter dreams began to crumble. It took money or rich parents to drift around and get into small adventures and at the rate he was going he would be broke in a week.

That night he found a small roadside bar, a green and white aluminum-sided double-wide that had been added on to so many times it now resembled an overgrown children's fort. The parking lot was full of motorcycles and dusty pickup trucks. He planned to get drunk and plot his next move.

The place was an alcoholic gulag heavy with the aroma of vomit and spoiled beer, suitably smoky and dim. Half a dozen bikers were milling around, drinking and palming dope and swag under the tabletops as a posse of loggers looked on, running ruined fingers through sawdust-filled beards and waiting for the inevitable fight. Through it all, a thin waitress circled the room with a rag in her hand, taking silent drink orders and shoving the occasional meat hook away from her ass.

Fitch overheard a man in tan overalls and mushroomed corks lecturing one of the bikers about Detroit, insisting it had a skyline. "Paris of the Midwest, Jack. And you gotta see the pimps, man, some stylized motherfuckers. Plus you got the Kronk and Motown. I'm tellin' you, skip Milwaukee if you got to."

The biker told the man he was fucked and walked away, grabbing a chubby woman in black leather chaps and shoving her into a booth where they sat staring into the guttering orange-globed tea light, drinking gin with crushed ice.

Fitch took a seat at the bar and ordered a double bourbon, drank it quickly, ordered another and another until he couldn't feel his hands and a fat man with the face of a walrus stood and shouted, "I am a pacifist Negro!"

The blonde next to the man said, "No, Paul, that is a lie. You are from Cleveland."

"Okay then, I can do nineteen pull-ups and I want some pussy," the man shouted. Several rough male voices answered back that they had some for him and so he sat back down and growled at his beer bottle as the blonde stroked his arm, trying to prevent any further blurts.

The bartender leaned against the drip rail, smoking with a pained expression as he watched the men and women lost in their drink voids, some still trying to tell stories that had been told dozens of times, groping for new details or insights—some twist that would make the whole thing seem fresh and worth listening to. It was the sort of place where everybody knew their role, and Fitch, with his relatively clean clothes and pale arms, stood out and was the subject of several whispered conversations. A pair of bikers who had already made him for a narc or maybe an undercover game warden out to clamp down on poaching began plotting his disappearance.

The bartender asked Fitch if he was just blowing through.

He nodded. "I'm on the road."

"I got you, one of those grand jack-off types."

"Careful."

The bartender gave him some glower and brow. "What then?"

When Fitch didn't answer, the bartender pulled out a cigarette and a book of matches and asked, "Ever see a match burn twice?"

"You need a new act."

"I get by. Look around. I'm good at my job."

Fitch had a look. There were many drunk people, some severely—eyes scotched over, drooling into their collars.

"An interesting crowd."

"You think so?"

Fitch looked around the dim bar again. "It's a bit of a dick farm."

The bartender nodded and dumped well vodka into a Styrofoam cup ringed with shallow teeth marks and drank it down with his eyes closed. "I wouldn't want to be a woman," he said. "Not here at least, not tonight with all these bikers."

They were interrupted by a large unshowered man with bulging eyes and a lumpy, misshapen gut. He banged on the bar and said, "I've got some bad news, Chief."

The bartender said, "Wife came back?"

"Worse, the commode's clogged and I gotta pinch a loaf. I'm off my medication and—"

"You can stop right there, Barker," the bartender said, slapping a well-used plunger into the man's hands. "I want that back, you hear? I don't want to find it stuck to somebody's windshield like last time."

Barker tossed a mock salute and clomped off toward a small alcove in the corner bouncing the plunger off tabletops and chairs, humming to himself.

The bartender fixed Fitch with his bloodshot gaze. "In the meantime," he said, setting a saucer of water, a shot glass, one olive, and two matches on the bar. "Here's another trick for you. Without touching the saucer, put the water in the shot glass."

Fitch stared at the olive and saucer of water and shook his head. He was too drunk, the bar spinning black and brown around him, bottles gleaming as he tamped out a cigarette and reached for the matchbook next to the saucer.

"I'll give you a hint. Light the matches," said the bartender, eager to display his cleverness.

Aware that all he'd had to eat that day was a box of stale powdered donuts and some jerky, Fitch plucked the olive up and tossed it into his mouth and was about to suck the water from the saucer when the bartender stopped him.

"No, not like that. Watch." He replaced the olive and made a show of grabbing the matches and sticking one in the center of the olive alongside the pimento. He set the olive and match on the saucer, lit the other match and touched it to the one stuck in the olive. As the match flared he clamped the shot glass down over the olive and waited. Fitch watched as the flame, slowly starved for oxygen, sputtered out. As it did, the vacuum sucked the water up into the glass.

"A little science," said the bartender, scooping the whole mess into one of the slop sinks.

"Not bad," Fitch said, even though he knew the real mind was the first guy to figure out the bit with the olive and matches.

At the other end of the bar a logger grunted for beer and the bartender got him one, refusing to give any change. When he came back he said, "Lots of these loggers suffer from short-term memory loss. Bar-chain oil." He made a drinking motion, screwed a finger into his temple, and stuck his tongue out. "Branches fall on them. I mean why else would you come back to a place like this?"

"I saw the sign and those big moths flocking around the lights, plus I was thirsty."

"Once you get past the lights there's no pussy here and what pussy there is has been spoken for several times over, the odometers have been fucked with, plenty of country miles. Hell, the Treehouse is ten miles down the road and full of naive Slavic women, many of them unhappily married to long-haul truckers. And every last one of them can cook."

"None of that for me."

"A rolling stone gathers no moss, is that it?"

Fitch took a drag and tipped his drink. "Something like that."

Two bald bikers began tossing quarters at a small cup near the cash register. Above the cup was a cardboard sign that said "SINK ONE & WIN DRINK ON HOUSE." The floor beneath the bar was littered with quarters and every once in a while a coin would take a mean bounce and roll back down the bar at Fitch and his double bourbon. He knew it was time to go when a coin tossed by a lantern-jawed biker named Rex ricocheted off the cup, bounced back to the bar, and rolled down toward Fitch, where it circled his empty glass three times before swirling heads-down in front of him. He reached out to take the quarter but stopped when he saw Rex making his way down the bar through the haze of cigarette smoke, ready to whup some ass. The bartender gave Fitch one of those universal looks that said run, and so he slid off the bar stool in a drunken blur and stumbled into the night.

Just outside the door Rex clamped him in a tight, leathery bear hug, bathing Fitch in a warm fog of beer and sweaty cowhide.

"You're not from around here, are you," Rex said. "Either you go away or I will pound you till I feel no malice."

Fitch said he understood and tried to meet Rex's gaze, worried that at any moment a few of the man's hog buddies would appear and drag him off to some abandoned trailer in the woods where they would hook him up to car batteries with roach clips or beat him with shovel handles for laughs.

"It's totally up to you where we go from here," said Rex.

"Okay, I give. Uncle and all that."

"I'm not looking for an apology."

He gave one last squeeze and then with a weary sigh released Fitch. "Now disappear before you and me dance and we see what's what."

Fitch backed away as Rex went to relieve himself behind a VW Camper van before checking on his bike, a heavily chromed black Harley softail with dual dyno kickout tailpipes and a saddlebag with red stitching that read "Rex Talionis" across the top.

The stars were out, sprayed across the black sky like busted teeth, the moon sitting low and bright over the treetops. As Fitch fumbled around for the keys to the Dart he saw a woman walk out of the dark woods. With her mass of tangled blond hair and torn clothes she looked as if she'd been ravaged and tossed from a moving car and had come back for more. She walked straight at him, the moonlight glowing behind her, casting weak shadows across the gravel lot.

"Hey," she said. "I know you."

"Me?" Fitch said.

"No, Fuckwad, me." Fitch turned around and saw that it was Rex.

"I get the strays," he said, shoving Fitch to the ground and grabbing the woman. He spun her around, laughing as she struggled against him. "First I'm gonna buy you a bunch of drinks," he said, dragging her toward the bar. "Then I'm gonna introduce you to some friends of mine who like to party and after we've had some fun I'll take you for a ride."

"I don't want to ride," she said.

He cuffed her roughly on the back of the head. "Hey, do you think I take just any hole for a ride?"

Fitch looked on, knowing that whatever "fun" Rex had in mind would most likely be ugly and sporadically violent. So he summoned some of that old gridiron cream-'em-in-the-earhole fury from his days as a strong safety for the Massilon Tigers and charged Rex with everything he had, bulling his head and lowering the boom of his shoulders. They went down in a tangle of adrenalized arms and legs. Rex immediately started swinging and caught Fitch with a few weak blows to the face and chest. Fitch answered by gouging at Rex, his thumb finding the soft cave of an eye socket.

Rex screamed and rolled away, reaching for something in his boot. Fitch jabbed him with a quick roundhouse to the throat and followed that up with a good old-fashioned military ear boxing that sent the biker to his knees howling.

Ready for the coup de grâce, he closed in only to have Rex stagger to his feet and charge, elbows whirling in jagged arcs. Fitch tried to duck but a vicious elbow to his temple sent painful shock waves up and down his spine as if he'd just been slammed headfirst into hard, wet sand by a killer wave. Rex connected again. Blood fluttered behind Fitch's eyes and his vision whirled with giant orange sperm that gave way to an electric blackness that faded as Rex began kicking him in the ribs, raging about his blown eardrums.

Fitch crawled for his life, trying to escape the fury of Rex's stacked-heel blows, which were landing with increasing fury. He slithered under a pickup truck and surfaced on the other side groping the bed for something to lay upside the biker's thick skull— some kind of tire iron or ball hitch to get at the meat and stop his charge. Instead he found a can of Quick Start carburetor ether. It would have to do, and so in one fluid motion he blasted Rex between the eyes with the ether. Like a man who'd had his cord cut and didn't know it yet, Rex continued to stand, his face clamped down into a Leninesque scowl as he took a few more steps. Fitch blasted him again and this time he toppled, ripping at his eyes and mouth. Fitch stood over him, the can still poised to strike, wondering if he'd fried Rex's retinas with the ether or, worse, killed him. But after retching up a foamy delta of beer and half-digested chili dogs, Rex groaned and passed out. Worried that he'd pull a Hendrix and choke on his own vomit, Fitch rolled him onto his side and draped a burlap sack over his shoulders.

Then he stood to see if there had been any witnesses to the fight. There was nothing—just the silhouette of the woman walking toward him against the glare of the bug-encrusted bar lights. "You're the one that I want," she said, coming closer. "Yes, I definitely know you. You're—" Without warning she collapsed between a Ford and an old yellow International.

Fitch bent to pull her to her feet. She was drunk or tripping on something and not the devil woman he'd first taken her for, even though he did have a thing for witchy women and her sudden appearance confirmed a lifelong suspicion that out-of-the-way bars were hotbeds of random sexual encounters. He'd just never found the right out-of-the-way bar or rescued a woman from some sorry biker gang bang.

"You, you, you," she said into his neck. "You came to my rescue, mister knight in shining armor." Her shirt popped open, displaying a butterfly tattoo between her breasts and, still lower, the fold of her paunch. He caught a whiff of sex and sweat that sent his blood flooding to all the wrong places.

"We haven't met," Fitch said. "I drift, I mean, I'm a drifter."

She laughed and stood uneasily, brushing twigs and fern leaves from her hair. "I'm a lady who knows." She bit her lip and stopped giggling.

"Knows what?"

"Things." She came closer. Her eyes were staring off in different directions and she had a gap in her teeth. "That your car?" she asked, pointing at the Dart.

He hesitated and then nodded. "That's my ride," Fitch said, trying to rally some pride for the pitifully square car leaking oil onto the dusty lot. "You said you knew something. What do you know?"

"I suppose you want examples?"

"That would be nice."

She laughed, tried walking, and nearly fell again. "I know what you're thinking." She did that thing with her lip again and she had him.

"Yeah?"

"I know that you'd like to wash your face between my legs." She opened her shirt and flashed her breasts at him. They were large and white, not to mention the tattoo crushed between them. Outstanding breasts. They could have been in a magazine, pressed against some chrome or tumbling in the hay, a little sunlight breaking over them. Plus there was something interestingly wrong with one of the nipples—it was too large and drooped oval. Fitch bent to have a closer look, hoping to find more sexy imperfections.

She whispered in his ear. "I knew you'd save me. I could see it in your aura."

Fitch blushed. If this was what the hippie chicks were like he might have to consider letting his flattop grow out, get himself some of those love beads, stop showering, and work on his b.o. "Do you wanna go for a ride?" he asked.

She pointed at the Dart and laughed. "In that?"

"It's better than it looks."

"It's for shit," she hissed. "My old man drives a hog. He could mess you up and break every bone in your body if he wanted. He knows the arts. He can catch flies with chopsticks. He's killed three men. There may be more, but I don't ask questions, because he's got a wicked backhand."

"Hey now, I just asked if you wanted a ride. There's no need to go criticizing my wheels and siccing your old man on me."

"You're right," she said. "We're on the outs anyways. I've been trying to put all that behind me, but things keep happening to me. Like tonight, for example. How did I end up here? And what about this dirtbag?" She stood over Rex and tried to spit on him but could only manage a ball of white foam that drifted wide right and curled dust when it landed. "I suppose I should kick him," she said. "Smash his nuts or something permanent like that. I don't think men like this should be allowed the privilege of reproducing. I'd like to plant a tree in his ass and watch it grow. It's the only way anything good's gonna come out of him."

"It would take a long time."

She shook her head and gave up on further violence and trying to spit on Rex again. She staggered back over to the Dart, where she did some complicated kung fu stuff over the hood of the car, clapping and making hissing noises.

"What's that?" Fitch asked.

"I put a curse on it. You don't need that car. That car will kill you."

"Curse? What kind of curse?"

"You'll see," she said, grinning. "I'm doing you a favor. I'm generous with my gift. Like I said, I know things before they happen. I anticipate phone calls and bridge collapses. I predicted Kent State. But in my dream it was three dead. But four people I know are dying. You don't have cancer, not yet at least, but I wouldn't rule it out. It will start in your colon. I can tell you that. I've changed my name three times and—"

"Okay," said Fitch. "So you have a gift." He looked at the Dart with its bald tires, dangling tailpipe, and dented grill and decided that the last thing it needed was a curse, valid or not. "I want you to take that curse off."

"I'm afraid I can't do that."

"Well, how about you try."

"Come here," she purred. "I want to give you something for killing that man for me."

"He's not dead," Fitch said.

"Yet," she said with a slight giggle. "But he will be in three days."

Her prediction made Fitch nervous and so he went to check on Rex and found him still breathing. His legs stirred gravel. There was some general moaning and rasping coming from somewhere deep in his chest. Fitch figured that, contrary to the woman's forecast of death, the biker would be up breaking laws and drinking beer in no time.

"He's going to pull through."

"His buddies will find you then. It will not be pretty."

On this matter she had a point and so Fitch quickly moved the Dart, hiding it under some low branches on a rutted turnoff next to a collapsed deer carcass with something squirming around inside it, mining bits of rotten meat. When he returned to the parking lot he found the woman standing at the edge of the woods, shimmying at him, hips moving like some stoned Nancy Sinatra singing about her boots.

"Hey, you," she called, before ducking into the fringe of trees and motioning for him to follow.

Fitch entered the woods, concocting all sorts of backwoods sex scenarios. He wanted to smell her again and run his tongue over the tattoo down into the fold of her stomach, lower and lower, and come back up around her spine in some kind of buzz saw cross-sectioned equatorial love move. Of course, he'd settle for quick and dirty and maybe even something painful.

When they came to a small clearing she stopped and tossed her hands around in a general manner. "Look," she said. "It's all around us."

"Trees," Fitch said. "How interesting. Now, about that curse. I've already got play in the steering column. It burns oil and there's this grinding sound that troubles me. I don't know any good mechanics."

"You worry too much," she said and scampered away deeper into the woods. He stumbled after her and nicked his head on a tree limb because he was still thinking of her humpers and how if he could just find her he might have a chance of seeing them again, but she was gone, swallowed by the black forest. He called out a few times and chased her over a ridge, down into a boggy creek bottom where mosquitoes and gnats rose in buzzing clouds to assail him.

Just as he'd begun to give up hope he heard her voice. "Over here, silly rabbit," she said. He turned and saw her face hanging in the dark, taunting him. He moved toward her, tripping over exposed roots and low-lying vines, his shoes spongy with stagnant creek scum, only to find her gone again.

Ten minutes later it began to occur to him that not only was he lost but he would never find the woman unless she allowed herself to be found. Worse still, he'd begun to suspect that perhaps she was leading him into some ambush and that at any moment a pair of in-bred backwoodsmen would spring from the bushes, club him to death with pine knots, and sink his body in a bog.

He swatted at mosquitoes, hoping to catch one more glimpse of the woman before he called it quits, but a thick ground fog began to twist and wend its way through the already murky woods. He heard grunting and out of the corner of his eye saw something large and dark moving and feared that it would be just his luck to get mauled by a bear or gored by a horny elk. Or worse, meet up with a Sasquatch. He hadn't given the Bigfoot stuff much thought, but as he stood there in the damp, dark woods the possible existence of large, smelly apemen seemed beaucoup real. He didn't want to be carried off to some dank cave to be shrieked at by a family of them and then later forced to face the press and recount his story, insisting that he was a trustworthy and productive member of society who stood to gain nothing by going public with his abduction.

He stood still for a very long time. The last of his horniness gave way to fear and then panic as he finally attempted to retrace his steps, swimming through the underbrush toward a faint light he could see hovering in the distance, remembering something about will-o'-the-wisps, wondering if that's all the girl was. But after half an hour of bushwhacking he found a narrow game trail leading back over the ridge. By the time he managed to claw his way out of the woods and felt the road under his feet he no longer could remember her face, only her loopy voice and of course the breasts.

Somebody had smashed the Dart's windshield and kicked out the taillights. But he was too tired to care and crawled across the front seat, brushing glass off the vinyl before passing out.

The next morning he woke with cubes of glass pressed to his

cheeks and wood ticks burrowing their snouts into his flesh. He studied their greedy blood-swollen bodies and wondered if they were part
of the curse or just the sort of thing you got for lurking around the
woods at night. He punched the Dart's cigarette lighter and started
coaxing the ticks out. Most of them waddled off and dropped to the
floor mats, frantically scratching over the bits of broken windshield
before Fitch brought his boot heel down on them. The more stubborn
ones he let dance on the hot coils of the cigarette lighter until they exploded, peppering his arms with their warm insides. He licked some
of the blood. It tasted good and got him to thinking of the woman,
wondering if she was still waiting for him as he scanned the woods
through the web of broken windshield. But there was no woman. His
ribs ached and his face and neck were full of red knuckle blossoms
from his tussle with Rex that would soon rot into purple bruises.

After he'd rid himself of the last tick, he checked his wallet again,
kicked out the rest of the windshield, and began brushing the glass
out the door when he noticed a strange backpack in the backseat.

He grabbed the pack and set it on the hood of the Dart. The bottom was wet and smelled like liquor and so he opened it. Inside were
dozens of small airline bottles of scotch, bourbon, and gin, most of
them smashed. There were also three cans of Squirt, a leatherbound
book covered with weird symbols and signs, two pairs of striped athletic socks, a sack of marshmallows, a pouch containing a pair of
ivory dice and a pack of playing cards with naked women on them,
a bottle of Romilar cough syrup, and a black knit ski mask. He salvaged what liquor he could and set the rest of the items out to dry,
drinking a can of hot Squirt after brushing away sticky flecks of glass
from the rim. Then he ate the marshmallows, washing them down
with a tiny bottle of Jim Beam and some cough syrup. He looked
down and next to the delicate remains of a dead toad pressed into
the road tar there was a dime. He smiled—his luck was back.

Then he examined the book. It was hand-titled "Book IV"—the
Roman numerals a clever touch. There was a crudely drawn Mayan
calendar on the first page, under which was written: *It's the end of the
world and I feel fine*. The following pages were filled with neat, tight

script, the margins populated with strange symbols—pi signs with small bird heads protruding from them, slashes, squares bisected by rectangles, clefs, crescents with stars at both tips, signs shaped like staffs, and many circles bounding minute stick figures. One symbol had been repeated many times. The symbol consisted of three circles arranged in a delta or upside down triangle. The author of the book had taken great pains to reproduce them in many colors and sizes. Below one such rendering was a short paragraph about how the symbol was first found on a cave wall and then three thousand years later on a painting. The accompanying explanation of the connection escaped Fitch's hungover brain and so he skimmed ahead to the dated entries.

He read one. *Ate breakfast*, it said. *Tasted good. Love oats. Must remember to chew more. Must remember my name is not Abe or Jeb or Hey or Jack or Buddy or You or Captain or Chief, et all. Easy to forget. But then what is a name? I have been up here so long and she has been gone so long nothing means nothing . . .*

. . . Put milk away. Believe expiration date has been tampered with—a trick to get you to buy more. Comrade in California, codename Fishboy, confirms this. Wonder if tobacco companies are in on this. Well-known fact they put ground glass in Skoal and have smoking chimps . . .

. . . Terrible conspiracies out there, underarm deodorant, Ziebart, lip balm, the repeat step on shampoo bottles, Pepsodent for a Whiter Smile! Things that melt in your mouth and not in your hands.

. . . Looked out window. Birds but no agents today. Things not what they seem. Clicking in phone. Things never what they seem. Weatherman is often wrong, but he has nice hair, bright smile and points well and everybody buys it . . .

. . . Checked on crop. Crows eating seedling. Bad luck to kill them, this from comrade in Peshawbestown who explained crow/raven link, something about their use of tools, deceptive nature, and breeding ritual . . .

. . . Met man with steel plate in head today. Said Army gave it to him and that it stopped wristwatches, made pins dance, hurt during full moons, and interfered with his television reception. Could not confirm this, but he did have strange scars above his eyes . . .

Whole pages were dedicated to describing the precise and proper way of frying bacon—the man who was not Jeb or Abe preferred it undercooked and believed there was a conspiracy among local diner owners to overcrisp bacon. There was mention of a group called the AWAKE Brigade that the author promised would take action and snap open eyes all over the country, after which a period of great re-assessment called The Coming would follow. There was other vague revolutionary mumbo jumbo, but Fitch favored the long-winded di-atribes against a woman named Jane, who had somehow wronged the author. She owed him money and had kidnapped a German shorthaired pointer named Buck from him. He described her as a bird of prey and feared her powers of seduction, going on at some length as to the blondness of her hair and the firmness of her thighs and breasts. Despite the author's many and sundry objections to her, she retained an air of mystery. Who was she? Where could she be found? And what was it about her voice that drove men to such de-basement? If that wasn't enough, there was a pen-and-ink nude sketch of her in one of the margins. Great detail had been paid to the breasts, with finger rubbing and fine hatching around the aureoles. But the artist had gotten the eyes all wrong; they were uneven and lizardlike, looking off in different directions.

Fitch stared at the sketch, wondering if the woman he'd chased into the woods had been this Jane. After all, it had been dark and he'd been drunk, his brain scrambled by the curse, those breasts, the gap in her teeth, and the beating from Rex. He looked up briefly into the jigsaw of trees and brush, momentarily transfixed by the swarm-ing zigzag of deerflies and mosquitoes zipping about on their blood maneuvers. His ribs hurt. There was a knot on his head and he had not gotten laid.

He flipped through the rest of the book and found a map of Mexico taped to one of the back pages. On the opposing page was a hand ren-dering of the same map, titled "True and Sovereign State of Mexico, Containing Hidden Territories and Secret Lands for Those in the Know." Most of it was the same but there were a few spots, marked with red peace signs, that, according to the lengthy legend, indicated

Hidden Territories and Secret Lands. A page and a half of elaborate directions that began *Down to a sunless sea. So twice five miles of fertile ground, then five miles meandering with a mazy motion* ended with a long list of secret passwords and the names of people in the know. Fitch studied the map and noticed that several large *J*s denoting places where Jane had been spotted or was known to have spent time. He flipped back to the sketch, trying to discern if the woman he'd rescued the night before had been this Jane. He was not sure.

Still curious, he waded into the woods as birds hopped from tiny branch to tiny branch and a ground squirrel twittered. He ventured deeper and called out, "Jane." But there was no answer and so he went back to the Dart, took one last look at the book, stashed it and the bag in the back, and drove east toward home, dodging the cubes of glass that periodically sailed off the hood at him like hail.

His luck ran out on an empty strip of Route 20, ten miles east of Harper. The Dart blew a rod and no sooner had he steered it off the road when he heard a soft whoosh and saw flames shooting from the grille, buckling the paint. Fitch sat behind the wheel locked in disbelief. Black smoke fingered its way out the vent louvers and billowed through the knocked-out windshield, stinging his eyes and drifting over the molded plastic dashboard, which had begun to ripple with the heat. He snatched the backpack and his duffel bag full of clothes from the backseat and ran screaming from the car, sure that at any moment it would blow and he'd be skewered by flying lifter rods, pelted with hot motor mounts, and blown clear off his feet when the gas tank exploded.

He retreated and when there was no dramatic explosion he crept closer, transfixed by the angry Halloween-colored collars of flame whorling off the Dart's burning radials. Perhaps, he thought, he was the victim of some grand cosmic plan to grind him up and spit him out. Maybe this was the final gutter bounce, the rock bottom Geena had always warned him about whenever they spotted old liver-spotted men in moth-eaten tweed coats Dumpster diving or pear-shaped women in Dacron dresses dragging trash bags around the bus station, looking for a place to sleep or maybe some lonely guy to buy them a ticket to anywhere as long as there was a handjob some-where down the road. "They still have a ways to go," Geena would say. "That last step to the gutter's a long one."

He started walking. It was hot, the sun a seething match head in the cloudless vault of blue, burning for him. He tried thumbing a ride from the occasional flatbed full of Indians that sped past him. No luck there, and so he began looking for a patch of shade—a rock or tree, anything that would allow him to escape the sun.

A mile down the road he guzzled one of the travel-sized gins and washed that down with more cough syrup. He resumed his aimless march, half wishing an air-conditioned bus would appear on the horizon, pop its hinged doors open for him, and take him to Reno, a town he imagined to be full of crafty drifters he could apprentice himself to. He looked up and saw the glint of a distant jet and the milky white contrail splitting the sky. The jet was no air-conditioned bus but it did get him to thinking of escape to some faraway place like one of the spots on the map in the book he'd found in his car—a place where he could just be, maybe loaf and live off the land a lit-tle, meet interesting folks, and basically get by with a minimal amount of hassle. The more he thought about it, the more it seemed that the sudden appearance of the backpack and the strange book were too great a coincidence to go unnoticed. Add to that the curse and the subsequent fiery destruction of the Dart and it seemed to Fitch that he'd stepped out of the random flow of his life into a place where anything was possible—even a ride out of the high desert, where he was disappointed to find no mirages, no shimmering lakes littered with topless women waiting to pour cold beer down his maw. It was just rock and sage and dust.

So he walked, letting the Romilar and gin melt away his fears of a hot, stranded death as he spun grand escape plans and with great ef-fort forced his limbs to move, remembering to hoist his thumb and look friendly whenever he saw the flash of an approaching car.

An hour later a silver-haired man pulled alongside Fitch in a Buick Skylark and said, "Hop in, soldier. Let's start with a name."

"Fitch."

He crushed Fitch's hand. "Larry. I'm ex-Marine."

"So?"

"So mess with me and I'll kick your ass into next week." He smiled, tossed a map out of the way, and slapped the vinyl seat.

Fitch got in.

Not wanting to swap war stories or hear some hastily barked comparison between the Korean conflict and Nam, Fitch kept silent about his two tours of duty as he smoked the last of his cigarettes and thought about quitting.

"My car blew up. Maybe you saw it back there."

"The Dart?"

"I don't know what happened."

"Well, it's charcoal now and there's a bunch of Indian boys frying snakes on the hood. Was it insured?"

Fitch shook his head.

"Typical," Larry said.

They rode through the dry rock wasteland of the John Day Wilderness. Raptors drifted overhead, their shadows flickering across the canyon walls like dark crosses.

"I hope you're not in a hurry to get back," Larry said. "I'm a scenic route kind of guy. Freeways give me migraines."

Fitch adjusted a vent toward his face. "I have nothing to get back to."

Larry shook his head in disgust and said, "Typical."

From time to time he swerved around ancient ranchers puttering along in stake trucks laden with alfalfa bales, and Fitch clutched the backpack containing Book IV to his chest, closed his eyes, and imagined the Skylark violently remodeled by an oncoming tractor trailer. Larry turned out to be quite the chatterbox, jawing about his plans to open a knife-and-gun shop. Fitch listened, happy when Portland finally came into view.

UPON ARRIVAL AT the trailer Fitch started planning his escape to Mexico. He knew a few things. One, that he would need money and, two, that he wasn't going to work or answer to some boss for it. He was done with paychecks, punch clocks, pensions, lunch breaks, FICA, and fuck all else that came with making a straight go of it. He'd tried all that and been shown the door and maybe it took nearly frying to death in the desert for him to wise up or maybe it was the book and that map and nude lady working on him, but he figured that there had to be a better way. What he had in mind was some sort of one-time-only crime that would finance his escape. It was a subject he'd been contemplating like crazy since the war.

CHAPTER TWO

On the way back from the lake Frank stopped off at a gas station to top the tank. He pumped and looked around. A group of teenaged boys were huddled near the ice machine pointing Swiss Army knives and skateboards at one another. And there was a chubby woman in black stretch pants sobbing into a pay phone who caught him staring and pointed at him. In the car behind her three small children sat with their faces pressed to the window, smearing the remains of what looked like a Tootsie Roll against the glass. He pretended to fiddle with the pump but when he looked back she was frantically waving him over.

He set the gas cap on the trunk and walked across the lot, wondering what she could possibly want from him.

"Do you have a quarter I could borrow?" the woman asked. He fished around in his pocket and gave her two, watching as she fed them into the slot before putting her hand over the receiver and thanking him in a soft whisper. Then she turned away from him and apologized to the person on the line in a tiny voice that made Frank cringe.

He walked back, finished pumping the economy, and was checking the cupping on his rear tires when a police cruiser swung into the
station. A tall, flabby-jawed cop got out, angrily squelching his hip
radio as he slid a long, black Maglite from his holster and approached
the teens. When he spotted the cop, one of the boys slapped down
his board and skated off. The rest stood their ground as the officer ordered them to empty their pockets. They quickly dropped their haul
and scattered, leaving behind a few shoplifted packs of Twinkies,
several bent candy bars, and an issue of *Guns & Ammo*.

Frank went inside to pay. The cashier looked at him, blew the hair
out of her eyes, and scratched at a purple hickey on her neck. She
had cheap rings on every finger and a necklace with her name
spelled in fake gold script; Melissa. Frank pegged her for twenty-five,
one kid maybe and definitely unmarried, taking night classes at the
JC and hoping to become a nurse or paralegal.

"Pump six," said Frank, sliding a twenty-dollar bill across to her.

"Never a dull moment around here," Melissa said, pointing outside. "Last week it was the Chicken Man undressing behind the chip
rack, flashing customers, and then Sammy found a deer hoof in the
rest room. Somebody wrote "Imagine" on the mirror with soap too,
but I don't think it was a reference to that John Lennon song, more
a comment on the hoof."

The cop came in and sauntered up behind Frank with his chest
puffed out, hands gunslingered on his holster. "If they come back I
want you to call me," the cop said.

Melissa nodded. "What was it about this time?"

"A disagreement over whose mother wears army boots. But I
think we've come to an understanding."

"Well, I told them to take it outside and they took it outside,"
Melissa said. "That's progress."

The cop grunted and dropped the Twinkies, a Three Musketeers
bar, and the magazine on the counter. "I've recovered some evidence," he said. "I hate to blame the parents, but this is where it
starts."

"Snack food and *Guns & Ammo*?"

"No, the life of crime. If I were you I'd demand that Sammy get you one of those bulletproof stalls like they got over at the Chevron."

"We have our own system," Melissa said, pointing at the counter below, where a gun lurked. She handed Frank his change, flashing him a dull smile. He lingered a minute and then went outside and saw that the phone shelter was empty. Where the woman's car had been idling there was a small pool of radiator fluid. He tapped the edge of the green pool with his shoe and felt around his pocket for the car keys, his fingers brushing the finger bone. An unexpected chill went up his arm and stayed there even as he slipped back into the stream of traffic, where, as if by habit, he scanned license plates and studied drivers, most of whom were locked in thought or listening to the radio. The few that did return his stare seemed slightly irritated by the intrusion. A mile down the road Frank realized he was headed in the wrong direction, away from home, and took the first right into a narrow parking lot to turn around. He wasn't sure why he'd made the mistake but instead of correcting he paused at the lip of the road, thinking of the woman at the pay phone and the desperate look on her face as she'd taken the quarters from him. Something about the whole episode stirred up another piece of unfinished business that had been looming over his retirement for quite some time.

Instead of correcting his mistake and heading home, he took a left and headed for the trailer park to see Anne Blackwood, a woman whose husband, Jimmy "J. B." Blackwood, Frank had arrested four years ago for distributing several kilos of pure uncut heroin. As he drove, houses flicking by in the late afternoon sun, he wondered if maybe Anne had something to do with the state he'd been in—if whatever unresolved mess he'd created with her was part of the weight he felt pressing down on him whenever he contemplated the end of his days in the Bureau and what came after.

J. B. had killed a man and tortured several of his former partners. One of them, a man named Carl Dixon, had aided the FBI with its investigation after Blackwood forced him to eat rat poison at gunpoint and then mistakenly left him for dead at a rest stop. Dixon rat-

ted for real and Frank and a dozen other agents stormed the Blackwood house before sunrise with warrants and guns. He remembered
how on the night they'd come to arrest her husband, Anne had
greeted him in the bedroom doorway, her face dull with sleep, almost as if she'd been expecting this moment and now that it had arrived she seemed already bored with it and ready for the next part of
her life to begin.

Despite the black eye and split lip, she looked beautiful standing
there with her youngest boy cradled in her arms, shielding his eyes
as flak-jacketed agents rushed through the house, securing dark
rooms with revolvers and racked riot guns. She locked eyes with
Frank and slowly pointed to a walk-in closet. He immediately understood and motioned for Agent Brown to kick open the louvered
door while Frank covered him. For a minute the room was filled
with the chatter of wire coat hangers as J. B. emerged from behind
several dry-cleaning bags. He was naked and holding a revolver at
his side. Several flashlights danced over his pale and well-built
physique, the powerful shoulders and hard stomach marred by
burnt-match-and-spit tattoos of serpents, dice, and daggers. His eyes
were hard and black like apple seeds. He was ready to mix it up and
die.

Frank shouted and advanced across the room, keeping him dead
to right, prepared to blow J. B.'s hip joints out if he made some crazy
move to escalate the situation. It was a delicate moment, one that
Frank had come to appreciate. The bad guy had a choice. Either he
could acknowledge that it was all over and let himself be taken or
else he could make one last move to save a little face. Frank could
see J. B. sizing up the situation, even looking down at the floor, perhaps to imagine how the carpet might soak up his blood should he
decide to say fuck it and make a struggle of things.

Instead he grinned, dropped the gun to the carpet, and said,
"Hello."

As soon as an agent kicked the gun clear, Frank gave the signal
and two jacked-up baby-face agents approached J. B. with zip cuffs
and a body chain.

"Floor," Frank said, pointing. "Floor now!"

J. B. got on the floor, every muscle in his back strung tight, all hardwire and gonads, still ready to pop up and take a beat down or bullets. But he didn't, and as Frank dragged him out to the idling van, he turned to see Anne standing on the front porch looking not at her husband but at him. Her cool, unwavering stare masked rocket loads of relief as the van door slid shut and swallowed up the father of her children.

The whole thing should have ended that night. But a month before his trial J. B. skipped bail and disappeared, leaving behind a wife and two small boys, and it became Frank's job to watch over Anne, check in from time to time and call her to ask how she was getting along and if she'd heard from her husband. The theory was that sooner or later J. B. would come back and try to see his family and that's when they would grab him. At the very least Frank figured he'd make a phone call and arrange to have money sent—they almost always did. One thing he'd learned was that bad guys loved their wives and missed their kids just as much as the next law-abiding joe—an Achilles heel that allowed them to be scooped back up into the system.

Blackwood, however, was a pro. He did not come back or make any sort of contact with his wife or former friends. During the first few months of his disappearance Frank trailed J. B.'s now ex-wife down narrow dirt roads at odd hours of the night, expecting a rendezvous, only to watch her sob against the steering wheel in between gulped cigarettes. He followed her to work, drafting behind her in his government-issue sedan as she went about the ordinary everyday errands of a life. He took some pleasure in the fact that the woman with the black eye and split lip who'd given up her husband in that dark bedroom had tried to make something better for herself. Because in Frank's experience most people in her situation did not try for anything better and instead wallowed in the misfortune, usually making things worse for themselves.

In the aftermath, what the government hadn't seized the bail bondsmen laid claim to, until Anne found herself living in a dim and cramped trailer, barely scraping by as she tried to raise her two boys. She'd started a small cleaning service, working long hours and encouraging her more understanding clients to pay cash. Frank admired her for maintaining, for not slipping back into the freewheeling lifestyle she'd known before the arrest.

She displayed no curiosity when Frank told her that a man matching her ex-husband's description had been sighted in Seattle and Billings, his hair peroxided, driving a late-model Ford van. Nor did she flinch when he reported that J. B. was a suspect in a violent convenience-store robbery west of Pendleton in which the cashier had been pistol-whipped and beaten with an ice scraper.

Blackwood was out there and he would come back—Frank was sure of it.

But then an odd thing happened: Frank found himself looking forward to his meetings and phone conversations with Anne. Even as the search for her husband got back-burnered and other more urgent cases piled up on his desk, he made a point to keep up with her and over the years had more or less gotten involved with her life. While he'd done nothing to encourage the friendship, he'd done nothing to stop it from happening. He couldn't put his finger on exactly when the routine visits had become something else, but they had and he was careful to hide any trace of it from her. Perhaps it was the time she'd asked if he wanted something to drink—ice tea, Pepsi, or beer—and he'd answered, "Beer," watching her smile as she popped two cans and walked into the living room with them, wanting him to follow. He did.

Another time he stayed for dinner and after the boys had gone to sleep they watched *The Poseidon Adventure*, talking late into the night as Shelley Winters swam for her life in the upside-down ship. The difference between them was that Frank remembered Shelley Winters as the sleepy-eyed bombshell in *Night of the Hunter* where all Anne saw was the hysterical fat woman clutching at her fat neck and blubbering about her schlub of a husband.

Another time he discovered a pile of unpaid bills and shut-off notices on her kitchen counter and offered to loan her money. She refused and so he simply returned the next week with several crisp hundred-dollar bills and slipped them into her purse when she wasn't looking.

On each visit he made a point of mentioning her ex-husband, asking a few questions. Had J. B. made contact? Any strange phone calls? He pretended to take notes, even though her answers were always the same and he knew her well enough to trust that she wasn't feeding him lines.

Then one hot July afternoon she stopped him at the front door and asked point-blank what the hell it was he thought he wanted. He looked her straight in the eyes and said, "I'm just doing my job."

"What kind of job is that?"

"Helping people."

She curled her lips and said, "Bullshit."

Frank flinched and looked down at his tie, swiping at some imaginary lint, drinking in his scuffed shoes. She had her answer. He excused himself and walked to his car, the question bouncing around his head the whole way home. He wanted to steer into traffic and have her come to his rescue, cradle his smashed body—only then would he be able to look her in the eyes again with cop authority. But as his grip loosened on the steering wheel and he reached to adjust the volume knob on the radio, the feeling passed and he knew he would be okay and could go back to being Frank in a day or two. Nothing had been lost. All he had to do was maintain and it would pass. It had to pass.

He stayed away the rest of the summer, until Anne finally called the Bureau and, after telling him there was nothing new to report, mentioned that her boys missed him. He stopped by that very same afternoon and then again a month later. Little by little he erected the elaborate firewall of excuses that allowed him to keep seeing her with a minimum of guilt and the comfortable veneer of normality.

Now, as he turned and heard the familiar crunch of his tires on the gravel entrance of Middling Oaks Trailer Court, he kept telling himself over and over that he should wheel the car around and never come back. He would be retired in a week and could no longer hide behind the flimsy see-through satin line that he was "just doing his job"—a job that required him to ask the same routine questions about her ex-husband's whereabouts before they could talk about anything else.

The fact was he no longer thought of Anne as just another interesting and basically well-intentioned person for whom he felt a small amount of pity. It was much more than that. He enjoyed the messy life she'd managed to carve out for herself and there were times as he watched her standing under the cheap frosted light fixture in her torn Seahawks jersey, her arms covered in bright Palmolive suds, that he wanted something more from her and was sure she'd thought the same thing occasionally—and that all it would take was one firm and determined move to part the invisible curtain they'd erected. But every time he arrived at her trailer, his head full of sex—imagining Anne straddling him, dressed in one of those faded tube tops she liked to wear low, biting her lip and pressing her work-chapped hands against his shoulders as she ground away at him—she would mention a man she was seeing or ask him about his wife and family and Frank would ask his cop questions and leave the trailer giddy with his suppressed desire, vowing to jack off more than once a week or pay special attention to Clare, but not so much as to arouse her suspicion. He was content to twist between wanting it to happen and not wanting it to happen, the whole thing just dangling there, waiting for him to neglect it and let it die as he had so many other fleeting desires. And even though he'd pushed it around his head enough to know that he would not be taking advantage of her. He would not be like the other men he knew who had cheated on their wives and took guilty pride in confiding their infidelities to other men over a couple of beers and some baseball game on the television or while teeing up the Titleist on the eighteenth hole. Every time Frank unscrolled the fantasy he would inevitably come to the part where he would have to sneak past Clare and feed her lies about how he'd worked late on a case and then stopped off at the gym for a quick workout and shower. What bothered him was not that he'd be forced to deceive her but that she would buy his story because he was Frank and she trusted him. No matter how many times he rehearsed the deed he couldn't get it to end any other way or, for that matter, imagine balancing the guilt and sneaking around that would surely be required. And so he maintained—burying himself in the parade of cases, the routine phone calls, briefings, surveillance, and visits to the lab.

As he topped the trailer court hill a couple of boys astride mutilated Schwinn ten-speeds tailed his car down the winding narrow streets, past dozens of cramped dandelioned lawns disfigured with broken toys and rusty jungle gym sets. The boys peeled off down an alley lined with propane tanks and piles of wet cardboard boxes.

A few residents had attempted to dress up their lots by planting crooked flower beds around fake wishing wells or bordering the cracked cement walks with painted rocks and submerged tractor tires. To Frank, the stab at picket-fence perfection seemed a tiny and desperate measure, as useless as wind chimes. In the rare instances that he actually took note of the place, he imagined Clare's standard singsong appraisal of bad real estate, a simple "Ewww."

Anne's trailer was one of the ones that tried: the grass had been cut recently, the boxwood had been trimmed, and there were even plastic window planters full of dahlias, asters, and cockscomb lolling bright orange, pink, and yellow over the edge, the window glass cloudy with their spilled pollen.

He parked behind a faded purple Gran Torino with a missing bumper and flaking chrome trim. The air filled with the jabber of daytime television and the distant drone of weed whips and lawn mowers.

At a nearby trailer an old man sitting on a lawn chair raised his cane at Frank. He waved back and crossed the street toward Anne's place.

Her car was gone and so he walked around to the side of the trailer and spotted her oldest, a thin-armed boy of seven named Rory. He was sitting on the back porch dropping Japanese beetles into a coffee can filled with gasoline.

Frank waited a minute, trying to decide whether he should flip up the gate latch, walk back, and say something to the kid, tell him he'd stopped by to see his mother or something like that. Instead he scanned the trailer's small aluminum-framed windows before walking back to the car, relieved by her absence and still not sure why he'd come.

As he pulled away, the boy looked up and waved hesitantly. Several metallic green beetles clung to his fingers, glinting in the sun as they tried to get free. Frank waved back, watching as Rory quickly shook his hand over the gasoline.

■

DURING FITCH'S SECOND tour of duty he met a fellow grunt named Ricks, a muscular black guy from Philly whom everybody called The Brick. One night on patrol The Brick confessed how he used to pull the occasional armed robbery when he was short of bread or wanted to impress a lady with a gold watch he couldn't exactly afford. "Nothing to it," The Brick said. "Just need yourself a set of stainless steel nuts and a gun—any old gun will do. The trick is you gotta mean it. They look at the gun, and then they check ya out, see if you're some kinda cold-blooded killer. See, what I do is this." The Brick rolled up his sleeves and stood twitching his muscles in the moonlight. "Now do you think some bubblegummer minding the register is gonna fuck with me? Hell no, man, they gimme what I want. Sometimes I don't even gotta ask. Sometimes it's like I got ESP."

And so it was with The Brick's simple advice coming back to him that Fitch idled away his afternoons casing banks and credit unions. He watched the tellers take smoke breaks, crushing the butts out with their heels, looking for hose runs, and checking their makeup in small oval mirrors before going back to work. He imagined them scampering around the polished lobby floor as he pointed a gun at them. Maybe he'd even cut one from the herd and take her with him on some criminal spree where she'd eventually grow to admire him for his views and bravado. He got as far as buying a black ski mask and practicing in the mirror until the wool mouth hole was damp with spit and smelled like rotten crotch and he realized that he didn't have the charming banter to be a bank robber or the in-your-face menace The Brick had demonstrated for him years ago in the jungle. His criminal streak, like available-light photography, was best when circumstances cooperated. So far the various crimes he'd considered refused to frame up and take shape—he'd scoped liquor stores and gas stations with bad intent and, after badgering his few low-life friends and part-time criminal acquaintances to no avail, went to speak with Boris Sparks, a veteran armed robber who hung around the Yamhill Tavern playing Yahtzee and acting as a reluctant fence. Fitch had once helped Boris move a steel claw tub, a dozen bags of quick-set cement, and a large plastic-wrapped duffel into a basement. Boris had tipped him an extra fifty and a twelve-pack of Rainier to wipe his brain clean of the job. Fitch said no problem, even as he helped Boris lift the duffel into the tub and felt the unmistakable outline of a hand.

The Yamhill Tavern had high ceilings and white stucco walls scaled with cheap beer mirrors and sickly neon signs that buzzed. At the bar there was a row of battered men drinking draft beer from short glasses and lying about their wives and the celebrities they'd met, while the bartender, a large woman with orange hair and silver rings trapped on her pudgy fingers, looked on sneering and snapping a scuzzy bar rag at them when they went too far or lighted her on a tip.

Fitch ordered a drink and watched a group of young college types gathered around a shriveled Irishman in a tweed coat who was muttering incoherently about his childhood, something about his drunk Da and luvely, luvely Mudder. Every once in a while he would gargle a beer and launch into long, lilting descriptions of a grassy hill or Mudder's tawny hair or a friendly priest who got into his cups and sang Sinatra tunes. The kids were taking notes on napkins, nudging

and winking at one another, drunk on the fleeting and deep connections they'd manage to extract from the Irishman's high bullshit.

A trim gent sitting next to Fitch loosened his tie, pointed at the
Irishman, and said, "I hope he chokes on glass. I know that's un-
Christian of me, but I'd really like to see him choke."

Fitch pushed a dollar across the bar, nodded at the old shammers,
and drifted to the smoky little nook toward the back of the bar where
a crowd of men sat huddled around a roundtop rolling dice from
padded cups. He found Boris. He had the long, sad face of a jour-
neyman boxer, drank Cutty Sark, and wore a pea coat and wool fish-
erman's cap year-round. Fitch broke the ice by telling him he'd run
into Auer, a mutual friend and odd-jobber who dabbled in petty
crime but claimed it was merely an intellectual pursuit.

"Tell me, is he still hoarding those prescription forms I gave him?"

"He went back to school."

"At his age?"

"He's only thirty."

"It's all that rum and cured meats. Hard on the skin," said Boris.
"Well, wish him luck for me. We're all rooting for him. I harbor no
ill will toward the man."

"Who's that?" asked a large bearded man.

"Brad Auer," Boris said. "Stubby fellow, used to carry a book
around all the time, was good with locks and counter girls. Remember?"

"Why would I wanna root for that son of a bitch?" said the
bearded man. "He owes me seven dollars or a new pair of shoes."

"He was disrespectful to my sister," said another.

A man Fitch knew only as Screech said, "Are we going to roll or
talk?"

Boris hushed the crowd, gathered the dice into the cup, rolled,
and waited for his score to be tallied.

Later, after Boris had won and lost a few more times, he stood unsteadily and pointed at the bathroom, saying, "I gotta drain the pipe,
kid. You can wait or watch."

Fitch said he'd wait.

Boris returned and Fitch waited until he'd finished adjusting his cap in a beer mirror before he asked for a little advice, hemming and hawing about it.

"Advice about what?"

He looked around, "Well, uh, you know . . ."

"Here's some," said Screech. "Buy low, sell high."

"Well," Fitch said. "The thing is I'm broke and . . ."

"Take a number and get in line." Boris laughed. "Relax, I'm just breaking your stones, kid. You looking for some work? Is that it?"

"More like advice on a job."

Boris smiled. "You mean?"

Fitch nodded and the old thief pulled him close. "I had dreams just like the next guy. Now look at me, I'm living on past glory."

A thin man with the veiny bulging head of an infant looked up from his score pad and said, "He's not up on all the new violent tricks."

Boris agreed. "I blame it on narcotics. Those guys are taking from Peter to pay Paul. They like couches and aren't into planning. You're not a doper, are you, Fitch?"

Fitch said that he was not.

"Convictions?"

"Vague ideas, nothing strong."

"I meant jail. Have you done time?"

"No, I have not."

"I hope you're not looking for a mentor. The last kid I took under my wing drove a getaway car into a telephone pole and got his head chopped off."

"You mean Topper?"

"After Topper. Topper, I'm happy to report, sells office furniture and is married to a thrifty Honduran woman who runs a tight ship and makes a mean omelet. She uses this special kind of pepper and what she does is she chars them before putting them in the omelet. I keep encouraging her to open a little drive-through omelet shack."

"I'm just looking for some advice is all." As he spoke, a woman on her way to the rest room said to no one in particular, "I hate these shoes."

Boris stopped to watch her before nodding at Fitch. "When I was your age I was a master fur trader. Had ladies up and down the coast and never lost sight of the fact that I did the crime for the pussy." He gulped his scotch, ice, and quickly signaled for another. "Next question."

"What about banks?"

"Never had the stomach for them. Tellers can really hit the high notes if you scare them and, you see, my mother was a yeller, she used to scream and yell all the time, so that shit's like Kryptonite to me in high-pressure situations. I just freeze up like I'm twelve years old."

"Gas stations?"

"Not worth the hassle and you have to worry about explosions and getting whacked with crescent wrenches. I robbed a church once and wouldn't recommend it. Like I said, I'd advise you to think big— a one-shot deal of some sort. Get in, get out, because I gotta tell you that the long-range forecast for a life in crime is not good."

"Get in, get out," Fitch repeated.

"Ideally you wanna do one great thing and then kick up your heels," said Boris.

"Anything else?"

"Yeah, stay away from strippers. I dated one once. They've got nice skin, but you can't save them no matter how much money you throw at them. And the sex is never as good as you think it's going to be. This girl was always cold and refused to wear sweaters. A big problem because I was raised in a house where if you touched the thermostat my old man would crack you with a yardstick. Sure, I got to see her fry eggs in skimpy numbers but my gas bills doubled and I had to pull extra jobs. So where did that get me?"

"I'll keep that in mind."

Boris wished him good luck and went back to his game.

Before Fitch could leave, the bearded man stood and pressed a napkin into his hands. "Be a good cunt and give this to Auer," he said. "Tell him I don't want to have to come looking for him at that fancy college of his. Tell him he left a sour taste. Tell him I do not suffer fools. Tell him—"

Fitch stopped him. "Perhaps you should tell him everything in the note, that way I can just hand it to him."

"Just make sure he gets the note." The man loomed over Fitch breathing beer and stale cigarettes, his eyelids crusted with yellow fat scales and dead skin. "And forget that crap Boris told you about the one big score. It's better to be a steady earner. Think singles and doubles."

Fitch told him he'd think about it. The man grunted, pulled his shirt over his stomach, and waddled back to the table.

Outside he folded the napkin open. It said "*Cui bono?*" There was a phone number beneath. Baffled, and not wanting to see Auer, he let the damp wind take the napkin up the street, where it crashed and melted into a puddle beneath a leaking fire hydrant.

He still liked the one-big-job idea.

In the weeks following his chat with Boris, Fitch spiraled into a bleak bout of postdivorce and jobless despair. He sat around feeling sorry for himself, doing push-ups, eating kipper snacks, waiting to be evicted, and wondering how long it would be before he'd have to find some crap job like raking asphalt or folding boxes. In fact, the more he sat around doing nothing the more his admiration grew for the drifters, hippies, and common bums who loafed through life.

And then there was the book he'd found in the Dart. It sat on the table taunting him like some exotic relic from the world of the recently turned-on and paranoid dreamers who Fitch believed had figured a way out of the drudgery. Perhaps the book was a wake-up call, a road map out of the aimless mess Fitch found himself mired in.

Then a candle in his darkness. While flipping through the *Oregonian* he found a small article about the trial of a man named James Edwin Bennett Jr., who'd attempted to hijack an Eastern Airlines jet. After demanding half a million, Bennett had been overpowered by the crew, taken into custody and tried, found not guilty by reason of insanity, and sentenced to a mental hospital. Fitch read and reread the article and even went to the library to search for similar news articles on hijackings, and what he found was a lot of angry Cubans, a couple of Black Panthers, and the usual assortment of Middle Eastern zealots ready to die for some dry patch of the Promised Land. But it was the homegrown and apolitical would-be hijackers who interested Fitch, guys like Bennett and a guy named Arthur Barkley, who'd asked TWA for the unreasonable sum of a hundred million dollars only to be shot in the leg by the FBI and carted off to a nuthouse. Fitch quickly determined that the failure of these crimes could be traced back to the skyjackers' lack of a clearly defined plan and their reliance on guns or delusional threats to get what they wanted. But perhaps the single biggest reason for their uniform failure was that they had no clear escape route once their demands had been met. On the rare occasions when all demands had been met, the men predictably tried to commandeer the jet to some third-world country or Canada, where they were arrested after tense negotiations or "neutralized" by sharpshooters.

By the time Fitch left the library he'd already begun entertaining the idea of skyjacking a plane. The problem of escape was easy enough—he'd use what Uncle Sam had taught him and jump the silk, loot and all. The hard part was going to be coming up with a suitable threat that would not involve accomplices or guns or a lot of violence. What he wanted was the potential violence without having to wave a gun around and take hostages.

After a couple of long nights he settled on the idea of hijacking the plane with a bomb because a bomb did not discriminate, especially at twenty thousand feet. The whole jet, himself included, would be held hostage, thus eliminating the annoying rogue acts of heroism that had tripped up others. So he built a bomb out of road flares and bright red wire and spare parts he'd salvaged from an old RCA television someone had abandoned in the adjacent lot. He bolted the whole thing inside an Electrolux display case he'd nicked from his two-day sales seminar. When he'd finished he stood back to admire his work. It looked ominous when viewed in brief snatches, especially the way the wires embraced the road flares.

He set about testing it, riding buses with the briefcase and handling it in a fragile manner that suggested the presence of explosives. One night on a deserted crosstown bus he opened the briefcase and scared the shit out of a woman with mysterious stains on her slacks and several hospital ID bracelets circling her wrist who'd insisted on taking the seat next to him although there were only three other passengers on the bus. Her pockets were full of scraps of paper with notes and bits of scripture scrawled on them.

"I have a bomb," he told her, opening the briefcase and giving her a quick glimpse.

She snapped out of her fog just long enough to stare at the coils of wire, the long cherry-red flares made to look like dynamite, and the copper breakers he'd rubber cemented between them. Pure, unadulterated fear flickered across her face as her knees began to vibrate and her face crumbled into a pale, twitching mitt.

Fitch grinned and shut the case, anticipating her scream. Instead she shouted, "And whosoever was not found written in the book of life was cast into the lake of fire."

Sensing trouble, the bus driver eased off the gas and looked back at them through his mirror.

She rose and took a seat up front next to an old man clutching a grocery sack and hopped out as soon as the bus stopped in front of a brightly lit movie theater. Fitch watched her go, scraps of paper fluttering from her coat and taking wing down the avenue, where they would be found the next morning by puzzled schoolchildren.

The bus pulled away and the woman stood there, pointing and shouting something at him until she was just a normal-looking speck in the movie crowd.

Back in his trailer he paced, did push-ups, drank beer, and tried watching television but nothing could erase the confidence the bus experiment had given him. It swirled through his chest like some idiot wind filling him with the same dark confidence he'd experienced creeping down dim jungle paths, his finger on the trigger of his M16. Even the sight of Barbara Eden in her sheer jinni scarves and billowing Scheherazade pants did nothing to distract him from plotting and replotting the hijacking. No, for the first time in years Phil Fitch felt focused and sharp, his mind a criminal laser beam relentlessly obsessing over the details until it was no longer a question of *if* he could pull off the skyjacking but a question of *when*.

He odd-jobbed around, stockpiling what cash he could, allowing himself a mere five dollars a day for food, subsisting on dented discount cans of baked beans, small boxes of raisins, fried onion sandwiches, tap water, and day-old donuts. At night he worked on his plan, studying the mistakes of others until the plan became a fixed and unquestionable part of his routine. Just the idea of hijacking a plane and escaping to Mexico had already rendered the world anew for Fitch. He had hope. Crappy food tasted better and entire days passed where he experienced a certain giddy lightness, like walking out of a dark movie theater into a bright spring day and noticing tulips or a pretty girl in a skirt with a shy smile and tangled brown hair.

He read the strange book he'd found and thought of the woman who'd lured him into the woods and of Jane—wondering if she was still out there, waiting for him to break free and get to her somehow as he studied the pages of Book IV, looking for clues as to her whereabouts. Mexico City seemed to be the most likely place, so he looked that up in a *World Book Encyclopedia*—crowds, pollution, street musicians, poverty, and some bit about the altitude. If he managed to pull off the skyjacking, he'd go looking for this Jane.

He stopped seeing his few friends, let his phone service lapse, and tacked towels over the windows. He pawned two clock radios and the black-and-white television and practiced his landing by jumping off the deck late at night, his tiny crash cushioned by the crabgrass and lamb's-quarters that had colonized his neglected lawn. And when Lonny Ramp, the trailer park beer hound, came calling with a case of Oly he did not answer the door. He was too busy and knew that Lonny would want to chat and nose around the trailer, asking vague but prying questions until he got around to hitting Fitch up for a few bucks. He put in for several bogus changes of address with the post office, tore up his driver's license, burned his military ID, along with his library card. By Halloween he was officially lost, a chalk line of a man.

He rehearsed, and after dozens of twenty-dollar milk runs with the briefcase he knew the patterns of the stewardesses and the exact moment when the pilot would level off and snap the plane into autopilot.

He worked on his appearance in the mirror, darkening his closely cropped hair with a box of Nice 'n Easy hair coloring until it was Betty Page black and rubbing moist tea leaves into his face and neck until he looked like an Egyptian. The suit and sunglasses topped it off. He no longer felt like Phil Fitch or any of the other poor saps trying to make a go of it chasing after some kind of watered-down forty-hour-a-week life. He was Dan Cooper, the man with the plan—the man with the bomb, who, if he got what he wanted, would jump and never be heard from again provided he could find the hidden spots in Mexico and drum up this Jane chick. Or maybe he just wanted out—he did not know.

CHAPTER THREE

exico was Mexico, the streets flush with starving dogs, trinket peddlers, old women selling novena candles, pale German tourists, whores, fruit vendors, and children who milled around the gringos like pigeons, hoping to be tossed coins. Cooper searched for both the Hidden Territories and the Secret Lands—the book didn't make the distinction entirely clear. He bummed around Chiapas and Tabasco, inquiring furtively about the existence of Secret Lands and of Jane. On the Sea of Cortés he discovered a topless beach and a group of old Broadway performers who'd bought a string of condos in a lush canyon and were experimenting with bee sting therapy to cure their aching, kicked-out joints. In Colima he thought he saw Jane crossing the street but the woman turned out to be a drug-bunny nurse from Saint Cloud who was looking for El Hombre and was disappointed to discover that Cooper was not El Hombre and therefore useless. She told him to get lost and drop dead.

And in Comita a ragtag group of students cornered Cooper on the streets with their vacant stares, calling him Irving—he didn't know why—but within minutes they'd shortened it to Irv and were giving him familiar pats on the arm, flashing peace signs, and slagging President Ford. They'd built a camp in the jungle full of geodesic domes in the hope that Buckminster Fuller, or Bucky, as they called him, would come visit and explain the Green Bank Formula to them and apply his Dymaxion principles to their camp.

One of the women even hugged Cooper and whispered, "Come as you are."

"How's that?" Cooper asked, lost in the tangle of her unwashed hair.

"My name is April," she said. "Like warm showers. Would you like to see our camp?" She had armpit hair and tattered cargo shorts with a Che Guevara patch stitched over the back pocket. He quickly agreed to go with them.

After buying a month's supply of cigarettes and two fireproof boxes for his money, he checked out of the hotel. The toothless man behind the counter stopped to guzzle something from an old bleach bottle before taking Cooper's money, wiping his mouth on his sleeve and yelling over his shoulder to an efficient-looking woman in the back room who darted out, snatched the pesos from the man, and shoved them into her apron.

"*Los rastros felices, señor,*" said the man, laughing and pointing at the hippies waiting for him on the street. They were tossing a Frisbee and doing handstands to entertain the children.

He followed April and her crew up a muddy trail to a narrow valley where a clearing had been hacked from the jungle. There were trailers and tents decorated with spray-painted slogans and stoned thoughts. Wet sleeping bags hung from the trees like cocoons, and dozens of well-fed dogs were sunning themselves on rocks and scratching at fleas. A hairy couple sitting inside a tepee reading R. D. Laing paperbacks looked up and waved at him. Still others, dressed in bright orange caftans and swami robes, milled around a broken-down VW bus discussing Dylan's *Tarantula* and passing fatties with dirty fingers. There was music in the air, smoldering campfires, bits of ribbon fluttering on sticks, old piñatas stranded in trees, pit toilets, wind chimes made from tin can lids, half-built drums, tire swings, and stone paths that led nowhere. The air was heavy with mosquitoes and bot flies. Not paradise, Cooper thought, but weird and interesting enough to hang around for a while until he could figure out his next move.

April introduced him around as Irv to many a blank stare or a dazed "Cool."

She told him that she was into smoking opium and had once been a promising Jane Austen scholar at Columbia but had dropped out after meeting Huey Newton at a Black Panther rally. She'd come to the camp hoping to do some good and find herself.

"So where are you?" she asked. "Have you found yourself? Are you on the path?"

"I'm getting there," he said.

"That's totally okay and cool," April said. "You'll fit right in up here. We are trying to do some good, or at least that's what I've been told."

"What sort of good?"

"Reba says we must better ourselves before we can better our world. Reba says we must create mysteries and not solve them."

He nodded. He'd heard the community outreach, peace, love, and understanding blather before and knew that all it took these days to make someone a committed liberal was to see some third-world women pounding laundry on river rocks.

After the tour Cooper excused himself and scurried out into the jungle, where he buried the fireproof boxes, covering them with stones to deter curious monkeys. When he returned there was hot food waiting for him. He ate and April showed him to a sagging canvas pup tent with Day-Glo runes painted on it. Inside he found a backpack full of dirty T-shirts, a red wool brim cap, and a small, tattered book on yoga with Zen koans scribbled in the margins.

"That's Salinger's," April said, grabbing one of the T-shirts and sniffing it. "Yep, it still smells like him. Salinger sure liked his Brut."

"I don't want to sleep in another man's tent."

"Don't worry about it," April said. "He wandered off last month and we don't know what happened to him."

"Without his clothes?"

"He liked to meditate in strange places. I've decided he's wandering the earth dispensing kindness and correcting people's posture," said April, dragging the backpack from the tent. "Anyway, it's all yours now. I think you're going to like it here. I think you're going to fit right in."

"Why?" he asked.

"Because you need us and because it is a beautiful thing," she said with a cryptic grin.

He crawled in, arranged his gear, and passed out.

A week later Cooper still had not left the valley and had more or less decided to stay, won over by the campers' impossibly sincere belief that they were creating something special in the middle of the jungle. Although he still hadn't mastered the lingo or when to flip a soul shake instead of a hug, he'd been accepted and, after spending many a night listening to idealistic dope speeches on how they wanted to change the world, he sometimes felt the urge to dig up a little of his loot and let April buy the poor village kids shoes and Wiffle ball bats. He held off because the campers claimed to be *not into money*. Instead he asked April for an audience with Reba, the camp matriarch. He wanted to show her Book IV and hear her thoughts on the map.

Reba received him sitting lotus in front of a roaring fire. She was a short, full-figured woman with plump, sunburned cheeks, a Jewish Afro, intense black eyes, and small, darting hands

"Take a load off, Irv," she said, patting the ground beside her and dismissing April. "As my father used to say, let's chew the fat."

He sat and listened to Reba's story. The camp was her second attempt at communal living, the first being a loose art collective called Greenerburg. Greenerburg had been founded by a bitter old man named Byers Hilton, who'd once mixed paint for Norman Rockwell and claimed to be a sculptor. He sunbathed in the nude and scoffed at her art, castigating her for relying on blacks and grays. "Okay, I'm depressed," Reba said. "That's what he used to say. And 'Rain clouds equal death. It's been done before—well-tilled soil, salted earth. Move on or get out of the way.' But his favorite," she said, putting a hand on his thigh to make sure he met her gaze, "was 'Simple, banal, reductive.' Do you have any idea how many times I heard that, Irv?"

Cooper blinked and lit up a cigarette. He wanted to show her the book and couldn't figure out what this art creep had to do with anything. But she went on. "And do you know how it feels to have your breasts poked with a damp paintbrush?"

He didn't answer and she took a deep breath. "I was fresh from a divorce, you see." She went on to describe the other artists in residence, an emotionally fragile and angry group who made for interesting nights full of dramatic exits and tearful confessions and plenty of why-I-paint soliloquies. "I lasted three months before quitting and fleeing back to Brooklyn," Reba said. "I founded a food co-op and tried to start a Synergistics study group in my temple but was told by Rabbi Siegel that I was a troublemaker. So that's the short version of how this all started, or how I avoided selling Tupperware, clipping coupons, and saving for some canned cruise full of recent divorcées eager to start the game over again. I've been around that block. I'm a seeker, Irv. I want to make the world a better place. I have a mission and that makes me a dangerous woman. Now let me see this book I've heard so much about."

He handed her the book and watched as she skimmed a few pages, stopping every so often to quiz Cooper about his travels and wave his cigarette smoke away from her face.

"Have you seen Moab? Ever been to Oneonta? How about White Sands? Did you know you can stand at ground zero? It feels like the end of the world and wasn't as dark as I expected."

She kept on with the questions and he answered with a series of noncommittal shrugs.

"Take your time," he said, gesturing at the book. He leaned over the fire, hoping to foil the gang of mosquitoes circling his sunburned neck.

She skimmed a few more pages and then began firing questions at him regarding the book. Who was this man not named Jeb? Was this a ploy to get the reader thinking about Jeb Stuart?

"I don't think that's the point," Cooper said. "He said his name's not Jeb."

"Did you know," Reba said, "that after the Civil War thousands of Confederates tried to set up a New Virginia in Campeche and Tampico? Right here in Old Mexico."

Cooper said that he was not aware of that fact.

"An utter failure, as you might have guessed, Irv. Another defeat for those Confederate dreamers and something your average South-erner won't admit to because it might take some starch out of their argument that had Lee gotten that letter sooner the South would have prevailed. Well, they managed to muck things up quite nicely down here without the Union and Ulysses S. Grant. They were doomed to fail. Read your history, Irv, and these threads will become clear to you. You do read, right?"

"I prefer the pulps and some select magazines."

"So it's cheap thrills you're after?"

"Mostly a good story."

"And what about this?" She pointed at the book.

"Well, uh . . ."

She clamped the book shut. "Do you want my opinion?"

He started to speak but she cut him off. "What you have here is the ramblings of a sour academic with a prescription drug habit and overactive imagination. Just the sort of half-baked reasoning that serves as inspiration to less nimble minds. We here know better, Irv."

"I just thought maybe you'd heard of one of those places."

"What places?"

"These," he said, leaning over and thumbing a few pages until he came to the map.

She glanced at it. "If it's a hippie Shangri-la you're looking for— look around and you'll see we're in the building stages. What exactly *are* you looking for?"

"I don't know, a place to escape the world, leave my troubles be-hind, and kick my feet up for a while."

"And what troubles might those be, Irv? I'm a good listener, adept at putting myself in another person's sandals."

For a half second he considered telling her about the plane and the bomb and how he'd basically put one over on the Man. Surely these folks had heard of his crime, perhaps they'd even seen the artist's rendering of him on the FBI's Wanted poster, a copy of which he'd remembered to remove from the book before allowing Reba to examine it. The sketch on the Wanted poster made him look men-acingly cool, like one of the bad guys on *Dragnet*. He could spin the whole thing into an act of civil protest, explain how Uncle Sam had shaved his head and sent him to Vietnam, put a rifle in his hand, and told him to kill for love of God and country. It would all be a lie, but they might buy it and let him stay as their resident rebel.

"Is there something you want to tell me, Irv? I'm here for you—we are all here for you," she said.

He looked into her damp eyes and tried to lie in an earnest and forthright manner. "Well, most of my troubles stemmed either from lack of work or low-quality work. Do you know what I mean?"

"Exactly what kind of work are we talking about, Irv? Are we talking metaphorically?"

"The kind that wasn't getting me anywhere, soul-sucking, punch-the-clock-and-earn-a-few-bucks sort of work."

"Sounds to me like you didn't like the path you were on. Am I right?"

He nodded. "I came to the conclusion that work's basically social welfare."

Reba smiled. "I won't argue that point."

"I did a little thinking and got angry about my situation and knew that if I didn't do something quick and take action I'd end up just an-other cog in the wheel."

"Irv, I sense there's another reason you've found your way to my camp."

"Well, then I found that book."

"Yes."

"And I guess you could say I dropped out and sorta started looking for Jane."

"I'm confused."

He reached over and flipped the book open to the sketch of Jane, pointing out a few choice passages and watching as she skimmed them. "I was hoping to find her in one of those places described in the book."

"And?"

"So far she has eluded me."

"So she's the Maguffin in all this," Reba said, poking a finger through her curls. "The reason you've run off to Mexico. For your sake I hope you didn't leave any women and children in your wake."

Cooper said that he had not.

Reba sighed and then continued her lecture. "Well, I wouldn't spend one day of my life looking for this Jane. Do you want me to tell you about women who pose nude for artists? I have some insight into what drives them to disrobe. Needy, vain, and cowlike. Suppose you did manage to track her down in some dingy atelier. What then?"

"I guess I hadn't thought it out that far. I liked the drawing and that bit about how she keeps her nails painted black."

"If you want my advice, and you're going to get it, you'd do well to focus your attentions elsewhere. Which leads me to my next question. Have you ever heard of R. Buckminster Fuller?"

"Yeah, the dome guy," he said, pointing over his shoulder where one of the half-built domes stood against the night sky like some massive golf ball skeleton.

"Well, Irv, do you know that he is none other than a raging optimist? The most important original thinker of our time!" She grabbed a stick and sketched a tetrahedron in the dirt between them. "Did you know that's the basic building block of the universe? It's a naturally occurring shape."

"Don't know much about geometry," Cooper said.

She stared at him coldly, Book IV trembling in her clenched paw, inches from the fire. "You would do well to steep yourself in this great man's philosophy. I don't mean to sort bruised fruit on you here, Irv, but we take pretty much anybody who can tolerate the mosquitoes and understand the beauty of Fuller's Dymaxion Map of the World. And you look capable of both."

Worried that in her excitement she might pitch the book into the fire, he reached out and took it from her.

"All I want to know is if you are with us or against us, Irv."

"Well, I'd like to stay, if that's what you're asking."

"Okay."

She then inducted him into their cause with a brief ceremony and gave him a dense tome by Buckminster Fuller, telling him that if he wanted to crew on Spaceship Earth he would do well to study the words of the Master and stop rooting around for Secret Lands and Hidden Territories.

"Get on board!" she said, wrapping her soft arms around him and squeezing until he squeezed back. He thanked her and joined the others in the tepee, where he got stoned and listened to April sing Carole King songs with sloppy bongo accompaniment.

Months peeled by and Cooper got to know his fellow campers, who when sober had painfully short attention spans. They came from powerful East Coast families and had attended Ivy League schools, where they'd studied global politics, accounting, and fashion design before dropping out. Most of them had never worked a real job. Instead they relied on Western Union and sizable trust funds to finance their nomadic lifestyles. They played chess and Go, sang protest songs, and hatched schemes to declare themselves a nation, one that would have no national anthem and certainly no currency except for ideas and sex. Cooper disagreed with their stance on anthems, pointing out that it was always the country with the stirring anthem that seemed to prevail in times of war. Did anyone know the Polish national anthem? Could any of them hum a few bars of the song the Zulu nation had bravely taken into battle against the English?

A large dude whom everybody called Princeton Bob accused Cooper of being a fascist.

"I'm not advocating war," said Cooper. "I was merely pointing out a few historical facts."

Princeton Bob loomed over Cooper, sneering down through his overgrown Prince Valiant cut. "War piggy. Oink, oink, oinky," he said, tucking his arms across his sweaty chest as if he'd won some debate point.

April stepped between them and said, "Can't we all just get along? I mean really, put the testosterone away."

Princeton Bob backed off and Cooper hung around trying to think of some witty comeback but the damage had been done and only April would meet his gaze.

He went back to his tent and tried to read the Buckminster Fuller book Reba had pressed on him and found it to be some tough sledding—heavy on the science and short on drama. He ditched it and picked up Book IV as he smoked the last of his cigarettes and studied the Jane sections, trying to figure out her connection to this AWAKE Brigade. But he kept getting sidetracked by the long-winded antitechnology rants that bubbled up along the margins at odd junctures. He learned that the AWAKE Brigade, although seemingly small and sub-rosa in nature, had executed several violent protest bombings, egged a Republican senator, and dumped trash on the lawns of various cabinet members. Other groups had taken responsibility for the acts—all part of the plan because the AWAKE Brigade was not about responsibility. According to the book, the AWAKE Brigade was about foment. Jane had something to do with fundraising and long-term planning but had split with the group and become, in the author's words, a "Free Radical."

Cooper inquired around the camp about Jane, no small task, being as half the campers had given themselves new names to signify their newfound freedom. A woman calling herself Magnolia said that her name had once been Jane and that she'd been a cheerleader for the University of Nebraska but that she'd let herself go and could no longer do a cartwheel. She was blond and had strong legs.

"I was naturally peppy," Magnolia said. "Then I dropped acid and I saw that peppy and hopeful was a terrible way to go through life."

"Have you ever owned a German shorthaired pointer?" Magnolia stared at him blankly, pulling on her sun-chapped lips. "It's a dog," he explained. "The woman I'm looking for had a German short-haired pointer."

She giggled and told him that he was being silly and that interrogations bummed her out. "Are you a cop?" she asked. "I hope you're not one of them undercover pigs. I dated a cop and it was a totally weird drag. When we were doing it he baby-talked and wanted me to pee on him."

"I'm not a cop."

"Sure thing, officer." She stuck her finger in her mouth and brushed his cheek with it. "You need to loosen up a little."

He tried and spent his days patching leaky trailer and tent walls, gathering firewood, boiling lentils and beans, and taking small hikes out into the jungle to check on his stash. Often he rose early to watch the camp women practice yoga because he loved the way they sat, arms clamped about themselves, their rib cages swelling with yogic ecstasy, sweaty skin glistening in the golden first light. He'd tried joining them but couldn't master the breathing and Magnolia's constant and overly calm corrections annoyed him. He was not good at clearing his thoughts or thinking of nothing. In fact, the opposite happened and he thought of everything at once and it reflected in his erratic breathing.

Late one night during a full moon Reba gathered the campers and told them about a dream she'd had. Her dreams usually featured Bucky playing some racquet sport or tucking into an enormous lunch of oysters and melon ball soup, and the campers would help her interpret the dream. But this one was a Buckyless reverie about Reba's attempts to swim with a large sea turtle in a kidney-shaped pool. In the dream the turtle tried to talk to her but could manage only a few dry croaks and, in what Reba thought was a telekinetic rage, caused several large stones to roll into the pool. "It was the strangest thing, but I woke up feeling energized. My palms itched and I had this bruise." She rolled up a sleeve to reveal a small crown-shaped bruise on her arm. She looked around, her face flickering with reflected campfire before pointing at Cooper and asking, "What signs and wonders do you make out, Irv?"

Cooper stalled. Most of the time he just watched and listened, trying hard to avoid being labeled a fascist, Nazi, or consumer drone. But Reba kept staring at him, waiting for a response.

Finally he said, "The turtle wants something."

"Yes, that goes without saying, Irv. Can you be more clear?"

He looked around at the eager faces of the campers, awaiting his answer. "A display or monument?"

"Too vague," Reba snapped. "Shall I go through it again or is this beyond your interpretive skills, Irv? What sort of monument? A monument to what? What does the turtle stand for? Explain yourself." She fixed her heavily lidded eyes on him and folded her arms across her chest, causing her breasts to squish out at odd angles. Cooper heard the impatient tinkle of ankle bracelets as several women leaped up and went to fetch their drums.

"Was it a tortoise in your dream?"

Reba shook her head. "I see where you're going with the tortoise, but I'm sorry to say it was just a very large turtle and I have a very long life line, Irv. No death for me. Get on with it."

"A rock garden, perhaps?" he offered.

She rolled her eyes. "I'm not sure I see the connection, Irv."

He glanced over at Marla, a skinny, lank-haired woman from Chicago who was fond of crystals and quoting John Lennon. She held a tattered copy of Fuller's *At Home in the Universe*. Something clicked as he studied the back jacket photo of the owlish visionary hovering over one of his geodesic domes with a questing expression on his face,

"An environmental tribute," he said, hoping she'd tire of quizzing him and move on.

"Hmmm. I think you're on to something, Irv," she said, suddenly excited. "Something in the manner of the Minton Turtle or the Nazca drawings—primitive etchings, celestial offerings that I firmly believe doubled as runway markers for extraterrestrials. Are you trying to say that if we build it he will come?"

He shrugged and a chorus of appreciative sighs went up and the campers began to blurt.

"I know the secret of Easter Island and can help with the logistics," somebody said.

Another, "I've read the Voynich Manuscript."

"This sounds like work."

"I sing the body electric."

"I didn't come here to move rocks."

"Hey, Jude."

Reba put a stop to the blurting and huddled with the senior camp members and by midnight Cooper's suggestion had been transformed into a massive building project. The rock garden, when viewed from the sky, would resemble the revered Bucky. The hope being that the philosopher would pass over the camp, see his likeness, and be moved to pay a visit. There was much hand-wringing over the use of charred logs to render the philosopher's black spectacles when a sensitive environmentalist named Nancy began denouncing Cooper as a tree killer.

April came to his rescue and led him to the creek, where she lay down on the moonlit bank and pointed to the shadowy outline of several large fish suspended in a deep pool. Cooper lay down beside her and watched the fish rise and fall, trading places in the invisible current, snouts pointed upstream.

"Do you see?"

When Cooper said he did not, April smiled, slid on top of his back, slipped her arms around his neck, and whispered, "They're on their way, they have a purpose in life. Don't you see, they fit right in." As she spoke thick strands fell over his shoulders and punctured the still surface of the stream. He rolled to face her, his hands gliding inside her camisole and running up the warm cup of her spine and then down to her breasts. She pressed her hips into his and kissed him. "I want you to help me with the others," she said.

"I don't understand."

She sat up and shucked her camisole and dirty cutoffs, motioning for him to strip. He did and soon felt the hot slide of her body and the tingle of her damp hair as she hugged him. "I have plans for this place. I need you to help me move them, get them off their asses."

"You mean the campers?" he said, putting his face between her breasts.

She nodded. "I want to help the village."

"It looks fine to me," he said, going back to his breast work. "They have a movie house, refrigeration, and sewers. I'd say they're on their way."

"No, not that one. The Indian village on the other side of the mountain, La Tontería."

"I haven't been down there."

"Well, I have. The children play with dead birds and bite one another. They live in mud huts. I think the Catholics are circling and it won't be long before the Baptists smell a battle and bush-plane a nice couple in to teach them about baby Jesus and the end of days."

Cooper felt the lust leaking out of him as she went on, listing the shabby living conditions, the lack of electricity and indoor plumbing, not to mention the burden of the women, who spent their days pounding maize and looking after children. The same things could be said of the camp, but he knew to keep his mouth shut if he wanted some of April's loving. And he wanted.

"You have ideas," she continued. "Like tonight with Reba and the rock garden. She put you on the spot and, well, I don't know about a rock garden, but it was something. You answered her and look what happened."

"I was just groping and I'm a tree killer."

"A fascist tree killer."

"Heil, Hitler," he said.

She said, "Let's stop that and start this." With a sigh she sat back and he was in. They didn't move for a long time, and when she did, it was a slow, slippery build, her dark silhouette twirling against the moon as the stream sucked by and he tried not to think of what the fish might be doing or what this incredibly small but intense moment of fun would cost him in the long run. He forgot about all that when she bent down and took his nipple in her mouth, telling him to go deeper and let go.

He did as he was told, and after, as they lay there smearing mosquitoes dead against their sweaty bodies, she told him how she'd been rejected from the Peace Corps because she'd refused to write the application essay and then later at a séance she saw Jayne Mansfield's ghost and something called ectoplasm.

Cooper said, "Well, I've seen some strange barf." He coptered his shirt above them to ward off the bugs. "A buddy of mine got lost in the jungle for a couple of days and came back puking caterpillars."

"Like, real caterpillars?"

He nodded. "Dozens of these little green dudes. We took pictures and then stomped them with our jungle boots and rifle butts."

She quietly pointed at the small tattoo on his shoulder with the motto *De Oppresso Liber* scripted over it. It was supposed to be a dagger stabbing a beret but had always resembled a slug and a baseball bat. "What's *De Oppresso Liber* mean? It's military, isn't it?"

"No."

"I knew it."

"Knew what?"

"You were a soldier. You've killed people," she said.

Worried that she'd heave some hippie spit on him and stomp back to the camp and blab to the others about how he was a baby-killing Uncle Sam Aim High soldier boy, he stammered, "I'm not proud of it. All in all it was a pretty bum deal."

She sighed and told him he didn't have to explain, that her father was an air force colonel whom she still loved despite the fact that he ordered young men to drop bombs on people and shine their shoes for a living.

"What does it mean?"

"To free the oppressed," he told her.

"Well, see, you could turn that around," she said. "I like that—free the oppressed. It sounds kind of groovy when you take it out of context."

She also promised not to tell the others about his being a soldier as long as he agreed to help her.

Cooper thought about it. Oregon and all the humdrum crap he'd left behind seemed another lifetime. He wasn't quite a carefree, take-it-easy, life-happens hippie, but he was getting closer day by day and had no compelling urge to leave the camp and look for Jane just yet. And so he agreed.

Over the next couple of months the Grand Jungle Bucky slowly took shape, the campers happily clearing brush, rolling boulders into place. But without air support it was impossible to tell if they were working to scale and Reba was constantly fretting that some other quasi-celebrity like Ernest Borgnine or Lawrence Tierney would fly over the camp, see his own likeness reflected in the jumble of stones and greenery, and get the wrong idea. But no one flew directly over the camp and Reba's frequent letters to Bucky went unanswered. Cooper snuck down the mountain with April to visit La Tontería, the village she'd told him about. They held babies and tried not to gawk at the sagging huts, tattered clothes, and gap-toothed smiles of the villagers. In halting Spanish they asked a couple of old men sitting on grease cans what they could do to help. Even though the men said they were curious about toaster ovens and the New York Yankees, they were *afortunado* and could think of *nada* they needed. April, however, remained unconvinced and suspected that the men were simply too proud to accept aid. Cooper kept his doubts to himself even as they snuggled down next to a smoldering fire and watched the monkeys sneak from the trees and skitter across the rock garden, pulling up zinnias and sunflowers, shrieking out complicated primate dramas and pecking orders.

THE CAMP'S ABILITY to absorb the frequent and often strange visitors—lone middle-aged men who'd heard about the camp and decided to investigate, curious Dutch tourists with their guidebooks and pale legs, acid heads, swagmen, bindle stiffs, grifters posing as peaceniks, artifact hounds, junketeers from Florida, and the just plain lost—was tested when a man calling himself Baron arrived late one night in a battered old school bus full of his followers. They smelled of sex and carried large hand-bound "soulcheck" journals tucked under their arms. At first nobody paid them much attention, assuming that after some couscous and fried jicama they'd be gone within a week. Only Magnolia rose to greet them, pointing out where they should park the bus and pitch tents if they intended to stay.

Baron's aides-de-camp, two AWOL marines named Sapp and Tergent, stomped off the bus pointing like conquistadors as they surveyed the camp. In their wake trailed assorted hippie flotsam. Others stayed on the bus and slept, including an enormous fat woman named Ethel.

Baron, who resembled a faded linebacker who'd dropped acid one too many times and seen things he shouldn't have seen, listened to Magnolia's sketchy instruction with a deep grin slicing across his broad face. He shouted to no one in particular that he had proof that UFOs were responsible for a rash of cattle mutilations in Texas as well as the sudden disappearance of a small lake in northeastern Ohio where as a child he'd chased tadpoles.

Then he toured the camp with several of his followers, poking the long red frog gig that doubled as his walking stick into the fire pits and nodding to himself.

Cooper, who'd been waiting for April to return from her nightly dip in the creek and slip into his sleeping bag, heard Baron and his crew counting falling stars and giggling outside his tent.

He rose to investigate and saw Baron leaning on the frog gig with a giant pair of army binoculars slung around his neck like General MacArthur.

"Good evening," Baron said, scratching at his ear dandruff. "Just arrived and was admiring the sky. You can call me Baron. We are currently on a hejira that has delivered us to this pleasant valley."

"What for?" Cooper asked.

"Several of us seek masters and we rely on the comfort of strangers while on this arduous quest. We see this as the only way to connect with the folk and get our message out, so to speak. Do you grok?"

Before he could answer, one of Baron's followers poked a flashlight into Cooper's eyes and shouted, "It's not him. His pupils are slow to react."

Baron spoke calmly. "We've startled this creature from his slumber. Give him a chance to muster some spirit."

For a minute Cooper thought that FBI agents posing as hippies had discovered him. But upon closer inspection he noticed Baron busily tossing small seeds into his mouth. He knew FBI agents were fond of their Teaberry gum and the occasional cigarette. But seeds? An unusual habit. Not to mention the canker sores ringing the man's mouth and the frog gig. No, Cooper figured, not only was this bird a true believer in his own private cause but he'd no doubt been rousted out of many small towns by flat-topped cops on the lookout for strange vagrants come to ruin Main Street with their manic curbside predictions of Armageddon or pitiful storefront mooching.

"You do have a name, don't you?"

"Irv," Cooper said, "they call me Irv. It's a camp name and I just never got around to correcting them. It's short for Irving, I think."

"Well, I'm sorry, Irv, but Chet here is looking for someone and it seems you're not it."

"Looking for what?"

"I'm afraid that's not on the table tonight, Irv. Perhaps some other time, after you've gained our collective confidence. But perhaps you can tell me about this place."

"What do you want to know?"

"Do the women wear undergarments or are they into bra burning and letting their armpit hair go unbarbered?"

"It's fifty-fifty. You get used to the armpit hair."

"Now, what about the food? I've had it up to here with solar-oven fare and homemade yogurt."

"It varies."

"Vague, but we'll hope for the best," Baron said. "Now, are you hip to Jorge Feingold and the Children of the Sun?"

"They some kind of rock band?"

"No—I'm afraid they're a sorry bunch of chanting vegans. We'd heard great things about their camp and went to see firsthand and, well, we were sorely disappointed. Chewing grass and sprouts is dead-end nutritional advice. We tried to introduce them to vitamin K and brisk walks but couldn't rouse them from their dark yurts. They had lots of answers but were asking all the wrong questions. And Jorge—did you know he has very small hands? Why, they're doll hands, always a sign of some hidden character defect. Many famous actors are short and have small hands too. Now, tell me about this Reba woman I keep hearing so much about."

Cooper briefly explained what he knew of her past.

Baron licked his lips and adjusted the dirty coils of friendship bracelets circling his arm. "Perhaps she is my soul mate. How are her teeth? Does she prefer soup or salad? Does she want the whole man or would she try to change me, put me in a suit, and push me into the workforce? What are her views on Atlantis? Does she walk with a limp? And what's with the domes? I'm listening, Irv."

Cooper told him about Reba's devotion to Buckminster Fuller.

"Never heard of him," said Baron. "Must be some local guru because I'm not familiar with his teachings."

Cooper pointed to the field and the dark outline of rocks glowing in the moonlight. "That's him in profile."

Baron went up on tippy toes to see a few monkeys cavorting on the portion of stones that formed Bucky's neck folds.

"It's a rock garden," Cooper explained.

"Well, imagine finding idolatry way up here," Baron said with a disapproving glance at his followers. "I thought the Catholics had rooted it all out. What's this Bucky guy's method of dispersal? Tell me he's not some street preacher or grinning pamphleteer doling out his tracts to the mentally halt and lame."

"He writes books."

"And?"

"They start out fine and then I get lost or tangled up or maybe it's just that they're boring. All I know is that I can't understand them."

"A common enough complaint. Take heart. Perhaps these words will act as balm." He cleared his throat and spoke in grand tones. " 'We shall be known by the delicacy of where we stop short.' That's Robert Frost, a man to be read on many levels, as all the great ones are. Does this Buckmiser fellow dwell in the abstract? Is his vision icy?"

"As far as I can tell he builds geodesic domes and ponders the great problems of our time. He's got world hunger boiled down to greed, border skirmishes, and banks."

"Domes?"

Cooper pointed at the dark silhouette of the dome just beyond the trailers.

"I'll tell you right out he stole the idea from the Eskimos," Baron snorted. "Not the first time the red man's been had by the white man."

"He's supposed to be some sort of visionary or cultural prophet. You really should ask Reba, though. I just crash here."

"Irv, I've met only a few true visionaries in my lifetime. Jim Jones is one such man, although he's given to the occasional fit of Bible thumping and vodka. I expect great things from that Texan."

"Another time," Chet said before loping off into the dark, eager to put his flashlight into other faces.

Baron swatted a pack of mosquitoes drilling on his forehead. "Let me speak collectively, Irv. We, I mean our group, draw our inspiration from many sources. What you might call spiritual diversification. Why, Ethel, for instance, worships a cinder block obelisk in Grand Rapids, Michigan."

"Who's Ethel?"

"The plus-size woman on the bus, but never mind that, tell me about your past. What unseen force drew you to this buggy Eden? You look half soldier to me."

Cooper tried to ignore the man, wondering, as he glanced down to make sure that his tattoo was well covered, if April had somehow let his secret slip.

Baron waddled over, planted the frog gig in the dirt, and asked to see Cooper's hands. Cooper held them out in the moonlight for inspection. Baron bent over his palms and sniffed. "Six," he said.

"Six what?"

"I'm afraid you've killed six men in the Southeast Asian conflict."

"I've never been there."

Baron grinned. "Don't crap a crapper, son. You've got Nam written all over these paws of yours. Why, I can still smell the rifle grease."

"But . . ."

"Hold on a minute," Baron said. "I think we can call the last one an accident—shots fired on a lark at some colorful jungle cock to impress your fellow soldiers with your marksmanship. Well, I'm sorry to say they missed and snuffed a life."

"I never shot at a bird."

"Ah yes, the madness of war," said Baron. "Tell that to the Vietnamese. I'm sure they'd understand perfectly. Kill 'em all and let God sort them out, is that it?"

Cooper felt himself getting angry and blurted, "They were shooting at us. I saw my buddy catch one in the cheek. It was kill or be killed, a trap around every corner."

"I gather the Vietcong are very antlike and crafty, fond of pits and tunnels."

"They can put a point on bamboo."

"And I suppose that's your justification? I can see right off that you're not the sort of person I'd like to bunk down with during a blackout. I'm afraid your inner looter would emerge."

Baron snatched the frog gig up again and patted Cooper on the shoulder. "Our chat is over. Good night, Irv. Don't worry about that sixth man. We have plenty of time to lift this burden of yours."

"Right on," a voice said.

"Ahisma," someone whispered.

"So mote it be," said the woman in plastic shoes.

And with that, Baron and his followers tottered off into the dark to search for Reba. Cooper crawled back in his tent to wait for April.

CHAPTER FOUR

rank Marshall pushed back his chair, loosened his tie, and stared at the small flower arrangement on the table before him, while Harry Arluck, a lanky, red-faced agent with silver hair and confident, booze-shot eyes, toasted his retirement, punctuating each barb with a tilt of his empty Budweiser and a friendly wink in Frank's direction. It seemed to Frank that the only thing keeping the inevitable maudlin nosedive at bay was the clatter of the busboys clearing the dinner mess into large gray slop tubs and the bustle of waitresses dumping coffee into waiting mugs.

Thankful for all the distractions, he turned his attention back to the vase, poking at the spray of fern to see if it was real (it was) and the roses, one red and one white with pink edges. The roses were no longer tight. Instead the petals were sprung wide, revealing pistil and carpels. Frank knew that the arrangement had served for several days and that tonight it would be flicked into the trash along with the crumpled napkins and spent globe candles. He stuck his thumb into the halo of pollen fanned around the vase, leaving his fingerprints as he mashed the waxy yellow granules into the cheap tablecloth and tried hard to listen to Arluck fumble for moments of phony sentiment between the half-drunk laughs and clink of silverware.

His wife, Clare, sat beside him, smiling her practiced Realtor smile and giggling as Arluck blathered on. In the dim light of the restaurant the others appeared as strangers to Frank even though he'd shared office space with them and made jokes about crime-scene photos, marveling at the carnage and unintended irony of a blood-stained Sorry game box in the upper-left-hand corner of one or the languid, peaceful sleep of the strangled mob informant who'd died clutching a dog-eared copy of *How to Win Friends and Influence People*. So he coaxed his good-sport smile out with the knowledge that there wasn't an agent in the room that he'd call a real friend. He wished they'd just give him the gun and be done with it—let him go without the speeches and whispered promises of staying in touch.

He pushed his thumb into the red rose again, admiring the softness of each new fold—a little mystery that forced him to keep probing its dark center even as petals dropped and the rose ceased looking like a rose and more like a blown eye socket. He continued his destruction as Arluck ran down the list of his achievements, stopping every other sentence to bust balls: "Frank put away Peltz and broke the Boswell murders . . . he can't type, but he can hold his liquor . . . and okay, he got lucky with Gangemi and Franconi . . . Frankie does not wear a dress, the man's got whiskers, and some of you in this room'll know what that means. And he knows who really killed Kennedy, King, and Ruby, and as far as I know, he's the only agent to have been spit on by Squeaky Fromme . . ."

Frank attacked the white rose next, knowing that the rest of the evening would be an endurance test of sloppy farewells and teary hugs from the wives and women agents, most of whom considered Frank some dinosaur from the agency's old-boy days. And that was okay with him. He'd learned early on to play the game, keep his enemies within the Bureau close, and avoid office politics. But the truth was that something had been lost and he did not know what that something was, only that he woke most days with it sitting on his chest and couldn't figure out whether it was the job or the loom of his mandatory retirement that had changed or him. Despite what others said, he was not looking forward to quitting as he slogged through the late innings of his career—the endless phone calls, computer problems, paperwork, case file updates, endless meetings with superiors, or dozens of new tech specialists who had invaded every field office. They were younger than Frank and as bland and humorless as their suits suggested, but they would get ahead. Frank was certain of it, just as he was certain that his whole career had been one large case, a stream of crimes, questions, and murky motives that when all was said and done offered no easy answers and very few happy endings. It was a conclusion that every agent in the room would come to sooner or later because part of the job required that you plug into the never-ending hum of the large crime story that employed them all, the statistics of which could be boiled down into facts and figures that he supposed said something deep about society and human nature. But down in the trenches the whole thing felt more like a machine designed to leave bodies in its wake and keep agents at their desks late into the night pondering files brimming with toxicology reports, counterfeit plate proofs, entry-wound conjectures and mushroomed slugs, fibers from a '79 Ford, boxes of tape-recorded conversations, phone and credit card records, VIN numbers, photos of gruff-looking men in suits standing outside certain restaurants, ransom notes, hair, soil, blood, saliva, and semen samples, eyewitness statements, and even the bits of flesh that arrived in clear plastic bags from the lab, like the pieces scraped from under the fingernails of a fifty-year-old oral surgeon who'd been beaten and drowned in his own lap pool simply because he'd had the bad luck to have the wife of a drug dealer die during a routine wisdom tooth extraction.

Clare slipped her hand into his lap and stirred him back to the party. Arluck finished up by making a gun with his hand and pointing and firing it at Frank. "We got you a little something, Frankie," he said, snapping open a black case to display a brand-new Heckler & Koch 9mm. "Just in case the squirrels give you trouble."

Claps and hoots filled the room and Clare pinched him. "You okay?" she asked.

He nodded, snapping out of it just in time to toss Arluck a polite wave. "I'm fine," he said, but it was too late because she'd spotted what was left of the roses.

"Frank," she hissed, "look at the mess you made. I mean, you've ruined them. What were you thinking?" He looked at the bare stem and then the red half-moon stain under his thumbnail, shrugged, and said, "Nothing."

As he watched her sweep the bruised petals into a napkin and stow them inside her purse he reached into his pocket and nudged aside the loose change until he felt the cool smoothness of the finger bone.

She snapped her purse and looked at him impatiently, letting him know that he'd embarrassed her, as Arluck made his way through the tables toward them and she was forced to bury the little incident with a smile.

"Hello, Clare," Arluck said. He slapped Frank on the shoulder and set the gun down in front of him. "I had them put extra long grips on it and custom sights."

"It looks great," Frank said, popping open the case.

"Thanks, Harry, that was sweet," Clare said.

Arluck pulled a chair over and collapsed into it. "Now, I don't know about that," he said. "But it looks like the big guy's getting sentimental on us?"

Frank shook his head and noticed folks gathering their coats and searching pockets for car keys. "I'd better go make the rounds, the early birds are starting to fade," he said.

"Go on," said Clare. "Harry'll keep me company, won't you, Harry?"

Arluck nodded. "Hey, Frank, if you see the waitress, send her over. I'm about three scotches shy of good company. Five away from inappropriate limericks."

Frank laughed and went to say his good-byes, dipping his large frame over tabletops to shake hands and politely grin at bad jokes, parting shots, and awkward introductions to significant others, wives mostly, who smiled and asked him about his family and then only half listened as he told them about his daughter, Lucy, who was living in Seattle. He kept moving, bon mots and nifty conversation closers flowing effortlessly in his quest to be done with the night and get out.

Agent Hawkens told him to come by the office and see him, making the universal stroke-off sign for paperwork and rolling his eyes. "You're not officially out just yet. We still have our tendrils wrapped." Then he told Frank about his son who was working as a freelance cult deprogrammer. "His first job was this timber exec's wife who'd run off with Rajneesh."

"The Rolls-Royce Swami."

Hawkens nodded. "They confiscated seventy-two Rolls-Royces and a dozen air-hockey tables. Now that's what I call enlightenment."

"Did he get her?" Frank asked.

"The wife?" Hawkens said, nodding. "Yeah, she was banging the swami, even helped plan that salmonella in the salad bar, trying to rig the election. It almost worked and I tell you what, it put me off salad bars for a while." Hawkens gulped his drink and straightened his tie. "Well, my boy had to chloroform her, and when he brought her back the husband served her with divorce papers and shipped her off to a sanatorium."

"So he likes his work?"

"He has his complaints like we all do, but he's never bored. You should see his hotel bills. He writes everything off as a business expense," said Hawkens. "He's taking notes and plans to write a how-to manual. And after that a field guide to cults and cult leaders, a handy pocket reference that will help people identify some of these groups. He's very ambitious. Now, what about Lucy?"

"She's in Seattle," Frank said, "working temp jobs and finding herself."

Hawkens smiled. "Music to a parent's ears."

"She'll be okay. She's got good instincts."

"Don't they all," Hawkens said, letting him go with a wink.

He moved on, thanking Bob Depalma and Special Agent in Charge Woodrell for coming. Woodrell told him about a lake that the Fish and Wildlife Service had stocked with golden trout. "I'm giving you this on the hush, hush," said Woodrell, drawing Frank a quick map on a napkin and handing it to him. "Your retirement present. Try corn niblets with a worm and you won't be able to haul them in fast enough."

Frank said a quick good-bye and circled back to his table to find Arluck gone and, sitting in his place, Tim Peck, who was chatting up Clare, his hands folded politely on the table in front of him.

Peck had been with the Bureau only three years and was still green, eager to right wrongs, full of all that good stuff every new agent charged into the job with. He had a pudgy, enthusiastic face and was always trying to shake a few pounds. He stuck out because he was smart and perhaps a little body shy, unlike the ex-military guys, former detectives, and overachievers whom the Bureau seemed to attract. They called him Pitter Patter behind his back because he wore pastel ties, had a high voice, and was not married or divorced. It didn't matter one way or the other to Frank whether or not Peck was gay because he approached the job with old-fashioned head-down vim and vigor, quietly solving the tough and unglamorous cases tossed his way. He was also constantly pumping Frank for information on the D. B. Cooper case, wanting to know what he thought had become of the skyjacker. At first Frank thought the younger agent was slyly busting stones—going on about an old unsolved case—but after he'd helped Peck out a few times, showing him ways to slip stuff past the SAC and how to smooth things over with the local sheriff's department, he realized that Cooper's crime had put its hooks into the younger agent. Frank, for better or worse, was one of the few guys left who'd been assigned to the case and who endured Peck's endless questions and far-fetched theories.

He sat down and nodded at Peck.

"I'm gonna find Tim a house," said Clare. "Two-bedroom Craftsman or—"

"Something like that," Peck said.

Frank watched him blush and knew that he had no intention of leaving the cheap one-bedroom he kept south of town.

Arluck returned clutching a tumbler of scotch, ready to talk shop, and Clare, sensing a round of guy talk, stood and made her way across the room to speak to Fran Drucker, the wife of one of the agents.

"You really think he got away?" Peck asked.

"Who?" Arluck asked.

"Lemme guess," Frank said. "Cooper, right?"

"Of course," Peck said, nodding. "What else is there?"

"That was a long time ago," said Arluck. "He's probably dead now. All that money can and should get you in trouble."

"Tropical island," Frank said. "Or maybe he didn't run, maybe he stayed local and bought himself some acreage and watched the grass grow. The mistake the Bureau made was in assuming he'd done something like this before and that he'd do it again."

"Mistake?" Arluck roared. "We don't make mistakes!"

"I'd say it was his first time and that's what made it the perfect crime," said Frank. "He just put all his chips on one number and spun the wheel. You gotta like his guts."

Arluck said, "If he did make it to some tropical island, he's probably knee-deep in booze and LBG's. I know I would be." Peck looked at him blankly. "Little brown girls—Jesus, Peck, don't act so fuckin' innocent or else they're gonna promote your ass."

Peck blushed as Arluck tossed back his scotch and signaled the waitress for another.

"No, really," Peck said. "I want to know if you think he survived."

Frank shrugged. "I hope so, but I doubt it. It would be nice to know we haven't been looking for a pile of bones all these years. Maybe someday we'll pass each other on the street, but I don't hold my breath. It's a frigid fucking trail. But I still go by the shelter and look at their faces, see if maybe he's found his way back."

Arluck spun his empty scotch glass. "What the fuck are you talking about, Marshall?"

"The bums. I keep thinking maybe that's how a guy like Cooper ends up."

"My uncle's a bum in Lake Tahoe," Arluck said. "Not a bad place to be a bum. He eats pretty good."

"Ski bum?" Peck asked.

"No, a bum bum. Carries all his belongings in a garbage sack, writes poetry on napkins, eats ketchup, shares malt liquor, and mutters. He's the real deal and he's happy as hell. We visit him once a year and bring him a change of clothes. He calls me Freddy and tries to kiss my wife, says he could make her happy."

"Well, I don't believe in coincidence," Peck said. "I don't think you're just going to run into this Cooper panhandling on the street."

"Ah, bull semen!" Arluck shouted. "You want coincidence, Peck, I've got some coincidence for you. Lincoln was elected in 1860. Kennedy in 1960."

"Yeah, and both were assassinated," Peck said. "I've heard this before."

Arluck waved him off and charged ahead. "On a Friday, with their wives sitting next to them and bullets in the back of the head. I'm not making this shit up. Lincoln was killed in the Ford Theater and Kennedy in a Lincoln convertible."

"Made by Ford," Frank added, getting in on the act. "You want more?"

Peck threw up his hands, grinning.

"Both men were succeeded in office by southerners named Johnson," said Frank. "One born in 1808, the other in 1908. The names Lincoln and Kennedy have seven letters. And the names of their vice presidents, Andrew and Lyndon Johnson have thirteen letters. Lee Harvey Oswald and John Wilkes Booth have fifteen letters. I've got more."

"Okay, okay, I give."

Arluck said, "Strange shit happens out there, Peck. Work the job long enough and you'll see."

"A butterfly flaps its wings over Brazil and there's a tornado over Texas."

"What the hell does that mean?"

"Sensitive dependence on initial conditions. Order in the chaos that is impossible to detect," said Frank. "Some guy jumps out of a jet and I get a 9mm instead of a gold watch tonight. They have equations for this stuff."

Arluck pounded the table. "Woodrell ever tell you about the Hoyle case?"

Peck shook his head and let Arluck continue. "Ten years he looked for that guy. Hoyle's thing was he'd take cruises and put the moves on lonely old women, marry them, and take all their money. He killed three of them. We called him the Cruise Artist because he had impeccable manners and was an internationally ranked bridge player."

The waitress arrived and set fresh drinks down in front of them, spilling a little of Arluck's scotch on her uniform.

"Now, this Hoyle," Arluck continued, "was supposed to have some sort of magnetic gaze."

"Like Manson?" Peck asked.

"No, that would be the crazy-as-a-shithouse-rat gaze, Peck. Do not confuse the two. Not in this line of work. That would be a mistake."

"He was also a good listener," Frank added. "Which as you know is catnip to women. He wore a pinky ring and could foxtrot. Left a trail of broken old hearts and empty bank accounts, that's how he charmed his way on to the Most Wanted list."

"And let's not forget the three dead ladies," Arluck said. "He chopped the last one up, stuffed her into a Samsonite, and tossed it overboard."

"And what was the coincidence?"

Arluck looked at Frank and winked. "Woodrell's mother took a cruise . . ."

Peck laughed.

"True story," said Frank. "You never know how the case is going to sort out. Some solve themselves, others just fade away until you forget about them. Point being, you can't let a little thing like coincidence put you off. Things line up all sorts of ways. The good cops—

I mean the ones that slam cases—are the guys who refuse to let patterns take over."

"What he means," said Arluck, "look at things the same way twice and you get locked into thinking one way when the bad guy's thinking the other way. But that's only half the job." He gave Frank a look of grim joy before continuing. "Then there's the rest of the mess, mothers and wives—the ones who think their husbands and sons are somebody else and you gotta tell them how they shot somebody or grabbed a little boy from a park and left his body in the cattails or how they've embezzled a million dollars and disappeared with their twenty-year-old secretary. At first they don't believe you, so you tell them again, maybe show them some photos until they get that look and you know it's time to leave."

"You don't ever get used to that," said Frank.

"I've done a few," Peck said.

Both men nodded and looked around for their wives as Rispoli and Jerry Brown joined the conversation. Rispoli was drunk and fingering his pack of Marlboros, wanting to light up. He was currently undercover and the butt of a lot of Serpico jokes around the office because he'd let his hair grow long and was sporting a ratty porn star mustache.

Brown, neatly dressed as always, pulled up a chair and said, "Here's to the old school, Frank."

Frank tipped his drink to that. He considered Brown not only a solid agent but a stand-up guy. He'd graduated top in his class at Annapolis and cracked several high-profile cases in the organized-crime division. The press loved him and he had become the Bureau's "go-to guy" when there were cameras around and the Bureau wanted to put its best diversified face forward.

"Sit down," Frank said, "Peck was just pumping us about D. B. Cooper."

"That's a shocker," Brown said.

"And ancient fucking history," said Rispoli. "Everybody knows the guy ate it on the way down."

"You tell him about that woman in Arizona?" Brown said.

Peck waited to see if they were fucking with him. "What woman?"

"The one who claimed to have been Cooper's mother, what was her name?"

"Darlene Dink," Frank said. "She'd also dated Elvis and Buford Pusser and supposedly had an affair with one of the Kennedys. Their love child's in an institution, drooling into his pajamas—one of them idiot savants who can carve small wooden animals."

"Sent Frankie boy naked Polaroids of herself," Arluck said. "I told him he shoulda sent the beaver shots into *Hustler* with a little number for D. B. to call."

When the others finished laughing, Peck said, "Was there anything to her story?"

"Darlene's story had a lot of holes," Frank said. "They all did, but it was my job to follow up any nut that claimed to be Cooper or married to Cooper or shared a beer with him or gave him a ride or square-danced with him. Hell, one guy told me he was Cooper in another life and then there was the speed freak who said he'd stabbed Cooper. I've got a file of letters this thick. You name it, I've heard it."

"So nothing?"

"There was one guy, though."

"Yeah?" Peck said.

"Buy me a cup of coffee and I'll tell you about him."

"There's always one," Rispoli said. He polished off the rest of his vodka and leaned in close to Frank, asking, "You got a minute?"

Frank nodded and started to ask him what was the matter when Rispoli vibed Arluck sitting there with his radar up. "Nothing," he said, trying to play it off. "I'll get you later." He tamped out a cigarette and said he was going outside to smoke even though Peck had already pushed the ashtray across the table for him.

He left and Arluck clapped his hands and said, "How about we talk baseball?"

"Okay," said Brown.

"Where were you born?"

"Saint Louis."

"And so that makes you a Cards fan?"

Brown shook his head. "Nope, I'm a Dodgers fan."

"As a rule I don't trust people who don't root for the team they grew up with. It shows lack of loyalty."

"Well," Brown said, "have you ever been to Dodger Stadium?"

Arluck said he had not.

"I could look at that grass all day. I been using the Scott's Turf Builder on my own lawn—you know, trying to get that deep green, experimenting with different mowing patterns."

"Well, that's still not an excuse," Arluck said. "Me, I was born an As fan and I'll die an As fan. Vida Blue, I'm for you."

"I suppose you have views on the DH," Brown said.

"It's wrong."

"I disagree. It prolongs careers. You gotta hate the Yankees, though."

"Everybody hates the Yankees. I'm not fond of the Astros either. Scott's fine, but those uniforms—what the hell were they thinking?" He turned to Peck. "Peck?"

Peck said he didn't watch baseball.

"Where you from?"

"Cincinnati."

"Shit, the Reds and you don't watch baseball?" Arluck made a V with his fingers and jabbed them toward his eyes. "I'm going to be watching you, Peck."

Peck smiled uncomfortably as Arluck ranted about other un-American activities such as drinking Canadian beer and rooting for Ali.

Frank raised his hand to stop them. "A perfect reason why we don't talk baseball." They were quiet a moment. Frank watched a woman perched on a bar stool nearby. She had nice legs and knew how to smoke, letting the cigarette linger inches from her lips before taking another drag. Got him to thinking about Marlene Dietrich.

"Painful," Arluck said, giving him a wink and a nudge, indicating the woman.

"Who's going to track down leads on the Cooper case?" asked Peck.

Frank shifted. "I'm retired. But if you want, I'll pass you the file. It's out of gas, that is, unless some solid-gold tip comes in. Then maybe they'd throw a few man hours at it."

"This some kinda hobby of yours, Peck?" Brown asked as his wife, Leona, appeared behind them, coats draped over her smooth arm. "I mean, it was kinda before your time, wasn't it?"

Peck nodded. "When I was younger I wanted to escape like he did."

"Don't tell me you had a bad childhood," Arluck said. "My old man used to chase me around the house with a band saw blade and I'm a better man for it."

"No, it's not that. I just liked the idea of being able to get away like that."

Frank eyeballed him. "Like what?"

"You know, jump out of a plane with all that money and never be heard from again."

"Only thing Cooper accomplished was getting the airlines to re-design planes. What's that thing called?" Brown snapped his fingers, trying to remember.

"A Cooper Vane," Peck said quickly. "It prevents the hatch from being dropped while the plane's in the air."

Brown chuckled as his wife tapped him on the shoulder. "Yeah, the Cooper Vane. Guy jumps out of a plane and that's probably all he got for his troubles."

Frank rose to say good-bye.

Brown did the same. "You know," he said, "I've been sitting here trying to think of something to say all night and all I could come up with is something my father used to say. Whatever it is that gets you up in the morning, don't let it go. Does that work for you?"

"Only if he lived a long and happy life."

"Don't know about happy, but long, yes, he lived a long time, maybe too long," he said.

"Well, I've got a few things," Frank said.

"Listen, you ever wanna go to a game—"

"Yeah, I know, call. Right?"

Brown smiled and they shook hands, knowing Frank would never call

He let Brown's hand drop from his grip, hating these moments of false wisdom. Brown nodded, hooked an arm around his wife and led her to the door past the pod of pimple-faced busboys in stained aprons who were waiting for the party to end.

Frank sat back down and listened to Arluck explaining the dead-case file to Peck and how the Bureau let things slip, especially if there were no victims left to complain and stir the pot. "Things get reshuffled and reprioritized," he said. "One year they get their ass in a crack about paperhangers and so we go after paperhangers. Next year it's the drug dealers and so we go after drug dealers. Then it's kidnappers. Hell, it gets to the point where we're just chasing our own tail."

Frank suddenly remembered a tattoo of a snake swallowing its own tail he'd seen on a young street kid who'd been a witness in a kidnapping case. She'd startled Frank by fixing up into her scabbed fist behind a pizza shop and then asking Frank if he wanted to fuck her. He gave her twenty dollars instead and bought her a coat, insisting that she pick something out that wasn't black. All these years later and all that remained when he tried to conjure her face was the tattoo—solitary and black like a bruise or delicate brand against her pale skin. He recalled how the whole incident had sobered him with the knowledge that a large part of the job was sorting through the menagerie of the lost, stolen, and counterfeit, the guilty and innocents who'd been caught up and hijacked, shot, stabbed, held for ransom, accidentally dismembered, kidnapped, chopped to death, blackmailed, beaten with blunt instruments, disappeared, lied to, coerced, bribed, tortured, and deceived. He glanced over at Peck and thought, if you didn't know this going in, you sure as shit did going out.

"Come on, Frank, anything else?"

He looked at Peck. "About Cooper?"

And so, with Arluck chiming in, Frank covered the case again, the whole thing bubbling out of him just like the bedtime stories he used to read to Lucy, the words long since burned into his brain. He went over the discovery a few years back of the bundle of bills with matching serial numbers that had washed up along the banks of the Columbia and how subsequent searches had been unable to find any additional clues.

Peck pulled out a small notebook and jotted down a few notes. "I've been wanting to ask you about that."

"We figure the money was part of a stash he intended to come back for," Frank said. "Or maybe he landed in the river and drowned, but that doesn't explain how come we didn't find more."

"Did you check the deeds along the river?"

Frank thought, trying to remember through the ground fog of booze and party fatigue. He wanted to go home but when he looked into Peck's eyes he saw the same look he himself had when he used to talk about the Jane Doe in the pond. This wasn't just idle shoptalk anymore. Even Arluck sat silently, waiting for Frank to answer.

"What do you mean?" he asked Peck.

"If he meant to come back for the rest of the money he must have thought it was in a safe place, a place he was familiar with, maybe a friend's house or something like that."

Arluck cut in. "What good would checking the deeds do? If you haven't noticed, Peck, it's a big fucking river with thousands of miles of drainage. The money could have come from anyplace."

"I was just thinking that if he hid that little bit, maybe there's more somewhere else."

Frank sniffed his fingers. They smelled like dead rose. "Two hundred and ninety-four twenty-dollar bills—about six thousand bucks—and if I remember right, the thinking at the time was that it could have been a decoy."

"Decoy?"

"Enough to throw us off his trail and make us think he'd drowned or something. Only it backfired and got lost until that kid decided to build a sand castle and found the money."

"So you didn't check the deeds?"

Frank rubbed his face. "I don't remember."

"If you think there's something we missed, have a chat with Woodrell about it," Arluck said. "Tell him you wanna be put on the Cooper case, and after he gets done laughing his ass off he'll stick you on the tip line."

"It's okay," Frank said. "It's just it's late and I'm too tired to re-member, but if you've got a question, call me. I can't guarantee I got any answers for you, but I'll do my best."

Peck nodded.

"You heard the man," Arluck said, pointing at Peck's notepad. "Now put that away."

Clare came over and pulled Frank aside and told him that he should at least make an effort to mingle and thank people for coming.

So he followed Woodrell and Sanitsky out to the parking lot, say-ing good-bye and thanking people for coming, and just as he was about to go back inside he saw Rispoli leaning against the cinder block wall smoking, flicking his Zippo open and shut with trembling hands. He made his way over through the tip and glare of headlights.

"You okay?" he asked.

Rispoli took a long drag and squinted. "Actually no, I'm not okay," he said, running a hand through his sweaty hair and shivering. "Thanks for asking, though."

"You wanted to talk to me before?"

"It's nothing."

"You sure?"

Rispoli shrugged. "Yeah, I'm good."

Frank didn't push it. All he really knew about Rispoli was that he'd worked a lot of the organized-crime stuff before going under-cover and that lately there'd been talk about him being a little too undercover. Creeped up with the criminals—no longer in on the act but part of it. An awkward silence descended on them as they watched a skinny Mexican kid toss leaky trash bags into a spattered Dumpster, where they landed with a hollow gong.

Arluck poked his head out the door, saw them standing there, and motioned for Frank to come back inside.

"You'd better go," said Rispoli.

"Somethin' you wanna tell me about?"

Rispoli shook his head. "I wouldn't know where to begin and you wouldn't want to know even if I could."

"Go on, I'm listening."

He started to say something but stopped, tacked on a smile, and instead said, "Forget it, you're retired, Frank."

"What's that mean?"

"Nothing, except you made it to the end and there was a lot of love in that room."

"Horseshit."

"Well, okay, respect. You did the job right and that's gotta count for something."

There it was, Frank thought, the night, his career, maybe even the rest of his life in a nutshell. He'd put his head down, laid his shoulder to the wheel, and where had it gotten him? "No," he said. "I don't know what counts for anything anymore."

Rispoli took a drag and winced, chucking the half-finished cigarette away. "Well, that's fucking depressing, Frank."

"You change your mind and wanna talk . . ."

Rispoli's sucked-out stare spoke volumes even as he told Frank to have a good one and strolled to his car without looking back. Frank returned to the restaurant and watched Arluck yakking away at Clare, who was holding the black Heckler & Koch case away from her body as if it might explode. She looked over and tossed him a tight smile—the green light to get out of there.

Before leaving, he found Peck again and told him to call, that he'd tell him everything he knew about Cooper and some stuff he didn't exactly know for sure but believed to be true. He meant every word.

CHAPTER FIVE

At first the campers thought that Baron was just another colorful nut who would shuffle down the road dragging his flock behind him the moment some better opportunity presented itself, but as the rainy season approached, Baron and his crew showed no sign of pulling up tent stakes and continuing their hejira. The bus remained double-parked between the unfinished dome and Reba's busted VW Camper van, its side panels cloaked with speedy green vines. Saplings had sprouted from the bug-clogged grillwork and birds had built nests under the side-view mirrors. Someone had soaped the word CROATOAN across the front windshield and the only sign of life was the occasional squeal of leaf springs whenever Ethel moved to yell out the window to complain of the heat.

Reba began to feel increasingly threatened by Baron's chatty and haphazard campaign to undermine her matriarchal authority. Not only did he refuse to read any of the Buckminster Fuller books, but also he went around camp dismissing them as elitist, loudly proclaiming his preference for Isaac Asimov, who in his reckoning would someday run neck and neck with Einstein. Whenever campers argued with him he'd make small zapping noises and call them Reba-bots.

He carried a large soup spoon in his pocket and was quick to paddle food down his throat only to feign injury at cleanup time. And when Magnolia asked for help pulling the long-rooted weeds that seemed to grow overnight in the vegetable patch, Baron would go into one of his fogs, clutch at his back, and say, "Bad lumbar. An old nine-pin injury come back to haunt me. My nickname was Mr. Three Hundred, and I had the generous sponsorship of Trout's Ford, Lincoln, and Mercury. But that's all gone now." Then he'd offer one of his acolytes' services.

He pressed Castaneda paperbacks on people, demanding that they know the identities of their four enemies and rambling on about the crack between the world of *diableros* and the world of living men.

Several of Baron's women followers began going topless. Old and veined in odd places, the women were walking conversation stoppers and mosquito magnets.

Cooper became suspicious when, during one of his periodic strolls into the jungle to check on his stash, he ran into Delroy, one of Baron's minions, tapping on rocks and digging small holes. Worried that Delroy might accidentally stumble on the money, he cornered him, demanding to know what he was up to.

"I seek Montezuma's lost treasure caravan," Delroy said.

"It's not here," Cooper said.

"Well, my research tells me the caravan marched 275 leagues north of Mexico City and then west toward some mountains."

"I didn't know we were 275 leagues north of Mexico City."

"Depends on your definition of a league. As far as I know, there's no historical consensus." He went on to explain how the treasure would be covered with layers of guano and small animal bones and how he'd invested in a pallet load of solvent to clean the gold with.

Cooper trailed behind until he was sure Delroy had no interest in the soft hillside where he'd buried the fireproof boxes of hijacked loot. In Delroy's opinion, no right-minded Aztec would bury his nation's fortune in simple topsoil. So Cooper returned to the small wooden tool shack to resume work on the gas generator that April had picked up at a flea market. The generator was to be the first step in her rural improvement project, providing Cooper could get it to run.

The shack was a jumble of paper oil quarts, machetes made from rusty mower blades, petrified glue pots, seized flocking guns, hex wrenches, nippers, and stiff tack clothes made from old tie-dyed T-shirts. Over the single window hung a Tecate poster featuring a señorita in a low-cut Mayan tunic and on the door there was a schedule for the 1954 Cleveland Indians.

Having made little progress on the generator, Cooper was tilted back in the swivel chair, admiring the busy knit of mud dauber tubes attached to the rafter boards, when Baron appeared. "Wait until dark and they're snugged into their barracks before you gas them," Baron said, pointing at the nests.

"I don't want to do that," Cooper said. "I kind of like the way they come and go, always in a hurry to improve on what they got."

"They're insects, they don't know any better. Have you spotted their leader yet?"

"You mean the queen?"

Baron nodded.

"No, I have not."

"When you do, kill her and then note the confusion. Remember, small ripples lead to tidal waves. I say you tamper with their election, exert your influence. It's always bothered me how successful this matriarch business is."

"I just like to watch."

"Watch all you want, you won't learn anything. Trust me—I've looked long and hard at the insect world for answers, and let me tell you, it's highly organized but empty and cruel. Busy is about the best you can say for the whole lot. Don't forget we have dominion over them."

"How do you explain spider webs?"

"Let's not go down that road," Baron snapped. "Besides, I didn't come here to talk bugs. I've got orders from April."

Cooper turned to face him, not liking the sound of it one bit.

"I know about the pagan village and her plans."

"La Tontería?"

Baron nodded. "She has decided that they need radios."

"What happened to damming the creek and setting them up with a catfish farm?"

"I talked her out of that," Baron said. "We can't have little chiclets falling in and drowning. Mess with mother nature and we'll have the elders wringing their hands over *agua diablos* and bad omens. I think hi-fi is a good start, give them a taste of the BBC or, radio waves willing, maybe a little Paul Harvey—give them *the rest of the story*." He slapped the generator. "Now, let's get this mother running. Have you seated the brushes and checked the filters? And what about this pull cord? We need to get our fingers on some good nylon bonded cord. The jungle's not kind to cotton."

Baron was a natural mechanic, and as soon as he got the generator up and purring, they took the camp car down the mountain to buy radios for the villagers. The car, a rusty Mercury Colony Park wagon with a crumpled front bumper and busted dual-action tailgate, sputtered and swung back and forth across the road. Baron complained about the bumpy ride, giving Cooper a hard time for steering with one hand draped over the wheel like a pimp.

They successfully bartered with a local junk peddler for eight badly damaged clock radios, a large sea-band all-weather radio, a spool of lamp cord, and a box of salvaged socket plugs. Baron refused to accept the junk peddler's as-is terms and instead cajoled the man into shaking on a twenty-four-hour satisfaction guarantee.

Halfway back to the camp the car sputtered out and quit. Cooper tried all his usual tricks to get the wagon going but the car refused to cooperate. Baron sat watching his peace offering to Reba, pistachio ice cream, melt into a froth. He tossed the ruined ice cream into the jungle and said, "Let's have a look."

He circled the wagon, his hands hovering inches over the ticking engine as he read the Detroit Chi and muttered to himself. He sniffed the tailpipe, put an ear to the carburetor, and even dipped his finger into a spot of oil and tasted it.

When Cooper asked what he was doing he replied, "Diagnostics. Part of the problem is that business with the gas pedal. That little flutter you were giving it. My mother has the same problem. You don't want to tease the carb. I mean, I hate to criticize another man's driving but . . ."

"I don't know what you're talking about."

"Well, there it is," Baron said. "Looks like I hit a nerve." From his pocket he produced a flip-top tin of aspirin and dropped a tablet into the gas tank. He dried the carburetor with his shirttail, fiddled with the distributor cap, and pulled a vacuum tube, plugging it with a golf tee he'd found rolling around on the floorboard of the car. Then he sat under the shade of a large tree to consult his watch and eye the stalled wagon.

While they waited, a column of ants threaded themselves across the road. Bored, Cooper dropped oatmeal cookie crumbs in the shape of an A, trying to get the ants to form the letter. He'd once watched a beautiful Seri Indian woman fool a string of ants into a series of pulsing loops with a bottle of vanilla extract. But these ants remained on their stubborn course, unswayed by his oatmeal raisin cookie. Only one ant stepped out of line to lift a crumb before rejoining the queue.

"They respond to vibration," Baron called out from his shade. "I find a Popsicle stick pounded in about this far and then bowed on top with another such stick does the trick. All that vibrating turns their tiny ant brains to mush and they go into an earthquake panic. Same with chickens and earthworms. When it comes to predicting natural disasters I'll take a rock hen any day of the week. All that talk of dogs warning their owners is propaganda from the American Kennel clubs—old ladies looking to push their breeds on the public."

Cooper looked around for a Popsicle stick or paint stirrer and found nothing and so he watched the ants disappear into the jungle, imagining them beating out little ant work tunes with their feelers as they zeroed in on the melted pistachio ice cream.

Baron rose and began shaking the car, the struts groaning and popping. Then he reached in and turned the key with a flourish, grinning as the engine roared to life.

"Hey, it worked," Cooper said.

"Of course it worked. Now steady pressure on the gas pedal."

When they reached camp, April was waiting for them, her hair tucked under a faded red bandana. She hugged Cooper and then inspected the radios while Baron gabbed on about the plan to run the radios off the generator and give the villagers news of the world and music.

"Remember," Baron said. "Charity's a dish best served cold."

"What's that supposed to mean?"

"Leave it on a doorstep and ring the bell."

Cooper took the radios back to the shed, where he worked late into the night replacing frayed cords, mending bent antennas, blowing dust from the delicate speaker cones, and wondering why they just hadn't bought a bunch of battery-operated transistors. He got six radios running and tossed the others under the tool bench with the rest of the junk.

The next day he hiked down to La Tontería with April and Baron, who'd contracted Molto, the most servile member of his flock, to wheel the cumbersome generator and crate of radios down the rutted jungle path. April was in high spirits and sang the whole way, even accepting Baron's requests for a Blood, Sweat, and Tears tune.

A light rain started, drizzling down through the heavy green canopy, causing Baron to remark, "This is going to play hell with the reception. I hope you haven't overbilled the project."

Cooper assured him that he'd thoroughly tested the radios and was fairly certain they could pick up some stray signal. "But I'm not makin' any guarantees," he said.

As they hit the outskirts of the village Baron sniffed the air and said, "I'd feel better if we consulted a *bruja* before we get started with the radios and pollute these simple folk with rock music and Bromo-Seltzer commercials. There's mucho big magic afoot here."

Before they could stop him he barged into the nearest shack, demanding an audience with the local *bruja*. An old woman chased him out into the street, denouncing him as a *loco piojo* and spitting on his shoes, much to the amusement of the ancient wrinkled men watching the spectacle from a nearby log bench.

"What sort of village is this?" Baron shouted.

April told Baron in a motherly tone to be quiet, and much to Cooper's surprise he shut his mouth and stepped away from the old woman. A crowd gathered and a man with curled, callused hands and long black hair appeared, introducing himself as Manu, the village *autoridad*. April explained that she'd brought radios and a generator as a gift, telling him how they could get weather reports, listen to music—anything they wanted. She did not want anything from them, she reassured him several times, nor had she come to ask them to work clearing trails in the jungle or to trick them into signing on as porters for some ill-fated scholarly expedition.

Manu agreed and allowed Cooper and Molto to begin hooking up the radios.

Baron, meanwhile, had stationed himself under a tree and was locked in an elaborate evil eye contest with the old woman. She had him on the psychic run—rubbing his temples and calling out to Molto to loan him some pagan spell to turn her into a toad. The village children were no help. They pestered Baron, pointing at the coins in his penny loafers and asking him about his binoculars. Every now and then he would reach out and granny thump one who got too close.

When the moment arrived to fire up the generator, April took a minute to recheck the connections before giving Cooper the sign, and after a few stubborn pulls the generator finally growled to life with a gassy cough. Molto wiped mud from the extension cord and sank the ends together.

For a second nothing happened and Baron rose flapping his arms about in the rain like a large flightless bird. The woman backed away, spitting in his general direction one last time.

April looked at Cooper. "Do something," she said.

So he reached down and carefully wiggled the cord and a loud snarl of static rippled through the village. Baron immediately stopped his flapping.

"It works," April shouted, rushing around twirling dials and knobs until she had all six radios playing "Lara's Theme."

Although she expected the villagers to break into dance or gather around her in a swarm of gratitude, they stood frozen as the slow, leaking strings and brooding horns struggled over the drone of the generator. For the better part of an hour she and Cooper sorted through the radio dead zone, trying to get a response from the villagers, some of whom had gone back to work as the rain broke, others submitting to Baron's spiritual quizzes, which he administered in loud, harshly enunciated English.

Midway through a static chopped version of "96 Tears" one of the radios began to melt and spew sparks. The sparks struck a grass mattress that quickly sprang into flame before anybody knew what was happening. Cooper smelled smoke and turned in time to see a man rush out of the shack. His hair had been singed into a frizz and he was shouting as flames crept up the old and highly flammable burlap coffee sacks that served as makeshift window treatments.

The crowd scattered to fetch buckets but they were too late and the water did little except to push a rich, creamy blanket of smoke into the air. Babies cried, old men shook their heads, and the teenagers stood transfixed by the flames coiling up the shack's support beams in search of more thatch. Cooper tried comforting April but when "96 Tears" gave way to the stupid thud of "In-A-Gadda-Da-Vida" and the shack collapsed, the "no-goodwill mission," as Baron called it, was officially over.

Manu pointed to the trail and told them to get out, that they were no longer welcome in the village.

Later that night Cooper woke to find Baron scratching at his tent with the frog gig, looking vaguely satanic in the moon shadow. "I've come to collect and draw on our deep brotherly bond," he whispered, motioning for Cooper to be quiet.

Cooper rubbed his eyes, his head still muzzy from the homemade wine he'd consumed with dinner and the peyote tea he'd shared with April in a futile attempt to stop her from pulling at her split ends and humming "In-A-Gadda-Da-Vida" as if it were some sort of penance.

"Arise, Irv," Baron commanded, waving his hands about in a complicated pattern.

He groped for his shoes. "What's with the fancy hand movements?"

"You're either a natural resister or I am out of practice."

"What do you want?"

"It's better I show you."

Cooper hesitated before following Baron into the heart of the camp, where he saw the bus. It had been cleared from its viney mooring and was sitting like an overgrown soapbox derby car, ready to drop down the hill. Figures moved about sleepwalking or tripping on something, he couldn't tell.

"What's going on?" Cooper asked.

"I'm afraid this is our exodus. It's on to greener pastures with a few new flock members, Irv. Do you dig?"

"No, I don't dig."

"Very well." Baron went over to one of the small four-wheel camp trailers and grabbed the tongue, knocking away the pillar of stones beneath it, feverishly motioning at Cooper to help. "If you don't dig, can you at least give me a hand with this heavy mother? I don't want to bulge any more discs."

Princeton Bob and Magnolia stumbled out of the shadows, holding hands and moving with a weary, zombied deliberateness. Cooper thought about taking this opportunity to fuck with Princeton Bob or maybe even punch him but figured that going off with Baron was a more fitting punishment.

He tapped Baron. "You got me out of bed to help you steal a trailer?"

"I've cleared this with Reba, Irv, and the short of it is I'm to play the camp scapegoat and that involves borrowing this trailer and sneaking out under the cover of night." He dropped the trailer tongue, took up the frog gig, and poked Cooper in the chest, saying, "Now, why don't you chuck it all and come with this—you're either on the bus or off the bus. If you're on the bus and you get left behind, then you'll find it again. If you're off the bus in the first place, then it won't make a damn. In other words, you don't wanna traipse through life being a last-chance Charlie, do you? This place is over, man. Paris is burning—chuck it and get out."

Princeton Bob and Magnolia began droning, "Chuck it, chuck it all, chuck it . . ."

"I'm going back to bed," Cooper said, taking one last look at their slack-jawed faces and deciding that he didn't want any part of whatever Baron was up to. "I think I'm going to sit this one out," he said.

Baron shook his head and lowered the frog gig. " 'So we beat on, boats against the current, borne back ceaselessly into the past.' Is that your plan, Irv?"

"I have no idea what you're talking about."

"Humans are pattern-seeking animals. What pattern do you seek?"

Before Cooper could answer, Baron backed away, trembling as something large ambled out from behind the dome.

It was Ethel, the bus hermit, wearing nothing more than a cotton sheet printed with little lambs frolicking over picket fences, wrapped toga style around her immense rolls of fat. Cooper stood frozen, marveling at the lava lamp–like ooze of her shoulders, the thick shelf of stomach and breast, and her arms, square like flour sacks, that terminated in tiny pale hands. She closed in, panting with the effort, swinging one thick leg in front of the other, her eyes fixed and determined.

"You've done it now, buddy boy. Ethel's anxious to get on the road," Baron said. "I have no control over this gal—she's all want and need. Four hundred bills of pure id."

"Call her off."

"I lack those skills," he cackled. "I'm afraid you've stepped into the eye of the hurricane this time, Irv."

Cooper turned to run, but Baron brought the frog gig up to his throat, stopping him before he could shout and warn the slumbering camp denizens. The maneuver allowed Ethel to snatch Cooper off his feet and smother him in a chubby, vinegar-scented bear hug. Trapped inside the sheer jiggling wave of her, he struggled for breath only to surrender and let himself be carried across the field to a large stone, where she set him down, took his face in her hands, and kissed him lightly on the lips. He tasted butter and chocolate and looked up blinking at the sheer mooning blot of her as he groped for words.

"Deliverance," said Ethel in a soft and pleasant voice. "You don't have to thank me. You wouldn't like where we're going anyway. We're on the road to nowhere."

Cooper made no move to get up as she smiled at him and trudged off to put a shoulder to the trailer, rocking the rust-locked tires until the thing began to move slowly toward the waiting bus. A small ramp was lowered from the bus's emergency door as people teemed around Ethel like worker ants swarming a pale, helpless queen, pushing and dragging her slowly up the ramp to safety.

When they were done Baron waddled over to Cooper and pried a wheat penny from the slot in his loafer. "A small token of our time together," he said, handing him the penny. "See you down the road some time."

"Happy trails."

Baron grinned. "And then some." He hustled back to the bus and climbed aboard, the doors swallowing him from view like a magic box.

Cooper watched them go as Chet crawled behind the wheel, adjusting the bus's mirrors before releasing the clutch. Gravity did the rest and the bus silently disappeared down the hill, with the trailer in tow.

The next morning they found a note from Baron tucked inside a signed first edition of *Journey to Ixtlan*. The note said, "Our services are needed in Chihuahua, ASAP. Please accept this book as partial payment for the trailer and stew pot—all regards, The Baron, et al."

There was much talk of kidnapping or worse, foul play facilitated by brainwashing techniques Baron claimed to have learned in Sri Lanka. Cooper stepped forward and gave his account of the past night's events, leaving out the kiss from Ethel and how maybe he could have stopped them.

A month went by with no word from Baron or the missing campers, but reports of petty thefts dropped off and in her nightly fireside chats Reba referred to Baron and his followers only as those wretched, trailer-thieving Roma.

The monkeys returned to the rock garden and at night Cooper listened to them. He was growing restless and tired of the camp's lazy routine. Yes, he was in Mexico, an important man hiding from his big crime, but that feeling had recently begun to fade and it dawned on him that he was going to need more entanglements and some adventure, because lounging around Reba's jungle commune was beginning to feel a little too much like work. To make matters worse, April had been avoiding him since the radio incident, somehow blaming him for the faulty wiring that had incinerated her dreams of making a difference in the world. She spent most nights getting stoned, staring at the campfire, and talking about Austen's *Emma* and how she wanted to go back to school someday or maybe open a muffin shop or bead store.

Two months after Baron's hasty departure, a woman named Jane turned up at the camp. Reba, perhaps sensing Cooper's growing restlessness, had put word out for Jane over the hippie grapevine, but as she introduced them Cooper saw that Reba was taking some pleasure from his disillusionment. The woman calling herself Jane was old, her hair a frosty tangle of gray, her face sagging here and there like a balloon left out in the cold. She wore too much topaz, her fingers and throat webbed with cheap Mexican silver jewelry that clacked and tinkled at her slightest move. She'd put on a few pounds in the hip department since the fetching sketch of her Cooper had stared at so many sleepless nights. She was also crazy or a little light in the head, a terrible combination of menopause, cheap acid, and a case of sunstroke she'd come down with while drifting on a pontoon boat in the Sea of Cortés with a Mexican industrialist who refused to let her off until she agreed to marry him—a long and confusing story that Cooper had a hard time following.

"To the hammer, everything looks like a nail," Reba said, stepping between them, a little too pleased with herself.

Cooper ignored her as Jane asked him if he was a Fed hoping to arrest her for antigovernment activity, saying, "To tell the whole truth and nothing but the truth, all that stuff was just a pose, a fashion statement. You see, I had my eye on this guy and he was, like, very committed to the cause and I was totally not committed, if you know what I mean. I mean, I liked his beard and the way he wore his sandals and so I started going to meetings and before I knew it I was involved with this AWAKE thingamajig and all these unshowered men with big plans for anarchy, protest marches, and LSD in the drinking water. Before I dropped out and tuned in I was just a housewife, ironing socks and packing lunches like the rest of the horde."

"Perhaps Jane would like to see the book, Irv," Reba said.

"What book?"

"Oh, it's nothing," Cooper said.

"Nothing is never nothing," Jane said. "I thought everybody knew that. Nothing is always something. Where have you been?"

"Never mind then," Cooper said. "I think there's been a mistake."

"What do you mean?"

Without thinking, Cooper said, "For starters, you're too old. The Jane I'm looking for is younger."

"What do you mean too old? I've maintained myself. How old do you think I am?"

"I'm not going to answer that."

"I think you should show her the book," Reba said. "It might clear some stuff up for you."

Jane poked him in the chest. "I have a right to see this book, don't you think? I mean, you asked and here I am, and now what? Don't think you can jerk me around, pull my daisies. I've been around the block and I'm telling you, I'm the one and only original Jane."

Cooper started for the creek, telling them he was late for a nap, hoping to shake them. But they tailed him down to the water's edge, picking his liver out about the book, until he began to wonder if this Jane wasn't some waste case Reba had coaxed up to the camp to prove that his search for the mystery lady was little more than a pointless sexual snipe hunt.

When he saw that there would be no peace until he showed them the book, he led them back to his tent and flipped through the moist pages until he came to the sketch.

"This you?"

"Oh my," she said, blushing and clutching her throat. "I thought this had been destroyed in the police raid."

Reba chimed in, "Wonders never cease."

Cooper gave her a buzz-off look and pulled Jane aside to quiz her at length. One thing the camp had taught him was that things were never what they seemed. And he was himself knee-deep in the deception. So he quizzed Jane about the dog and was surprised to find that she held her own, answering his questions correctly until she'd convinced him that most of the stuff written about her in the book was false.

"It was my old man's psychotherapy journal, or perhaps it would be more accurate to call him my young old man. I was twelve years and three months his senior," she said. "His beard falls out and I get blamed. He went around telling people how I'd crawled inside his head to break his heart. We were the Frank and Ava of the underground movement, fighting and falling in love. I have mostly fond memories because I was in it for the sex, but it's clear he never got over me. I guess that's the risk you take with younger men."

Cooper asked what happened.

"I got old," she said. "Happens all the time. You men and your ability to spawn. I'd like to see you go through the change. Men are mostly weak."

Cooper nodded—he'd heard enough. He took the book back from her and wrapped it in its canvas bag. Jane kept talking until Reba stepped in and asked if she'd like to eat.

"Depends."

"Rice and steamed dandelion greens?"

Jane left, but not before extracting a promise from Cooper that he would destroy the book. Desperate to be rid of her, he agreed and spent several days doing his best to avoid her.

A week later he retrieved the fireproof boxes from their shallow grave, and the minute he shuffled a pack of the twenty-dollar bills he knew that it was time to go. Traipsing back through the dark jungle he saw the camp in all its shambling glory—the peeling khaki paint, the wet cut-off jeans and peasant blouses drying in the trees, and the piles of garbage they'd been too lazy to bury or haul down to the village dump, where it would all be recycled by Indian children and junk dealers.

He found Reba. She was alone, drunk and sitting in a partially collapsed lawn chair with a small lizard perched on her knee and a jug of wine within easy reach. "I noticed it's always the green that seem to go first," she said, picking at the broken bands hanging off the lawn chair.

"Sun absorption. You don't get that with the white ones."

She thought about it a moment and then said something to the lizard before taking a slug of wine. "Do you want some?"

He shook his head and started for his tent. He was afraid she'd ask about the burlap sacks containing the money. "I know you're leaving," she called out. "I have a sense for these things. I hope it's not the crash of this Jane dream of yours. I only meant to help."

"No," he said. "It's time I hit the road."

"Just as well," she said. "I fear this place is doomed to suffer the same fate as Nashoba. Those Scots and slaves made it four years before their little communitarian experiment crumbled. I give it another year or two. I figure we'll either be discovered by tourists or else stagnation will set in. Splinter groups will form. But then again, Rome did not fall in a day."

"I thought it was wine and sodomy."

Reba sighed. "Well, a new order rises and the cycle repeats itself. You should have that printed on a card and hand it out to remind folks where they've been and where they're going."

With that, Cooper wished her good night and left her to the wine and lizard. He did not look back.

■

AS HE DROVE home from the party, making the familiar rights and lefts and catching lights, it began to sink into Frank that the banal ritual he'd just escaped from marked the end of his career as a government man. He thought about the articles on retirement Clare had set aside for him, the ones intended to prepare him for the inevitable with their talk of money market funds, rising health care costs, second mortgages, the importance of diet and exercise, wills, and second careers. He had zero patience for the whole business of what was optimistically advertised as the Golden Years. The photos of grinning gray-haired men clutching scuba diving gear or the liver-spotted women wearing denim skirts with inappropriate slits, standing in front of the junk-filled antique shops they'd opened, made Frank dread old age. They were the same insufferable people who dragged golf bags around lush country clubs, grinning like fools, socializing at tented cocktail parties, gulping multivitamins, subscribers to *Fortune* and *Smithsonian*. They watched *Matlock*, wore copper arthritis bracelets, gave advice on where to get the best steak, pulled straight Republican at the polls, and let on after a few too many Gibsons or G&Ts that they still enjoyed sex. Frank wasn't about to sun and fun the rest of his life away on some treated wood deck, waiting for his hair to gray and go and his teeth to loosen as he gummed oat bran muffins and worried about his prostate. Sooner or later he'd have to figure something out before Clare started riding him and making little comments about how it was time to get on with the rest of his life.

Other guys he'd known from the Bureau had made tidy fortunes setting up private security businesses or playing the market. They traveled—cruises mostly, a little bone fishing in the Gulf of Mexico and Southeast Asian junkets that Frank believed to be shorthand for sex tours featuring slim-hipped thirteen-year-old girls or boys. He'd been too busy to plan, figuring that whatever was supposed to happen next would happen and he'd adjust and move on. Only now, as he pulled the car into the drive, he wasn't so sure.

He turned to Clare and told her that he felt tired.

"Retired?"

"That too," he said, killing the engine and waiting for the feeling to pass. It did not. She leaned over and gave him a kiss—nothing behind it, just a dry pressing. "You did good," she said. "I never know how to act at those things. Everybody lies and tells you to stay in touch when it's the last thing they want."

"Well, it's done. Tomorrow I am a zero file."

She turned to him, her hand already on the door latch, the other gathering her purse. "I'm cold. We can talk inside if you want."

He told her to go on, knowing she was eager to check the messages on the machine, hoping some buyer had called with a last-minute counteroffer on one of her listings. It was more likely her mother with some exasperated complaint about her father.

She got out and headed for the door. He followed, tripping the security lights he'd installed behind the juniper bushes at her request after a house down the street had been broken into and ransacked by stoned teenagers. He still remembered the argument they'd had when he told her how the neighbors would complain and how in the end the lights wouldn't be much of a deterrent because, in his experience, if someone wanted to get into your home bad enough, they were going to get into your home, lights or no lights.

Frank froze, half embarrassed by the paranoid brightness of the lights as Clare keyed the door and continued inside without him. He heard her purse drop on the carved trestle table, followed by the clunk of her shoes against the oak floor.

When he turned to make sure he'd rolled up the car windows he saw something small scamper along the cinder block footing and disappear into a knot of shadows cast by the bushes. As he waited for whatever it was to come out and show itself, the security lights clicked off, stranding him in the dark. He listened to the thrum of crickets and peepers for a while until he heard a rustling sound and a rabbit emerged from under a juniper bush, quaking. If he moved, the rabbit would bolt into the neighbor's yard and probably set the dumb black lab to barking or else it would get hit by a car and he'd have to watch it rot for a week guiltily. So he stood there, not moving a muscle, until he heard a car approaching and he turned, instinctively following it up the street, trying to catch the plate numbers—H8 something—a maroon sedan with a bad exhaust pipe and dented front bumper. When he looked back under the juniper bush the rabbit had vanished. There was nothing else to do except go inside and have another drink, maybe sit in his chair and hope the heavy feeling he felt pressing down on his shoulders would lift and allow a few hours of sleep.

But the feeling was still with him when he startled awake several hours later. He sat up. The bedroom appeared dim and familiar, all the shadows in their right places and Clare's sleep warm body nearby. The air smelled correct, even his clothes sat folded neatly on the black Windsor chair they'd bought at an antique shop from a small, neatly dressed man who kept polishing his glasses when asked whether or not the chair was a reproduction.

The framed photos on the dresser glinted like dark mirrors, reflecting what little moonlight leaked through the clouds outside. His legs ached and twitched and he felt oddly lucid, as if he were meant to be up at this hour staring out the window, waiting for something important to happen.

He shuffled the blankets off and slid his feet to the floor, feeling better already and yet wincing at what he knew could all too easily become a habit. Perhaps it was already a habit, he didn't care as he made his way downstairs, expertly navigating the dark hall and landing until he was in the kitchen.

The bottles rattled as he opened the liquor cabinet and reached behind the frosted fifth of gin and the sticky pint of peppermint schnapps, feeling for the smooth neck of the Smirnoff.

Standing at the sink he gulped down a juice glass of vodka and listened to the purr of the refrigerator and the pop and grind of his shoulders as he poured another shot and tossed it back. Then he ate a few antacids, crunching them down, and swished his teeth clean with another half a jig before setting the glass in the sink. Only then did he walk his routine circuit, checking windows and doors, eyeing the front hall closet, where he briefly allowed himself to imagine a burglar or bad, knife-wielding man hiding in there, nestled between the rain slickers and mothballed coats. He chided his urge to open the louvered door and check for the phantom intruder and instead went into his office, where he lowered himself into the swivel desk chair, the liquor already warming his belly, melting away the nervous twitch in his thighs and the tightness in his throat. He sat there for a long time, staring at the phone and thinking of Anne Blackwood and the way she'd fixed him with her dead eyes all those years ago when Frank had come for her husband. It bothered him that he should so easily conjure her without knowing what he wanted or exactly what it was he intended to do about her. She wasn't even a victim in the worst sense of the word, just a woman tangled up with the wrong man and left to sort out the pieces.

With that he took the one file he'd lifted from the office before his retirement. It was the pond girl's, Jane Doe #5966–7, long since zeroed. The case had not even been the Bureau's until Frank had made it one by arguing to the SAC that she'd been the victim of a suspected serial killer operating along the Oregon border—his only proof being that she was young, female, possibly a hitchhiker, and dead. She, too, had gotten under his skin, but in a different way, teasing him with the utter absence of leads. Thirteen years later, the finger bone and thin file were the only evidence that she'd ever existed.

He opened the folder, its edges foxed and dimpled where paper clips had held notes, site photos, and shots of her skeleton resting on a black body bag, the eye sockets like empty egg cups. He leafed through the various medical reports and lists of scant leads he'd chased down into quiet dead ends over the years. The pages of missing-person reports filed during the time the girl had gone missing brought back the many awkward phone calls he'd made to the relatives of the missing, a pool of names, each of them anxiously waiting on any news—even bad—of their vanished. He recalled one woman whose daughter Maggie, a shy freshman at Reed, had disappeared from her dorm room. The woman told Frank about a disturbing phone call she'd received long after she'd given up hope of ever finding her daughter alive or even knowing what had become of her. Late one night a woman calling herself Margaret had called collect but had simply sobbed before suddenly hanging up. He'd heard dozens of stories just like it, stories of parents glimpsing their lost children in crowds or receiving mysterious postcards. But there had been no such breaks in the pond girl case or parents to step up and claim her. Only Frank and maybe a local or cop or two had shown interest in the case over the years, and now certainly there was nothing except these pages and her killer out there somewhere. He skipped past the forensic reconstruction photos and sketches as that nagging and all too familiar sense that he'd missed something or somehow failed the dead girl came back to him, as fresh and as haunting as the day he'd leaned out over that cold pond waiting for her bony hand to float into his. He quickly shut the file and stashed it back in the desk before heading up to bed, hoping the vodka would work its lethargic magic on his brain and let him sleep.

He woke the next morning and untangled himself from the sheet as weak bands of sunlight struggled through the blinds. The backs of his hands were puffy and he could feel the first cottony buzz of a booze headache descending on him. He rubbed his face, stood unsteadily, and remembered how in his younger days a night of drinking could be shrugged off with a glass of water and a greasy breakfast, followed by a two-mile run.

By the time he reached the bathroom sink he realized there was no reason to rush through his groom-and-go routine, no more sniffing his jacket collar before swinging it over his shoulders or checking his tie for grease stains as he gulped one last cup of coffee, said good-bye to Clare and loped out to the car, already blocking out his day—the endless follow-up calls, sit and grins with wary local cops, file work, briefings, and lost hours spent fucking around in front of the Selectric pecking out reports and expense sheets. This morning there was nothing except his swollen reflection staring back at him and all the time in the world to stumble downstairs and do whatever it was you did when there was no job to go to, no boss to please or clock to punch.

After pulling on a worn gray sweatshirt, he opened the closet and thumbed through his old waist sizes, searching for his work pants. For some reason he'd kept a couple pairs of the dark blue 32s from his first days in the Bureau, the 36s Sansabelts from back when he'd worked undercover, and a half-dozen 38s he could still squeeze into if he skipped a few meals, did his crunchers regularly, and got religious with the jogging. He'd held the line at 40 for the last six years, vowing to stop the expansion because he did not want to be one of those older men who took to wearing baggy clothes to hide their spreading asses and thickening middles. But today, for the first time in years, he stared at the pants strung up on their wire hangers and wondered why he hadn't just shoved them all into a garbage bag and hauled them down to Goodwill or dropped them at one of the nearby churches. What was the point in keeping them? They were depressing reminders that he was getting old and out of shape.

Downstairs he found Clare sitting at the kitchen table, dressed for work, scraping a grapefruit hull clean as she scanned time-share brochures. They'd been kicking around the idea of buying into a condo in Arizona because Clare's sister lived south of Scottsdale and they'd spent the last few Christmases down there. The lack of trees had bothered Frank and so did all the fake cowboy crap—the guys from Jersey strutting around in crisp Wranglers and clean white cowboy hats as they tried to puff their desk-softened bodies into some cock-armed approximation of a cowpuncher.

Frank picked up a brochure for a planned community called Red Rock Rim that extolled the virtues of desert living and had pictures of happy couples staring at cacti or sitting poolside next to impossibly blue water. According to the copy, relaxation was the number-one concern of Red Rock Rim's inhabitants. Relaxation was one of those quasi-mythic activities Frank had taken great pains to avoid. He was suspicious of folks whose main goal in life was to relax and take it easy and was himself never more tense or unrelaxed when on vacation and being told by Clare that no, he couldn't check in with the office, he had to sit and relax with her, enjoy the sun. He took one last look at the brochure and wondered why the folks at Red Rock just didn't lie down and take the big sleep.

"Good morning, you," Clare said, snatching the brochure back. "I was reading that."

He mumbled a rote apology and poured himself some coffee. "I don't like people who like the desert," he said.

"You're just being stubborn."

"I'm not being stubborn."

"Then give me an example. And by the way, the coffee's bitter. I'm going to buy one of those grinders and use whole bean from now on, okay?"

He nodded, took a sip of coffee, and winced. She was right. "Okay, Mel and Carol Fargo."

"They don't count. Mel's an embezzler and Carol's a scheming enabler. Nobody likes them. Did you know they're being forced to sell their house to pay that lawyer?"

He thought a minute. "Okay, Tommy Fingerle."

"What's wrong with Tommy?"

"He's got a tan all year round. He's fifty-five and still calls himself Tommy. He wears a Speedo and some kinda high karate cologne." Clare winced. It was true, but Frank continued anyway. "And he's always going on about how alive the desert is, how it's teeming with life, and he's smug about the dry heat. But when I ask him what's so great about dry heat, he tells me about the arthritis clinics and retirement communities. I mean, what kinda proof is that? Arizona's a good place to live because it's got a lot of death barracks where you can play shuffleboard and Bingo?"

"He's got that time-share in Tucson, doesn't he?"

Frank nodded. "He handed me a Bible once and told me it was the best book he'd ever read. Two months later I caught him saying the same thing about the new Stephen King. Plus he golfs, and you know how I feel about golfers."

"Okay, so your dislike of the desert is based solely on Tommy?"

"And others like him who get righteous about where they live. It's the same with Californians and New Yorkers."

"It was just an idea. What about Florida? Jill Tuttle and her husband have a time-share there and they absolutely love it. I just think that we could use a break in the winter, and now that you're retired there's no reason why we shouldn't." She pulled a few glistening pieces of pulp from the grapefruit skin and popped them between her two front teeth.

"Florida?" He groaned. "It's swamp and strip malls now anyway. We've got that here, what do we need Florida for?"

"We'll just stay put then. We won't go anywhere unless someone dies or gets married. Does that sound good to you?" She shook her head angrily. "A little break in the routine and you get nervous. What's wrong with trying something new?"

"I try new things all the time and I'm not going to defend myself."

"I'll settle for you telling me where you'd like to go," she said. "We can start with a vacation and maybe a rental after that—ease into it. Or do you dislike somebody from Florida?"

He took another sip of coffee before giving up and splashing the rest down the drain. "Troy Mace is from Tallahassee."

"I know his wife," she said. "I see her jogging in this tight pink outfit with racing stripes. Now, what's wrong with Troy besides the fact his wife's pushing fifty and still shows her ass off in public?"

"Nothing wrong with Troy, he gave me a fair price on the Buick. It runs good. Maybe he took pity on me or it was because he knew I was FBI and was worried about selling me a lemon."

"Well, there you go—you and Troy can hang around used-car lots and keep people honest."

"I'll think about it," he said.

"I'm serious about this, Frank." She got up to go, tossing the grapefruit into the trash and rinsing her bowl. "Oh, and I forgot, there's a message from Lucy on the machine. I've already called her back but I promised her you'd listen to it."

"And?"

"All I got out of her was that she's still temping and working at the museum part-time."

"She plan on coming home anytime soon?"

"You can call her and ask. I said we were planning to take a weekend and come up."

"Fine, as long as I don't have to go to that market and watch them toss fish around again."

"Noted." She grabbed her date book and took the portable phone into the small room just off the kitchen that doubled as her office, saying, "I've got calls to make, could you . . ." She pointed at her coffee cup. "I don't know what I'm doing wrong."

He said okay and turned his attention to the coffeemaker, dumping out the bad stuff and rinsing it before reloading it with a dash of table salt to cut the acid.

After a bowl of bran flakes with a banana sliced over the top, he hit PLAY on the answering machine. The first message was from Harvey Minogue, a tenant in their Center Street rental, who sounded tired and drunk or perhaps both. The message was a long and overly detailed story about how the garage door had mysteriously somehow sort of broken itself and the toilet not flushing. It was followed by Lucy wishing him a happy retirement. Thinking he'd heard a man's voice in the background, he replayed the message, hoping it wasn't Dylan Wallace's.

He remembered the weekend his daughter had first mentioned Dylan, telling them how serious she was about him and how he was this totally amazing and brilliant artist, producing performance pieces mostly—something to do with mannequins and tape loops. Frank wasn't listening, already not liking the guy because he wanted to get into his daughter's pants, plus the word *artist* hoisted all sorts of red flags. He kept his mouth shut—part of the deal he'd struck with Clare to let Lucy make her own mistakes and learn from them, or something like that. Of course, this didn't stop Frank from running Dylan's name on the database and learning that his real name was Hiram and that he'd been arrested once for shoplifting in Tulsa and cited for a DUI. Even though the charges had later been dropped, Frank expected the worst, imagining Lucy dragging home some smirking leather-jacketed bad boy for them to meet.

He was not disappointed.

Dylan swept into their house wearing a long black duster coat, black stovepipe boots, and silver rings on his fingers. He was tall and skinny and might have been wearing eyeliner, although Frank couldn't tell and didn't want to ask—he would have preferred the smirking bad boy he'd been prepared to dislike and intimidate. Once he got past the kid's costume, he noticed an angry, seething calm about him, the kind he saw in forty-year-old men who'd realized they hated their jobs and families and wanted out but who didn't have the guts to do anything about it.

Frank made nice while Clare put on her welcome-to-our-home act, taking his coat and offering iced tea or Coke. After tea and small talk they went into the kitchen, picked at a cheese ball, and Frank asked Dylan what he intended to do after graduation.

"I'm sorry but this interview's over," Dylan said.

Frank's face reddened and Lucy giggled, teasing him about being stiff and overly protective.

"I think I deserve some sort of answer," Frank said, trying to put an eyeball on Dylan but getting only the top of his head.

Clare, who'd been rinsing lettuce in the sink, smoothed things over by asking Dylan to describe his art. He couldn't and Frank gleefully listened as he stammered out some vague speech about how art wasn't about answers. "I like to think that I create little mysteries with my work," Dylan said. "Does that help?"

"I think so," Clare said, although Frank knew better.

Later, after Clare had pulled him into the pantry and insisted in a stage whisper that he make an effort—try to see what Lucy saw in him and be nice—he asked Dylan if he wanted to see his woodshop. The kid barely nodded but followed him out to the garage, still wearing that damn coat, even though it was eighty degrees and muggy out.

In the woodshop Frank pointed out what was what and waited for Dylan to say something—ask a question about one of the machines. Instead he stood there nodding, a sly sneer dancing offstage as Frank explained how his father had been a great woodworker and how he'd inherited the lathes, saws, planers, and drill presses from him. He didn't give a shit what the kid thought of the machines, he was just biding his time, waiting for just the right moment to ask him about the road trip Lucy had mentioned they were thinking of taking together after graduation. All through dinner Frank couldn't stop thinking of the girl in the pond, her body dumped there perhaps after just such a road trip. And so he showed Dylan the planer, even kicking it on for him and running a plank through it just to hear the buzz as it squared the corner. He snapped the planer off and cleared his throat, trying to meet the kid's gaze as he asked about the trip. "I heard Lucy mention something about it and all I wanted to know is what you've got in mind."

"It's a possibility," Dylan said, scowling. "But there won't be any plan. We're gonna, like, keep it open, you know, see where the day takes us. Don't worry, it'll be all-good. I mean, I'll, like, take care of her. That is what you're asking, isn't it?"

Frank forced a smile. "Well, it's more like it would be nice to know where exactly you plan on going. I don't think that's too much to ask."

Dylan stared at his shoes a moment. "Does our lack of a clearly defined goal bother you?"

Frank picked up an old table saw blade, put his finger in the arbor hole, and spun it, saying, "See these carbide teeth?" Dylan blinked and for a flash Frank imagined tossing the blade at his face and then helping the kid out to his car with vague directions to the nearest hospital. "They cut without tearing, that's why they're so expensive. It's important when making fine furniture."

As the threat slowly dawned on Dylan, Frank looked out the window and saw Lucy. She was laughing, her brown hair swinging back and forth across her face as Clare broke match after match trying to light a citronella candle. He wondered what someone so light and happy saw in this lanky drip of kid standing before him. He shoved his hands deep into his pockets and felt the finger bone there as he recognized Dylan for what he was—a test, the antidote to all the smiling jocks Lucy had dated in high school and the long-haired guitar player she'd seen during her junior year at Oregon, the one who told Frank he had an interest in celebrity murders and suicides and was working on a demo called "Songs for Bob Crane." Lucy had chimed in about how brilliant he was, wanting to play a tape for Frank, and Frank had thought, Not on your life.

The trip with Dylan never happened. Lucy graduated and moved to Seattle and took a temp job with flexible hours while she volunteered at the museum, hoping to land a full-time job in the research department. Dylan followed her, but they kept separate apartments, or at least that's what she told her parents. If it was a lie, Frank was happy to be lied to. They broke up soon after the move, got back together, and then broke up again, and the one time Frank had asked his daughter whatever had happened with her and Dylan, she'd laughed and told him that they were just friends and that he'd gotten *weird* on her a few times. He didn't ask her to define *weird* because his cop brain had already quick cut through the possibilities, graphic and grim and, despite the fact that it was his daughter, sexual in nature. No, he'd seen enough weird to last a lifetime.

While the Mr. Coffee hissed he played the message a third time and decided that the voice in the background was most definitely not Dylan's but probably that of some other guy he'd try hard to like when the time came. With a fresh mug of coffee he went out to the woodshop and waited as the fluorescent lights flickered on. He thumbed a layer of dust off the radial arm saw before going to the long hard-maple work benches, scarred from his father's many projects, a good number of which sat just inside the house and were regularly commented upon by guests. Woodworking was to have been Frank's hobby. He'd even taken a few classes with the chronic putterers and odd-jobbers—men with half glasses and thinning hair who passionately debated saw blades and Finnish carving tools the way other men argued about the AFC. The hobby had never taken hold and instead existed as another nagging undone thing Frank meant or needed to do with his free time. He stared at his tools and the half-assembled martin house he'd never finished and the pile of ¾-inch oak flooring he'd intended to make into a deck table but had never gotten around to finding plans for. There was dust everywhere and spiders in the aluminum frame windows busily trapping cluster flies in their triangular webs.

He dug out the Milwaukee drill and found a piece of a two-by-four and proceeded to bore a series of holes in it with a spade bit, admiring the simple power of the tool, its ability to create useless holes. When he grew tired of that, he replaced the bit and sunk screws in the wood, careful not to strip the heads. He was killing time and trying to find the energy to start something he might finish, like the flower boxes Clare hinted about every spring during their ritual journey to the greenhouse for flats of pansies, dusty millers, phlox, and mulch and several pots of herbs that grew uneaten on the back deck until frost wilted them.

Clare came out to tell him she was going to a showing and that she didn't know when she'd be back. "Have fun," she said, jingling her car keys at him. "If you have time, I've always wanted a picket fence."

"I'll get right on it," he said.

She smiled and blew him a kiss, and as she pulled out of the drive, part of him was happy to see her leave. Even though her job selling houses had started out as a sideline it was now a full-time job. It had changed her. She became overly involved in her clients' lives, fielding late-night phone calls from them as closing dates loomed, talking them down off the ledges of buyer's beware and seller's regret. She went on and on about people he'd never met, filling up their small talk with stories about how the Greens were selling their three-bedroom ranch because their eldest daughter had cut her wrists in the basement or about the Swangos, first-time buyers with unreal expectations who wanted a view, dry basement, four bedrooms, and garden space but were not willing to pay market price. Then there were Al and Judy Geng, who were retiring to Florida and selling everything, even the furniture, now that Judy had become obsessed with Danish Modern. Frank knew more about his wife's fellow Realtors than he cared to know—Cecil Ott, for example, a retired geography teacher who'd lost his hand in a revolving door and now had a small mechanical hook attached to a putty-colored plastic tube that fit over the stump. He joked that part of him was made in Korea, the rest in Eugene. He specialized in acreage and handyman specials and drove a silver Lincoln with leather seats and chrome rims he called Luanne. He kept a tape measure clipped to his belt and still subscribed to *Popular Mechanics* and went around proselytizing about ham radio. Or Olive Meyer, the firm's top seller in Clare's book, a bitch on wheels who could sell an Eskimo ice cubes. She'd been divorced twice, held degrees from Yale and Berkeley, spoke Portuguese, collected botanica, and kept threatening to move back to Boston or the East Coast—civilization, as she called it—where people didn't use the word *pop* when they wanted a tonic. She often had her picture featured in strip ads, telling people to check out the new listings and ask for Olive, *The Agent with Smarts*. Two years ago she'd been *The Agent with Energy!!!* but that, she had decided, made her sound hyper and had elicited several lewd comments from recently divorced clients who wanted to find out, over drinks and dinner, just how much energy she had. Clare had so far avoided titles and worked in a poorly lit office that still smelled of cigarette smoke from the previous occupant, a man named Grant Dawson, who'd quit real estate to open a liquor store only to be shot during an attempted robbery. He was sometimes held up as a cautionary tale, a horse head in the bed to all those who endeavored to dream of a career outside of real estate.

In the shop Frank reversed the drill, backed out each screw, and tossed the wood into a scrap barrel—another hour dead and unaccounted for. The sun was still behind the clouds, shading the back deck and allowing him to see inside his own silent house through the sliding glass door. The floors shone, glass gleamed. Everything was in its place.

A squirrel dropped off the crab apple tree and started across the deck but froze when it saw him standing there with the drill in his hand like a gun.

Now what do I do? Frank thought.

CHAPTER SIX

After leaving the camp Cooper bought a used Camaro from a dealer in Mexico City and tooled up and down the coast, never staying in one place too long. When pressed, he used his old name, Fitch, even though he still thought of himself as Cooper or D. B. Cooper, after some UPI jackass had run a story identifying the hijacker as D. B. Cooper and it had stuck. It was cool with him—D. B. sounded just as bad and crazy as Dan Cooper and both were better than Phil Fitch.

It was the tail end of 1976 and Bicentennial fever had crossed the border. American tourists wore flag pins and went around bragging about American-style democracy and Betsy Ross. Part of him thought he was missing some big party by not being in the States although about the only thing he wanted to see in the states was the annual D. B. Cooper Day, a ragtag festival held in a small town called Ariel, Washington. It was nowhere near where he'd actually landed, but just the same, the attention-starved locals had seized on his crime and started a celebration that attracted the curious, the crazy, the drunk, and the bored the day before Thanksgiving to watch sky jumpers parachute down into a muddy field behind the general store. Along with one of the original Wanted posters he'd filched from a bail bondsman's office in Tijuana, he kept a press clipping on Cooper Days between the pages of the now-discredited Book IV. The lead read: WHERE IS HE? And was followed by a short recap of his crime and then some colorful bits about the faithful who gathered to observe the anniversary of his jump and how he'd become a folk hero of sorts. One David Frankel, a thirty-two-year-old expediter, was quoted saying, "I'm a little jealous of how he took a powder. Let me tell you, there are days I'd like to jump out of a plane." It was followed by a quote from FBI agent Frank Marshall, who said, "It's dead wrong to romanticize Cooper's crime, but I'd still like to think he's out there somewhere and that we're gonna get him." Next to a photo of the crowd there was a sketch of Cooper jumping out of the jet, the money strapped to his back, grinning and giving a thumbs-up to the world. It didn't look a thing like him, especially not now, after so long in Mexico. But there it was, proof that he was famous for at least one day a year. Gone but not forgotten.

He piloted the Camaro up narrow mountain roads and then over to the Yucatán, where he stayed in hotels with nosy bellhops—small and slightly feminine men with long fingernails good for slipping pesos into their pockets without others noticing. These bellhops all had cousins eager to provide any services Cooper lacked and it took him a while to learn the art of delicate refusal, plus the power of a small tip to ensure his room wouldn't be looted while he was out.

The only things he missed about America were Jean Shepherd's rambling late-night radio show, club sandwiches held together with tasseled toothpicks, morning box scores, Best mayonnaise, snowstorms, and housewives who looked like Lee Remick—Oregon was full of them—maintained highways, majorettes, and maple candy. Both his parents were dead—rain, I80, a Catalina with bad brakes and a bakery delivery truck. There was Geena Rae, still a kid when she'd slammed the flimsy trailer door in his face and left for good. And as for his sister, she'd run off to India and fallen in with a bunch of drum beaters who believed in reincarnation and practiced *vasti* in dirty rivers. They'd never been particularly close, not since the thing with his Schwinn back when he was ten.

He replayed the jump over and over until it seemed to him part of another life, an act that could never be repeated, at least not by the deeply tanned face staring back at him in the mirror, getting older every day. Inside the cocoon of the Camaro it was too easy to shrug off thoughts of the future. Days tripped into weeks, weeks into aimless months, and the aimless months into several blurry years of shabby roadside hotels, Pemex stations, near misses with livestock, dim tavernas, chatty hitchhikers, haggling with crooked shade tree mechanics, fish tacos, and warm nights with the windows down, his arm fluttering in the wind, smashing mosquitoes and moths as he admired the desert moon or the face of a pretty girl in a passing car.

In December he pulled into a tiny seaside village. Tired of the road, he had vague notions of finding some sort of base of operations until he could figure out what it was he was supposed to do with the rest of his life.

There were hundreds of villages just like it sprinkled up and down the coast, but as he sat eating breakfast on a brick patio overlooking the ocean, his head pounding with cheap beer and several ill-advised shots of tequila he'd shared with a vacationing phys-ed teacher from upstate New York, he simply decided to stay for a while—sort things out and plot his next move.

The village consisted of nine poorly paved streets, two churches, several cantinas, three run-down hotels that had trouble keeping maids, a general store with aluminum picnic tables out front, pigeons, and a bank with bullet holes in its brick facade. Near the water, fishermen sold bags of shrimp, shark steaks, and clams from plywood stalls. Flies hovered in greedy knots. Indian women prowled the street selling beaded necklaces while their children offered bags of warm flatbread sweetened with sorghum. Dogs lurked in the many trash-filled back alleys, stepping over smashed fruit and flattened Tecate cans on the hunt for discarded chicken bones.

On a green bluff overlooking the ocean stood an abandoned half-built hotel that was surrounded by an overgrown par-three golf course, dozens of dead palm trees, and crushed shell paths that led nowhere. A stoned American hawking tie-dyed T-shirts and sunglasses told Cooper how three dentists from San Diego had planned on opening a posh resort only to forsake the project when they ran into more Mexican red tape than they had budgeted for, not to mention several untimely and gruesome accidents at the construction site involving locals.

"That was it for development around here, dude," he said.

After breakfast Cooper hiked up the winding dirt road to the abandoned hotel. Glue-sniffing teens had tagged the crumbling stuccoed walls of the hotel with dense spray-painted declarations of love and anarchy. Spider webs hung in the glassless picture windows and stray cats darted through empty door wells in pursuit of mice. He walked out to the point and looked down on the village spread out below him like a brightly colored beach blanket, the sun beating down on the whitewashed church walls, glinting off storefronts and parked cars. A hot wind raced off the bay, rattling loose roof tiles and sending dead palm fronds twirling across the cobbled walkways as Cooper ducked under a damaged brick arch into a courtyard that was now little more than a boiling riot of weeds littered with bags of seized cement, crushed vent pipe, and cat shit. On a ledge he found an old rain-warped cigar box and opened it. The box contained a rusty pocketknife, a tooth, several dead beetles, and a broken Boy Scout compass, the needle frozen West. The tooth looked human and there was a gold filling nestled between the crowns. When he touched the sharp little roots, Cooper felt suddenly cold and looked around as if the box's owner might lurch out of the weeds and club him to death. He dropped the lid, left the box, and went back to the edge of the bluff, where he leaned against the stone wall and watched the silent white rows of waves come in off the bay and break against the sandy curl of beach. And just like that he decided to cool his heels in the tiny village.

He rented a room at the hotel and paid cash for two weeks up front, scrawling an illegible squiggle of vowels and consonants on the room waiver. When the man behind the desk asked for his name and a credit card just in case, Cooper said, *"No más,"* and dropped a peso into the man's trembling hand to shut him up. Unlike America, where money often invited prying questions and whispered suspicions, palming a few pesos here and there insured *mucho silencio.*

A month later he bought a small beach house nestled in a bank of trees a mile from town, its red tin roof just visible from the crushed-shell road. It had polished saltillo tile floors and a narrow kitchen with an old Magic Chef four-burner and tin cabinets decorated with tiny paintings of deserted islands with stranded castaways on them. But what sold Cooper on the property was the constant whirr of the ceiling fans, which reminded him of a certain hotel room in Saigon where he'd waited, naked except for his dog tags, as a Vietnamese bar girl washed herself in the bathroom before coming to him. Her nipples were the color of dark plums and her straight black hair was heavy with Mai Tais, Marlboros, and the cheap cologne of the soldiers who'd come before him. He remembered the way her breath had felt on his neck and how after they'd finished she'd laid with him staring up at the fans, watching them chop the sweltering air and billow the white gauze curtains as guilt ballooned in his belly and her stilted and robotic small talk turned to money, spoiling the brief moment of calm that had surrounded him.

Steep green mountains bounded two sides of the village and at night all sorts of creatures would descend out of the jungle and knock over trash cans—rats as big as dogs, monkeys, snakes, and lizards. There was a lot of gun toting among the locals and stories of evil spirits that would steal the fillings out of your teeth if you were foolish enough to nap on the beaches. Children disappeared all the time, and whenever anybody created a stir about it, America got most of the blame. Ran off to the USA to clean toilets, was one he heard a lot. Even the little ones were accused of scurrying north for exciting careers in the fruit industry and scraping dishes at diners and hotel restaurants. And although the beaches were uniformly gorgeous, there were just enough sharks to keep the tourists in check. The sharks, however, did nothing to deter the hippie backpackers who hung around the general store trying to steal ice or bum cigarettes before continuing on down the coast to join their brethren in noble drop-out activities like marijuana cultivation, deep thought, and squatting. They sometimes nodded at Cooper as if he were one of their own and drew him tiny maps indicating parties or gatherings, giving him passwords and advice on where he could crash without hassle.

On the rare occasion when he was asked about his limp, he blamed it on an old war injury. "Nam. Claymore," he said. "I was one of the lucky ones. I lost friends though . . ."—conversational poison to the hippies and info that elicited merely a shrug from most locals. And when asked where he got his money, he pointed at a bottle of Coca-Cola and in butchered Spanish claimed that his father owned the company but that, after signing a no-compete clause and agreeing to exile in Mexico, he'd received a lump-sum payment. It was a big fat lie but one most Mexican men, themselves disposed toward constantly stretching the truth, were only too willing to believe, especially when he was the one buying them rounds of cheap warm *cerveza* and answering their questions about American women.

He was dogged by rumors about his true identity: CIA operative, fallen missionary, mobster, bagman, famous writer, West Coast doper, black-balled archaeologist, tax dodger, trustafarian, AWOL soldier, cuckold, and so on.

He let his hair grow, quit smoking, and hunted the cafes for old American newspapers left in folded heaps by the tourists. The crosswords were always half finished, but he could not complain. In addition to papers he snagged whatever books he could—bad poetry, repair manuals, how-to tomes, lurid road trip sagas that ended with double-crossed bloodshed in small desert towns. But his favorites were the dime store pulps featuring soiled ex-cops named Ace or Jack who went around kicking down doors and slapping whores. They wore battered fedoras, guzzled gin from short glasses, wolfed black-and-blue Delmonico steaks in dimly lit diners, and bedded agreeably chubby women who wore garters and left lipstick prints on their cigarettes. The books made Cooper long for a world he suspected had never existed, and for a while he briefly toyed with the idea of setting up the village's first private investigation office—not that he wanted to investigate anything or anybody but figuring that, if they did come looking for him, the first place they'd come looking would be his office and he'd slip out the back.

He'd met a woman named Inez, who worked at the local cantina selling bottles of beer and tamales from a straw basket. Her trick was to walk through the crowded bar with the bottles still wet from the ice bin pressed to her thin cotton dress, wordlessly offering them to the eager men. She had cruel cheekbones, never smiled, and had long dark hair that she washed in the cement trough he'd rigged up outside his back porch to catch rainwater from the frequent storms. She walked his house barefoot, smelling of the limes she kept in her work apron, and was not impressed by Cooper's money or the fact that he did nothing to earn it. She asked him very little about America, and when she did, it seemed out of politeness and her boarded-up sense of self, a sense that reached no farther than the small village and certainly not to America.

Three years ago Inez had lost her husband in a fishing accident. Eaten by a shark. His finger and left thigh had washed ashore two days later. They never found the rest and the villagers believed his ghost haunted the mangrove swamps.

Some nights Cooper would walk with Inez out to the beach and watch the cruise ships pass, their lights blinking red, white, and blue. He did not ask about her husband and she did not ask about his leg or the botched tattoo on his shoulder or the odd book with symbols on it that she sometimes caught him reading.

Over time the routine of their affair became a sturdy and suitable stand-in for the over-the-top, heart-melting passion he read about in the secondhand romance books. Boil it all down, Cooper thought, and women were suckers for bad boys, dogs, children, and lilac, while men liked routine, roasted meat, cars, and lingerie. Somehow in all that mess love and happiness could find a place to put down roots. And there were times when he was between her legs, sliding swiftly in and out of her, sweat rolling down his back, that he thought he loved her in a simple and wordless way. And so he lived in the moment, forcing himself to pay attention and gather memories even as his groin tightened and he felt the inevitable fluttering of his heart as Inez began grinding her hips into his. But sometimes when they finished and he swept the hair from her face, she'd look away from him and stare out the small bedroom window toward the dark blue of the ocean, perhaps thinking of her dead husband or of his ghost or maybe of nothing at all. He never asked. Instead he let her hair fall back over her face.

He told no one, not even Inez, about the plane and the fake bomb rigged inside the briefcase or how he'd landed in the rainy canopy of fir trees and brush thinking himself dead on impact, imagining the weeds and trees growing right through him and then the coons scattering his bones. Instead he'd risen, and after untangling himself from the chute and packing it away, he forced himself to move until he was warm again and he'd mentally marched the pain in his knee to a dull grinding ache that hurt only when he stopped. Later, he built a small fire and ate a Hershey's bar, taking care to pocket the wrapper and kick the fire out, burying the coals with moss and pulped wood. And then he began walking again, lucky to find a narrow country road and a junked-out trailer with a Plymouth Fury parked out front next to a tarped DeSoto. The keys were just sitting there on the stained bench seat, waiting for him. He took the Fury, pushing it out of the drive and down the road.

By dawn the next day he'd made his way to Moe Dipner's farm, where in the back pasture he stashed a sealed drywall bucket containing forty thousand dollars in the trunk of a broken-down and abandoned Ford Galaxy, with another ten thousand salted away in a nearby discarded Frigidaire.

Moe was an old war buddy of Cooper's who'd managed to foul himself up in some top-secret government chemicals the flyboys had brought into base camp. Word around the camp was that they intended to introduce the chemicals into the water table and if that didn't work they'd drop it over rice paddies and contaminate the food chain, where it would work its way up and wreak havoc with the enemy—typical government scheming. When one of the camp dogs licked a canister and fell dead, Moe had orders to move the pallet with the forklift. Ray-Banned spooks in sweat-dampened linen suits watched as Moe missed the slots and poked clean through several canisters. The chemicals ate his hair and caused his eyes to milk over so that while he wasn't legally blind, at least not according to the petty and exacting VA doctors, the world appeared to him as a gauzy white blur.

An immediate medical discharge followed. In the years following, Cooper (still Phil Fitch to Moe) had stayed in touch, dropping Moe breezy letters updating him on his travels and made-up bits about women he'd met on the way—lonely underwear models or Moe's favorite, disgraced nurses. Moe was an ardent subscriber to *Penthouse Forum* and had tried for years to no avail to see one of his fantasies into print. They almost always involved generously proportioned women who wore foam curlers in their hair and enjoyed disrobing in kitchens and doing provocative things with cast-iron skillets. The rejection slips faulted him for his narrow fetish and encouraged him to splice in a horny teenager or two or maybe some sexy stuff with food items, but he refused.

Strange sores appeared on Moe's legs and back, and despite his many retellings of the chemical mishap, the VA doctors attributed the sores to poor hygiene, lack of exercise and too much sodium nitrate in his diet.

There was, he'd learned, no official record of his chemical mishap and no matter how much he protested or phoned the so-called higher-ups in the Veterans Administration he got the runaround, dished from doctor to doctor, collecting new prescriptions that were supposed to help but only gave him the piles and made his teeth ache. He wrote letters and phoned old war buddies, asking them to corroborate his story. The response was underwhelming. The few who did write back sounded worse off than he was and closed their letters with loan requests or disjointed suicidal poems. He spent his days sitting on his large wraparound porch fending off the Realtors who papered his mailbox with friendly offers to sell and tucked cards in his window frames where the glazing had cracked and pulled away from the glass. He couldn't bring himself to sell the land or the house—he'd grown used to the square familiarity of the newel post, the creaky pine plank floors, and the stubborn front door that opened with a little pull to the right and up. He knew the cow trails well enough so that, even as blindness encroached, he could still stroll around the property when the trees were budding or sneak down to the back pasture and creek, where trespassing teenagers held parties. Whenever Moe heard the teenagers' cars crunching along the cindered easement road, he'd put on his knit cap, pull on his boots, and crawl down the dirt path, feeling his way along the ruts until he could see the blurred orange of their campfire or the aluminum flash as they tipped beer cans to their faces. He'd spent many a night squatting behind the old Galaxy, picking rust flakes and listening to the teens shout along to Cheap Trick and Iron Maiden as they scratched pentagrams into the ground with smoldering branches and taunted one another into intimate wrestling matches over important things like the last beer or who was a pussy or turd burglar. He had no intention of running them off like his neighbors did—not even as they stumbled past his hiding spot to vomit in the burdocks or even when they filled the creek with junk, rolling tractor tires into the water, heaving car batteries, and shoving old appliances down the bank. One morning when he went to assess the damage he saw the Frigidaire sitting at the bottom of the flooded creek, the door bent open and Cooper's bucket rolling down toward the riffles, spooking suckers and crayfish into the shallows. A white and watery blur, but had he waited and his eyesight been better he would have seen the bucket catch on a rock and the lid pop off and the bills tumble down the creek like sunken rafts.

Down in Mexico the years passed pleasantly for Cooper. He tried to teach himself the guitar with the Dot Method but lost interest. He was, he decided, completely without rhythm, soul, or hand-eye co-ordination. He liked the radio, especially the Texas stations that somehow found their way south playing swing bands and Willie Nelson tunes like "River Boy" and "Crazy." Every once in a while he picked up a college station with tentative deejays who read liner notes in a monotone and thought nothing of following a zippy Ramones tune with some Funkadelic or Gregorian chants, before sliding into an astral-noise collage that sounded to Cooper like his tin roof in a windstorm.

He checked out Guatemala but did not like the spiders or the way the men were always hanging gobs of spit from curbs and street signs. It was no wonder everybody was sick. He kept waiting for a fight to break out or for some clever soul to introduce spittoons. Panama was too hot and buggy, although he did enjoy the canal and watching people eat rice with their hands in restaurants. For a while he even toyed with the idea of going to Bolivia and robbing banks like Butch Cassidy but ruled that out when an old cowboy told him how bloodthirsty the Bolivians were—public hangings, torture, and the like.

And so he kept returning to the village and his cabin under the trees, where the air smelled like dead minnows and beached shrimp. Over the years Cooper made a few casual acquaintances and for better or worse befriended Ernesto, a short man with large, hairy ears and a flabby paunch that he patted when making grand statements or sizing up menus. He claimed to be the illegitimate child of an American flying ace and a Mayan princess and referred to himself as a royal half-breed. He spoke fluent English, raided the occasional tomb for artifacts to sell, and took tourists sightseeing up twisty mountain roads in his wrecked Ford Bronco. He did not ask questions about Cooper's past and was easily distracted by schemes and projects, such as their plan to erect fake stone ruins in the nearby jungle and charge the rubes ten bucks a pop. Ernesto had already agreed to dress up like an old Mayan chief and run around whooping and threatening human sacrifice. Cooper envisioned trinkets and T-shirts, maybe a girl selling ice-cold Cokes and tacos. They'd make a killing. But after a long, hot day of hauling stones into the jungle, they gave up on the idea and retired to the cantina to get drunk and endlessly rethink the plan only to have it fade away to the junk heap of all their other half-great ideas. It kept them busy and that was the point.

After a few years Cooper even stopped worrying about the strange Americans who would show up from time to time in the village, alone, dressed in cheap suits or ill-fitting Bermudas. They were not agents sent south to get him but merely lost men who, like him, were looking for a little sunshine, uncrowded beaches, and brown girls with bright, easy smiles. And so he made a point of parading Inez past them and watching as she ripped their hearts out with her faraway eyes and sad mouth.

He enjoyed chatting with the occasional tourist, catching up on what he was missing back in the States—how Carter was just Ford with a better smile. And then how not only was Reagan going to bust the Communists, he was going to cut taxes. Most of the time he just listened as some insurance salesman or retired autoworker from Detroit complained about his sunburn, the crowded buses, or the lack of work ethic in the country.

During the village's many festivals he and Ernesto would watch the pale tourists dance to the mariachi bands. After logging many hours on his bar stool perch, Cooper had come to the beery conclusion that white people, especially Americans, had no business dancing to anything except polka or country western. It baffled him that devout wallflowers—vacationing Americans and their whiter Canadian brethren—became consumed by dance fever whenever some half-good mariachi band struck a chord or somebody punched up the tired bing and bong of "Girl from Ipanema" on the cantina Wurlitzer. The worst were the folks from Wisconsin and Iowa, whose gyrations came off as a sort of palsied freestyle that bespoke years of stoic repression.

And so it was on a throbbing and moist night, while waiting for Inez, they observed a batch of fresh tourists cut loose.

"There go Minnesota," Ernesto said, pointing to a couple dressed like suitcase missionaries in high-water permanent press slacks, thick-heeled shoes with sole guards, and black rim glasses. They were doing some half-remembered *American Bandstand* step from their youth, grinning lustfully at each other as they knocked strings of dried chilis and tomatillos off the wall.

"Check out Kansas," Cooper said, calling Ernesto's attention to a stiff-backed gent in a high-panted linen suit who thought himself his own private Fred Astaire, trolling for his Mexican Ginger.

Ernesto snickered and waited for Cooper to buy him another *cerveza* so they could get back to telling lies and spinning wild plans. But Cooper ignored him. Inez had promised to meet them and he was eager to see her cut a swath through the men standing in the square, hoping that she'd worn something low, thin, and white and that she'd let her hair down.

Instead she came to him in the night and led him into the bedroom, where she took her top off and pulled him to the mattress, pressing herself tight against his chest. As he dragged his lips across her neck and shoulders, tasting the sweat and Sauza, he wanted to come clean, tell her about his crime, and take her back to Oregon with him to grab the rest of the cash he'd stashed in his buddy Moe Dipner's abandoned pasture. They'd figure out some way to wrangle her a green card and then move someplace nice like Miami or Charleston and start something.

He waited until she was naked and up on all fours shivering in anticipation of his touch. He'd learned that she liked the blind, swirling silence as he lined up behind her, making her wait for everything to begin as he marveled at the way the moonlight seemed to light her from within and the quivering wet fold between her legs, glistening for him. He leaned close and could smell her as he fought the urge to rush the whole slow ritual—get to the end, the part where Inez would flop to the mattress and stare out the window, thinking of her dead husband. But he wanted this time to be different and so he brushed a hand between her legs slowly and began to tell her how he'd hijacked a jet back in America.

"Mmm," she said, as he leaned across her back and wrapped his arms around her. He couldn't tell whether or not she was listening and so he pulled away and began again, telling her how he'd built a fake bomb and boarded a plane and made his demand.

She reached between her legs and guided him into her, her hands rough and insistent. And he told her the rest, the story just gushing out of him as she moved against him, sweat beading along the shallow valleys of her ribs. He told her about the escape and how he'd been on the Ten Most Wanted list and about the money and the run south to Mexico and how he'd crossed the border in the trunk of an old Cadillac driven by an auctioneer named Freddy "The Tongue" Parks, who had agreed to smuggle him across for twenty dollars and a barlow knife with a mother-of-pearl handle that Cooper's father had given him.

"*Más! Más!*" Inez said.

He grabbed her hips and swung himself into her until it felt as if he were falling and he told her everything, recounting his short and futile search for the secret places on the map and how he'd settled in the village after seeing the beach and the small house with flowers growing beside it.

She finished, her spine stiffened, and she pushed her face into the mattress, humming, her flesh loose and hot as Cooper let himself go. "Goddamn, that was good," he grunted.

He collapsed on the bed next to her, not even noticing when she threw his arm off. He picked up the story where he'd left off. She listened, gazing out the window at the ocean, absently running a thumb across her nipples.

When he was done with the story she rolled toward him. "I do not believe you," she said. "All these years you keep this secret and not tell me? How could you?"

He smiled. "So you've heard of D. B. Cooper?"

She shook her head. "I have not heard of D. B. Cooper."

"Everybody's heard of D. B. Cooper. They wrote songs about me. They thought I was dead. I mean, where did you think I got the money from?"

He ran his hands across her damp thigh until she flinched and reached for the sheet.

"The lottery," she said.

"Lottery?"

"Everybody in America plays the lottery."

"No, I took my money, Inez."

"Took?"

"Put the airline in what you might call an untenable position."

"I do not understand."

"I said I had a bomb, Inez, just like I told you."

"Bomb?"

He nodded. "It wasn't really a bomb—but that was all part of the plan."

"Plan? What plan?"

She sat up, swept the hair from her face. "I want to see it."

"See what?"

"The money," she said. "I want to see this money. Prove it to me that you take this money from the plane."

He couldn't squeeze under the bed fast enough to grab the sacks of bills.

"I am D. B. Cooper," he said, tossing a few bundles of twenty-dollar bills on the feather pillow. They landed with a satisfying whoosh and he watched as Inez examined one of them, grinning.

"There's more," he said. "There's a lot more. They gave me every-thing I asked for. I took hostages. I scared them, had them by the short and curlies, and they screamed uncle." He tried to remember what else had happened but the details had slipped away from him and all he could recall with any certainty was the cold finger of fear popping up his spine as he'd climbed out onto the stairs, the wind and rain and that split second just before he let go of the rail and flew down into the night. He told her about that—how he thought he would die. But she was too transfixed by the banded stacks of money and so he sat down beside her and stared out the window at the dark ocean; the weight of his deed lifted, the proof scattered across the bed for a Mexican girl who could not love him to examine. He knew that now, and still it was okay, because he'd uncorked his story for the first time and nothing had changed.

After a minute, she said, "I believe you."

"You do?"

She nodded. "You are a desperado."

"Hey."

She made little guns with her hands and fired at him.

"It was a bomb, Inez."

"Whatever," she said, piling the money at the foot of the bed in a neat little wall. He waited for her to say something else—ask another question or tell him how brave he'd been, but she just pulled on her dress and told him she was going.

At the door she kissed him lightly on the cheek and said, "Good night, Mr. D. B. Cooper."

She left him standing there in the hot room, naked and dusty from his crawl under the bed frame. He wanted her again, right there in the doorway, wanted to seal his confession, make her promise not to tell anyone in the village, throw some kind of sex lock on her and make her his forever and ever. But she walked away like smoke.

He followed her outside, the elation he'd felt while telling her about his crime replaced by a strange emptiness that grew as he watched Inez disappear down the dark footpath, a shadow among shadows.

■

ON THE MONDAY after his retirement party Frank loaded his toolbox into the car and drove over to the rental to see about the toilet and the garage door Harvey Minogue had described as having just "sort of broken itself," whatever the hell that meant. Frank was suspicious even though Harvey had been a good tenant for them—paid his rent on time, kept the yard looking neat, and called whenever there was something he couldn't fix. As far as tenants went, he was a keeper, although Clare often suspected him of having some creepy dark side simply because he was forty years old and unmarried and watched too much television. Frank wrote him off as a harmlessly weird man-child who collected comic books and had probably never been in a fistfight his whole life.

The rental sat at the end of a sloping street lined with alder, gnarled sugar maples, and crooked cyclone fencing trimmed with morning glories and tattered garbage sacks. It was a small two-bedroom bungalow with peeling powder-blue shutters, a detached single-car garage, and a half-dead apple tree shading the cramped backyard. Clare had saved up her first few commissions for the down payment, pouncing on the house before it made it to market, and they'd sunk a couple of grand into it—bought a new washer/dryer, had the chimney reflashed and lined, hung gutters, painted inside and out, and ripped up the mauve carpeting and had the pine floors redone. She'd been after him for months about cutting down the apple tree in the backyard, but Frank conveniently never got around to it. He didn't have the heart to kill it even though each fall the deformed and worm-ridden apples it dropped in the yard attracted swarms of yellow jackets and were a pain in the ass to rake up and bag.

Harvey met him at the door wearing a stained blue Jedi Master T-shirt, his billowing pear-shaped body filling up the frame as he sighed and pushed his thick horn-rimmed glasses back, magnifying his bagged and bloodshot eyes.

"I guess I shoulda called first," said Frank, setting the toolbox down on the cement stoop. "I keep forgetting to do that."

"Well . . ."

"It's in the lease or something like that."

"It's okay," Harvey said, unlatching the screen door. Frank grabbed the toolbox and followed Harvey as he lumbered into the living room and collapsed on a green plaid sofa, his pale belly wagging out. The television was on, the radio in the kitchen blaring something about all hits, all the time. The shades were drawn and the air was a sour mix of spoiled food and defeated Glade room freshener. Frank looked around, waiting for Harvey to explain the mess of takeout food containers and pizza boxes covering the coffee table, not to mention the dozens of empty Gatorade and Heaven Hill vodka bottles, the various mugs of unidentifiable scummed-over liquid, or the trail of dirty clothes leading toward the darkened master bedroom.

"You okay?"

"Stephanie left me," Harvey said.

"I don't think I've met her," said Frank. "Was she living here too?"

Harvey nodded and looked up at Frank, who was standing there trying to decide whether or not he should mention the mess to Clare. "I didn't know that."

"Doesn't matter now," Harvey said, his chin trembling. "I've got to get myself together, get back to work. Blow the stink off, like my mother says." The phone rang. He picked it up, shouted, "Stephanie?" and slammed it down.

"Well, I'll just take a look at that toilet," he said, eager to just get the job done and leave Harvey to his breakdown.

Harvey sat up and clicked off the television. "You know, she kinda looks like Stevie Nicks. We met at Kmart. She works in the toy department."

"Look, Harvey, I'm just here to fix that stuff you've been calling about. You do want it fixed, right? I mean, that is why you left the message, isn't it?"

"I guess so."

"Okay. Then as your landlord I will fix these items," he said, grabbing his tools and heading toward the bathroom.

The phone rang and again Harvey picked it up and shouted, "Stephanie?"

The bathroom was surprisingly clean—no clogged drains or disturbing stains in the tub or come-stiff washcloths. There were towels neatly folded over the bars and above the sink a small cartoon of a grumpy-looking man in a bathrobe with a caption that read: "Smile once in the morning and get it over with."

On a hunch Frank opened the medicine cabinet and found a smorgasbord of pill bottles—Stelazine, Elavil, and dozens of others he didn't recognize. In the trash basket lay several empty Nyquil bottles. Evidently, being Harvey involved a daily chemical balancing act, Frank thought as he shut the mirrored door quietly and got to work.

The chain was an easy fix; he rigged it with some bailing wire and adjusted the ball cock so the flapper sat flat against the bottom. He flushed the toilet a few times and then, satisfied, told Harvey it was fixed, before going out back to see about the garage door.

Something was seriously wrong. The whole door had been knocked out of its tracking, the frame splintered. "Son of a bitch," he said, turning to go back inside and ask about it. But Harvey was already standing there in his socks, hands shoved down the front of his sweatpants, rearranging his balls.

For a moment Frank considered marching him into the bathroom and shoving some pills down his throat. Instead he pointed at the mangled garage door and said, "This doesn't look like it broke itself."

Harvey pulled a hand out of his pants and adjusted his glasses. "Well, uh . . ."

"Looks like somebody hit it. Is that what happened, Harvey?"

He nodded. "It was Stephanie. She took my car and half my record collection. I don't know where she went off to. She just got in the habit of borrowing it to drive up and see her mother in Vancouver and umm . . ."

Frank gave him the eye and waited for him to continue his ramble. "Well, last Saturday she drank, like, six wine coolers and started telling me how, like, we weren't good for each other and how she was worried about her weight and our age difference. What do they call that?"

"May-December."

"Yeah, May-December," Harvey said. "See, when she left I kept thinking this was one of her mood swings. Little things set her off, you know, like fluorescent lights—she's sensitive to them and all kinds of high-end frequency stuff, and I've got to be careful what kind of music I play. Oh, and she likes to throw things when she gets in these moods. I mean, watch out—"

"Look, it's none of my business. I'm just your landlord, Harvey, but if Clare sees what you've done to the house she's not going to be happy about it. Do you understand me?"

Harvey nodded and looked up the street expectantly as Frank bent to have another look at the door. He tried to lift it one more time, and when it wouldn't budge he briefly thought of just letting it stay broken, even though he knew Clare would get on him about it. "I'll have to get somebody else out here to fix it," he said. "You're gonna have to pay for it or get this Stephanie to pay."

"I expected that."

"Maybe you should call the police about the car too."

"No, I'm gonna give her some time before I do that, see if she comes to her senses."

"If she took your car, maybe she's already come to her senses."

"You don't know Stephanie."

"I know she's a bad driver," he said, pointing at the damage. "I don't think I wanna know much more."

Harvey laughed. And that's how Frank left him.

On the way home he saw one of Clare's For Sale signs standing in the front yard of a low-slung brick-and-board ranch with plastic deer grazing behind a bank of overgrown wisteria. As he idled at a stoplight, he remembered how he'd first met Clare at Paul Wilson's house.

He'd not yet joined the Bureau and was still working for the local sheriff's department, setting speed traps, writing tickets, and tipping his wide-brim hat to small children and women. He'd pulled Paul Wilson over for running a light and after he'd given him a warning they got to talking, Paul telling him several good jokes he could take back to the station for the guys. Then later he ran into Paul in the sporting goods department, testing spin-casting rods. They agreed to hit the river together and became friends and occasional fishing buddies.

Paul ran a small manufacturing company that made a series of electrical clips for Boeing. He and his young wife, Cassandra, lived in a large house with gleaming bay windows, expensive shrubs, and a kitchen full of blenders, stainless steel shelves, German knives, and Fiesta ware. They threw theme parties from time to time and it was at the Wilson's Hawaiian Night party that Frank had met Clare.

He'd arrived early, only to have Wilson steer him into the bedroom, where he put three loud tropical shirts on the bed.

"Pick one," Wilson said. "Because you've somehow managed to look like a cop."

"Sheriff's deputy," Frank corrected.

"Whatever, just pick one. I can't have you walking around here making my guests nervous."

He chose the blue one with a walleyed parrot staring at an orange sun through a wall of foliage.

"Good choice," Paul said, ushering Frank out to the backyard to help him dump sand into the clam pit and light the tiki torches.

They raked back the embers and hosed down the hot rocks and then spread seaweed over them and a layer of chicken wire as the pit began to hiss.

"I wouldn't want to be a clam," Frank said.

"No, it wouldn't be my first choice," Paul said, clapping sand from his hands. "A salmon maybe, if you're talking reincarnation, or maybe one of those turtles who live forever. Less trips."

Frank thought about it a minute and then laughed. They placed partially shucked corn on the chicken wire and dumped five bushels of clams, raking them evenly to the edges. Paul handed him several packages of hotdogs. "For flavor. Don't worry, I got a deal on them and nobody'll eat them."

They flung the hot dogs over the clams, the sight too strange to joke about.

"We're going to skip the chickens," Paul said after consulting *The Joy of Cooking*. "Says here we need a bucket or two of seawater. You don't happen to have any seawater on you?"

Frank pointed at the hose and said, "You've got pickling salt, right?"

Paul nodded and went to get it while Frank stood over the bed of clams, steam rising, shells already clicking open, exposing the meat. Paul returned with a box of salt and stirred some into a bucket filled with water. "Does that taste like ocean yet?"

He dipped a finger in and sucked. "Maybe."

Paul dumped more salt in. "Okay, it's the Red Sea now." Then he stood and splashed the water over the dying clams and for a few seconds the yard was transformed into a beach at dusk, the dim outline of trees hemming in the sky, dunelike, the sound of cars out on the road like waves breaking and rolling away.

They unfolded a heavy green tarp and set it over the clam pit, anchoring it with stones, and waited.

Paul consulted the book again. "Says here the tarp will puff up when the clams are done."

Ten minutes later the tarp began to move, steam luffing out the edges, darkening the stones and dewing the grass.

"It's the clam souls that do the puffing out," said Paul.

"Could be the hotdogs."

"I didn't know they had souls."

"Many. Legion."

Cassandra emerged from the kitchen in a tight cotton dress that showed off her shoulders to press a napkin-wrapped drink into Frank's hands and drop a pink plastic lei around his neck.

"Loosen up, Frankie," she said. She had long blond hair and bright green eyes. Her arms were firm and tan and Frank had to train himself not to stare too long at any one part of her. She knew this and made a point of flirting with him, even with Paul around. Frank had even stopped wearing his gun and cuffs when he visited them after shift because Cassandra seemed a little too interested in them. It embarrassed Paul when she would ask Frank to cuff her, the shiny steel rings creasing her skin and summoning delicate blue veins to the surface. Not only did she scare Frank but she took joy in making him uncomfortable.

They weren't alone long, as the other guests began to arrive, the men standing around clenching beer cans and staring at the clam pit while the women greeted Cassandra.

Clare arrived on the arm of a tall, rather dim-looking man named Hugh Moody, who had curly hair and rubbed his stubbled jaw when he spoke. He wore an Accutron watch and kept looking around the party to see who was there and nodding his head to the Safaris playing on the hi-fi. He worked at a bank and rode a Vespa.

Frank pointed and asked Paul about Clare as she floated down the cement path, flashing her smile. Paul laughed and began shouting for Cassandra, who'd just stepped out of the house holding a bucket of melted butter for the clams.

"You were right," Paul said.

"I'm used to it," she said, dipping her finger into the butter and pushing it into her husband's mouth. "What am I right about this time?" She dipped her finger again and came at Frank, but he put his hand over his mouth and tried not to see if Paul was watching.

"Sheriff Frank and Clare," Paul said. "He's already asked me about her."

"Look, I didn't mean it that way," Frank sputtered. "I just asked about her." He'd begun to blush and now wished he'd freshened his drink or gone to stare at the steaming clam pit with the other men.

"She's younger," said Cassandra.

"How much?"

"Six years, I think, but that's nothing if you make a connection," she said. "Don't worry, I'll get her to dump that creep Hugh. She just needs a little encouragement. I'm gonna tell her there's a new sheriff in town."

She laughed and then leaned over to whisper something to Paul but ended up kissing him. Frank looked away in embarrassment, his eyes tracing the walkways that threaded between the boxwood and immature fruit trees toward the pool, where bunches of flowers floated in the deep end like fragile life preservers.

Later, after the clams had been eaten and people were down by the pool doing the limbo, Paul dove on the grenade and dragged Hugh Moody inside to show him his record collection while Cassandra shepherded Clare over to Frank, who'd just finished explaining the intricacies of a citizen's arrest to a drunken wedding photographer named Willy, who'd confessed that his business partner dabbled in pornography.

"You'd never know looking at him," Willy said. "He told me he picked it up in the war."

Cassandra sat between them, wrapped a tan arm around the photographer, and asked about his dog, a golden retriever named George who often posed for photos with children.

Both Frank and Clare feigned interest in their drinks until Cassandra turned to them and said, "Go on, get out of here. You two know what to do."

"Walk?" said Clare, pasting him with her eyes and a smile. He liked the small gap between her two front teeth.

Frank nodded and followed her down past the pool toward the duck pond.

"I'm under strict orders," she said, reaching up to strip a nearby branch of its leaves, dropping them one by one like bread crumbs as they walked past other couples talking in the shadows, some smoking, others just sitting out the limbo and drunken laughter.

"Cassandra?"

Clare nodded. "She likes to play the matchmaker. We're not her only project tonight."

"I didn't think so."

She stopped to look at him.

"And what about the guy you're with?" He could barely make out her face in the dark, but he knew that he'd asked the wrong question, a cop question.

"Hugh?"

"I'm sorry. I shouldn't have asked that."

"No, it's just I need a minute to think about it."

"Fair enough."

"First, explain the hotdogs," she said. "They were in the buckets and I wanted to taste one, but Paul stopped me. At first I thought he was joking because he does have a strange sense of humor, you know."

"They were for flavor. Recipe called for chickens, but we skipped those."

"Oh," she said. A comfortable moment of silence descended on them as they walked down the sloping backyard toward the pines. "They want to do a fondue next month and, to tell you the truth, I don't want to sit around and watch people eat off sticks."

Frank agreed and together they watched the people mingling by the blue light of the pool, drinking and laughing and shimmying under a limbo stick held by two grinning bald men.

"So are we following orders?" he asked.

"I hope so." She floated closer. "You asked about Hugh."

"No, I . . ."

"No, really, it's okay. We go out and have dinner a few nights a week. He talks and I listen. Besides, if I know Cassandra, I bet she's already filled you in."

"A little."

"Well, it's nothing. No sparks or anything like that. It's pretty simple, really." She adjusted the flower in her hair. "Hugh's a banker who wants to be a folksinger. What about you? Are you really a cop?"

He explained the difference between the sheriff's office and the Portland police department to her, and she seemed genuinely interested. It was Frank's experience that law enforcement was seen by most folks as a personality defect—a compensation for some lack and therefore not a job but a crusade to correct one's self-image. When people found out he was a cop they would suddenly became nervous and confess small crimes they'd perpetrated in their youth or else ask him long hypothetical questions about the law and its possible repercussions. But when he finished, Clare was smiling, still interested. "So basically the difference is the hats, right? Now tell me about girlfriends—how many?"

"A few, but the job's a problem, especially now."

"What do you mean?"

"Just that it's my experience that women are attracted to bad men. Blame it on Marlon Brando."

"Maybe you just have high standards."

"They must walk upright and have a pulse."

She laughed and reached up to pull her hair into a ponytail, exposing the pale oval of her armpits. "Well, I'm pretty successful in that department. I used to run steeplechase."

"Isn't that the same thing as cross-country?"

"Many people make that mistake. It involves hurdles and water hazards. You can do it on a horse too."

"Perhaps you're overqualified."

"Enough, I'm beginning to feel as if we're trapped in a *Thin Man* movie." She slapped his shoulder lightly. "Too much witty banter." Her hand lingered and then slipped away and he wanted it back, having nearly forgotten what it was like to touch a strange woman in the dark. He wanted the moon to shine on them and strand them in this moment a little longer or maybe forever.

"Time's up," she said, pointing to the deck, where her date, Hugh, stood searching for her, trying to look nonchalant but not carrying it off.

"To be continued?"

A moth with large black eyes on its wings bounced between them as Clare leaned over and kissed him roughly on the mouth. She tasted like strawberry-scented rum. By the time he could respond, she was already walking away along the pond, spooking frogs into the water and dumping her drink so that the ice caught the flicker of the tiki torches. The moth followed her and Frank stood a long time in the dark waiting for her to return and finish the kiss.

She did, and two weeks later they met for dinner, where she told stories about her now ex-boyfriend Hugh and his rich family and their suicides and his retarded twin brother whom they kept in an institution and visited only on holidays. Frank told her about his plans to apply to the FBI and how he'd already spoken to a recruiter.

In July they took a trip to the Oregon coast and stayed in a small hotel, not noticing the sand in the sheets and the shower with very little pressure and missing grout. They took walks on the beach and searched junk stores, and at a nearby roadside bar that served beer in cans and had small plastic bowls of stale pretzels on every table, they met a man named Dennis from Michigan. He had the snarled face of a football coach and ended his sentences with a dismissive wave of his hands. After several beers Dennis told them he had inoperable cancer and planned on killing himself sometime in the next month or two. "Depends on the pain," he said. "That and my supply of pills."

"Is it bad?" Clare asked, putting her hand on his sunburned arm.

"The pain or my pill supply?"

"The pain."

Dennis snapped a pretzel. "A dull ache mostly. Some days I can't feel my lips or maybe my arm won't work right. You ever sleep wrong and wake up feeling like both of your arms have been cut off?"

"I hate that," said Frank.

"That's what it's like and when the pain gets to be too much I'm going to wash down a dozen pills with a bottle of Teacher's and go for a swim."

"Drown?" asked Frank.

"It's supposed to be very peaceful."

"They say the same thing about jumping off a cliff," said Frank. "The catch is, you don't meet many survivors."

"At the very least, there won't be a body to deal with. My goal is to end up as fish food, ashes to ashes—that sort of thing. I don't wanna go staring up at one of those hospital drop ceilings mooching for morphine."

Clare shivered and said, "Let's change the subject."

"There's a dead sea lion with gulls all over it on the beach," Frank said. Clare shot him a look.

"I've seen it," Dennis said. "Now, have you two been clamming yet?"

"No, but we met at a clambake. Does that count?" Clare asked.

"Well then, I'm going to teach you how to clam."

They hit the beach with trowels and plastic buckets, Dennis showing them how to read the small sand craters and which way to dig. He told them about his son, who was living in Canada and working as a seeder. "He knows I'm here," he said. "And he approves of my decision to end myself."

They watched gray waves roll and break against the sand for a while and then Frank asked how he'd discovered the tumor.

Dennis rapped a knuckle against his forehead. "I was out mowing the lawn and I felt something slip up here. Next thing you know I'd crashed the mower into my neighbor's garage."

"Have you gone for a second opinion?" Clare asked.

"A second, a third, a fourth, and each doctor tells me it's like a spider." He spread his fingers and wiggled them. "I'm so goddamn sick of hearing them tell me about how the tumor resembles a spider. What about a hand? Yes, I've got a tumor shaped like a baby's hand and it's squeezing me to death. I'd like that better."

Gulls wheeled overhead and waves brought long lines of sea foam that made a pleasant popping sound as the water retreated and stranded it

"My uncle had a tumor the size of a grapefruit in him when he died," Frank said. "Fruit was all anybody could talk about at the funeral."

Clare slapped him on the arm, but Dennis laughed. "Here's to spiders and fruit. Now, dig deep and fast—there's a geoduck down there."

He pointed at a slick little hole in the sand and Frank went to his knees, digging furiously. Seconds later he'd wrenched the large and stubborn clam from its hiding place and lay back on the wet sand, caught up in the beauty of the clouds rushing overhead.

On the way back to their hotel room Clare kissed Dennis good-bye lightly on the cheek and told him she was okay with his decision even though it made her sad. They made plans to meet for breakfast the next morning and later, under sandy sheets, Frank told Clare that he loved her.

CHAPTER SEVEN

Around noon Walt called Frank to ask how retirement was going. Frank could hear his father-in-law walking through the house, shutting doors behind him and talking to the dog, affectionate insults mostly and questions about treats.

"It's going," Frank said. "Do you know a garage-door man?"

"What do you mean?"

Frank explained the situation with Harvey and the broken door.

Walt grunted and said, "Sounds expensive. Hold on a minute, I think I've still got the number of the guy who put the automatic in for us, provided Mary didn't toss it into file thirteen. What else?"

"You called me."

"Any plans?"

"I'm baiting my hooks."

"Just be careful my daughter doesn't draft you into that real estate hustle of hers," said Walt. "You should see the junk mail I get from those folks. Remortgagers too. It's all a great big pyramid scheme, you know. I'm betting on a crash."

"Imagine me showing a house."

Walt chuckled.

"Here's the bathroom," Frank said in his FBI voice. "And here we have a yard." He heard a dish clatter in the background and then Mary began yelling about her back pills. Walt excused himself and set down the phone. When he came back on he said, "Business as usual here. What about on your end?"

"Clare's at a showing and I've got to go by and see about this job."

"What job?"

"Loss prevention over at the mall."

"That was fast."

"I don't think I'm going to take it."

"This Clare's idea?"

"Bingo," he said, explaining how at Clare's urging he'd dropped a résumé on the toy-clogged desk of a frazzled secretary a week before his retirement, not thinking he'd get a callback. The fact that he'd gone in to see about the job would be enough to get her off his back if and when she started in on him about doing something besides puttering around the house and helping her father with that fool boat of his—a thirty-six-foot Grand Banks that Walt had rechristened the *Weaver's Beam*.

"Sooner or later I'm gonna have to find something to do," Frank said. "I mean, it's not like I can lie around the house dreaming up projects to keep me busy."

"I suppose not. Although shoplifters would be a step down. What about after?"

"I've got to head into the office to do some paperwork."

"You mean the Bureau?"

"Lace up some loose ends," Frank said. "Mickey Mouse stuff. How's the boat coming?"

Walt vented about the price of hardwood and brass fixtures and then they arranged to meet at the marina to start work on the deck-house.

"So I'll see you down there?" said Walt.

"Sounds like a plan."

After he hung up, Frank took a short nap and woke with his face stuck to the couch, vowing not to take any more unearned naps. In the kitchen he ate a ham salad sandwich, standing over the sink to catch the crumbs. Then he dressed and went to see the head of security at the mall.

He hated malls, hated the way they reeked of perfume, new leather, and whatever oil they sprayed all over the elevators, and he hated the zoned-out look of the shoppers doing laps, browsing sale racks, and running up credit. The only people who seemed to be enjoying themselves were the teenaged girls who patrolled the polished cement concourse whispering about cute boys and trading lip gloss because they were at the height of their powers, and the mall, with its bright lights and busy din, was like a movie set.

The parking lot was packed with minivans and seagulls circling discarded french fries and popcorn. A few women walked with fresh bags, fishing around their oversized purses for keys, looking like they'd forgotten something.

He found the security office and waited to be buzzed in by a patchy-haired man named Mr. Jimmy, who met him at the door and ushered him into a nautical-themed office. He wore a blue blazer, tasseled loafers without socks, and some sort of copper bracelet around his suntanned wrist. He smelled like scotch. Frank checked his watch—two o'clock in the afternoon and the man was on his way. It spoke volumes about the job.

Mr. Jimmy said he was impressed with Frank's FBI experience—it had caught his attention when he'd grabbed the résumé. "Mostly I get rent-a-cops and ex-cons," Mr. Jimmy said. Then he went into a long story of how he'd once tried to join the police force but had failed the physical exam. "Asthma," he said. "Couldn't haul my ass around that track fast enough for those cops. And pull-ups—forget about it."

"I don't think I could pass it either," said Frank, letting the man off the hook. He listened as Mr. Jimmy ran down the job basics as if he were still surprised that a man with Frank Marshall's experience would want or even need a job busting the shoe kipers, purse stuffers, and teen vandals who stalked the mall.

"I'm interested," Frank said with little conviction but, just the same, willing to lead the man on a little.

"Well then, let's take the tour," Mr. Jimmy said, jingling some loose change in his pocket.

And so Frank followed him along the box-littered narrow back alleys and hallways that connected the mall's department stores and retail shops. When Frank noted some baroque gang scrawl on a loading dock wall, Mr. Jimmy stopped and said, "I don't smell blood like I used to with that stuff. My policy is that as long as it's not visible to the public they can tag away. I think this one stands for death or something like that." He practiced his golf swing, his hands gripping an imaginary club.

In a drab cement-block room he showed Frank the video monitors and the two-way mirrors they'd installed in the dressing rooms. "We're not technically supposed to have these," he said as they watched a man with gigantic pimpled thighs shimmy into a baby-blue Speedo and stand flexing in the mirror, baring his teeth. Other visitors to the dressing rooms did curious things with the straight pins they pulled out of the dress shirts, and one man entered the room with a pile of slacks only to sit on the narrow bench, stare at his reflection, and sob.

"What's wrong with him?" Frank asked, after the man still had not moved to try on the pants.

"Unless he decides to steal something, it's none of our business," said Mr. Jimmy, brushing lint from his sleeve. "You get used to it after a while."

"Used to what?" Frank asked.

"Waiting for people to do bad things."

They walked down the hall and met the large, humorless woman whose job it was to monitor the women's dressing room. She had short brown hair, thick glasses, and small hands that were busy working knitting needles in her lap.

She nodded briefly at Frank before going back to her knitting, her eyes flicking up every now and then to the bank of black-and-white

video feeds of empty dressing room hallways waiting like badly carpeted prison cells.

Mr. Jimmy explained the complicated and too-clever-by-half code
they'd devised for use over the PA system when alerting security
guards to crimes in progress. The signal for shoplifters in the shoe
store was "Paging Dr. Marten, paging Dr. Marten." A "blue light special" was a flasher or suspicious person lingering around the chain of
fountains in the center of the mall.

"We get too many of those," the woman said, shaking her head.

Back in the office Frank told the man he was interested and would
think about it, maybe get back to him in a week or so, selling each
lie until they shook hands.

Frank couldn't get out of the mall fast enough.

He drove over to the FBI field office and pulled into the garage. A
car he didn't recognize was parked in his usual spot and so he pulled
into one of the visitors' spaces.

Inside the steno pool, phones rang and flashed red as Connie Nova
looked up from her Selectric and snapped her gum at Frank. She had
big brown eyes, wore tight slacks, and practically ran the office, refer-
ring to the agents as her "boys." Other women despised her and Frank
knew this was a sign of her power because she was physically splendid
and knew how to wear clothes. The women who hated her did not.

"Look what the cat dragged in," she said, giving him a flirty smile
before hitting the return bar.

"I'm back."

"Sure you are," Connie said, going back to her work.

He paced down the hall to the bullpen, ducking into various of-
fices and waving hello. He saw Rispoli behind a desk, squinting at a
pile of reports, his long hair pasted to his forehead in sweaty curls.
Frank waved but didn't go in.

He found Agent Hawkens at his desk, phone pressed to his ear,
scribbling like mad. Hawkens, who specialized in kidnappings and
extortions, was an amateur cryptographer and a nationally ranked
Scrabble player.

Frank took a seat. As he waited for Hawkens to finish up the call he scanned the corkboard above the agent's desk. It was papered with dozens of ransom notes. One was signed "Seekers After Smooth Things" and demanded $100,000 and the publication of one of the Seekers' unpublished essays, entitled "Free the Scrolls!" Another note was signed simply "Jim, the man who kidnapped your son," with a P.S. requesting that the police not be involved in any way, shape, or format. Worst were the notes from various student radical groups because they were heavy on the symbolism and grave predictions about the fate of the earth or democracy. They seemed unable to arrive at any concrete demands, nor did they threaten any violence, instead alluding to the possibility of further unrest, which if left unchecked would rapidly descend into anarchy, a state that all student radicals seemed to have romanticized and saw as a necessary stage in their revolution. The notes displayed perfect punctuation and a fondness for metaphor, which in criminal terms did not always achieve the desired effect and often left the reader confused.

Hawkens hung up the phone.

"You busy?"

"Some cowboys down in LA are demanding passage to India. One of them says he's a Hindu or something like that. They've got posture and the baby-face negotiator down there wants to know what to do. I told them to pray—the bad guys, I mean. Paint it black, let them know the consequences of their desires."

"They affiliated?"

"Not that we know of. They robbed a bank last night and there's been a standoff, tense negotiations. All of it textbook. Fifteen hostages and you know how those SWAT boys get when they've been staring at crosshairs too long."

"Let God sort 'em out."

Hawkens made a gun of his hand, fired, and winked at Frank. "So you're out?"

He nodded.

Hawkens slid a folder across the table. "There's stuff for you to sign and a contact sheet in case the office needs to ask you any questions about ongoing investigations."

"I'm not going anywhere."

Hawkens laughed. "Well, you remember Firmin, right?"

"Finished up at the Seattle office, didn't he?"

"Sort of. He put in his twenty, said he was taking a vacation, and then poof—he vanishes and we never hear from him again."

"What do you expect from a guy who collected hotel soap and miniature flags?"

"Woodrell thinks he hired himself out as a sniper or something. He was one helluva shooter. I saw him shoot aspirin once. This was before they lowered the standards for the gals and bunchings still mattered, but I'll be damned if he didn't hit every one of those Bufferin I tossed." He leaned across his desk, his eyes darting to the hall. "I've heard they're looking for him, using a couple of former agents from the Seattle office."

"Maybe it's something simple."

Hawkens shook his head and pinched his fingers. "The file on him's this thick, Frank. I don't think they're chasing after him just to hand him a pension. My wife met him once and said he had dead eyes—some kind of woman's intuition bullshit. Used to be I didn't believe in that stuff, but I tell you, as I've gotten older I've become a believer."

"I don't rule it out."

Hawkens knitted his hands behind his head, nodding. "Last spring my wife wakes up, starts making coffee, and then just tells me like it's some sort of fact that her mother's passed. I look at her and say, 'Pearly gates passed?' and before she can answer, the phone rings. It's her sister with the bad news."

"Women know things."

"And Clare?"

"Sell, sell, sell," Frank said. "She's going to have us rich if I don't watch it."

The phone rang. "LA," Hawkens said. "How much you wanna bet somebody got shot or else they've asked for something else?" He picked up the phone, punched the extension, listened a minute, and then began talking in a calm, rational drone. "Tell them you no longer believe in the fellowship of man. . . . That's right, you've got it. . . . If they piss and moan, give them some statistics, point out the snipers—make sure they know what ballistic-tipped bullets do, how these men aim for the heart or head, point out the barricades, paint a grim picture of all the possible bad outcomes. . . . I know it's negative, but it's best to let them know where you're coming from. . . . Well, the positive message is out. . . . Deader than disco. . . . You don't wanna go down that road, trust me on this. . . . Just look where all the let's-be-friends I-understand happy couch talk got them in Pocatello . . . Three dead and six injured. I repeat, three dead and six injured. You're not there to hold hands. . . . What you wanna do is wrap your brain around the worst that could happen and do everything in your power to avoid that scenario. . . . It's gravy from there. . . ."

Frank picked up the folder, shook hands with Hawkens, and left him to his negotiations.

He made the rounds, shaking hands, bullshitting about investigations, and lying about his retirement plans. It was a low-key goodbye to the office that looked plain and normal to him now that he was no longer under its tarnished spell. Still, he took it all in—the agents at their fake-wood-grained desks, phones cradled to their ears, pencils going, the flutter of fluorescent lights, the perpetually water-starved horsehair palm next to the drinking fountain that Frank used to water, faded cartoons depicting G-men interrogating aliens and talking dogs in fedoras, a photo of J. Edgar Hoover under which someone had taped a sign that read: "Size 12, likes to dance," the chipped grid of ceiling tiles, the hum of teletype machines, and the clatter of nails on typewriter keys. Only the sanctity of unsolved crimes made it special and every last agent knew that.

He stopped by his old desk and found it stacked with file boxes and two reams of copy paper that somebody had spilled coffee on, causing the paper to wrinkle and fold like old skin. Without thinking, he shut the desk lamp off, turned his back on the cracked leather office chair, and saw Peck leaning against the door, a file folder clamped under his arm.

"You got a minute?" he said.

"I've got nothing but."

Peck stepped in, his eyes darting around the empty office. "Well, I made some calls," he said, pointing at the folder. "Actually, a lot of calls."

"On what?"

"That thing we talked about at your retirement party."

"You mean Cooper?"

Peck nodded.

"I thought that was just party talk."

"Nope, like I said, it's been a little hobby of mine for quite some time. I want to prove he didn't survive."

"And if he did?"

"Well, then I want to find him or something he left behind."

"Like I told you before, I just happened to be out there that day. I wasn't even one of the primaries on the case. I got wet and cold and found nothing."

"Except for the girl."

"What girl?"

"The one in the pond."

Frank snapped up straight. "Who told you about that?"

"Agent Brown." Peck blushed. "It was nothing, really. I just asked him something about the Cooper case and we got to talking. I'd rather not . . ."

"No, go on, I'd like to hear what Agent Brown thinks of me."

"Just that you spent a lot of time on the case even though it was cold from the jump and not under our purview. I don't think he meant anything by it."

Frank pointed at a chair and told Peck to sit as he thought a moment. "Well, maybe I did get a little too involved. There were hundreds of us searching for Cooper and I just happened to find those bones in the pond. The only reason it made the papers was because of Cooper and, yeah, the crime hooked me. It would have hooked anybody who'd seen the site. It was the middle of fucking nowhere. Plus, I knew the sheriff wouldn't do too much about it because everybody had her figured for a prostitute or crazy hippie chick who'd met the wrong ride."

"There were no good leads then?"

Frank shrugged, remembering how he'd pored over missing-person reports for months after the discovery. "A few, but none of them went anywhere. I worked it hard for a while but then it stalled on me. Happens all the time," he said. "Next time ask Brown about the Maguire case."

"I don't understand."

"Sooner or later you get a case that gets you. The pond girl was the one for me, and Maguire is Brown's own little sticky mess. When I first joined, an old agent named Ray Riskin took me aside and handed off one of his unsolved cases to me, made me promise to keep an eye out and give him a call if something popped. I remember him telling me how the case kept him up at nights—gave him a reason to go to work every goddamned day and claw through all the other bullshit."

"What was it?"

"Some guy in a van snatched this boy from Ankeny Square and disappeared without a trace."

"Anything ever turn up?"

"Not a thing," Frank said. "What happened was, the family finally declared the boy dead then. Two years later Riskin had a stroke and died."

Peck was quiet a minute. "That's funny, I would have guessed Cooper would have been the case that stuck with you."

Frank shook his head. "I didn't exactly feel any sort of righteous anger about what he'd done. In fact, I kind of admired his cleverness."

"Ahh, Bureau cardinal sin number one."

"Isn't that why you're obsessed with the case?"

"No comment," said Peck.

"Fair enough." Frank leaned back against the desk. "Just remember, I'm retired."

"I could talk to Woodrell about it—that way we're not sneaking around."

"I wouldn't do that. The Bureau tends to frown on stuff like this. Might look like I'm digging up material for one of those true-crime books. First tell me what you've got."

Peck looked around and toed the door shut before opening the folder. Inside was a survey map of the Columbia River drainage with tiny metes and bounds along each lot and several circles in red ink, lists of numbers, and some photocopied pages from the original Cooper case file concerning the discovery of some of the hijacked money in the Columbia River by a kid trying to build a sand castle.

"That money washed up here, right?" Peck asked, pointing at a spot on the map.

Frank took a look. "So?"

"Well, I checked deeds upstream and on some of the drainages going back to the hijacking and found a few interesting things—nothing concrete, but worth checking on—and I wanted to run them by you before going any farther with this." He pulled out a few sheets of paper with notes on them. "Do you have the time to listen to my crazy theory?"

"I'm listening."

As Peck continued, pointing at the map and lists of names, Frank felt that old electric snarl of pieces snapping neatly into place and of connections being made. Peck explained how he'd rechecked the deeds on every river and creek upstream from where the bills had been found, his theory being that, had the money initially gone into the main river, it would have dissolved and been washed out to sea and that, given the condition of the recovered bills, it was reasonable to believe that they had only recently found their way into the river and that there was perhaps more of the money somewhere. "What I want," Peck said, "is for you to tell me whether or not I'm wasting my time."

Frank wanted to tell him he was and leave it at that, but when he looked at Peck he saw that it mattered. "No," he said, "you're not, but I still don't understand why you think there's more out there somewhere."

"Because he meant to come back for it when he ran out of money wherever it was he escaped to."

"We always figured that as a possibility."

"Okay, so say that six thousand they found was part of something larger—not much or else more would have been found—but say he stashed ten or twenty thousand. Even that's not enough to come back for."

"I don't follow."

"If he went to the trouble of hiding some money in case he got caught, he would've hid a lot more, don't you think? Otherwise it wouldn't have been worth the time and effort."

Frank thought a minute. "Maybe, maybe not."

"What I want to do is whittle this list down. I figure that he would have put the money not only someplace he knew but a place where he thought it would be safe." He pointed to several pages of land deeds and addresses. "It's going to take me awhile to narrow the list down, but when I do I was wondering if we could take a little field trip and knock on some doors. Now, you said there was one guy."

Frank looked at him. "I don't know what you're talking about."

"The other night at the party, you said there was some guy you thought had something."

"That?" Frank chuckled. "It turned out to be a big fat zero."

"Why did you like him?"

"Because he'd served and had some jump experience."

"And?"

"And he was at work that day. I checked him out top to bottom and nothing."

"What was his name?"

"Dipner or something like that."

Peck grinned and pointed at his list. "I've got his name right here."

"So?"

"So maybe you should take another look?"

"Better yet, cross him off the list. We looked at him hard."

"The son, right?"

"No, the old man. Of course we looked at the son and nothing."

"Well, it's his farm now."

Frank glanced at the map again. "You think I've got nothing better to do than wait around for you to call and ask me questions about dead cases?"

"Is this the part where you break my stones, Frank?"

"Not necessarily."

"Then you're interested?"

He laughed. "Okay. Call me when you get this list of names down and I'll see what you got." He watched as Peck meticulously gathered up the maps and papers and slid them into the folder, smiling.

"Oh, and one more thing."

Frank stopped.

"I got this call," Peck said. "The switchboard pushed it to me because I'm catching this week." He unfolded a memo slip from his pocket and handed it to him. "It was a woman asking for you."

Frank took the note and saw that at the top was the name Anne Blackwood.

"She say what she wanted?"

"She wanted to speak to you," Peck said, "and didn't want to leave any message."

"You tell her I was retired?"

Peck shook his head. "Didn't get that far. Like I said, she hung up before I could get any information. I called back, but there was no answer."

He handed the memo back. "Old case," he said.

"I know, I pulled it and had a look."

Frank let a little silence pass before asking, "Has there been any activity on it?"

"It's a pretty cold case. But the photos of what this Blackwood guy did to that convenience store clerk are quite vivid."

"I know that," Frank said, trying not to seem too eager but doing a shitty job of it. "And the phone log?"

"The last entry's a routine house call to the ex-wife on June 9." Peck paused. "But you already know that . . . it was you."

"Yeah, yeah," he said. "She was probably wondering how come I haven't been by to check up on her."

"Check up on her? Is this another one of your sticky messes?"

Frank tried to laugh it off and put the young agent at ease. "Not like that," he said. "She's just a kid."

"I didn't mean it like that."

"Well, are you gonna follow up on it?"

"I was hoping you'd tell me whether it was worth it or not."

"How about if I stop by and see what she was calling about?"

"Depends."

"Depends on what?"

"Depends on whether you'll show me where that money washed up and knock on some doors."

Frank wiped the sweat from his palm, held out his hand, and said, "Deal."

They shook and Peck left him in his vacant office feeling like he'd somehow been had and at the same time anxious to see what she'd called about as he strolled out of the office toward the parking garage, tossing insincere nods and waves. He'd expected to feel some blast of freedom leaving the office, a sense of closure that would put a spring in his step, but when he looked back over his shoulder he felt his future unraveling, twisting itself around his chest as he wondered how long he could hold out before going to see Anne.

■

AT FIRST COOPER tried to play it off, pretend he wasn't worried that he'd not seen Inez since revealing his true identity to her. But after a few days he couldn't take it anymore and went looking for her. He stopped by her apartment and knocked but there was no answer, no shifting of the curtain or thumps from inside to suggest she was hiding from him.

He went by the cantina and asked the owner, a short, balding man who scowled a lot and kept a cotton towel tucked in over his belt in a sanitary manner, if he'd seen her. The man shrugged his shoulders and said that she'd missed her shift and he'd been forced to wait tables—something he was *mucho infeliz* about.

After lunch Cooper swung by the Blue Dolphin hotel, where Rosa, a friend of Inez's, cleaned rooms and did a little catering on the side. She had terrible acne and long, beautiful hair that she kept in a braid. But all Rosa could do was shake her head and mention something about family and point to the mountains. He thanked her and nicked a pack of matches off her service cart. He was thinking of taking up smoking again.

At night he walked the beach, half expecting some piece of her to wash up at his feet, but there were only dead fish and chicken bones covered with crabs and farther up, where two massive rocks stood in the surf, some teenagers had built a bonfire. They were dancing around it, shooting off firecrackers, and running along the surf with giant sparklers, oblivious to his busted heart.

He spent the next day at the cantina with Ernesto, and rather than tell him about Inez's disappearance, Cooper let him drunkenly plot their petting zoo. By noon Ernesto had stubbornly latched on to the idea that they would import some tapirs from Panama and have a room where the tourists could watch them rip up live chickens and maybe a few of the stray dogs lurking around the village. He said it would be cathartic for people who'd been trapped on buses all day. "Takes care of our trash removal problems too," he said.

"The tapirs?"

"I've seen them eat the tires off a minibike. And they like motor oil too."

"Petting zoos are for kids. How in the hell are you going to have carnivorous pigs running around?"

"Details, details, details," Ernesto said.

"Impossible to insure."

"Have you ever seen a tapir?"

"That's not the point."

Ernesto shrugged and changed the subject, talking about his royal lineage while Cooper kept an eye on the street, hoping he'd spot Inez and stop the worried trembling in his gut.

"My weak chin's a dead giveaway," said Ernesto. "I've always been fond of purple and I make fists when I sleep."

"Horseshit," Cooper said.

"A very small country, perhaps a tribal king. Can you see it?"

"No, I do not see it."

Ernesto struck a Roman coin pose and pointed at a small, grimy Indian huddled in the corner under a heavy wool blanket, rubbing his mouth with nicotine-stained fingers.

"Did you see the way he cowered?" Ernesto whispered. "He sensed my royal blood. I could have been a king, held inspections, demanded taxes."

"Okay—a very small and desperate country. How about we leave it at that?"

"Go on, I'm listening."

"Plenty of crop failure and civil unrest," Cooper said. "You would have been the likely victim of a coup, dragged into the jungle and chopped to bits. End of story. Now can we talk about something else?"

"Still, I would have been king. How many men can say that?"

Exasperated, Cooper did the only thing he knew would distract him; he pointed to Ernesto's glass and asked if he wanted another drink.

"Oh, and one after that too."

They ordered another round. They even bought the Indian a beer, which he accepted without so much as a nod and proceeded to drink in tiny, delicate sips as if he were merely being polite.

"You know," Ernesto sighed, "I'm beginning to think there's more to life than beer and pussy."

"What's that?"

"I don't know yet. But seeing as how I've devoted my whole life to it with lopsided success, I still don't feel maxxed out. I've been having these dreams."

"I don't like listening to other people's dreams, so stow it."

"No," Ernesto said. "That's not what I'm talking about. What I'm talking about is that sometimes I wake up and feel like I've been missing something. Does that ever happen to you?"

"You're drunk." In the dark crankhouse of his brain, Inez was naked and looking at him through her hair, trying to tell him something. He drained off his drink, hoping to wash the cold hand of dissatisfaction off his back.

"That may be true, but it doesn't explain how come I keep getting this feeling. I mean, what are we doing here? What's the point?"

"I don't want to get into this now."

"Well, I need a mission," Ernesto shouted. "I need something good to come along and sweep me off my feet."

Cooper stood and did his customary check of pockets and then looked to see that he hadn't dropped anything on the floor. All was well. Ernesto asked where he was going, trying and failing to organize his face into something approximating hurt.

"Home."

"You're not going to talk me down off the ledge?"

"My advice is have another drink and then jump."

"I'm full of ideas."

"You are full of shit is what you are."

Ernesto began nodding. "I don't see anything wrong with that."

"Well, that's your problem, not mine."

With that, he left and wandered home along the beach to find a man on his porch and two others already inside, tearing up the place. Not exactly what he wanted to come home to, but par for the course. The whole way back he'd been thinking of Inez up on all fours, the belly chain she wore, the one with the tiny gold Mayan mask charm dangling above her pubic hair, just waiting for him to push it aside and grab her hips.

He thought about running. But where would he run to? Besides the fact that Inez could be inside, lashed to the bed frame, dirty gag in her mouth, cigarette burns on her thigh, desperate for him to

come to her rescue. But he knew that wasn't the case. The only reason to do anything was that the money was in the house. He did the
math and quickly decided that the life of a penniless vagrant expa-
triate did not appeal to him. Nor did the idea that he should just walk
away and hope for the best, pray the men ransacking his house were
just stupid vandals. Instead he stepped out of the shadows.

He'd never seen the man on the porch before, a short, fat dude
with squinty eyes that looked like they'd been punched out with an
ax handle.

The man whirled around, sizing Cooper up, making sure he saw
the knife. "The money, señor," said the man.

As Cooper looked around for a convenient weapon, he remembered something an old-timer had told him about bandits—that they
were like black bears and would run off if you put up a fight. He
ducked into the shadows and quickly loaded up his fists with stones
before stepping onto the porch.

He towered over the man, who in the half-light of the porch
looked like a large toad, his neck covered with moles and raisin-
shaped growths. That wasn't all. Cooper now saw that the knife,
which had looked somewhat formidable before, was upon closer inspection a tarnished butter knife.

"What are you going to do with that?" he asked.

The man raised the knife and let out a hiss and Cooper knocked
him in the chops with the rock. The man went down, the butter
knife clattering against the porch boards.

A second man stepped out of the door and onto the porch wearing a canvas tarp with a hole cut in the middle. He was stoop-
shouldered and had thin, greasy hair raked back over his ears. He
took one look at his fallen accomplice and produced a real knife.

Cooper went on the assumption that it was sharp and kept his distance, figuring he had one shot, maybe two, to park a stone against
the man's face.

When they squared off, the man walked right at him, batoning
the knife in flashy circles with a bored agility.

"Where is Inez?" Cooper asked.

The man squinted and swiped the knife out quickly. It flashed past Cooper's face, narrowly missing his left ear.

"Inez," Cooper repeated, careful to keep his hands down. He wanted the stones to be a surprise.

The man swung again and Cooper tilted away and brought his loaded fist up hard into the man's jaw. He didn't go down as expected. Instead he took a few quiet steps backward and smiled, blood framing the gaps in his teeth, snot dripping from his nose.

Cooper froze, waiting for him to topple, and that's when the third man got him. Cooper heard a whistling sound and turned to see a board screaming, hell-bent for his face. He felt his legs jelly as the delayed sting ripped into his skull. Bright Roman candles knocked around his brainpan for a few last seconds of consciousness before he started the long fall.

The man connected again, but Cooper was too far gone, his brain a crackling white mess, his sinuses full of blood and the sparky odor of chipped teeth.

IT WAS MIDMORNING when he woke, covered in mosquitoes and sand fleas. His right arm, which had lain in a patch of sun for hours, was fried to a blistered crisp and his face was glued to the porch boards with dried blood and drool. It took him half an hour to sit up, his head pounding like a steel drum. No great truths came to him, just the impending sense of doom, that when he crawled inside he'd find the money gone. There was almost no sense in looking. It did occur to him that Inez was responsible for the men and thus for his head and boiled ham of an arm and all the bullshit that would follow. All because he'd opened his mouth and showed her the money, when he should have left her staring out the window longing for her dead husband.

Of course, his Camaro was gone and they'd done a number on the house, countertops covered with half-eaten corn tortillas, banana peels, and the smashed remains of a dark rum bottle. They'd destroyed his LP collection against the wall and disarticulated the turntable. The couch cushions had been inexplicably slashed open to reveal nothing but beautiful pale latex foam. He kept moving and found the refrigerator door torn off, an unflushed turd in the commode, and some white gunk smeared on the mirror as if one of the bandits had been squeezing blackheads or scraping his tongue and had wiped the haul on the glass. He flushed the turd but it was stubborn and he had to get out the bent coat hanger he kept behind the door to break it up before flushing again. Then he checked out his head in the mirror. The blood made it look a whole lot worse, so he wiped it off with a damp towel and wrung his hair out and picked splinters from his face. After swallowing a handful of Mexican aspirin and as many vitamins as he could find, he continued the search.

In the bedroom he found the sack that had contained the money and wasn't surprised to find it empty. He sniffed it, the dank inky aroma of the loot still lingering. "Fuck me, fuck me, fuck me," he said, dropping the sack and numbly forging on with the inventory of loss.

He discovered the parachute where he'd hidden it, between the mattress and box springs. Book IV was lying open in the closet. He picked it up, sat on the bed, and consulted it.

It had been awhile since he'd read from it and he hoped now that it would inspire him to action. Instead he found himself reading about great hoaxes the author had perpetrated on his neighbor, such as smearing pie tins with mashed fireflies and then tossing them into the air, filming them on Super 8 and sending the footage to a weatherman on the local television station whom the author thought was a fraud, always hedging his bets and predicting rain or partially cloudy. And there was the bit about burying cow bones and shark teeth and then having some local punks dig them up. Fascinating stuff but at the moment useless to Cooper, who as he sat in his ruined house knew that he would have to go back to America and get the rest of his money from the broken-down Galaxy in Moe's pasture because there was nothing for him in Mexico now that Inez had betrayed him. He knew that if he stayed he'd end up like Ernesto—sponging off the tourists and making unfortunate remarks in public, one small step above the fogged-out acid heads and dropouts who sat around the town square chattering at unlit cigarettes and braiding one another's unwashed hair.

From the pages of the book he pulled out the old Wanted poster, folded it open, and stood staring at the crime sketch, wondering if the reward for information leading to his capture still stood. Probably not, he thought. And how would he turn himself in? He felt faded and old now that a trio of sofa-slashing bandits who carried butter knives and swung boards like Babe Ruth had suddenly snatched the simple life he'd found in the village out from under him. As it was, he'd been running out of money and would have had to return for the stash eventually. Inez, it seemed, had merely sped that process up. What the bandits had taken wasn't worth chasing after and possibly getting himself killed for. What mattered was whether or not Inez was crafty enough to try and turn him in and collect some kind of reward. He wasn't about to stick around and wait for that to happen.

And so he gathered up a few items—the parachute, Book IV, some clothes, and the empty money sack because he wanted to be able to sniff it and remember way back to the night he'd jumped and thought he was going to die. Even that prospect seemed preferable to his current ones. In the bathroom he washed his face again, tucked his hair back into a loose ponytail, and slathered his sunburned arm with lotion until it was as white as a bowling pin.

On the porch he saw the butter knife and bent to retrieve it, when he remembered to check his pockets for money. The bandits had done a slack job of robbing him—he had a grand total of $103 to his name. It would, he hoped, be just enough to buy his way across the border with one of these coyote outfits that smuggled illegals across the desert to America, where jobs awaited them. He remembered Ernesto claiming to have some connection with them, scouting out future busboys and fruit pickers for them in return for a small finder's fee. There was a better-than-average chance that this claim of Ernesto's would turn out to be utter bullshit, the product of too many beers and the need to feel connected with some dangerous criminal underworld. Still, he had to try. It wasn't like he could risk just crossing the border or hopping on a jet.

As he walked into town he tried to muster some anger over Inez's betrayal, but he kept circling back to his own big-mouthed postorgasm stupidity. What had he been thinking when he'd crawled under the bed and tossed the money around like rose petals, hoping to impress her? The money and his story of the crime had effectively plucked from her imagination the image he'd cultivated of a hangloose bum just tanning his heels in deepest Mexico. She had seen her chance and, without hesitation, hired or seduced three violent and stupid men to seize it for her. Who could blame her?

He supposed he should track her down, but given how little he knew about her other than the dead husband and the fact that she had a birthmark in the small of her back, it seemed folly to think he could find her. He was, after all, still a gringo and he'd never once met any of her family. By the time he made the town square he'd come to the paranoid conclusion that a good portion of the villagers not only knew about what had happened with the bandits but at this very moment were dialing up the American embassy and spilling the beans about the gringo—the desperado with the bad knee and the pile of money, the one who claimed to have hijacked a plane.

At Inez's apartment an old woman sitting on a milk crate eyed him as he trudged up the building's iron steps and knocked on the door. Of course, there was no answer and so he tried the knob. The door swung open with a metallic groan.

Her clothes were gone and so was the painted dresser and the photos of Faye Dunaway she'd taped over the bed. A ceiling fan swirled overhead, the breeze moving the strings of Inez's waitressing apron, which she'd left draped over a chair. He picked it up, felt fabric stained stiff with hundreds of beers and the juice of lime quarters. There was nothing inside and so he hung it back over the chair and left without closing the door.

He found Ernesto at his usual spot at the bar, munching on a pickled egg, taking his time with the jalapeños and onions, flipping them like hot coins before sentencing them to his mouth. Two field hands were passed out at the corner table and the bartender was sleeping on a small cot next to the clogged sink.

A big-boned American woman with bright red hair sat next to Ernesto, stirring the remains of a Singapore Sling with painted nails and pumping her legs back and forth like a child. Cooper had seen her earlier in the week hanging around the bait shop trying to rent a boat, flashing her freckled shoulders and white teeth at the dock boys.

"Lunch?" Cooper asked, pointing at the egg.

"Breakfast, lunch, and dinner," said Ernesto. "Meet Dolores, my American woman lady friend. We met last night. You ever been hit by ball lightning?"

"No."

"It was like that."

"Kaboom," said Dolores, taking Cooper's hand lightly in hers. She pressed it to her cheek and sniffed. "You smell good," she said.

Cooper told her it was the burn medicine he'd put on his arm.

"They should bottle it," she cooed. "I'd buy some. Do you have a name for it?"

"Ointment," he said.

"Dolores's husband left her," said Ernesto, his face gray with booze, no sleep, and whatever he meant by "ball lightning." "She's celebrating her divorce and thinking of becoming a hippie."

"No, no, silly, you've got it all wrong. All I said was that I believed in crystals and the power of the pyramids. Now, does that make me a hippie?"

"What do pyramids have to do with anything?" Ernesto said.

"A friend of mine sleeps with tiny pyramids over her breasts. They're a sign of power, evil, or prosperity, depending on your culture."

"Excellent," said Cooper impatiently. "Good to know that."

"My friend wants a C cup," Dolores said, looking a bit hurt. "And as for my husband, I've left him mentally, but as far as the state is concerned, I'll have to hire a lawyer. My husband collects legal minds and plays golf—get the picture?"

"Whatever," Ernesto mumbled, raising his drink at her.

Without warning, Dolores hopped off her stool and shimmied across the tiled floor, snapping her fingers at Cooper. "Come now and let's dance."

"I don't dance," he said.

Ernesto laughed. "I told you he has these rules for everything."

"I've never heard of such a thing. What kind of rule is that? You won't dance or you can't dance?"

"Both. I don't feel the music, but I like to watch." He wanted her to go away.

Instead she put a finger over his mouth. "Well then, we were fated to meet, because I am a very generous teacher. My first husband was quite the dancer. He had gifted hips, you see, and a little of his magic rubbed off on me before he managed to step in front of that bus. It was an uptown express. Very messy."

She giggled and then slapped his bad arm, causing him to leap up and do a little pain jig, which only encouraged her.

"There you go, you're getting the hang of it," she said, still shimmying.

"My arm," he gasped.

"Wisconsin," Ernesto shouted. "Canada. You're dancing Alberta, man."

"Shut your fucking mouth, Ernesto, and get off that bar stool. I need help. I've been run over by bandits."

"Such language!" Dolores squealed, rubbing her hips against Cooper. He could smell the rum on her breath and see her fillings.

"What?" Ernesto said.

"Now is the time for all good men to come to the aid of their party," Cooper shouted. "I need help."

"And I feel just like Leslie Caron," Dolores said, kicking her leg out, the tropical print skirt sliding up her thigh. She wasn't wearing any underwear.

Cooper's head began to hurt again. He was trying hard not to think of the stolen money or what the bandits might be doing with it—tequila, guns, silk shirts, and maybe some new chompers for the one he'd hit with the rock.

Dolores finally ceased her gyrations and began patting the sweat from her cheeks with a wad of bar napkins. Cooper pushed her aside and grabbed Ernesto. "Those men you told me about?"

"You mean the Panamanians with the line on tapirs?" Ernesto said, grinning. "I knew you'd come around."

"No, man, the coyotes, or whatever it was you called them. I need to make the crossing. I need to get back to America."

"You want to leave the village?"

"The whole goddamn country. I've got business to attend to in the States."

"What kind of business?" Ernesto pushed the rest of the egg into his mouth.

"I need—"

"Start at the beginning. You mentioned bandits. Did you kill one?" He paused to watch Dolores mop a line of sweat between her breasts and then smell the napkin before dropping it to the floor with all the other trash.

"They were waiting for me last night," Cooper said. "At first I thought drunk beach punks. But then . . ."

"What did they want? Bandits always want something."

"I didn't ask a lot of questions."

Ernesto squinted at him drunkenly. "I don't follow. They must have wanted something. I've been to your house and you've nothing to steal, man."

Cooper thought quickly. "Our business plans. They were after our business plans for the petting zoo."

Ernesto smeared egg yolk into the bar and nodded heavily as if he'd already suspected as much.

"What kind of bandits were these?"

Cooper pulled the butter knife from his shorts and showed it to Ernesto. "They used this on me."

Ernesto picked it up and tested the edge against his thumb, peeling up little worms of dirt and grease.

"Then they got me with a board," he said, pointing out the lump and gash.

"We should hunt them down."

"I don't have time for that."

"Vengeance will be ours!"

"Drop it," Cooper said. "I need your help."

"But you are an American. Just take the Camaro."

"They took the Camaro."

"Okay, then why not take a bus or fly?"

"You don't want to fly," interrupted Dolores, "or if you do, make sure you've got an American crew on that plane. Those Mexicans like to hotdog it on the landings. Plus, you have the siesta problem on long flights. They're very fond of autopilot."

Ernesto extracted a brown pill bottle from his shirt pocket and shook it in front of her. She snatched it and proceeded to wolf down several brightly colored capsules.

"Now, where were we?"

"I said I need to make the crossing—no planes, no buses or cars. I want to sneak back across."

Ernesto shook his head and pulled at his ear, dislodging a few crusty flakes of dead skin that he quickly brushed off the bartop along with the egg yolk. "Well, my friend, it's dangerous."

"I know all that. What I need from you is a few names, secret handshakes, whatever it takes to get me with these coyote fellows and into America."

"I suppose I could make some phone calls," said Ernesto. "They don't get many gringos, and one of them being a gringo himself, well, that might curry you some favor. Americans like Americans— everybody knows that. They will allow you to use the tunnel. And when you get across I have a friend who will help you get to where you've gotta go. Lou Brutus, the best there is."

"Best at what?"

"He's a freelance delivery man," he said, patting himself down and disgorging a snowstorm of toothpick wrappers, foil gum wrappers, several napkins with dense writing front and back, and finally a crumpled business card with several numbers spanning many area codes printed across the front.

"What the hell is that?"

He pressed the card into Cooper's palm. "Just say 'Thank you, Ernesto.' "

Cooper thanked him.

"You call and he'll get you to where you need to be."

Cooper took a stool next to Dolores. "Okay, what now?" he said to Ernesto.

"You want to do this now?"

"As soon as possible," Cooper said. "I'm packed and ready to go."

Ernesto squinted at the single bag Cooper had deposited on the floor and sucked at his teeth. "And what about your house?"

"It's yours until I come back for it." They shook hands on that, Ernesto grinning like some boob who'd just hit a trifecta at the track and wanted to push his luck. "And Inez?"

"You can have her too, but you might have to find her first."

"I see," said Ernesto. "A lover's quarrel and she calls in the bandits. How Latin of her."

"I don't want to get into it."

"Have you been cuckolded?"

"I don't know and I don't care. I hope she meets a few sharks, preferably angry hammerheads."

"It's going to be okay, my friend. Do you want a drink?"

"No, I don't. I need you to make this call for me, Ernesto—can you do that?"

"Of course," said Ernesto.

"Now."

Ernesto woke the bartender and asked for a phone, disappearing with it into a dim back room stacked with scum-frozen mops and busted bar stools.

Cooper heard him talking rapidly in Spanish as Dolores rose from her stool, lifted her dress, and straddled his bare leg. She smelled like rum and the Ivory soap girl all grown up and batted around by the world. He went to push her off, but then he felt her dampness and tried looking her in the eyes to figure out what it was she wanted, her pupils tiny, dumb black specks from the pills. A light sweat had broken out all over her body that was not, even in his current state, unpleasant. In fact, he wanted to touch her, but he knew that it would only encourage her and there was no telling what Ernesto might do if he found them humping against the bar rail like drunk college kids. Ernesto had a notoriously short temper, mostly around matters of his mixed heritage or lack of height, and with most vertically challenged men, he belonged to the swing-first, ask-questions-later camp.

"This will be our little secret," she said, biting her lip, having some pilled-up fun with his thigh and her wet track.

Despite the recent beating and theft, Cooper felt himself getting aroused and decided to go with it. Unable to resist any longer, he ran a hand across her sweaty shoulder and let it slide down into the cup of her chest until he was pulling and twisting one of her nipples, soft at first and then harder. She shoved her thumb into her mouth and began to suck as her body rocked up and down against his leg, hips quivering, her pupils dilating unevenly.

She finished with a shudder and pulled her dress down, wobbled, weak-kneed, back to her stool, winking at the now wide-awake bartender, who was straining fruit flies from the schnapps bottles.

A minute later Ernesto emerged from the back room looking rather concerned. "I pulled strings for you," he said. He motioned for Cooper to follow him outside, where he explained in hushed tones that there was some concern on the part of the coyotes that Cooper might be an undercover Border Patrol agent or, worse, a narco cop.

"So what did you tell them?"

"I told them you killed a man and needed to escape." Ernesto smiled proudly. "Strangled him with your bare hands and now you were facing a life on the lam. That sealed the deal. They have great respect for criminals. They will know you by your crime."

"What crime?"

"Hey, will you look at that!" he said, pointing to an empty Corona bottle lying in the dust. Inside, a roach and a wasp were squaring off, sticky with evaporated beer goo. The wasp was mindlessly stinging the glass walls as the roach gorged itself on beer syrup and dead gnats. "My money's on the wasp."

Cooper kicked the bottle under a bush. "What crime?" he repeated.

"Your crime of passion," he said. He made gurgling sounds and clasped a hand around his neck. "El strangler."

"But I didn't . . . I mean, couldn't you have told them something else?"

"Do you remember my advice about the schnauzers? If you'd heeded it, we'd be picking bandit flesh from their teeth and discussing clandestine burials."

Cooper looked at him. "What are you talking about?"

"Giant black ones. They guarded beer halls. A fierce and loyal breed with a nose for criminal activity." Ernesto leaned closer. "We had names already picked out for them—Fritz and Ilsa. Remember?"

"Ernesto, you're giving me a fucking headache. Just tell me what I need to know," he said. "I need directions, okay? Simple, clear directions. I need them now."

Ernesto nodded and began explaining the operation—how and when Cooper was to meet the coyotes and hook up with the free-lance delivery man Lou Brutus, who Cooper figured to be some sort of flunky drug mule.

Cooper gave Ernesto the keys to his house and told him to maintain the flower boxes and not to let the drip pans on the stoves become corroded with grease and spilled coffee. They shook hands as Dolores emerged from the bar, fanning herself with her skirt, her head bobbing in time with the private dope orchestra wailing inside her.

An old man walked past pushing a rusted wheelbarrow. Inside the wheelbarrow were three white chickens enjoying the ride, making subtle fowl motions with their necks.

Ernesto winked and hitched an arm around Dolores. "Happy trails," he called out as Cooper shouldered his bag and started for the road leading out of town.

Cooper kept walking, peeping into shop windows hoping to catch a glimpse of Inez or one of the bandits spending his money. Instead he got a lot of blank stares and cautious waves from shopkeepers and old women with too much jewelry, who regarded him now, as they always had, with a combination of suspicion, fear, and loathing. He looked up at the abandoned hotel perched on the hill. Sun bounced off the white stucco walls. For a moment he imagined he saw what the dentists had seen just before their dreams had crashed—a dazzling temple of golf and leisure and girls in string bikinis, the happy ching of cash registers. But then the sun ducked behind some clouds and he saw the vines creeping up the walls, the rows of empty windows and crumbled roof tiles, as a monster headache clubbed away the aspirin and resumed hammering his brain. He supposed there was a lesson in this retreat but he was too tired to venture a guess as to its meaning.

CHAPTER EIGHT

On a muggy Tuesday morning Frank went to see Anne again, fighting himself every turn of the way, regretting the lie he'd told Clare about going to see Paul Wilson—something he intended to do, but not before he spoke to Anne. Yes, he wanted to find out why she'd called him and to tell her he was retired and wouldn't be stopping by anymore. But most of all he felt foolish because his visits, if they hadn't seemed obvious before, sure as shit would be obvious now.

By the time he got to Middling Oaks the dull ache of a hangover had descended on him. Toxic vodka sweat dampened his already wrinkled shirt, trickling down his ass crack. His eyes ached and his jaw popped. He had not slept well. It had taken three glasses of Smirnoff to conjure a thin version of sleep. And there was Clare's pissed-off glare when she'd discovered the empty glass in the sink, sniffing it and shaking her head before telling him they were going to have a "talk" later, like he was twelve years old or something.

It hadn't stopped him, though, and as he parked in the dirt pull-off he took a minute to study his swollen, mazy-headed reflection in the rearview mirror, noting the dark luggage under his eyes and the high red glow of his cheeks that somehow made him look younger.

He checked his breath and was disappointed to discover that the mouthful of Listerine he'd gulped on his way out the door had already surrendered to the stale, pasty odor of soured orange juice and again the late-night vodka. It would have to do, he thought, as he gathered himself.

He got out, shut the door quietly behind him, and stared at Anne's navy-blue Taurus, the backseat crammed with mops, brooms, Ajax, buckets, yellow rubber gloves, and a Kirby upright. In the front there was a six-pack of generic paper towels and a half-finished cup of coffee dotted with lipstick stains in the cup holder, a bottle of Corn Huskers lotion, and an ashtray containing an ash-covered fruit pit sitting atop several worn pennies scraped out from under one of her client's refrigerators.

He walked up the short path and stood at the door a minute looking down into the flower bed, where a slug was making its way over cigarette butts and bits of broken glass toward a shaded crack in the slab.

He knocked and she answered wearing a tight red print top with a plunge front, her shoulders straining tight against the spaghetti straps. When she moved, the top pulled up and her belly peeked out. She was barefoot, her hair pulled back into a ponytail. Her pupils were tiny dots. Frank thought pills or a line or two of something, but then again, maybe it was not enough sleep and too much work. It didn't seem to matter though—she still glowed and worked him with that smile of hers and those eyes.

"You're a little late," she said, unlatching the screen door and holding it open for him.

"What do you mean?"

He stepped inside and let the thick aroma of Pine-Sol and cigarettes roll over him as he looked around the double-wide. The sink was choked with dirty dishes. A half-eaten coffee cake sat on the countertop with a jam-smeared butter knife stabbed into its curved side. Empty white wine bottles stood in a brown sack next to a full garbage can and there was a water bong on top of the refrigerator with a *Land of the Lost* sticker on its neck. He'd long ago given up the notion that a woman who cleaned houses for a living should be able to keep a tidy house or not need a little pot and cheap pinot grigio to relax and regroup for another day at the treadmill. After all, he knew that Anne was a hard worker who'd single-handedly provided for the boys, kept her chin up, and maintained her dignity.

"I called," she said.

"I know," he said, happy she'd got right to it and not let him linger there in the door the way she sometimes did, waiting for him to make the first move. "What's wrong?"

She sighed, pointed at the kitchen table, and said, "Sit."

He sat. On the table a deck of half-dealt tarot cards lay next to a set of ceramic salt and pepper shakers shaped like a rooster and a hen. Frank picked up the rooster and turned it over, spilling pepper on the table.

"Okay. I'm sitting, I'm listening. Now tell me what happened."

She looked over her shoulder at the small living room, where trapped flies and a half-dead wasp buzzed against a window that offered no view, just a fake redwood privacy fence and the top of a nearby trailer's television antenna.

"Jimmy called."

Frank pulled at his collar and placed his hands on the table to see if they were shaking. They were—because looking her in the eye was like getting all his angels to dance on a pinhead, and he did not believe in angels.

"Okay."

"He called me in the middle of the night and said he wanted to talk to me about something."

"Something?" Frank straightened and tried to recover. "Hold on, slow down, and back up. Are you sure it was Jimmy?"

She nodded. "I'm scared, Frank. I mean, it scared me to hear his voice like that, talking as if he hadn't disappeared." She reached for her cigarettes and struck a match, letting it burn awhile before pinching it out.

He studied her and was surprised to find himself giving her the same cold top-of-the-forehead stare he reserved for all the other folks he'd questioned over the years who'd found themselves on the wrong side of the law or caught up in nasty shit beyond their control.

She exhaled, pausing to pick a fleck of tobacco off her tongue. "He sounded different. God, it's been? . . ."

"Four years."

"And I thought he was gone for good, or I mean that's what I was hoping."

"What do you mean he sounded different?"

"He said he was back."

"Back where? Back here?"

"I don't know. He said he wanted to see the boys so I took it he meant he was back."

"It's possible."

"I don't want to hear that, Frank. You're supposed to tell me not to worry and that everything's going to be okay."

Frank ran his thumbnail under the table edge. "What happened then?"

"He started asking about our old house, wanting to know if I'd put his stuff in storage and, if so, where. He also told me he was fishing a lot and that it relaxed him and how he was a changed man. He went on and on about this spoon he was using."

"It's a kind of lure."

"That's right, you fish. Well, you two will have quite a bit to talk about," she said, a smile forming and disappearing quickly. "It sounded like he was tweaking or something."

"Maybe," Frank said, reaching for his customary notepad and pen, remembering only too late that he no longer carried them now that he was retired. "We know he beat that convenience store clerk's face off for three hundred dollars, a carton of cigarettes, and a twelve-pack of Old Milwaukee."

"I know. I don't need to hear the gory details." She looked up at him, her eyes hard and red. "Now, why didn't you call me back?"

"Well, because I retired." He let that hang, eyeing the overflowing garbage can, where two flies were going round and round on a wedge of lime.

"Retired?"

He nodded. "You're looking at retired FBI agent Frank Marshall."

It took her a minute to absorb the news and when she looked at him again her eyes seemed different to Frank.

"So you're not here because I called?"

"I didn't say that exactly. I came by to check on you."

She fixed him with a look—half grin, half something else. "Check on me—I'm not sure I like the sound of that. What does that mean exactly?"

"Nothing . . . it doesn't matter now."

"I bet it doesn't."

"Anne, look," he said. "I can make a call and get it taken care of."

"Get what taken care of?"

"J. B., your husband."

"Ex."

"I'm sorry, ex-husband. Of course."

"I had a legal divorce granted in his absence. I was nineteen when I married him."

"Okay, I get it," he said. "They'll want to put a trace on your phone and send someone over to interview you."

She frowned, examining a rough cuticle on her thumb. "Can't you do that for me?"

"I'm retired, Anne."

She looked at him and leaned back a little to take another drag on the cigarette, making sure he saw the belly pooching out. "That's it? That's all you're going to say?"

"It's pretty cut and dried. If you want, I can make the call and get the ball rolling."

"And have my house full of agents again? I don't think so. Isn't there another way to do this?"

"There's a protocol for these things."

"Well, I don't want that. Last time I was made to feel like a criminal because of what my husband had done."

"You did have knowledge of his criminal activity, and in the eyes of the law . . ."

"I should smack you."

"I'm merely telling you how the Bureau sees it. The important thing to keep in mind is that your ex-husband belongs in jail. And if he's in jail he won't ever be able to bother you or your boys."

"But what if he doesn't call back?"

"Then he doesn't call back and you go back to your life."

She laughed. "Yeah, right. In the meantime I get agents showing their guns to my boys, wanting to use the bathroom, and tossing cigarette butts all over the yard. I can't wait."

"You're exaggerating."

"Well, I don't want to go through that again. I'm trying to leave. I want to change my life."

He fingered sweat from his temple and tried to look her in the face but couldn't. She was right to want to change her life.

"Moving," she said. "Is there some protocol against that too?"

Frank shook his head and then after a long silence said, "Why?"

"In case you haven't noticed, I'm going nowhere here. I owe people money and I basically work to pay the bills," she said. "Besides, I have this friend in Aspen who says I could triple my rate for the same work and ever since she told me that I can't stop thinking how I'm selling myself short here."

He sat there quietly until she bumped the table to break his stare and said, "Well?"

"Well, I'm not going to stop you, but I think J. B. is the type of person that could find you wherever you went."

She leaned across the table, took one last drag, and stubbed the cigarette until the filter split. "What's wrong with you?"

"Nothing."

"You're sweating."

"It's stuffy in here. You should open the windows and catch some of that breeze."

"The house will smell like dog shit." She pointed out the window. "My neighbor has dogs and doesn't clean up after them."

He shook his head.

"How about I get you some water?" He tried to wave her away but she was already at the tap with a glass, holding her finger under the stream of water, waiting for it to get cool. "You sure you're okay?" she asked.

"I'm an old man who can't sleep and so I drink."

"It's called a hangover, Frank, and you're not that old."

"What I mean is that I feel old," he said, not sure what he hoped to gain by confessing his problems when by comparison her troubles seemed so unfixable and out of her control.

"Please, I don't want to hear it. I work for men like you. They buy expensive sports cars and go to Barbados with their third wives. They want the bathroom fixtures to shine and they don't like mold in the grout. Do you have any idea how hard it is to get that stuff white again?" He shook his head. "Hard," she said, setting the water glass down in front of him.

He thanked her.

"Amazing," she said. "Frank Marshall, FBI guy, hungover. I've always thought you guys weren't as straight as you pretended to be."

"The cat's out of the bag."

"If you want to know the truth, I woke up a little . . ." She made a fluttering motion with her hands and smiled, her lip sticking to her teeth. "Drunk or something like that, I guess. Do you want some aspirin or I have these great pills I found in one of my client's medicine cabinet . . ."

He put up a hand to stop her from going any farther. "This is fine," he said, taking a sip of water. "This is exactly what I needed. Now, I want to hear about this phone call."

"It's pretty simple. Jimmy called and I called you, just like I was supposed to do. I'm not trying to hide anything."

"Nobody's accusing you of hiding anything. You are the victim in all this. That's been clearly established."

She glared at him. "There was a time when you guys thought I was going to run away and meet him, right?"

"Yes, but we ruled that out and tried to help you," he said, impatiently. "The call, let's focus on the call, Anne. Did he say where he was calling from?"

She shook her head.

"Did you hear anything in the background, like, say, trucks or music?"

"No, he just asked about some stuff from the old house and when I told him I sold everything to pay the bondsman he got angry. I hung up and he called right back."

"Did you sell everything?"

She nodded. "What I couldn't fit in here, yeah. I didn't have a lot of time after I signed away the house."

"And did he say what he wanted?"

"Some key, I don't know—it wasn't like he was making a whole lot of sense. He sounded pretty messed up and kept talking about fishing, which was weird because I don't remember him being into anything like that. In fact, he used to make fun of this fishing show on TV, the one with the guy kissing all those bass."

Frank cut her off. "A key to what?"

She shrugged and pulled her leg up under her. "He didn't say, only that it was in this little three-drawer pull thingy we used to keep the phone on. I hardly remember it. Like I said, he sounded pretty messed up on something."

"Is there a key?"

"How should I know?" she said, slightly irritated. "I don't remember any mysterious key. He's crazy."

"What about the boys?"

"The minute he called I sent them to stay with my sister," she said. "And then I canceled my jobs."

"Probably a good thing until you get this sorted out."

She dropped her leg and shifted in the chair, turning away from him for a moment to glance out the window. "Yeah, a good thing until I can't make the rent this month."

"I can help if you want."

"I don't want your charity, Frank."

"It wouldn't be charity."

"In my situation, yes, it would be. I wouldn't be able to pay you back and then I would owe you something. You can call it what you want, but it's never just charity."

"But I thought you were doing pretty good."

She shook her head. "I've lost six accounts in the past two months and I really can't afford to be taking time off because of all this. About the only good thing to come of it is that my knees don't hurt so bad."

Frank leaned back to look under the table but couldn't see them. He blushed as he raised his head again.

"People want their floors hand-waxed these days," she explained. "The wives who enjoy seeing another woman down on all fours sweating up a storm. Husbands like that part too."

He shook his head. He'd heard this before and had counseled her to find other work, and now after several such bitch sessions he'd come to the conclusion that some part of her must enjoy what she was doing.

"So do you have this key?"

She bit her lip. "Goddamnit, stop asking me about that fucking key."

"It's important."

She sprang to her feet and ripped a nearby drawer from its tracking, dumping the contents to the floor. AA batteries, loose change, and scissors flew across the linoleum along with the other junk—coupon books, compacts and lipstick tubes, Legos, empty prescription bottles, and dozens of grease-stained pieces of paper with numbers and doodles scribbled on them. And keys—lots of them. "How the fuck am I supposed to know, Frank? I've got a lot of junk, just look around this place. Even if there was a key, I couldn't find it and I sure as shit wouldn't know what the hell it would open."

"Calm down," Frank said when he realized she was preparing to dump another drawer.

"Jimmy was crazy when I was married to him and he sounds even crazier now."

"Anne," he said, rising to stop her.

She pushed him away and began to cry.

He reached out and put a hand on her bare back and felt her skin ripple like cold sand under his fingers, her rib cage shuddering as she tried to stifle the sobs.

The touch surprised him. Normally he'd just sit and watch people break down and cry, knowing that nothing he could say or do would make things okay. He'd done it hundreds of times—broken hard news to families, victims, and bystanders—and had long since given up on sugarcoating. There was only the truth and he'd learned to drop it on the table without feeling and wait until the person either told him to go or got a grip and started asking the hard questions. Even Clare had given up expecting him to comfort her during her rare and fragile crying sessions. Frank was not a commiserator or, for that matter, a comforter and any anger she'd felt toward this fundamental lack in him had been tucked away during the first decade of their marriage. Frank offered only silence, rock-steady silence, and commonsense reasoning, exactly what Clare didn't want.

So it was odd that this tentative touch with Anne should change anything. But it did. He felt less awkward and stranded. Words came and he found himself saying, "I'll help you . . . it's why I came by. To see how you were, how the boys were, and . . ."

She turned to him and he couldn't finish the sentence. "I'm really a bit of a mess," she said. "I mean, the phone call got to me. I can't help it, but it really, really got to me and I know that's what he wanted, but I still can't help it."

"It's okay," he said, making no move to remove his hand from her back even as it slid under the shoulder strap and he quickly thought of sliding the whole damn thing off. "You can't let him get to you like this. Guys like J. B. like to play games. He probably just got bored and decided to drop some dimes into a pay phone and rattle your cage. That's probably all it is."

"I know, I know. But I really don't want my boys to go through it again. This time they're old enough to ask me questions about their father that I don't want to answer. I've tried really, really hard to put that old life in the past and become somebody different." She poked a tear off her cheekbone and smiled at him. "I just don't want to deal with this anymore."

"I do know that you just can't ignore the phone call and pretend it didn't happen. You should have told them."

"Told who?"

"The FBI."

"I wanted to tell you."

"Okay," he said, thinking quickly. "Before I do anything, it's important that you try to remember exactly what he said. Any little thing can help."

She nodded and wiped away the rest of the tears. "Okay," she said, breaking away from him. He followed her to the table and listened as she repeated the details of the phone conversation. Every once in a while he stopped to ask her questions or make her repeat a phrase or word she remembered her ex using.

When they were finished she looked at him with puffy eyes and said, "Can we wait a day or two before calling?"

"They might already be planning to send an agent out to the house."

"And if they don't?"

He stared down at the floor, his eyes tracing the vine-patterned linoleum in wasted circles, not sure what she was getting at or what the hell he was even doing in her trailer in the first place.

"What if I decided to wait?"

"I don't understand what you're asking me," he said, fronting her now like a cop, hands folded aggressively on the table between them.

"I just want to wait a day before I call again," she said. "If you're not going to be able to help me, I need to get my head straight first."

"It's not that I won't help you, it's—"

"I know you're retired."

"Even this," he said, pointing around to indicate his visit, "is something they'd frown on. So just you asking me to turn a blind eye, that's asking a lot."

"I know." She was quiet a minute. Outside a car rattled by and Frank thought he heard the distinct thud and flutter of a bird crashing into one of the trailer windows. "Please, Frank, I need some help until I can figure out what to do."

"Okay," he said, nodding. "But only on one condition." He waited for her to nod before continuing, careful not to take a "law-and-order lecture" tone, as his daughter called it. "If they do send an agent out for follow-up, you shouldn't mention that we talked. It wouldn't be good for either one of us."

"Why?"

"It would only distract them from their job."

"You mean you'd get in some sort of trouble," she said, tossing him a crooked little smile.

"It's a possibility."

"I understand."

"Okay then."

"Okay what?" She picked up a tarot card and tapped it against the Formica. "Can we wait?"

"*We,*" said Frank. "*You* can wait, but eventually they'll contact you. They have to contact you. I can't stop them from doing that, nor do I want to."

She smiled at him again and set the card down. "That's right, you're not even supposed to be here. Isn't that what you're supposed to say, Frank?"

"I'm not going to say that either."

"You're here and not here, is that it?"

Before he could answer she winked and told him she wanted to take a nap but had been afraid to before because she kept imagining her ex-husband pushing in a screen while she slept. "It's these pills I took, they're making me feel like all I want to do is sleep. Will you stay?"

"For a while," he said.

She stood and he followed her into the living room, where she slumped into the worn velour couch cushions.

He found a green and white afghan and was pulling it over her shoulders when she slipped an arm around his neck and pulled him into a clumsy hug. His hands automatically floated up and across her back, her skin warm and inviting. His breath shortened and the room began to swirl.

"Thank you," she whispered into his neck.

He didn't speak or move, afraid that any word or grope would break the moment. Then her lips brushed across his chin and met his for a quick tear-salted kiss. Frank knew that if it went any farther he would lose control. He did not want that to happen. But still he met her halfway, fumbling to return the kiss, only part of him realizing he'd completely forgotten how it all worked. His hand swept up her spine to the nape of her neck as he sunk a knee into the couch, not sure if she was pulling him down but, just the same, wanting to feel some other part of her body against his. And then, just as soon as it had begun, she turned away, her head falling back to the couch cushion.

He stood and forced himself to look at her before the guilt swept in and caused his face to redden.

"I could feel you wanted that," she said, grinning.

He didn't say anything and she nudged him in the thigh with her bare foot. "Just nod, Frank, it's okay, really, I don't mind. I'm used to men looking at me that way when I come to clean their houses and their wives aren't there."

"It's not like that." He looked away as the room came back into focus, his heart downshifting.

She poked him again. "Well then, I want to hear you tell me what it's like."

He wanted to ask her what would happen next but knew that was a stupid question and so he backed away from the couch, feeling foolish, not for letting it happen but because she'd seen right through him so easily and was enjoying his discomfort.

"Come on, I want to hear you say it."

"Yes," he said, clearing his throat, "but I shouldn't have, not now, not with what's going on."

She reached up and shook her hair loose. "Well, it happened because I wanted it to happen. You're not the only married guy I've kissed. You're not that special, Frank Marshall." She smiled at him and snugged the afghan up around her shoulders. "Now I need to sleep." She pointed at a remote control sitting on the chipped coffee table. "Can you hand me that? I like to have the television on."

He handed her the remote and watched as she flipped the channel to the *Phil Donahue Show*, where a bearded man in a corduroy suit was offering child-rearing advice. Next to him sat a worried-looking mother strangling Kleenex in her lap as Phil shuffled index cards and adjusted his too large glasses.

Frank stood there, waiting for instruction or some word from her that would break the banal television chatter.

"See how the noise helps?" she asked. He stared at the television, trying to conjure some witty remark to get him out of the moment.

Instead she said, "In case you hadn't noticed, I just let you off the hook so you don't have to hover."

He apologized and thankfully retreated to the safety of the kitchen table, where he watched over her, replaying their kiss and brief clinch, letting his imagination run all the way to them fucking. Ten minutes later her eyes began to flutter as her breathing leveled out, and her face went slack with sleep.

He waited and then quietly raked the contents of the tossed junk drawer back, setting out the various keys on the counter. After he'd slid the drawer back in place he arranged the keys in a neat line and studied them, trying to put the phone call into some sort of perspective. Part of him believed that Blackwood was nowhere near and had called merely out of spite or some twisted plea for attention. If he was indeed back, why not just surprise her and look for the key himself? The more he thought about it, the more comfortable he became with his promise to her that he would wait and say nothing until she was ready.

He had a look around the trailer and entered the boys' room first. In one corner a platoon of drab-green army men were waging an unevenly scaled battle with several *Star Wars* action figures crouched around a half-built Lego hut and an overturned laundry basket. From there he walked down the short hall to Anne's cramped bedroom. He clicked on a light. Dirty clothes lay in color-sorted pyramids. On the dresser stood several burned-down candles set on pickle jar lids to catch the wax, a tattered *People* magazine, and a wine glass with a sprinkling of dead fruit flies that had drowned in the dregs and were now fused to the glass like tiny fossils. He pulled back the quilted comforter to reveal the cover sheet, staring at the slightly stained and wrinkled middle where she slept night after night. He ran a hand over the mattress and then without thinking lowered his face to the bed sheet. He sniffed, catching the slightest whiff of her, the odor triggering the salty kiss all over again until he felt himself getting aroused and quickly stopped.

When the phone rang, he started to his feet and went into the kitchen, where the answering machine picked up and some guy named Drew left a terse message wanting to know why Anne had canceled the appointment on him. After turning the phone ringer off, he checked and found her still sleeping, her hands twitching slightly against the afghan. On the television the bearded man in the corduroy jacket had just finished telling the woman that she shouldn't be afraid of discipline. "Children crave it," he said. "You need to set limits on unacceptable behavior."

He turned the volume down, dropped a shade, and stood watching her in the gloom, realizing for the first time since he'd entered the trailer that he felt oddly focused and sharper than he had in weeks. It was the kiss and the fact that he no longer needed to hide anything from her. That was as far as it needed to go. He'd still be able to go home and act normal around Clare, small-talk her into thinking he'd gotten back on track, and for the moment that was all that mattered.

He scribbled his home phone number on a Garfield notepad and set it next to the deck of tarot cards, careful not to disturb them. Then he went to see Paul Wilson, some to cover his ass with Clare and some to reconnect with an old friend and maybe decompress from what had just happened.

It had been years since he'd seen Paul and he was shocked when his friend answered the door, nearly bald and paunchy, his normally piercing blue eyes dragged down and dulled with dark circles and small white polyps that struck Frank as a sign of arterial blockage and an unhealthy diet.

Paul had divorced Cassandra and moved to one of the pricey new subdivisions east of town with his second wife, a Rolfer named Sharon. Five years ago he'd sold the manufacturing company to a group of lawyers who were looking for something to do with their money and eschewed conventional investment strategies. In two short years they drove it into the ground, laid off all the workers, and were forced to sell the machinery to pay the bank. A wholesale florist and small interior design firm now operated out of the building.

"Sheriff Frank," Paul said, ushering him into the house. It was just like the old days, Paul with that guilty half grin on his face and Frank playing the dour lawman as he stepped into the high-ceilinged and overly dramatic foyer—fake brass, beveled glass, and oak trim.

"Smells like a new house," Frank said.

Paul shook his head and led him into the kitchen. "Well, I'm becoming increasingly dissatisfied with the workmanship."

Sharon came out of the den to say hi. She was a hugger and Frank fumbled to return, nearly choking on the patchouli oil she'd drowned her pulse points with. "It's so good to see you again," she said, stepping away to let him have a look. She was a large woman with loads of ash blond hair and freckles who did not resemble Cassandra at all.

"It's good to see you," he said, remembering that the last time he'd seen her had been the awkward postdivorce dinner where Clare had spent the entire night asking Sharon cutting questions and nudging him under the table any time Paul leaned over and gave his new second wife a deep kiss. Afterward, both men agreed to never do that again, Paul pulling him aside, making a hissing sound and clawing at the air. "Cat fight," he said. They had a laugh and that was that.

Paul slouched at the breakfast counter while Sharon in her soothing voice told Frank she didn't like the way he was carrying himself. "You're tense, aren't you, Frankie?"

"Frank's always been tense, hon," said Paul. "He's a cop, remember."

"Not anymore, I retired."

"Once a cop, always a cop," Paul said. "You are what you are."

"The negativity he throws off," Sharon said, pointing at Paul. "But we're working on that, aren't we, hon?"

Paul shrugged, picked another clump of icing, and let it melt on his tongue.

"All in all I feel pretty good," said Frank.

Sharon pressed her palm to his spine and made a clucking sound. "I'd say you're overdue for an adjustment. You've got this knot right here. How have your bowel movements been?"

Paul rolled his eyes and threw up his hands. "Sharon, please."

"I didn't come over here for an adjustment."

"Technically, I would want to Rolf you. Some people become very emotional when I release stored-up tension. Did you know tension can poison the muscles?"

Frank stepped away from her touch. He'd always associated tension with alertness, and alertness in his line of work was a necessity. "Really, I'm okay, Sharon."

"You're not sleeping, are you?"

"How did you know?"

"Oh, she's good," said Paul. "She's got what they call hot hands in the business. Show Frank how you can heat up your hands."

"I'm a healer," she said, rolling her eyes. "But Paul sometimes mistakes me for a circus performer. Isn't that right, Paul?"

"Okay," said Paul. "I want to give him a tour of the house, see what he thinks. It's falling apart on us."

Sharon winked at Frank. "See how he exaggerates and invites stress."

"Let's just see what Frank says."

So he gave Frank the tour, grumpily pointing out the crooked door frame, several drawers in the kitchen that were off track, a couple of popped bathroom tiles, and some bad corner bead.

"Where is the job pride?" Frank asked.

"A lot of the blame has to fall on the unions. You don't want to get me started, but we probably overpaid for the house because of the location. But then, location . . ." He shrugged, throwing up his hands, unable to finish.

They walked down a long corridor that smelled of fresh paint and carpet glue. Paul opened a door. "And this," he said, "this is going to be my rumpus room." He clicked on a light to reveal a bare room with knotty pine paneling.

"It's empty."

Paul grinned. "That's because I haven't decided what kind of rumpus I want to commit down here. At first I wanted to have a wet bar and pool table over there, but now I'm not so sure."

"Wet bar?"

"It just means I'll have plumbing—couple of sinks and drains, stuff like that. But I've scotched that idea and I'm leaning toward one of those home entertainment centers with surround sound. Watch movies in style. Maybe an air-hockey table over there and a couple of dart boards."

"You're too old for air hockey."

"I've been thinking the same thing. But I remember enjoying the game." He turned out the light and shut the door. "Do you wanna take a walk and see if I can find this contractor?"

Frank checked his watch. "What do you have in mind?"

"He's been dodging me and I just wanna wag a little chin with him, express my dissatisfaction with the work on my house, and see if I can't get someone over here to address my concerns."

Frank said okay and they took a walk around the subdivision, stopping here and there to talk and fill each other in on their lives. He considered telling Paul what had just happened with Anne, but he didn't want to explain how or why he'd been over there in the first place or what exactly he intended to do about it, because Paul would only bust his stones and start in on him about wanting to fuck her.

They passed a herd of shirtless landscapers rolling sod across a dirt lot. A boom box that had been spray-painted blaze orange was blasting Bob Seger's "Night Moves." Paul tapped Frank and sang along: "Little too tall, could've used a few pounds . . ."

One of the sodders yelled, "Snake," and a shirtless guy with tattoos rushed over with a pickax and chopped the snake into writhing gray-brown bits. They watched as the men gathered around, kicking bits of snake at one another with their steel-toeds.

"So," said Frank, making an effort to focus on his friend and not Anne.

"So what?"

"So how've you been?"

"Besides this business with the house, I'm pretty happy," Paul said. "I sold the business in the nick of time. I'd already made my nut. The writing was on the wall—competition was only going to get worse. Not to mention the constant labor-management tension. I don't miss it one bit."

"And Sharon?"

"She's got me on a new diet. I've lost fifteen pounds since Easter. Hey, what's your secret in that department?" He reached out and patted Frank on the stomach a few too many times.

"I don't have one."

"Ever been to Paris?"

Frank said that he had not.

"The only fat people there are Germans and Americans. What gets me is that the French eat and drink like fucking Vikings and they're skinny as shit. Then there are the women . . . I'm not even going to get into that."

"It all boils down to genetics anyway."

"Tell me about it," Paul said, pointing at the salt-and-pepper chevrons of hair clinging just above his ears. "I knew this was going to go sooner or later, and lucky for me, Sharon likes bald men."

As they walked along the freshly paved road Frank asked Paul if he'd kept in touch with Cassandra.

"Last I heard she was selling shoes in Cleveland. It's not what you think—she has her own store and is doing quite well for herself. She became ambitious right about the time I was losing steam with my work and sometimes I think that's why we ended up splitting."

"I've heard Cleveland's nice."

"Well, it's supposedly turned a corner," said Paul. "People no longer refer to it as the mistake on the lake. Cassandra's happy there—she's remarried, you know."

"I hadn't heard that."

"A younger guy, a lite-jazz deejay at one of the local FMs. But hey, she's happy, I'm happy, so what's the point? How are you and Clare doing?"

"The same."

"Good same or bad same?"

"I don't know."

"Something you want to talk about?"

He looked at Paul, sweat beading on his forehead, and said, "No." He was thinking of Anne curled up on her couch, trying to remember exactly what she'd said to him so that he could affix some meaning other than pity or tease to the kiss.

"The thing to keep in mind is that it's best to be happy no matter what the cost. Some people call that selfish, but I'm of the opinion that the sharpest knife hurts the least and honesty's not always the best policy. Our divorce was what you might call a mixed grill of goods and bads. Good—no kids were involved."

"And the bad?"

"Bad—I sometimes miss her social graces. She was very poised and could charm anybody. Do you remember the parties we used to throw?"

"I remember."

Paul winced as they rounded a corner into a cul-de-sac filled with lumber trucks, scrap-heaped Dumpsters, and piles of topsoil waiting to be spread for lawns.

"And what about you?"

"I'm not going through a midlife crisis, if that's what you're asking."

"Deny, deny, deny."

"It's not that at all," Frank said. "I'm getting adjusted to civilian life."

Paul batted a hornet away from his face. "Okay, if you say so, but let me tell you, I ignored Cassandra and in the end she never forgave me for it."

They came to a half-finished house surrounded by pickup trucks, bunks of two-by-fours, and a blue Porta-John on whose door somebody had scribbled "PAYROLL." Nail guns popped, Skilsaws whined, and men bent over tape measures, deftly marking the deck with carpenter's pencils.

"That's his truck," Paul said, pointing to a two-tone Chevy parked beside a skid of shingles. "You may want to stay down here. This could get ugly."

"I got your back."

"I like that."

They entered the house through the garage, ducking between stud walls as carpenters in dirty Carhartts paused from their work to shake their heads and rev saws for no particular reason.

On the second floor Paul cornered a tall man in a white hard hat and began shouting about his chimney, complaining of leaks, crumbling mortar, and a damper that wouldn't open. Frank stood back and watched as the man slowly set his clipboard down and unsnapped his tool belt. He had the thick fingers, long, ropey job arms, and punched-out face of a salaried laborer who'd just recently brownnosed his way into a position of authority.

He let Paul finish and then got in his face, growling, "I told you I'd send somebody to have a look. A lot of the work you're complaining about was done by a subcontractor who got eighty-sixed."

"I'm not buying that excuse."

"That's the unfortunate fact."

"And another unfortunate fact is that it's been two weeks since I asked someone to come out and have a look."

"We're on a deadline."

Frank watched Paul suck in his gut and step up. "I didn't come here to question your craftsmanship," he said. "But I'm not the only one in this subdivision with complaints. You don't want us to get lawyers involved."

"I'd be careful if I were you because, if I remember correctly, the river-stone chimney was your idea. It deviated from the blueprints and we were forced to improvise."

" 'Careful'? What do you mean by 'careful'? I hope you're not threatening me."

"This is a job site. Accidents can and will happen, buddy."

"Is that so?"

"You could slip and fall or maybe take a framing hammer to the temple, but I sincerely hope it doesn't come to that."

"Come to what?" Paul shouted, poking the man in the chest with his finger.

"When all is said and done," said the foreman, "just remember you touched me first." He moved quickly, shifting his weight back like a boxer prepping a jab. Then he grabbed Paul's finger and twisted. Paul gasped and dropped to his knees.

Frank jerked into action, his jaw locking, fight blood rushing into his limbs as his hands folded into fists and he charged. The man saw him coming and began twisting Paul's finger harder until he was writhing around on the plywood floor, swearing, desperately trying to pry his finger loose.

"You want, I can snap this," the man warned. "I'd stay back for your buddy's sake."

But Frank moved closer.

"Back off!"

"Let go of him," Frank said calmly.

"Fuck you," said the man.

Frank put a hand behind the man's neck, grabbed a clump of hair, and punched him twice in the throat. He felt something crunch and shift under his knuckles and watched as the pain registered in the foreman's eyes and he let go of Paul and fell to the floor, clutching at his throat, sucking air through his crushed windpipe. Frank leaned over and stepped on his hair, made sure the man knew there was a lot more hurt if he wanted it, that all he had to do was get up. But the man closed his eyes and shook his head slightly and Frank knew he was done.

They raced down the stairs together, jogging all the way back to the house, where they stood on the back deck, adrenaline flooding each of them. Through the sliding glass door they watched Sharon doing chi gong in the sunroom, eyes closed and her arms moving in impossibly slow and languid arcs.

"I don't think I'm going to tell Sharon about this," Paul said, working his finger up and down. "That was pretty slick. What was that, some kinda karate kung-fu shit you hit him with?"

Frank shook his head. "It was called 'Two to the throat and then run like hell.' So what happens now?"

"I'm sure personal-injury lawyers will descend," said Paul, still trying to catch his wind. "Maybe you should leave and we'll pretend you weren't here."

Frank nodded and they shook, promising to stay in touch. Paul told him to give his best to Clare as he walked him to his car.

With his hands still shaking from the fight, Frank stopped off at a small, airless bar and ordered a double vodka. At one end of the bar a man whose face looked like a peeled log sat talking to a plump woman who was clutching a pink vinyl cigarette purse and nursing a highball. And there was a furry-looking guy in a worn corduroy jacket combing his hair with a large green comb and muttering to himself.

Frank swished the vodka around his mouth until his gums went numb and his tongue felt heavy and swollen. He ordered another and the bartender slid off the beer cooler and got him one, free pouring until the vodka flooded over the lip of the shot glass and soaked the napkin beneath. Frank sipped the top off and set a five on the bar. He knew he had to get his head straight about Anne before he went home. It was just a kiss and now as he thought about it in the smoky air of the bar it became less and less. No, Frank thought, the correct thing to do would be to tell Peck about the phone call and turn the case over to the Bureau on the q.t. and just step away from the whole mess and back into his life. But by the time he finished the shot and listened to the man with the bad face tell the plump woman that although he was currently down on his luck, out of work, and being sued by his second wife, he could make her happy, Frank felt his resolve to do the right thing begin to slip. He'd wait for her to call and see what happened next. But first he needed to go home and pretend that nothing had been changed by something as small as a kiss.

CHAPTER NINE

The bus ride north took three days and was punctuated by erratic and desolate stopovers where riders waited. The desert passed by in a rocky brown blur of buttes, mesas, and shambling gas stations. Cooper sat alone, watching the ebb and flow of passengers at each stop—the old men who climbed aboard cradling chickens in homemade cages, women with tick bites and scars on their arms, mothers with stick-thin children and rotten teeth, stooped laborers who slept on the bench seats, their belongings in modest canvas sacks.

Near Ciliacan a man in a stained white linen jacket insisted that Cooper buy a busted wristwatch.

"You're passing up a whale of a deal, Jack," said the man. "It's digital and all it needs is a new battery. It's got a minicalculator. You gotta hear the alarm. It's made in the USA and cost me fifty bucks brand-new, but I can let it go for fifteen, figuring in the cost of a new battery."

Cooper said no three times before the man left him alone.

For a while he rode behind a pretty dark-haired girl with pink plastic thongs strapped to her feet. She leaned her head against the dirty glass, watching the power lines loop by outside as the bus wound through the blighted white-gray desertscape. When he wasn't admiring the girl, Cooper tried to imagine people and animals scratching out some kind of fried existence amid the stubble of sage, listing cacti, and sun-bleached rocks.

On the second day two Mormon boys in pressed white shirts and dark pants boarded, took seats up front, and began consulting their dog-eared copies of the Book of Mormon, arguing about the pre-mortal realm as the bus groaned up to speed. After a stop they floated back a few seats, pointed at Cooper, and said, "I spy crumbling ramparts."

The thin one spoke first. "I am Elder Elkin and this is Elder Ford. Would you like to hear the Word?"

"How about some first names," said Cooper.

"Orrin," said Elder Elkin, who sported a severe haircut and large, funnel-shaped ears. "And his name is Mark."

"Sir," said Mark.

Cooper tried to give them each a soul shake, but they couldn't get it right and so he settled for a regular church clasp. The boys had weak grips, but he didn't mention it. He'd always had the impression that Mormons were soft people who liked their dairy products.

"Nice to meet you," Cooper said. "Now, what are you boys sellin' today? I've already passed on a wristwatch."

"The Word," said Orrin. "A new way of life."

He put a hand up to stop them, but they were already off and running with the spiritual tag team, pitching him God and the church, saying they could put in a save for his soul. Cooper sat back and let them get it out because he could see that they had grown up believing and that it had twisted them so severely that the church was now the only place for them. They were, in his estimation, a couple of basic well-intentioned believers and he could not bring himself to be mean or rude to them.

"It all sounds nice," Cooper said. "But I've heard it's Brigham Young's church now. They're making a push to be very American and sweep the crazies under the temple rug. Plenty of photos with the flag and inroads with the blacks and Koreans."

Orrin leaned in. "Yes, but privately many of us are fascinated with Joseph Smith."

"Now, his bit about taking many wives is a bold statement," Cooper said. "Plural marriage, I believe it's called. I admire that, but I'd imagine that even your basic farm girl would take some convincing. Am I right?"

The boys stared blankly at him and closed up their books, figuring Cooper for another lost soul who needed some time in the fire before he was ready to be pulled out for the hammer and tong of God.

Cooper continued. "Now, if I was in charge of this missionary junket you boys are on, I'd push the multiple-wives angle. It's a helluva selling point to your average nongay lonely bachelor types."

"What you're talking about, sir, is called polygamy and it gets entirely too much attention."

"Sounds like you've thought about it some."

"We are twenty years old," Orrin said. "We think about a lot of things." The bus lurched around a broken-down Gremlin as Mark began to feverishly consult his Book of Mormon, looking for answers.

"It would be good at first and then I can foresee a lot of bickering and problems at dinner," said Cooper. "And I imagine the laundry situation's a real circus. Then you have the honey-do problem. Poor bastard would be morning, noon, and night working on the wifely punch list and he'd be too tired to get any."

Orrin handed him a pamphlet. "This might speak to you."

The pamphlet depicted a shaft of heavenly light breaking through dark cloud and a red question mark hovering in the bottom right-hand corner. Cooper folded it and tucked it in his pocket.

"I think you should give him the puzzle, Orrin," said Mark. "It'll bring him around, break some of that mental ice."

"Do you like puzzles, sir?"

"Jigsaw puzzle?"

"It's a word puzzle. No assembly required."

"Well then, lay it on me, boys. It's a long ride."

Orrin fixed him with well-meaning eyes and spoke. "I'd direct you to Ezra, chapter 7, verse 21. It contains every letter of the alphabet save one," he said. "We do not think the omission is a coincidence, but I leave it for you to decide." With that they rose and took seats next to an old man in a crushed straw hat who was holding his dentures to the window and inspecting them. He refused the pamphlet, crossed himself, and went back to his dentures—zero souls captured for Salt Lake.

The bus labored through the landscape, small lizards and rodents scampered across the road as the moon melted over the plains, and men with work-black hands got on and off at every stop as if the labor force were being shuffled by unseen powers.

Cooper snoozed and worked on his plan, trying to assemble a neat little itinerary. He would sneak back across the border and make his way to Moe's and recover the rainy-day fund. After that, he didn't know. About the only thing he wanted to see in America was the D. B. Cooper Day festival he'd read about. He wanted to stand rib-to-elbow with the drunks, bored locals, and conspiracy theorists and watch the parachutes plunge to earth. Perhaps there would be some kind of rock band and he could shout out, "Freebird," or maybe a look-alike contest. He would enter and lose—the irony. After that he'd probably slink back down to Mexico and search for Inez or try to find some other small village to hole up in. He did not know.

At a gas station outside Nuevo Laredo he bought a piece of flatbread from a very old woman with enormous hands and a bandanna stretched over her skull. Her feet were fused into dirty sandals and she tucked the money away quickly before handing him the bread, muttering something in Spanish he couldn't make out.

A small boy darted by shooting an imaginary machine gun. Cooper fired back and the boy crashed into the dirt, wounded, holding his gut as wrecked cars and shuddering buses rumbled past, raising tiny cyclones of trash and dust.

He ate half the flatbread and tossed the rest near a sewer grate, where a plump rat promptly pounced on it, hissing as it scurried back to its sewer and leaving Cooper to contemplate the border town spread before him—a sparkling mess of buzzing neon, flickering lights, and crooked buildings. He let his legs pull him toward the light.

Two hours later he'd found the cantina Ernesto had described, nestled along a row of dusty shacks down a desperate side street. A hand-painted sign outside read "La Logia." Somebody had pasted a faded Woody the Woodpecker sticker below. Under a street lamp some children were playing mumblety-peg with homemade knives.

Cooper stopped long enough to watch a skinny kid take a blade in the foot after balancing the knife on his nose and executing a fancy spin move. He pulled the knife out and hopped around howling as the others laughed.

Inside the cantina a withered woman sat behind the bar with her head pressed to a radio playing ranchero music, her hips doing little cha-cha twitches that bothered Cooper because he immediately tried to imagine her years younger, but the dark whiskers curling from her chin and the string of bright yellow peppers hanging around her neck on a piece of twine stopped him short. Without looking at him, she stepped away from the radio, popped open a bottle of beer, and set it down in front of him. It was warm.

He pushed it back across toward her. "No, *cerveza*," he said.

The woman shook her head and held up a gnarled finger to indicate she wanted money. In preparation for just such an assault on his wallet, he'd transferred a handful of pesos and American dollars to his breast pocket. The rest he'd stashed in his shoe.

The woman began to mumble and clutch at a stone amulet hidden beneath the peppers, and Cooper, fearing some ancient spell or curse, reluctantly dropped two pesos on the bar and took a sip of beer. He did not see the old woman's hands move, but when he lowered the bottle the money had disappeared and she was back at the radio fingering her pepper necklace, hips swaying slightly. He immediately figured her for some kind of witch and gave her a wide berth, taking his beer to the far end of the bar, where a pair of rough-looking men in sweaty cotton work shirts were arguing over a small cartoon clipped from a paper. The cartoon featured a rooster wearing a flak helmet and jodhpurs. The bird was saluting and puffing his chest out at a long-necked buzzard. Between them sat a single kernel of corn. He moved on and set his bags beneath him and waited, as Ernesto had instructed he should.

The plywood walls of the cantina were stained with smoke and above each chair there were brown smudges where tired and dirty men had leaned their heads back. Roaches worked the perimeter, darting out to snatch wedges of corn tortillas and other unidentifiable treasures known only to them.

By ten o'clock the place was full of men in battered boots carrying plastic shopping bags under their arms. Most managed to avoid the old woman and stood in back by the tables, drinking from sacked bottles they'd smuggled in. They seemed to be waiting for something to happen, a fight or a police raid or a pretty woman to walk by, because they never let go of their bags and every time the wafer-thin bar door shot open the men stared into the blue-black light with hopeful expressions.

Around midnight a boy entered and began to howl just as Ernesto had described. Cooper was not the only one waiting for the sign; half the bar followed the boy out through a back door. Cooper moved quickly and soon found himself in a maze of cramped alleyways running between the broken-down tar-paper shacks and aluminum huts. Rats moved in the moonlight and he could hear radios playing behind the walls, babies crying, and women shouting. Every so often he'd spot a pair of eyes staring between the slats or the pale finger of a child groping at the passing line of men.

After a while they came to a door and the boy rapped on it loudly. Seconds later it swung open to reveal a large, dark room, the windows covered with newspapers, the floor a sea of buckled tiles and dirty welcome mats. Behind a card table a shrunken old man with round glasses, pinched black eyes, and a rubbery neck sat hunkered over a clutch of yellowed foolscap. He made quick snapping motions with his hands as the men lined up in front of the table. One by one they approached the old man and were asked a series of questions before being ushered into another room.

When it was Cooper's turn the man took one look at him, pointed his mechanical pencil, and said, "Rinche?"

The men in line behind him backed away and began drawing small apple knives that had been worn to vicious-looking points from hard use. Cooper imagined himself full of pruning-knife holes, his body consigned to some foul-smelling Mexican rendering plant or shallow desert grave.

"Rinche?" the man asked again.

He shook his head and then, remembering what Ernesto had told him, said, "El Strangler," and wrapped his hand around his throat and began to strangle himself. The old man began shouting and a pair of big men in stained polyester shirts blasted through the doorway, snatched Cooper up, and dragged him deeper into the building. He struggled at first but then gave in and let the men take him, suddenly wondering if Ernesto had misled him about the coyotes and their tunnel to America.

The men opened doors with his face, jostling him down tilted, dirt-walled hallways and hustling him past a roomful of blond women lounging around a fire pit and playing a game with dice and sticks and another room, where thin-armed boys in tight pants were having some kind of slap fight, and farther along he saw the men from the cantina. They were squatting on the floor and cradling plastic milk jugs full of water as a man lectured to them, pointing at a blackboard with crude mountains and human-looking cacti chalked on it.

They came to a small grotto lit by guttering candles and hissing kerosene lanterns. Several arched tunnels spoked off the space, dark air swirling out of them.

"Wait here," said one of the men. They let him go and disappeared into the gloom.

A minute later he heard another voice, urging him to enter one of the tunnels. "Down here," it said.

A flashlight blinked and he followed it, his feet splashing through cold puddles, unsure if a good mugging lay waiting for him at the end of it all.

"Halt," the voice said. There was some giggling and Cooper saw the faint outline of others behind the flashlight holder—an illuminated hand or elbow, some boots and knees. He heard the word *gringo* several times and *hippie*, a reference, no doubt, to his long gray locks and distressed duds.

The man holding the flashlight instructed Cooper to hand over his bag. He hesitated until he heard the familiar click of a pistol and he quickly dropped the bag. Several pairs of hands began tossing the contents onto a stiff wool blanket that had been spread over the damp floor. When they got to the book, Cooper made a grab for it but was brought up short by the cold poke of gun barrel to his throat.

"Okay, okay," he said, letting them flip through the book. The flashlight beam played across the pages of tight dark script, pausing on the Mayan calendar while somebody mumbled a rosary. Then they clapped the book shut. After some discussion, they put everything back in the bag and led him deeper into the tunnel, finally arriving at a well-lit room where he saw that his guides had been teenagers sporting black concert T-shirts and plastic cowboy boots. They exited the room in a ganglike scurry, wallet chains rattling and boot heels flashing.

There were other travelers in the room, sitting on folding chairs, smoking cigars, and checking watches. In one corner stood a man in a dark suit flicking dirt off his oiled shoes with a handkerchief while a striking woman in a flimsy see-through wrap dress looked on, filing her nails and frowning.

"Is this the way to America?" Cooper asked.

A man with spiky black hair, his jeans tucked into mud-caked milking boots, swirled across the room toward Cooper to shake hands. "The Americano?" he asked.

His were the soft, uncallused hands of a mortician.

"Sort of," said Cooper. "I'm trying to get back."

"Aren't we all? Today, My name is Hicks and you are a friend of Ernesto's, correct?"

He nodded.

"Well, that Ernesto's got a line on busboys. Your average Mexican

can work the daylights out of any American. I don't know where this lazy rap got laid down. Word leaks out about siestas and suddenly the whole country's a bunch of loafs. It's simply not true."

"You have to factor in the heat."

"Good point," said Hicks. "They do move slower, that's a scientific fact, but steady. Now tell me, what did it feel like to strangle a man?"

"I don't remember."

"They say that women block out the pain of childbirth."

"I don't know about that."

"Please, I'd like to know. I am curious," Hicks said. "You see, in my line of work, violence or the threat of violence is unavoidable. When there is mayhem to be done, I contract it out. It's a buyer's market down here. You don't want to know what ten American buys."

"Okay. What would ten American buy?"

Hicks giggled. "Well, let's see. Disarticulation. Fence posting. Strappado. Some nasty stuff with car batteries and caulk guns. Fifteen dollars and some of your more desperate types will creatively hobble a mark. And squassation! I've seen the Vigils of Spain and grown men made to crawl like seals. Now, about this crime of passion . . ."

Cooper stammered. "I was in a Sauza fog and he had a knife to my throat. It was kill or be killed."

"Of course," he said. "That's your story and you're sticking to it. Now, do you have the money?"

Cooper retrieved the money from his shoe and handed Hicks a sweat-dampened mix of pesos and American currency.

"Keep it coming," said Hicks.

Cooper set aside one twenty-dollar bill. A swell of nostalgia swept over him as he stared at the rumpled sea-green face of Andrew Jackson, and he knew that whatever awaited him on the other side he would be hard-pressed to spend this last skyjacked bill.

"Keep that," said Hicks. "Twenty dollars is a down payment on prosperity, a ticket to the American dream."

"A bus ticket is more like it."

"That too." He scooped up the rest of the money with his long fingernails, tucked it into his shirt, and said, "Tell me, were there any last words?"

Cooper shook his head, not sure if they were still talking about the man he'd supposedly strangled or some problem he'd like to vent before the crossing.

"My research into this matter indicates that this is a common human reflex when confronted with sure and certain death. There are some good ones out there. For example, Thoreau said, 'Moose. Indian.' Now, I've puzzled over that one, and the same with Sam Houston, who on his deathbed said, 'Texas, Texas, Margaret'—a statesman to the end. And don't forget Stonewall Jackson, who said, 'Let us cross over the river and rest under the shade of the trees.' Pure poetry!"

"This is your hobby?"

"Some people collect stamps. But yes, it is. So when Ernesto informed me that you'd actually strangled a man I thought perhaps you'd been front row center to some last great words."

Cooper thought quickly. "He gurgled a lot."

"Animal instinct. Base and common. Plenty of that noise around here. Just open your ears around supper. You'd think they could manage the beans and rice without the grunts. No, it sounds to me like you didn't give the soon to be departed much of a chance to sum up or leave you with some small mystery. Be on the lookout next time and prick up your ears."

"There won't be a next time."

"They always say that." Hicks laughed and pinched a bead of snot off his nose. "See those men over there?" He pointed at two well-dressed but ordinary-looking men sitting on folding metal chairs reading magazines. "You don't want to know what they do for a living."

"Oh yeah?"

"They kill people," he whispered. "There is always a next time for them."

"Hit men?"

"I didn't say that, but yes. It's just a job to them. Real salt-of-the-earth types once you get to know them."

One of the men looked up and flashed some crooked enamel at Cooper as Hicks gathered the group together and prepped them on tunnel etiquette.

Cooper stared at the woman in the wrap dress and got to thinking hard about the unwrapping as several heavily tattooed men with potbellies and semiautomatics tucked under their chubby arms appeared to stand guard behind the group.

"No last names," Hicks warned the group, checking his watch. "We will be departing shortly, and remember that on the other side we must maintain silence."

The group became chatty with anticipation. The well-dressed man standing next to the woman in the wrap dress told Cooper in a Calvados-and-cigar-laden rasp that they were going shopping in Beverly Hills and that they had a car waiting to take them to a private airfield, reservations at the Four Seasons, chilled champagne, and a Star Maps tour.

The men with guns yawned and leaned against the wall as the mistress checked her lips in a black compact and complained that she had to pee.

One of the hit men offered Cooper a piece of horehound candy from a waxed paper sack. He put it in his mouth and remembered that he did not like horehound candy.

Hicks opened a door and ushered them through into the humid maw of the tunnel. Naked twenty-five-watt bulbs hung from an extension cord and cast an anemic glow over the narrow wooden walkway covering the muddy floor. Overhead the ceiling was sheathed in sheets of Visqueen where cockroaches and millipedes skittered across the plastic, sliding along small rivulets of condensation.

The well-dressed man slipped a pair of sunglasses over the mistress's eyes and took her by the hand, leading her down the twisting tunnel as if she were blind. Cooper followed behind the hit men, listening as they disagreed in Spanish about the slant six versus the straight eight.

For twenty minutes they walked through the hazy damp air, fording muddy depressions and climbing over miniature cave-ins, scampering down hand-built ladders into large cement pipes. At a cramped section of tunnel Hicks stopped, his flashlight beam landing on a hole in the ceiling. He reached up into the space, slid several pieces of plywood away, and dropped a ladder down into the tunnel. "The end of the road," he said. He whistled a few bars of "Coming to America" and slapped one of the large gunmen on the shoulder, waiting as the rest of the group climbed the ladder into the dark space above.

They emerged into a low, dusty basement just as a bank of fluorescent lights flickered to life. The floor had been attacked by orange shag carpeting and the walls were covered with tin foil and small novena cards taped in cross patterns.

Hicks climbed another set of stairs and disappeared. They heard voices and footsteps above and then the door opened and Hicks climbed down clutching a large sack of black hoods, which the gunmen distributed to the travelers.

"A precaution," Hicks said as his men began slipping the hoods over people's heads.

Cooper's hood smelled like stale beer and Skin Bracer and when he asked for another one he felt the cold finger of a gun barrel fit itself neatly under his ear.

He turned and saw the gunman glaring at him. "You not like?" the man asked. "We can find another head for the mask, amigo." He had tiny pupils and the scarred brow of a professional wrestler and Cooper figured he'd shot and stabbed a few people in his short, violent life, so he slipped the hood back on and did his best to avoid the crusty parts.

Next their hands were threaded through a knotted rope and they were tugged out of the basement and into the night, where cars peeled by in the distance and dogs barked and Cooper thought he heard a woman's voice calling for someone named Shane.

Half a mile down the road a vehicle approached and skidded to a halt, gravel crunching under its tires, U-joints rattling.

He heard Hicks say hello.

And Cooper, sensing trouble, pushed his hood up and looked out with one eye. The truck's headlights silhouetted armies of looming cacti and crippled juniper trees with deformed beer cans and old plastic jugs under them like Christmas presents. The stars hung pasted in the sky and the night air came at him in warm gusts.

There were two men in a blue-and-white Ford pickup. Behind the wheel sat a pale, fat dude with timid muttonchops running down his jowls. Next to him was a man with a greasy baseball hat pulled over his stringy hair. A pump shotgun and a Louisville Slugger hung on a gun rack behind them.

The driver leaned out and stroked his muttonchops. "Look, Don, I think we just found one of them desert execution rituals I heard about on Jimmy Swaggert. Satanic in nature, no doubt."

The one called Don said, "Where's the strange demonic music? The buxom women and pentagrams?"

Hicks spoke up. "It's nothing of the sort. These are wards of the state hospital afflicted with a little lunar sensitivity and some mild facial deformity. We do not wish to frighten the populace. You fellows have a good night, now."

The passenger tapped the driver. "Melonheads, Bruce. Traveling under the cover of night. God sure does make his mistakes. Remember that thing the Millard boy had growing out of his neck. They said it was his unborn twin brother."

Bruce nodded and squinted at the gunmen, who were doing their best to conceal the rifles. He dug a finger into his ear, twisted, and then inspected it before wiping it on the cab ceiling. He said, "Shoot, it takes all sorts. Must be on their way to get their heads drained or something. Wish I had my camera."

The men giggled and for a minute Cooper expected to hear the rap of gunfire. Instead one of the men tossed a beer can and shouted, "Gawdamn freaks!" Hicks suppressed the gunmen with a look as the men punched the gas and sped away into the night.

They continued walking and arrived at a pole barn. Hicks hurried them through a large sliding aluminum door and told them they were allowed to remove the hoods. Cooper peeled his off and dropped it to the floor as he took in the barn. The walls were festooned with old bingo boards and election signs that read "DEL FRISK IS THE LAW!" And "ELECT GOODELL FOR SHERRIF," "TOM BED IS THE FUTURE," and "VOTE JIMMY SHOAT FOR COUNTY COMMISSIONER." In one corner chairs and tables were stacked neatly and in the other sat several busted voting machines with bumper stickers all over them proclaiming, "We've come for your daughters" and "Tastes like chicken," and a long one that read: "I do not recognize your law, jumbled together as it is by the nobodies of bygone centuries and I do not recognize the decision of the court.— L. Lingg." Another one depicted a fist clutching a shock of wheat with the word "RISE" written under it.

The gunmen started horsing around, trading gut punches, and laughing. Cooper remembered a story about Houdini dying of a ruptured spleen three days after letting a man punch him in just such a manner, but said nothing.

A black limousine pulled up outside the door in a cloud of dust and the well-dressed man and his mistress quickly stepped into it. Then a van arrived to collect the hit men. One by one the travelers were picked up and whisked away without so much as a good-bye or nod to Hicks and his men, until only Cooper remained clutching his bag, his face still smelling of stale beer and aftershave.

"End of the line, killer," said Hicks. "The bus station is that way about five miles. Avoid the thumb express. This county is downright hostile to hitchhikers. Those boys we ran into are just the sort to snag an unsuspecting traveler and tie him to a fence post or fling him into a cactus patch. My advice is to put Arizona in your rearview and avoid the Border Patrol."

"I'll make haste."

So he set off toward the glitter of town, groping his way along the flatness and watching for headlights. Locusts flew at him and tangled themselves in his hair. Snakes slithered off the blacktop to hunt mice as cattle lowed over the symphony of crickets and tractor trailers air braking in the distance. As he walked the dark, baked earth Cooper felt surprisingly unlike the fugitive he'd pretended to be all those years in Mexico. In fact, the man who'd jumped out of a plane for all the right reasons seemed to have vanished from him now that he was back in America, and he felt as if he'd been cheated out of a little criminal glory, a glory that he knew he had no chance of recovering. No, he thought, what was left was to get in and get out and then go back to what now passed as his life, even if that meant a petting zoo filled with carnivorous tapirs or the occasional chat with uncomfortable tourists who talked to him merely because they were happy to see a familiar pale face. He let out a deep breath and kept walking.

■

ON SUNDAY MORNING Frank drove down to the marina to work on the boat with his father-in-law, Walt, steering the Buick through the sparse traffic, rapping his finger against the dash to Monk's "Crepuscule with Nellie," anticipating the stuttered silent dead spots. By the time the tune trinkled to an end he was at the marina. He parked and got out, grabbing a lungful of damp river air as he tried to rub the kink from his stiff neck. He'd not heard from Anne and had ignored two calls from Peck and was trying not to think about it.

He walked across the lot. Sunlight broke in uneven spokes through patchy gray clouds while a slight breeze rippled the bank of maples lining the riverbank, their leaves already weak and yellow in anticipation of fall. He nodded at two boat jocks gathering their scrapers and orbital sanders in five-gallon buckets from the back of a panel van.

They nodded back and continued grumbling at each other, one sucking hard on a cigarette and wincing. "I'm tired of workin' for this asshole," the other man said.

The older one took one last drag and pinched out the cigarette. "Beats retail," he said. "This guy can bark all he wants, we're billin' and it's gonna be a tall one."

Walt was waiting for him at the gate, holding a brown sack with

Styrofoam cups of coffee in it. "Got some of the good stuff," he said. "You take cream? I couldn't remember."

"Yes."

They shook hands, Walt giving him the usual hearty clamp, saying, "Ready to get to work?"

Frank nodded and followed him over to where the boat lay drydocked. Walt had bought the boat from a recently widowed woman in the neighborhood whose husband had died of prostate cancer. The boat was one of several the man had owned and the one most in need of repair and therefore, as Walt said, "The price was right. I'd be losing money not to buy it." A harbor master Walt knew had inspected it for him and declared that it had "good bones" and that most of the work to be done was interior and cosmetic, maybe some updates on the engine or even a new one. Frank was skeptical the boat would ever see open ocean but was surprised at how much he enjoyed the time they spent prying up the boat's carpeting, caulking seams, and repairing damaged cleats.

After peeling away the blue tarps and folding them in neat squares, Frank pulled out the stepladder and climbed on deck. Walt scampered up behind, coffee sack clenched between his teeth.

They'd been working on the boat for almost a year. At first Frank had merely pitched in—awkwardly holding the tape measure as Walt scrawled measurements on scraps of two-by-four and stood pulling at his beard, staring at plans he'd copied from restoration guides and shaking his head, saying, "This doesn't make any goddamn sense!"

Gradually, they found a rhythm and by June they'd gutted the old cabinets, installed soffits, and hung new doors, the usual stilted back-and-forth between them disappearing, and for long stretches it was just two men working. They talked about all sorts of things, even the women, but mostly Walt told stories about his days as a geologist and the dirty tricks the oil company employed to get the natives to go along with their plans.

Before they had the first piece of top trim in place Walt's voice dropped to a solemn whisper as he told Frank how the oil company had wiped out a whole village down in Central America.

Frank had heard the story already, but still he listened, nodding in all the right places, letting Walt confess as he set a nail, remembering to blunt the tip so that it didn't crack the wood going in.

"The drillers hit some sort of gas pocket. Ostensibly, I was sent in to write checks, but what they really wanted to know was if any of the oil could be salvaged and, if so, were there gonna be a bunch of lawyers or witch doctors standin' in the way. The military had ordered that the bodies be left where they'd fallen. It was horrible—women collapsed in front of the well, children with toys clutched in their tiny hands, old men in their beds. And the smell, I'll never forget that smell. It got into our clothes and we had to burn everything, even our shoes."

Walt was quiet a moment, busying himself resetting the chop saw. Then he looked at Frank. "You ever smell that smell?"

Frank said he had but he did not elaborate.

They worked for a solid two hours, cutting and nailing, taking a break only after Frank ran a sliver under his thumbnail and couldn't stop the bleeding. After wrapping his thumb in a wad of paper towel, he went up on deck and sat watching the clouds soften on the low horizon. His thumb throbbed and the work had done nothing to dull the restless anticipation that had been with him since he'd rolled out of bed.

The sight of a gull alighting on a nearby piling brought the pond girl back to him. He remembered the chill as he groped along the ruined dock all those years ago, water bleeding up his arm as he waited for her hand to come into his.

Spooked, he climbed back down and found Walt sitting on one of the built-in storage bins reading an old newspaper. He looked tired, the red-faced eagerness he'd greeted Frank with earlier long gone.

"Something the matter?" Frank asked, reaching for the tape measure. He took a minute to appreciate the progress they'd made. All that was needed after the trim was some paint and stain and then they would be ready for the fittings and knobs.

"Did you know I cheated on Mary?"

Although he was used to the non sequiturs Walt frequently lobbed into conversations, he focused on peeling back the blood-soaked paper towel. "Look, Walt, you don't . . ."

Walt chuckled and waved him off. "Long time ago with this girl in Penang."

Frank tried to go back to work but Walt had already launched into his story. "A whole team of us had been sent to Malaysia to look for oil," he said. "I met her in this bar, a disco, if I remember correctly. She asked for cash up front and then she gave me the menu, like it was McDonald's. There wasn't much she wouldn't do. I picked the number six and we had a good time. You know, I never asked her name and it's always sort of bothered me."

"Why are you telling me this?"

"Don't worry, I'm not asking you to trade secrets with me."

"What secrets?"

Walt gave him one of his patented dirty old man winks and said, "Like I said, I'm not asking. It's just for some reason I've been seeing her face lately—the girl, I mean. At the time it just seemed like one of those things you do and sweep under the rug. I was drunk and lonely, but that's no excuse and even now if I could go back and take a mulligan on the whole thing, I'm not so sure I would. I was a very good boy after that and maybe I had to get it out of my system."

Frank made a tick mark on the wall. "Guilt warps the mind a little."

"Well then, I'm warped. I even thought about going to confession."

"But you're not Catholic."

"I don't think that's a requirement anymore." He put the level on the corner bead and shook his head as the bubble floated off true. "It came to a head yesterday."

"What?"

"This thing with the girl. I was out cleaning the grill when I see Peggy Dunne, our next-door neighbor, putting pine bark mulch down in her flower beds. She was up on all fours and had on these short shorts, do you know what I mean?"

"No, I don't."

"She's forty-something, short black hair." He set the level down and threw up his hands. "Hell, she had these little bits of bark that kept sticking to her thighs and I couldn't stop staring at her. Every few minutes she'd reach back and brush it off—that's when I started thinking about that girl in Penang. I must have been standing there for ten minutes when Mary caught me and I had to listen to her call me a letch all night. I can't help it—I've got these tiny desires that come and go and I no longer know why. One gets mixed up with another and I guess it's part of getting old."

"Happens to the best of us."

Walt nodded in agreement. "Sure as shit does."

Later, after the tools had been stowed and they were sharing a beer, Walt reached out his hand to thank him. But Frank knew that the handshake meant much more: it was a sign that what had been spoken of on the boat was to be kept between them, locked away in the man vault along with all the other transgressions and unacted-upon desires his coworkers and friends had unburdened on him over the years. Frank shook.

With a few hours to kill, Frank drove east out of town, through Gresham, past churches and gas stations and schools. The Buick ate the road as trees, trucks, and the brief, anxious faces of fellow travelers whisked by outside the window and Mount Hood loomed in the distance, high, white, and heavenly, lording over the dense roil of green. Twice he stopped at roadside bars, figuring he'd get a beer and find someone to talk to, but he couldn't bring himself to go inside, pulling up short of the doors with a tightness in his chest, as if he was still on duty and the only possible reason he could have for entering a bar before five o'clock would be to flash a picture of a dead girl around or maybe a grainy photo of an unshaven man, medium build, brown eyes, last seen with . . . or was it to stop his trembling hands and thoughts of Anne? But when he looked in the rearview mirror at his own grizzled reflection he knew that he'd somehow come unraveled. What scared him was how quickly it had happened and not knowing what if anything he could do to correct it.

By the time he arrived home it had begun to rain and his neighbor, Chap Taylor, a retired Fuller Brush man, was out clearing leaves from the drain grate at the end of his driveway. He turned away from Frank's headlights and tossed a quick hello wave over his shoulder before going back to the drain. Two years ago Chap's basement had flooded and Frank had helped him haul the waterlogged carpeting out of the basement. They'd worked late into the night peeling back the bubbled paneling and setting up fans. He remembered the look on Chap's face when they'd found an old photo of his wife behind the paneling, floating in an inch of dirty water. In the photo she stood on a dock dressed in green hip waders, smiling, still handsome for her fifty-three years. She'd suffered from lupus and heart problems and died during Lucy's sophomore year at college, and Frank's only memory of the funeral was of driving his daughter back to college after the service and marveling at her inability to listen to any one radio station for more than half a song. That and he suspected her of sneaking cigarettes when they stopped for bathroom breaks. It had been all he could do to not lecture her.

He parked the car in the garage, wiped his shoes on the coconut husk mat, and stared at Lucy's old ten-speed bike hanging from a joist hook right above his fishing gear. The tape had come off the bike's handlebars and a large black-and-yellow spider had spun a snarled web in the spokes. He blew on the web and watched the spider flinch into a ball.

Clare was on the couch wearing faded Levi's and a long blouse from Nordstrom that he'd bought for her last year for Christmas after she'd showed it to him and given him her size. She was glancing at a sheet of listings and watching a television program. On the coffee table sat a half-eaten salad and a wine glass trimmed with lipstick stains. She looked up at him and blew a strand of hair from her face, tossed the listings aside, and unfolded her legs.

"Where have you been then?" she asked.

"I was helping your father on the boat, remember?"

"How did that go?"

"It went."

"I don't like that he's being so cagey about his plans for that boat. He called and left a number for a garage-door repairman he said you needed. I asked him about the boat and he just changed the subject."

"No comment."

"Thick as thieves," she said, rolling her eyes. "Is there something wrong with our garage door? It opened fine for me."

After rinsing dried blood from his finger, he took a can of beer from the fridge and pressed it against his eyes before opening it. He drank until his throat hurt. "Harvey broke the garage door and I can't fix it."

"His lease is up for renewal in two months."

"Don't worry, it's taken care of, Clare. It was his girlfriend, or so he says."

"Harvey has a girlfriend?"

"Had. I didn't get into it with him." He took another sip of beer and put the can back against his aching eyes.

"Well, that's a relief. I was beginning to worry about him. He struck me as someone, well, let's just say I wouldn't want to look under his mattress." She shook her wineglass at him. "Can you get me another splash?"

He took it from her and went into the kitchen to refill it.

"What did you do after?"

"After what?"

"After the top-secret boat stuff with my father?"

"I took a drive."

She nodded and turned her attention back to the television as he emptied his pockets of loose change, dropping the coins into a clay pot Lucy had made for them in her high school art class. Her name was scratched on the side next to a crooked rising sun.

After slipping off his shoes, he sat down next to Clare, the hum of the road still buzzing in his palms, and for a moment he understood the allure of long-haul trucking and piloting large charter buses full of tourists to Vegas for weekend gambling junkets. It got you numb.

"Take a look at the ad on the table there," she said.

Frank looked at a section of the *Oregonian* that had been folded in quarters. Circled in yellow highlighter was the new Find-a-Home Realty strip ad. Instead of a smiling Olive it showed a cutout photo of Clare. She wasn't smiling, but under her face was the slogan NOW IS THE TIME TO BUY! CALL CLARE MARSHALL FOR YOUR DREAM HOME WHILE RATES HOLD. "Wanna know what I did for that?" She raised an eyebrow at him.

"I read in a magazine that you shouldn't joke about those sort of things."

He took one last look at the cropped photo of his Clare floating over the listings like a face on a milk carton and dropped the paper back on the table.

Clare filled the silence with the rest of her day, the phone calls, offers made, offers declined, and people whom she'd spent way too much time pacing property with. "The Donnelys made an offer on the duplex," she said, nudging Frank. "It's a good solid offer. And that Bob Milton finally came down off his perch and accepted market value for his tacky split-level. It needs a lot of work. Did you know he was a pilot for Northwest? Frank . . . hello . . . is there anybody in there? Just nod if you can hear me."

Frank grunted, rose from the couch, and while Clare continued her story fixed himself a chip-chopped ham sandwich with onions, horseradish, and mayo, looking up to nod at her over the counter.

"You're not listening to me," she said.

"I've heard everything." He grabbed another beer from the fridge, sat wearily at the counter separating the two rooms, and looked out the window where Chap was still out in the rain poking at the grate, his face stern and shadowy like a longshoreman's.

"Come watch this with me," she said, pointing at the screen where the actress was cradling her dead man in an alley while an old woman with a kind face looked on from a doorway. "I'll fill you in."

The scene shifted to the heroine delivering the bad news to a slatternly woman sprawled on a tangled bed.

"I can see it from here. That's her mother, right?"

Clare nodded. "Why must all alcoholic women get drunk and walk around the house in a slip?"

He finished his sandwich and beer and Clare groaned and said to no one in particular, "I didn't see that one coming." On the television the actress was buying a gun from a potbellied pawnshop owner. There was a close-up of her admiring the weight of the gun as the pawnshop ape scratched his perfectly grizzled jowls and looked on impatiently.

He put his dish in the sink and rinsed the empty beer can, setting it in a paper bag full of other empties. After drying his hands on a green- and white-checked tea towel, he went into the living room and stood behind Clare, watching as the actress slugged a punching bag with grim determination.

"I like that she's taking charge of her situation. She's determined not to be a victim."

"I think I'm going to go upstairs and read a little. It's good about the ad. I'm happy for you," he said, touching her absently on the shoulder. She turned, gave him a quick smile, and let him go.

Later she crawled into bed next to him and pressed herself against his back, stroking his stomach. At first he tried to ignore her and feign sleep but then he thought of Anne Blackwood and just as Clare was about to give up he rolled toward her and spread her legs apart with his knee, fumbling to lift her nightgown. He shut his eyes and pulled her on top, entering her quickly, Anne still floating through his thoughts. They moved wordlessly against each other as rain smeared down the gutters and eaves outside. She let him slide nearly out of her, waiting as he trembled beneath her, groping in the dark for her breasts. He shoved back and she let him have all of it, his motions becoming uneven until he gave in, and in the hush that followed he felt the weight wrap itself around his chest and squeeze him off into sleep without his speaking a word to her.

CHAPTER TEN

ooper called the number Ernesto had given him but got no answer and so he decided to keep moving north, hitching a ride with a woman from Yuma named Shelly who had a pierced nose and wore black combat boots with orange laces and claimed to be an antiques dealer. She made a point of telling him that she'd never picked up a hitchhiker and that her old man looked like Steve McQueen with long hair and tattoos. "He has a temper and fixes cars," she said.

He told her he'd been in Mexico.

"I'm really vibing on this conversation," Shelly said, catching a lock of windblown hair and sucking on it as her foot fluttered un-evenly on the gas pedal.

She dropped him in Tucson, where he fell in with a pod of bums he'd met behind the bus station fighting over an old air conditioner someone had set out with the trash. The men wore tattered blazers and funny hats and regarded him with suspicion as they traveled from shadow to shadow in the vain hope of avoiding another day spent under the relentless sunny broil of southern Arizona. It was

Cooper's hope that they'd lead him to some flophouse or perhaps even one of those free church meals with ginger-aled ham, over-cooked green beans, and Jell-O carrot salad. But when he suggested they pitch a penny or shoot even-odd to settle the air conditioner dispute, the men turned on him.

"You're not one of us," said one of the bums. "How do I know that? Well, for one, your fingernails are too clean and you're too jaunty."

"Jaunty?"

"He's an undercover reporter is what he is. I mean, look at his hair and those beady eyes. He's got us on the record, boys, so look out."

"No, I'm not a reporter, I'm looking for a ride," said Cooper.

One of them shouted, "Who, what, where, why, when."

Their leader fronted Cooper. "Just what the world needs is an-other heartwarming story about the less fortunate and how we used to be productive members of society. Pound-salt hack! I shot dope for twenty years. Hobart likes little girls. Vic here stabbed a man in Libby, isn't that right, Vic?"

"Twenty-six times," said Vic, a rheumy-eyed man with skin the color of wet cardboard.

"Look," said Cooper. "I just wanted to know if anybody knew of a ride out of this town."

The lead bum turned on him. "We don't believe in internal com-bustion engines, pal. We walk to wherever it is we want to get to."

They laughed and left Cooper to place yet another call to Ernesto's buddy, Lou Brutus. On the third ring someone picked up who wasn't Lou and told him to wait right where he was, that an escort would be by soon to take him to Lou.

Two hours later a man sauntered down the alley carrying a wooden tennis racket with no strings, which he pointed at Cooper. "My street name's Mother," he said. "State your business." Despite the heat and sun the man had on three T-shirts and flat canvas shoes with smiley faces inked on the white rubber toes.

"I'm a friend of Ernesto's," said Cooper. "He gave me the number, said this Lou would give me a ride."

"I don't know any Ernesto. Is he Mexican?"

"He lives in Mexico."

"Same difference. Now come on if you're coming," Mother said. "If you try anything I'll wrap this racket around your neck and strangle you." He swished the racket back and forth a few times and then offered his hand. They shook and walked, Mother telling him how he'd worked on fishing boats and how later he and his crew had poured form for the Saint Louis Arch. "Now look at me," he said. "I'm all worked out. My pride's so far gone that when some soft-handed dude refers to concrete as cement I don't get in his face and explain the difference anymore. How about you?"

"I figured the work swindle out a while ago and took decisive action."

"Did you marry up?"

"No."

"Embezzle?"

"That takes work."

"Hit the lottery?"

Cooper shook his head. "I'd rather drop silver dollars down sewer grates."

"Don't tell me you're one of them wandering Buddha types. I don't wanna hear none of that crap about how all a man needs is a good walking stick and a rice bowl."

"No, I took a lump sum settlement."

"Well, goody for you. I woulda been better off in life guarding retarded children at Kreppler's Home for the Challenged or collecting late fees for the Jeffersonville public library. But no, I went and worked with my hands and built things. Now, are ya hungry?" Mother flipped up the lid of a nearby Dumpster, rummaged around, and pulled out a pizza box. Inside was a cold anchovy and pineapple pie and Mother ripped off a piece, folded it like a taco, and began eating. Cooper took a slice from the grease-stained box and inspected it for bugs and stray hairs before taking a bite. The cheese tasted like plastic plates and the anchovies clung like salty little fingers to the roof of his mouth. But the pineapples were worth it; they burst across his tongue like sunsets.

Mother ate without chewing, swallowing the slice in greedy gulps and quickly shoving another piece into his shirt pocket. "Look here," he said, pulling out a bent half-smoked butt and sparking up. "You run into that shrimp Bragg, you give him this and tell him it's from me." He punched Cooper on the arm. "He puts up a fuss, tell him to shut his hole and pass it down the line."

"Who's Bragg? I don't know any Bragg."

"There's something wrong with his head—it got caught between his mommy's legs, I think. You just give him that punch for me. Remember, right arm, and make sure to twist and give him a little knuckle or, if you're so inclined, slap some of that Asian shit on him. Either way I want his soup arm aching. Do you know that Neil Young song, 'Everybody Knows This Is Nowhere?' "

"How's it go?"

"Forget it. You want me to sing for you so you can make fun of me. I know your type—stand around and make fun of people dancing and dog-faced women. Now let's go. Best not to keep Lou waiting—he's busy. He's got a schedule to keep."

Cooper asked where he'd parked.

Mother's brow drooped. "It's been the shoe leather express for me ever since my Vega bit the dust. Let me tell you that pride and craftsmanship took a vacation on that model, make, and year. Detroit rolled that baby off the assembly at beer-thirty on a Friday."

"Was it the transmission?"

"Nah, it was a three-speed and punks kept sticking potatoes in the tailpipe after I tripped one of their gang and smashed his skateboard to splinters. But that wasn't what did the Vega in. Bad gas or sugar in the tank is my suspicion, but there was no use in investigating something like that. It was the third bad thing to happen and I just took my lumps and moved on."

"I don't believe in the law of threes."

"Neither do I. Shortly thereafter I lost the apartment and the wife. Four and five, if you're keeping score at home. I am not bitter. I occasionally walk with Christ as it helps at the soup kitchens, plus I'm not a doper."

Mother took off swishing the racket in front of him and Cooper followed, still chewing pizza crust. They walked past a muffler shop featuring a giant revolving muffler and down a long and busy avenue lined with several dead or dying knickknack shops. They passed diners, Jenn's Hair Jungle, Pete's Great Frame-Up, and narrow brick stores that sold used vacuums and heating and air-conditioning supplies. The streets were full of old white-haired men who walked with a slowness Cooper attributed to swollen prostates and the tremendous heat billowing off the cement.

After ten blocks the heat and the pizza began to take their toll on Cooper. His sweat retreated, his vision wobbled, and his arms felt like lead balloons. He thought he saw crows following him, swooping down off high-tension wires, black against the blue sky. But when he looked again they were gone.

They came to a hole in the Cyclone fencing and ducked through it, emerging into a sea of smashed cars stacked one on top of each other. Aisles of discarded appliances lined an entire border of the lot and in the center of it all lay a collapsed scrap crane, a tower of busted oak pallets, and a pyramid of old oil drums containing various cancerous chemical stews that, judging by the body count, were irresistible to insects and small rodents.

Mother walked past the crane toward an urban campground populated by Pace Arrows and ancient Winnebagos set on cinder blocks. Mangy-looking dogs stood panting in front of a few of them and around the corner a narrow, potholed alley hooked back out to the street.

A woman, her face masked with cold cream, leaned out one of the trailers and shouted, "We don't want none."

They kept walking.

Parked at the end of the alley, under a listing plastic awning, sat a large butterscotch-colored panel van with bubble windows, chrome rims, flared running boards, sunroof, shag-carpeted dash, and dual exhaust cherry bombers. Airbrushed on the side of the van were two flaming eagles soaring over a lake of fire. On the other side there was a half-finished torso of a topless Amazon stringing a bow and a man riding a customized chopper.

Mother rapped on a window. The door slid open to reveal a pudgy guy wearing thick glasses and a T-shirt with a big zero on it. He had a wiry mop of black hair raked over in a swirl across his skull, a weak chin, and coffee-stained teeth.

"Hello, Mother," he said, stepping out of the van, his undone belt buckle clinking as he rubbed his stomach and squinted into the brightness. "You the one who called my answering service?"

"Cooper," said Cooper, stepping up to shake hands.

"Like Gary?"

"I guess."

"Okay, Cooper, my name's Lou Brutus. What do you want and how did you get my number?"

"Ernesto said you might be able to help."

"Yes, I remember, he called and told me you were coming. He said your name was Irv, though."

"Did he?"

"Which is it? Cooper or Irv?"

He thought quickly and decided he didn't give a shit, "You can call me Cooper."

Lou nodded. "Was my service courteous?"

"I don't understand."

"The gal on the phone, did she have good phone manners?"

"I'd say she was about average."

"That's what I suspected. Now, what did you say you needed?"

"I need a ride."

"A ride to where?"

"Oregon."

Mother interrupted. "Hey, Lou, you don't happen to have anything to drink?"

Lou pointed to a battered aluminum cooler just inside the van. "Grape Tang. Help yourself."

Mother went for it, taking up a crushed Dixie cup and drizzling some dark fluid from the spigot.

"Oregon?" Lou said. "Well, it's your lucky day, Cooper. Not only do I owe Ernesto—yes, hard to believe but I do—but I happen to be heading northwesterly."

"This tastes a bit off," Mother said, pointing to the cooler. "It's got a little whang to it. You sure this is Tang?"

"I spiked it."

"With what?"

"Avoid operating heavy machinery."

"Hey, man," Mother said. "I hope you're joking."

Lou ignored him and turned to Cooper again. "Where exactly in Oregon do you want to get to?"

"I want to be vague about that."

"I suppose you have a story to tell but no expense money to offer," he said.

"I wanna know what you spiked the Tang with, Lou," Mother shouted. "I don't even take aspirin. Reality's bad enough."

"Relax, Mother, take a holiday. You asked for Grape Tang, I gave you Grape Tang. Now deal."

"I'm not conning you," Cooper said. "I just need to get to Oregon and retrieve something."

"If it's lost love, count me out," Lou said.

"No, it's not that."

"Again with the vagueness. I like it. And still you haven't asked me why I'm heading that way or where exactly I'm going or where I've been. Why, I could be a serial murderer setting out on a spree or a traveling insurance swindler. The point is you don't know, do you?"

"Okay, what do you do?"

"I'm a freelance delivery boy. Coast to coast and under the table with an ironclad no-questions-asked policy. Just yesterday I delivered a pair of lemurs. Before that it was a briefcase to a man in Kingman. Now, what about you?"

"It'll give us something to talk about."

Cooper watched as Mother pried the lid off the cooler and fished around in the Tang until he came up with a handful of half-dissolved capsules.

"Dexatrim," said Lou. "I'm trying to shake a few pounds for the ladies. The waitress at Denny's told me I had a potbelly. And she was right. The post–high school years have been rough. Can you believe that I used to throw the javelin and wear a size 32?"

"Is that all you spiked the Tang with?"

"Merely boosters. Expect the real kick in the ass in about forty-two minutes."

Mother began to drool. "I can't feel my face and my toes won't stop curling."

"You're imagining things, Mother. It's much better than that."

Mother turned to Cooper. "You're on your own. I've got to go lay down and sleep this off in the library."

When he was gone, Lou asked, "Some Tang?"

"Maybe later."

"A real Stoic, set jaw, roll stone, grin and bear it. Life's a bitch and then you die."

"I like Tang fine with vodka or rum or just plain for breakfast, but I don't wanna end up like Mother until I get this ride stuff straightened out."

"Ending up like Mother would take some work, monumental bad luck, not to mention a matching IQ and body temperature."

"Couple of wrong turns and who knows."

"Perhaps."

Cooper asked about the zero on Lou's T-shirt.

"This?" Lou pulled up the hem, exposing his blue-veined gut. "I had a gross of them printed up back when I was a nihilist. I gave them away to skateboarders and those men you see hanging out at donut shops late at night chain-smoking and bitching about the government. Problem was people kept confusing nihilism with anarchism. I didn't sell too many. Since then I've scooted over to the skeptic camp."

"I have absolutely no idea what you're talking about."

Out of the corner of his eye Cooper saw a woman dart across the lot and execute a rugged-looking commando dive behind a pillar of tires.

Lou continued. "Not that it matters, but I subscribe to certain newsletters and belong to a dedicated but far-flung platoon of like-minded people. We debunk things and expose phonies. We recently made a move to topple the Masons but seem to have run out of steam on that front. Our ideological supply lines were too long and the Masons circled their wagons. We've decided to go after random church nuts instead and put a few victories under our belt. Just last month I had words with some of them Noah's Ark dingalings up in Colorado Springs. They have all sorts of numbers and measurements and meet in dank church basements to drink warm apple juice and discuss cubits. That astronaut Irwin's got them all hopped up about funding his expeditions to Mount Ararat. So I lied and told them I had some ark timbers I wanted to lecture about and then I bashed them with some cool, hard reasoning before they had me tossed out. Say, you don't have a gas card on you? I like traveling with a gas card."

"No."

"Big oil pretty much runs the show in this country. Do you agree with that statement?"

"It's likely."

"You bet your hippie ass it is. One of them sheiks calls up Reagan and shit happens—missiles fly, small Latin American countries get invaded and poked full of oil wells. You have nothing against credit cards, do you? What about bar codes? I've been meeting a lot of folks who fear some kind of bar-coded future where babies are born with them."

"I'm okay with those too," said Cooper. "Now, about this ride." He sat and removed the twenty-dollar bill from his shoe. "I have this. But I'd rather not spend it. The bill holds some sentimental value for me. But when we get to where we're going I'll give you five times that and split gas right down the middle."

"Sentimental value?"

"It's a long story."

"And I'll hear all the gory details if I give you a ride, is that it?"

"Something like that." Cooper pointed to the pile of tires. "Did you know there's a woman watching us over there?"

Lou ducked against the van. "Was she skinny and have chapped lips?"

"Is she your girlfriend or something?"

"She's delusional is what she is—not bad to look at in dim lighting and with a couple of beers in you, but she's completely Looney

Tunes. I can't help myself. Once you have a woman off her meds you don't want 'em any other way. They're unpredictable, emotional, and if you catch them on an upswing, hellcats in bed."

"She's not armed and out for revenge, is she?"

"Alice would only hurt herself. She's a cutter." He stood in front of the van and shouted toward the tires. "Alice, I'm not taking you with me. I was very clear about that, sugarpop. Now, we had our moment and I'll cherish the memories, but it's over—do you hear me?"

There was no answer and he crept back to where Cooper stood in the shade of the plastic awning.

"One night of empty, meaningless sex and I owe her something? I don't think so."

A crying sound came from behind the tires and Cooper looked over at Lou.

"It's a trap, plug your ears," he said. "She's a siren."

"Maybe she skinned her knee."

"I'm warning you, she looks like a praying mantis, and unless you want to be a cricket in her claws, you'd do well to keep your distance."

But the tiny sniffles and hitched-up sobs got to Cooper and he made his way across to her, stepping over broken glass and rusted coils that poked out of the earth like alien fossils. He found her sitting behind a wall of bald radials, a thin whip of a girl with nice hair, feathered back off her skull. But Lou was right; with her massive gray eyes, hard chin, and crooked mouth struggling to contain the jumble of teeth, she did indeed resemble a praying mantis.

She looked up at Cooper and knuckled a snot bead off the tip of her nose. "Who are you?" she asked.

"I'm a friend of Lou's and I wanted to see if you were okay." The van started up behind him. "It's Alice, right?"

She nodded and straightened her dress in a way that made Cooper's heart flood with pity. "I brought him some flowers," she said, pulling a limp collection of yellowed carnations and tattered tulips from behind her back. "All I want is to say good-bye. Is that too much to ask? Ever since he gave me that hickey he's been avoiding me even though I snuck up and I watched him sleep last night. You know, I could have smothered him with his own pillow but I restrained myself because I'm a good girl. I was brought up right."

"I can't speak for Lou, but the flowers are nice and I'm sure he appreciates you not feeding him the pillow." He took the flowers from her. "I'll make sure he gets these."

Her eyes dilated unevenly as she chewed strips of dead skin from her lips. "I haven't slept in five whole days after what he did to me. He read me poetry and took off my pants and it's like he turned something on in me that I can't turn off."

He started to say something but was cut short when the van pulled to a skidding stop behind him. The door swung open and Lou leaned across and shouted, "Let's deploy!"

Alice sprang to her feet and charged just as Cooper backpedaled and dove inside the van and Lou hit the pedal, tires spitting gravel as it scurried across the lot. They watched Alice chase after them, her arms windmilling in grief, tears sparkling in the sun, brighter than all the broken glass and bits of shattered chrome littering the crummy lot. For a moment Cooper believed that the creature he saw chasing the van would hound Lou to the ends of the earth.

When they broke out onto the main drag Cooper set the flowers on the carpeted dash. "These are for you," he said.

Lou grabbed the flowers, took a deep whiff, and lobbed them out the window, where they landed on the hood of a passing Lincoln Continental. The driver, a trim black man with pink palms, gunned past the van and shot them the finger.

"It's the thought that counts," Lou said. "Now let's blow this pop stand, Cooper. Anchors away and all that good shit."

■

FRANK PHONED THE Bureau and asked for Peck. He got a recording and left a brief message. Downstairs he drank cup after cup of coffee until his stomach soured and the inside of his cheeks peeled. He skimmed the headlines and checked the police blotter, thinking maybe J. B. Blackwood had made some violent mistake. But as he scanned the bulleted names and litany of their alleged crimes—DUIs, petty possession, shoplifting, domestic disturbance, break-ins, and bar fights—he chided himself for entertaining the thought that resolution with Blackwood would come so easily. It was more likely that nothing would happen, that the phone call and threat of a return was a one-time deal and Anne would be forced to fret and worry every time the phone rang or a car crept past her window.

He wanted to call Anne but decided to wait, putting it off by imagining that at this very minute her trailer was already full of agents peppering her with questions, chucking back cheese Danish, and guzzling her Folgers.

After glancing at the calendar and seeing the dates of their visit to Lucy circled, he called his daughter. As he accounted for his days he experienced the usual long, alien silences of all father-daughter talks and the small pangs of amazement and dread that this person on the other line was no longer his little girl but a woman who, like her mother, demanded not only his attention but his respect as well and whose demands he would end up ducking out on if she were still at home, the same way he ducked out on Clare. He'd learned to let them talk at him.

"Mom says you're coming for a visit next week," Lucy said brightly. "And Dad, I'm telling you now that I don't want to hear anything about how unsafe the neighborhood is, okay?"

Remembering the male voice on the message she'd left for him, Frank asked if there was somebody he needed to meet.

"Dad, please. That's another off-limits topic."

"Okay, okay, I was just . . ."

"I know what you're doing," she said, "but you're on a need-to-know basis." She laughed and quickly changed the subject, telling him about her boss, a tall lady named Cass who went around the office dropping inspirational memos and Ziggy cartoons on the workers' desks.

When he hung up he dressed to go jogging but couldn't bring himself to lurch out the door and down the street, so he dialed Anne's number and got her machine but did not leave a message. Worried, he peeled off his running shorts, changed back into a pair of khakis and a pressed denim shirt, and went to see why she hadn't answered the phone, all sorts of bad scenarios tilting through his thoughts.

He drove the whole way in a trance, the world crushed down to the twenty feet of blacktop hovering just off the car's hood as he cut east over the Burnside bridge toward Parkrose.

The blinds were pulled and her car was gone, but he knocked anyway. No answer. He tried the door and it was locked. Same with the windows and sliding glass back door—all locked and nothing to suggest anything bad had happened.

So he returned to the car and sat for a while, thinking and trying not to worry, although the fear kept poking holes in every logical explanation he could come up with for Anne's absence. She'd been concerned enough to send the boys away and call the Bureau and the longer he sat there the more he began to suspect that there was something she'd not told him or worse, that in his dazed state he'd forgotten to push her for details. It would explain the kiss and sly smile she'd given him—the one that punched all his buttons and made him promise things he had no right promising.

Before he could pull out, a rusted brown Reliant with a bad tailpipe slowed to a stop alongside his car. The windows were rolled down. A pair of naked speakers on the back dash were blasting "Over the Hills and Far Away" and the driver gave him a long, hard look.

For a minute he thought it might be Jimmy Blackwood and regretted not having tucked a gun under the seat. But it wasn't. The man behind the wheel had a wispy little mustache and the slouching demeanor of a nickel-and-dime dope peddler and occasional vandal who lived down one of the trailer park's dirt roads with his mother. Frank conjured up his best sucked-out-cop stare and gave the man a blast, pleased when the man tapped the gas and drove off, bobbing his head along to the lilting guitar.

He waited a while longer for Anne to return, watching two girls with pigtails shout at a trembling black puppy as it bit its leash and rolled over and pissed itself. Leaves blew from the trees and crab-walked across the windshield as plastic sunflower wind charms spun noisily from a nearby fence. But there was no sign of Anne and so he drove to a small downtown bar and had a few belts, hoping to kill the head cold he felt coming on.

From the pay phone he called Peck and told him that he wanted see him ASAP and that he didn't want to come into the office. Peck asked where he was calling from and Frank told him it was none of his business. They arranged to meet at a diner across town. Frank killed another hour listening to the bartender's muddled views on the legalization of drugs and Reaganomics.

When he arrived at the diner he found Peck in the back booth sipping coffee and playing with the creamer lid.

A few familiar faces looked up from their food to nod at him before going back to their folded newspapers or watching the street hustle and bustle outside the window. At the lunch counter a man dressed in Hefty sacks and bell-bottom jeans rocked back and forth laughing to himself. Four city workers on their lunch break sat staring at one another with work-bombed expressions and sagging eyes while a group of women in the booth behind them used napkins to dab the grease off their grilled cheeses and patty melts.

Peck's hair was gelled back gangster style and his aftershave cut a fragrant swath through the fog of burnt coffee and sausages. On the table in front of him sat a thick manila folder. Spotting it, Frank briefly worried that Peck intended to warn him about his recent contact with Anne Blackwood, that or give him some bad news. Plus he had a buzz on. So he smiled at the young agent, giving nothing away and ready for anything. A waitress he recognized zoomed over to their table. She'd been at the diner forever and moved with an authority many first-time customers mistook for rudeness now that her looks were gone and she had to rely on hustle and snappy comebacks. "Coffee?"

Frank said please and righted his mug and watched her splash it full. "I'll be back to take your order," she said, setting a smeared menu in front of him. He smiled, wrapped his hands around the hot mug, and watched her go, before turning to Peck. "Thanks for meeting me," he said, careful not to blast his boozy breath across the table, but just the same he knew Peck suspected he'd been drinking and had already decided not to say anything.

"You look well," Peck said, smirking. "The retirement glow, is that it?"

"Bullshit. Prom queens and sunsets glow. What you're looking at here is the slow, sliding fade of Frank Marshall. I'm having trouble sleeping. Not to mention the fact that I think I'm coming down with a cold."

"I'm sorry to hear that."

"Hell, I'm being dramatic."

Peck checked his watch. "Now what's wrong?"

"That case we talked about?"

"Cooper or Blackwood?"

"Blackwood," Frank said, choosing his words carefully. "I was wondering if anything else came in."

"Like what?"

Frank stopped himself when he saw the waitress approaching, pen and order pad out, hips cocked impatiently.

"Okay, boys," she said. She stopped, something pulling her out of the routine as she looked down at Frank in the booth, hands clasped calmly in front of him. "Where you been hiding yourself, hon?"

"Around."

She laughed and tucked a strand of frosted hair up. "Plenty of that. Now, what'll you have? And don't say the usual. I'm good but not that good."

Frank ordered a ham steak with mashed and chicken gravy, Peck cereal with yogurt. "I'm on a diet," Peck explained, mopping his shiny forehead with several napkins.

"I don't believe in diets," Frank said. "You eat what you eat and exercise and it'll sort itself out in the end. All those men's magazines are always writing about 'The Last Ten Pounds' and how to get tighter abs. I like my Last Ten Pounds, means I've lived."

"There's only one problem with that line of reasoning."

"Yeah?"

"My father dropped dead of a heart attack when he was forty. A lifelong bacon-and-eggs man and he didn't pass up many donuts either. He was happy, though, I'll give him that."

Frank squinted at him, trying to figure if Peck was busting his balls.

"You were saying," said Peck.

"Well, I went by to see her."

"Yeah, and?"

"Her husband called her, saying he wanted something."

"You believe her?"

"Of course I believe her. She was scared. I asked all the right questions, told her she ought to have her phone hooked up and all that, but she didn't want me to involve you guys."

"The Bureau?"

Frank nodded. "She called to talk to me and didn't know I was retired and I told her we could wait a few days, see what happened, only now I can't get a hold of her and she's not answering my calls."

"You worried?"

Frank paused and looked around at the people coming and going, blankly raising food to their mouths, and examining grease-spotted checks as they groped pockets for wallets. "Maybe," he said.

"Let me call in, see what's on the sheets," Peck said. "Maybe this Blackwood got himself picked up already."

Frank let him go without protest and when Peck returned, shaking his head, the waitress was right behind him, her arms full of steaming plates of food.

They waited until the waitress had set the plates down. "Nothing's come in," he said. "You want to take a ride after this?"

"I've already been by her house."

"No," Peck said. "I want you to show me where that Cooper money washed up. We can talk about this other thing on the way up."

Frank didn't know what to say, so he nodded and cut into the ham steak, hoping it would fill the void left by the retreating booze, stop him from wanting more. He watched as Peck spooned some yogurt into his cereal, neatly arranging the stuff in tiny white hills before collapsing it into the bran flakes. Frank knew Peck would circle back to Anne and maybe even gingerly offer him a way out but wanted something first. Showing Peck where the kid had found the Cooper money would be a small price to pay.

They ate without talking until Peck pushed his plate away, drummed his fingers against the tabletop, and asked Frank what Anne wanted him to do.

"Nothing. I mean, I told her she should report the contact, but she didn't want to do that and I stupidly went along."

"So," Peck said, snagging the check, "she must not be too worried if she doesn't want anything done. Did you ask me here because you think something happened to her or because you want me to get involved?"

"Both, I guess." Frank rubbed his eyes. "It's just I don't know anymore, and the more I think about it, the less business I have getting involved in something like this. I know what you're thinking, but that's not it."

"I don't think anything."

"Don't get me wrong, I've thought about it plenty, but I've been a good boy."

Peck put a hand up to stop him. "I would never think that, and even if I did, it's none of my business."

"Okay," Frank said, relaxing a bit. "Now, what's with wanting to see where the money turned up?" he asked.

"I'll tell you on the way up. You still got time, right?"

Frank smiled—he had all the time in the world. So they took his car, Peck asking him to drive him by Anne's trailer just so he could see for himself. But there was still nobody home, and after taking a quick look around, Peck asked if it was possible she split town. "I mean, her stuff looks like it's still in there, but maybe she just left."

"She would have called first."

Peck loosened his tie and undid a few shirt buttons before turning to Frank. "You want, I can call this in right now, have a couple of guys sent over. As long as you know there's gonna be questions . . ."

Frank thought a minute, remembering the look on Anne's face when she'd extracted the promise from him and suddenly he felt foolish—mad at himself for telling Peck he was worried.

"Well, it's your call," said Peck.

"Let's wait a day, see what happens. Maybe she's staying at her sister's."

"Fine by me," Peck said, getting back in the car.

Forty mostly silent minutes later, Frank turned down Lower River Road and parked in a dirt pull-off behind several pickup trucks and a Volvo crammed with gear. They cut through an easement that ran alongside some barbed-wired pastures and tilted barns, emerging on a sandy beach area littered with half-burned logs and snarled balls of monofilament line. The Columbia ran wide and slow before them and the air smelled like ash and dead fish.

A couple of fishermen standing hip-deep in the current nodded before going back to their heavy casting rods.

"Right over there," Frank said, pointing to a swoop of trees clinging to a cutaway riverbank. "We turned this place upside down. We even had the U.S. Corps of Engineers do a study."

"I've read the report."

"Well then, you know they think the money came from upstream and maybe even the Washougal River during one of the spring floods."

Peck smiled, his eyes following a bank of clouds as he thought. "I think this is gonna be interesting."

Frank waited for the young agent to get his fill of the place. His joints ached, and he could already feel the tight, bruisy sensation gathering in his lower spine that signaled he was indeed going to be sick. Still, he tried to push it out of his mind because he did not have time to get sick.

On the way back he asked Peck to pull the Blackwood case file for him.

Peck stared quietly out the window a minute before speaking. "What's this about, Frank?"

"Just do me a favor and pull the file and make a copy."

"Okay, but . . ."

"Don't get your panties in a bunch, Peck. I wanna see if Blackwood's still got any other family or old side pussy in the area."

"If you don't hear from her by tomorrow, I'm going to have to make a report."

"I know," he said, "I know. Now, do you wanna get a quick drink?"

"I need to get back, Woodrell's got me working with this ATF cowboy."

"Lemme guess," said Frank. "Ray-Bans, black leather, unfiltered Luckies . . ."

"Camels, but bingo on the rest."

"Just let him be the first through the door."

"I hope it doesn't come to that," Peck said, letting out a nervous laugh. "I've already heard all six of his gun-battle stories and how he and his old partner took down a cabin full of redneck patriots."

"Fucking typical."

By the time they made it back to the car Frank had begun to sweat again and his eyes felt as if they had weights on them. Peck popped the door and readied to go.

"You'll get me the file, right?"

"Call me," Peck said. "Just remember that when this Blackwood thing blows over I want you to knock on some doors with me. I've got a feeling he's still out there."

"Cooper?" Frank asked, again not sure if Peck was having some fun with him. "You've got to be kidding."

"I'm serious, Frank. I really think I'm going to find something."

"It's a dead case, but yeah, I'll knock on some doors with you."

Peck slapped the hood and told Frank to go home and get some sleep, that he looked like shit. True, but after Peck had pulled away he stopped off at a hotel bar for a cognac, thinking it might beat back the cold and open his already clogged sinuses, before going home to eat dinner with Clare.

The cognac didn't help, and as he sat in the hotel bar's padded club chair listening to a harp medley of Beatles tunes and staring at the empty snifter, he was beset by the nagging feeling that he'd forgotten something—an errand or a promise to Clare or maybe even something back at the river with Peck, where he'd been too distracted to even look around or pay attention to Peck's theories about what had happened to D. B. Cooper. As far as Frank was concerned, all that had happened all those years ago while looking for Cooper was that he'd found the girl's bones and not much else, not even a name or a good reason why she'd ended up lashed to a rotting piling under all that water. And so he snagged his keys off the bar, pushed a dollar over the drink rail, and headed for home.

In the car he fought the urge to drive by Anne's one last time and instead fished around the ashtray for a roll of breath mints, nearly swerving off the road. After the brief panic, he felt the worry settle around his chest like barbed wire and he knew that he had been worse than foolish for having let Anne flirt him into doing nothing.

CHAPTER ELEVEN

lare stood at the kitchen counter eating mixed nuts out of a can, waiting for Frank, and flipping through a *Better Homes and Gardens*, overwhelmed by the tips and wondering what woman could possibly have the time for making drapes or cranberry-pumpkin spice cakes. He was late, and the longer she stood there washing the nut paste down with some white wine she'd poured into a coffee mug, the angrier she got. It had been a long day. She'd closed on a handyman's special south of town in an "up-and-coming neighborhood" where the sidewalk buckled from tree roots and old women stood guard in front windows, eyeing strangers, ready to dial 911.

After the closing, the buyer, a recently divorced college professor named Russell, pressed a signed chapbook of his poems into her hands and asked Clare if she'd help him pick out furniture and wall-paper because he was blue-green color-blind.

She told him to call and left it at that even though both of them knew she was merely being polite and didn't want to ruin the sale.

When she finally heard Frank's car in the drive, she set the magazine aside, took one last sip of wine, and waited for him to enter through the garage.

He pushed open the door, looking bleary-eyed and soft-shouldered. A lot of the FBI man swagger was gone, replaced with something that she was too angry to put a finger on.

"Turn right around," she said. "We're going to be late. I'm not even going to ask you where you've been."

He picked up the nut can and saw that she'd eaten all the pecans and Brazil nuts. He tried a hazelnut and, as expected, immediately regretted it.

"I was with Peck, remember him from the party?" He started to launch into a little bit about how Peck was obsessed with Cooper but stopped when Clare leaned in and sniffed.

"At what bar?"

"I went alone, after I saw him," he said. "Now, what am I late for?"

"Dinner at my parents. Remember?"

"No, I don't."

"I can see we're going to have to have another little talk later." She went to the fridge and jabbed at the calendar. "It's written right here," she said.

"Shit."

An apology was required and so he coughed it up and tried to put a hand on her shoulder, hoping to slide into an apologetic hug. Instead she turned away from him and said, "Oh, and a woman called for you. She didn't leave a name or a number."

He looked at her and, before she could ask or give him some suspicious glare, said, "It's nothing, just an old case I was helping Peck with. Did she say anything else?"

Clare shook her head, and when he started for the phone, she stepped in front of him. "Don't even think about it," she said. "We're an hour late already."

"Clare, please, it's important."

"You're retired, Frank. How important can it be?"

He didn't answer, not with the face she was giving him, equal

parts I've-had-a-bad-day pissed off and gut-level distrust that everything he could possible say would be a lie. He put a hand on her
shoulder but she shrugged it off. "It can wait till tomorrow," she said.

He said okay, snatched his keys off the counter, and told her he
was ready to go.

"Change your shirt, you smell like a bar stool." She crinkled her
nose and pointed upstairs. "Put that navy one on I bought you last
Christmas and comb your hair."

He grumbled and marched upstairs, where he thought about giving Anne a quick call but did not. When he came down he found
Clare rummaging through her makeup bag.

"I thought you were ready," he said.

"Frank, please. I'm in no mood." She zipped the bag shut and followed him out to the garage, slamming doors behind her.

They drove across the Willamette without speaking. Gulls swooped
over the water as a voice on the radio extolled the virtues of Gold
Bond medicated powder and read the news in a halting dramatic style
that was oddly comforting. It wasn't until they pulled into the driveway of Walt and Mary's large stone house that she turned and gave
him one of her looks. "I hope you don't plan on going on like this forever."

Out the window he watched two cowbirds shaking leaves off a
nearby plum tree. He was about to tell her that not only did he need
to call Anne and make sure everything was okay but the greasy diner
food he'd had with Peck was still sitting in his stomach like a fist and
about the last thing he wanted to do was suffer through a dinner
with his in-laws. To top it off, he now had a full-bloom cold.

She poked him in the ribs with a fingernail. "Do you hear me,
Frank?"

"Go on like what?"

"The man who wasn't there, or whatever it is you're doing. You
should get up and go running with me or find a part-time job or I
don't know what . . ." She sighed impatiently. "I don't know why I
didn't see this coming. I should have known . . ."

"Seen what coming?"

"This tailspin of yours. Most people enjoy their retirements, Frank. They do things, spend more time with their wives or take up a hobby. They do something."

"Just calm down, Clare. I'm sorry about being late. It's just I think I'm coming down with a head cold or something and—"

She turned on him, cutting him off, her shoulders stiff with rage. "Don't tell me to calm down and don't turn this around so it's some-how all my fault. You're not okay. You come home smelling like liquor and tell me you're out helping on some old case?"

"I was . . ."

"If there's something wrong, I want you to tell me now. We'll get through it. We always do."

He shrugged, surrendering to the inexorable fact that no matter what he said she was going to pick a fight and would not be happy until he'd admitted to some wrongdoing or shortcoming.

"Okay," he said. "What do you want me to do?"

"I want you to snap out of it is what I want."

He pulled the key from the ignition, forced a crazy smile, and said, "Done. I'm all better. Was that our talk?"

"Don't condescend."

"I'm not condescending."

This only made her madder and so he let it go and followed her to the stoop, watching as she took a deep breath and got into character before swinging open the door.

T. J., her parent's hyperactive golden retriever, leaped up and clawed at them as Walt ambled out of the den, calling the dog a dumb blonde and tossing a gnawed piece of rope down the hallway for it to skitter after. "Come in, come in." Clare hugged him and he pulled away smiling to offer his hand to Frank.

The Goldberg Variations were playing on the stereo. Warm kitchen smells filled the house and the grandfather clock that stood next to the hat rack hung frozen at three-thirty. Scented candles flickered from windowsills, and on a small oak table Frank noticed a worn copy of the *Nation* folded open to a half-finished crossword.

They shook hands and the men slipped into the den while Clare went to the kitchen with her mother to complain about Frank's behavior and help get dinner out.

In the den there was a ballgame on the television with the sound off and a book on World War II fighter pilots on the coffee table next to the triangular golf tee games that Frank had steadfastly refused to learn. Every nook and shelf of the den was stuffed with puzzles of all sorts. At one time or another Walt had demonstrated his mastery of them to Frank and then watched impatiently as his son-in-law fumbled and gave up. Frank had no patience for stupid games.

Walt pointed at a drink sweating on a cork coaster between them. "Can I fix you an old-fashioned or a Harvey Wallbanger? I'm going old school tonight."

Frank collapsed into a heavy leather chair, kicked his feet up on the ottoman, and said, "I'd better not."

"What's the matter?"

"I've got a cold."

"Well then, you definitely need a drink. Take the hat cure," Walt said, going to the liquor cabinet. "What you do is get a hat and a bottle. Set the hat on the bed, open bottle, and drink until you see two hats. The next morning you're so hungover your body doesn't have time to be sick. Now, what'll you have?"

"No, really, I'm under orders to behave. I've been talked to."

"Clare?" Walt winced. "Don't wanna get on her bad side. We're having some wine with dinner, though, so you can make up for it there. I'll be your accomplice. Tell me how come nobody drinks rye anymore?" He held up a bottle of rye.

"I don't know the answer to that."

After setting the bottle back, Walt returned to his chair and picked up his drink as Frank asked how the boat was coming.

"The cabinets look great. I used oil even though the guy at the hardware store tried to sell me on the new water-based stuff. He made all sorts of claims but I didn't bite."

"Less fumes and easy cleanup."

"I'm still suspicious."

"Did you put her in the water?"

Walt nodded. "She's what you call sea-kindly, squats nicely and cuts water. I've already taken her up to the Saint John Bridge and back."

"Then what?"

"You know *then what*," he said, leaning close. "I'm really going to do it. Tomorrow I meet with the mechanic, and if he gives me the green light, I'm going to see how far I can get."

"Have you told Mary about the trip?"

Walt took a sip of his drink and shook his head. "She'd just worry herself sick and try to talk me out of it. She'd be happy if I just hung around the house, clipping hedges and fetching her pills. I've told her I'm not going to do that—end of discussion. She's got her plate collection, I've got my boat, and I'm not working on it just to lower my blood pressure. I'm not going to be one of those guys who sit around polishing brass all day and put-putting around the marina. I want to see the ocean, and what Mary doesn't know won't hurt her. I'm looking at a week from today, maybe sooner—do a day trip first, sneak out and steal back, see how she runs before I make the big one."

"The Strait of Juan de Fuca?"

Walt drained the old-fashioned. "Boy, I love the way that sounds. I have visions of whales following the boat and of catching my dinner while the sun sets. It's true what they say about the call of the sea."

"Sounds like you're gonna need an escape plan as far as Mary's concerned," Frank said. "Women know, they always know."

"I'm one step ahead of you, Frank. Last week I bought her some Wedgwood and she hasn't mentioned the boat. My guess is she's gonna circle back on me about it, trap me out in some lie. Believe me, I haven't heard the last of it, but if she gives me any more grief I may just keep sailing."

As if on cue Mary poked her head into the den. "Just leave the checkbook when you go, dear."

Walt laughed and picked up the fighter pilot book, pretending to look at a lantern-jawed pilot frozen in heroic pose next to his plane.

"Oh, hello, Frank," Mary said, giving him one of her cold appraisals that told him she'd been talking to Clare about him.

He smiled and said hello back as she crossed the room and closed the book on her husband's hands. "Dinner's ready," she said.

The men waited until she was gone before hauling themselves out of the deep chairs and trudging into the dining room. Walt turned the stereo off and locked T. J. in the back hall, before taking his seat.

They ate overdone lamb chops and pesto with a hint of curry, a recipe Mary had found in the latest *Redbook*. "Usually I skip right past them," she informed them. "But this one seemed so wrong I just had to try it. It's called Bombay Meets Bologna."

"What's wrong with regular pesto?" Walt grumped.

Mary glared at him and then traded exasperated looks with her daughter. "Something new for a change. It won't kill you."

"Medium," Walt said, chewing. "At these prices you want lamb to be rare." He picked some sinew from his teeth with a fork tine and passed the wine to Frank.

Frank filled his glass, drank, and pushed food into his mouth, only half paying attention to the small talk or the way his in-laws laced into each other with their tiny, well-honed jousts. Beside him sat Clare, stoically chewing and nodding along as Mary told a story about a friend of hers, Bess O'Herlihy, who'd given all her money to a televangelist and was now forced to remortgage the house.

"Bess is a dingbat," said Walt.

"She's lonely."

"Okay, she's a lonely dingbat," Walt grunted.

"I told her they were just going to build Bible theme parks with her money, but she wouldn't hear a word of it. She's gullible. Remember how she fell for the Grit scam."

"That boy was very charming," Walt said. "He had quite a sales pitch and that homemade suit of his didn't hurt either."

"He misrepresented himself. And for the record, I remember you bought a subscription too, Walter."

"I stand by Grit. Now, who was it that fell for the everlasting light bulb bit?"

"I don't recall," said Mary, smiling. "Well, what did everyone think of the curried lamb?"

"I need a minute, I'm still tasting it," Frank said. He reached for more wine.

"Some retarded group, wasn't it, dear?" said Walt. "Who ever heard of a thirty-year light bulb? And if they've just invented the damn things, how can they make that thirty-year claim?"

Mary stood to clear the platter of gnawed lamb bones floating in a lake of gray blood and rolling peppercorns. "Was the curry a good thing or a bad thing?" she asked.

"Frank's had too much wine," Clare said. "His judgment's impaired."

"I'd still like an answer."

"A good thing," Walt roared. "Not great, but good."

"Another success, Mary," Frank said.

They cleared the dishes and ate praline ice cream for dessert as T. J. scratched at the back door and Walt washed the dishes, pausing to give his opinion on Mondale. "It'll be another rout," he said. "Hell, Mondale-Kennedy would be a loser. It's this Cuomo guy they need, but I think somebody's got dirt on him."

"Skeletons in the closets," said Frank.

"They all got 'em. What we need is some firebrand to come in and stir the pot, but that's not going to happen. The only thing Mondale's going to stir is coffee. I tell you, it's the end of opposition-party politics in this country when you hear people say you've got to choose the lesser of two evils. What kind of crap is that?"

"There's always the LaRouchians, Walt."

"It's always the nuts that get the attention. Where are the good ideas? The freethinkers and risk takers? Screw the lesser of two evils. I don't want to live in a country of morons who think like that."

Mary threw a tea towel on the floor next to the sink and stepped on it. "Enough, dear, you're dripping water all over the place."

"Notice how I wait until the rinse sink's full before I run the hot water?"

"Your waste takes other forms," Mary said, winking at Clare.

Walt kicked the towel away. "You haven't answered my question, Frank. Where are the risk takers? I mean, if *Time* magazine says we are a nation of risk takers, how come I don't see any evidence of this?"

"I think they're talking mostly about sports."

"You're doing your part with the boat, Dad," said Clare.

"That's a recreational activity."

"It's a toy," Mary whispered.

"Always belittling," Walt said. "Landlubbers should keep their opinions to themselves. Now, who wants to dry?"

Frank stood and took a towel from the drawer while Clare followed her mother into the living room to look at a Christmas cactus that Mary suspected of having spider mites.

"They won't call it a toy when I hit the blue water."

"I'd like to see the way she rides."

"Come by anytime and I'll take you for a spin up the river. Meanwhile, one of the blue blazer set's already lectured me about wake etiquette. Captain Tom, the marina know-it-all, gave me an earful about my inappropriate wake."

"What about knots?"

"Another misconception. Sure, it's good to know a few, but boating's pretty much like driving a car now, point and steer, allow plenty of room to brake."

"So you're an old salt already."

"Har, har," he said, tossing T. J. a lamb bone. The dog crunched away and Frank was reminded of the sound the contractor's throat had made when he'd punched him. From there it was a hop, skip, and a jump to thinking of Anne and how he was going to finesse Clare on the ride home and get to bed without having one of their *talks* so he could slip into the den and phone Anne to see what she wanted.

■

THEY WERE HEADED north toward Utah, Arizona buzzing by in a hot, rusty swirl. Cooper gripped the armrests and braced his feet against the dash; it had been a long time since he'd driven on a well-maintained highway where obstacle-free speed was possible. Lou drove aggressively, tailgating when possible, refusing to signal lane switches, lingering in the passing lane as he took his hands off the wheel to air guitar and moan along to the Velvet Underground tapes playing at full woofer-rattling volume.

The van lacked air-conditioning and so they rode with the windows open, shouting at each other in between the snarling music.

North of Flagstaff Lou told Cooper he was headed to Oregon to visit his twin brother, who, according to Lou, slept with a pellet gun and had some monstro wolf dog trained to rip trespasser's throats. "Claims his competitors are always after his research," Lou shouted. "Or at least that's the picture he likes to paint. You live alone in a poorly ventilated cabin in the middle of fucking nowhere and that's what happens. We aren't what you call close. In fact, we're about as different as night and day. I haven't heard from him in a while and my guess is he got some hot lead on a fur sample or fresh tracks."

"He some kind of big-game Jeremiah Johnson hunter type?"

"A cryptozoologist," said Lou. "To be exact, he's the world's number-five expert on Bigfoot. Like I said, we're opposites. While I struggle to shed a little skeptical light on pseudoscientific crap, he runs around the country lecturing to Rotarians and Shriners about the existence of Bigfoot and the urgent need for funding."

"Does he have proof?"

"Proof?"

"I saw frozen yeti once in the Vancouver mall. It looked small and freezer-burned. Mighta been a gorilla, but you never know."

Lou looked over at Cooper sitting there with his hands braced against the dash, prepping for an accident. "Don't tell me you believe in Bigfoot."

"I hold out some hope," said Cooper.

"Hope's for dopes. There's no reason to believe in anything, let alone some screaming apeman trotting around the Pacific Northwest menacing overweight campers. I can see you need to draw a few lines in the sands of reason. Now, have you ever known, shared coffee with, or had sexual relations with anybody who's spotted a Big-foot?"

"No, but . . ."

"Hold on a minute. If you're going to tell me about the Patterson film, I don't want to hear it. My brother's been clinging to that bit of cinema his whole life. A large woman in an ape suit is what you're looking at. Hell, I see I'm going to have to take a base reading before you walk me through this soft-boiled belief system of yours, Cooper."

"What system?"

Lou silenced him with a hand. "Are you a member of the Flat Earth Society?"

"No."

"Spill your thoughts about UFOs. And spare me the Area 51 hokum."

"I've seen strange lights, but I was either drunk or high at the time."

"Typical," Lou said. "Most of the time it's swamp gas, weather bal-loons, air force shenanigans, or ball lightning. The rest you can chalk up to drug hallucinations and bad sci-fi movies. A sad, sorry bunch, but not as pathetic as those sea monster folks in Scotland. And don't give me that bit about Corinthians and the object in the sky. The Bible's no place to look for facts. Hell, you'd do better consulting the *Farmer's Almanac*. At least your pole beans would grow and you'd know the moon cycles. Are you with me, Coop?"

Cooper pointed at his ears and reached for the stereo knob. "The music, man."

"It's either loud or off, brother. What's it going to be?"

Cooper said off.

Lou stepped on the gas and crowded a blue Datsun with Nevada plates until it switched lanes. "My brother got tagged with that label young, and look where it got him. Hunched over a Vermont Casting stove, eating tinned fish, corresponding with Sasquatch freaks, and swapping plaster foot casts. Mom always said he lacked social skills. Painfully shy and withdrawn would be another way to put it. A chronic bed wetter and glue eater would be another. My *gifted* brother spent his toddler years staring at spinning pie tins and flapping his hands like a trained seal while psychologists filed through our living room pressing weighty academic tomes on my parents and dispensing child-rearing advice. But I flourished in the shadow of my brother's so-called genius. Now snag some of that Tang—it'll help us with the long, uncomfortable silences I feel are fast approaching."

Cooper crawled back and poured a small cup, staring at the inky fluid. "What's in it?"

"Some spay/neuter cat knockout I got from my defrocked veterinary friend. The Dexatrim's to keep the legs and arms moving. Keep up appearances and all that. Bottoms up."

Cooper drank and waited. He read the joke on the side of the Dixie cup.

Q: WHAT DO YOU FIND ON TINY BEACHES?

A: MICROWAVES.

When his ears had sufficiently recovered he asked for more music; it made the road better and turned his fear of highway death into glory even as Lou played "Sister Ray" three times in a row and said his foot had fallen asleep.

They stopped at a roadside rest stop billed as scenic and ate from a snack machine that dispensed treats with rotating silver coils. Lou shouldered the machine, trying to knock loose a PayDay bar hanging over the edge. No luck. They took in the scenic view. Red rocks and steep gullies filled with road trash—torn fast-food bags, Gatorade bottles brimming with fermented piss, animal bones, rusted oil drum tops, one sheet of drywall, and a crumpled cardboard sign that read "WHY LIE? I NEED A BEER." They took it all in and complained as a few camera geeks wasted film and struck canned poses against the guardrail, proof that they'd braved the desert.

Moving on, they threw rocks at a dying cactus until a sunburned man wearing green slacks and a sweaty tuxedo T-shirt told them that they were breaking environmental laws and that he was prepared to call the ranger and have them ticketed. "That cactus is over a hundred years old," said the man. "It's been on this earth a century."

"Well then, it's outlived its usefulness, is that what you're saying?" Lou said, grabbing another rock and heaving it at the cactus. The man shook his head and waddled off toward the bank of pay phones, holding a quarter up for them to see.

They got back in the van and peeled out, past the pay phones and the families sitting on picnic benches gulping soda and eating fried chicken from cardboard buckets.

They rode. Grasshoppers and lesser insects creamed themselves against the windshield in bright Technicolor splats. Dust devils spun across the road and then suddenly died. A gang of bikers zipped by, the wind pinning their beards back and flattening their cheeks.

"On their way to terrorize some small town," said Lou, pointing at the last of the bikers, a chubby wad of black leather and gray fur astride 1,400 ccs of fuel-injected fun. "The guy I bought this van from was a Gypsy Joker named Slab, and trust me, the name fit."

"That his artwork on the side?"

"Don't ask about the theme, it eludes me too—some kind of biker wet dream. I'd pay good money to see some shrink put Slab on a couch, but he got busted for defacing a post office box and had to sell off everything he owned to stay out of jail. How about you?"

"What's that?" Cooper said, squinting, the Tang cocktail doing a number six on his cerebral cortex. Tiny noises and rattlings became magnified. He could see the thin pink of his cheeks, and his nose felt as if it had been drilled clean and packed with dry ice. For a minute he thought himself a well-dressed bebop horn player. His hands appeared to be black and were able to keep time on the dash.

"It's just you strike me as the jailbird type is all I'm saying. Most guys you meet tell you right off what they do or where they've been to school or what famous person they're related to and what percentage of Indian blood courses through their veins. And you? Nothing. Let me tell you, the strong, silent types are an endangered breed in this day and age. Why, just the other day I read somewhere that Clint Eastwood's a real chatterbox in person. You can't shut him up."

"I guess that's why they call it acting."

"Good point. Still, I don't wanna know about that stuff. Give me the squint and a .45 and I'm buyin' a ticket."

When they reached the Utah border Lou pointed to a bullet-hole-ridden sign welcoming them to the Beehive State and said, "Okay, Cooper, now's the time to tell me if you've got any bench warrants. These Mormons are law-and-order types. Real sticklers for detail. They're fond of cutting off your circulation with tight cuffs and poking you in the kidneys with billy clubs."

"No."

"You sure? I've been burned before," said Lou. "Picked up a mulatto bank robber once outside of Elko. We ate at Sizzler and I dropped him in Salt Lake, where I heard he got shot trying to stick up a Wells Fargo with a tack hammer."

"I'm not a bank robber," Cooper said. "Do I look like a bank robber? I'm just a guy who needs a ride."

They crossed over into Utah.

"This bit about the money when we get there's got me confused. I hope you don't plan on hitting up family members for long-term loans. I'll tell you right now that I don't want any part of that money. The last thing I need is some thug uncle of yours chasing me all over the country on his souped-up Gold Wing for sixty bucks and the juice. If you insist on being vague I'm forced to assume the worst about you."

"I've had some adventures, a few snags here and there."

"Well and fine. Now, what sort of adventures and how do they relate to this money? And remember, I've heard every sob story there is about Western Union. And fuck traveler's checks."

The van swerved off the berm, kicking up dust contrails that caused the black Freightliner behind them to lay on the air horn. Lou corrected and the van dipped back across the two lanes. "So there's a stash. Is that what you're telling me, Coop?"

"I didn't say that."

"Hah, I read your body language. You're giving me a helluva lot of information without knowing it. Here's a tip—try some isometrics. A couple minutes a day to tighten and tone. See, muscle throws off perceptive body readers like myself. For example, take a look at this Arnold Schwarzenegger lunk and tell me what's on his mind besides barbells and schnitzel."

Cooper looked down at his slouching middle-aged gut and shrugged. "Okay, what am I thinking now?"

Before Lou could answer, the trucker cut them off, the yellow HOW'S MY DRIVING? sticker on the Freightliner looming large through the van's windshield.

"He's probably on the CB calling all his buddies to box us in," Lou said, beating on the horn. "It's all one big game of freeway death to these guys. Anything to break up the monotony." He eased up on the gas and changed lanes without consulting mirrors. "Back to this stash of yours. Remember, I can stop and let you off."

"If you want to drop me, drop me."

"I didn't say that now, did I?" Lou looked over, hurt.

"Whatever, it's your choice. Like I said, I'll make it right for you when we get there."

"There you go again with the shadowy past."

"I need to make a few calls first. I've been Mexi-KO'd and I need to get my bearings. Can you let me do that?"

"Okay, fair enough. I've got a buddy we're gonna stop and see. You can make the calls there as long as his mother doesn't find out."

Several hours later, on a stretch of highway just south of Moab, a mountain lion loped out of a ditch and killed itself on the van's bumper. Lou jumped on the brakes but it was too late, the lion thumped and tangled itself in the van's undercarriage in a jazzy jumble of thumps and knocks.

They stopped and Lou got out an ice scraper, a pair of channel lock pliers, and a rusty tire iron, which he handed to Cooper. They crawled under the ticking van to peel and scrape the lion.

A snub-nosed Bluebird bus with Arizona plates stopped and the driver, a balding guy with a smooth pink face and crushed ears, levered open the door. Over the din of hormone-laced high school abuse he shouted, "Need a hand?"

Lou held up a severed lion paw. "Suicidal puma."

"Well, I'll be damned," the driver said, flinching as bent paper clips plinked off the tilted mirror and paper balls bounced down into the vinyl stepwell, where the wind took them to join the other freeway trash.

One of the kids shouted out the window, "Hey, psychos, nice van."

A fat-necked kid dropped his Wranglers and pressed his pale ass to the window while his seatmate pointed and made retarded faces. Cooper gave them the thumbs-up and the bus driver swung the door shut and turned on the squirming rows of teenagers, shouting about his authority to turn this bus right around and head back to Arizona. Still the window abuse continued, until the driver threw up his hands in surrender and pulled back onto the road.

Lou flung the severed paw at the bus and shouted, "Give me five minutes on that bus, that's all I'm asking for. Five minutes and a little punk music to shake that herd mentality of theirs."

"They were just having some fun," said Cooper.

"I don't remember high school that way. They called me Butterworth. I ate a lot of knuckle sandwiches and suffered titty twisters."

"I've never understood titty twisters."

"What's to understand? They hurt and are the preferred method of abuse by future closeted gays with anger-management issues," Lou said, reaching under the van as bits of cat fur and gore began to simmer on the hot oil pan. "This stuff don't smell too good. Some asshole tells me cougar tastes like chicken, I'm gonna brain him. Now hold this and pull."

Cooper took the pliers and yanked a strip of mauled cougar belly from the U-joint. They scraped and poked what they could and when they were finished Lou told him he had puma blood all over his face. "It's not a friendly look."

"And you bear more than a passing resemblance to Roy Orbison," Cooper said.

"Not the first time I've heard that, Coop. It's the glasses that do me in, but I can't see without them."

"What about contacts?"

"Contacts are for pussies."

"Well, you've got blood all over your shirt too."

Lou looked down at the bloody handprints and grease smudges. "I can fix this," he said, sliding open the van door and rummaging around the back, where he found a pair of fresh zero shirts and some scented baby wipes with little teddy bears on them.

Cooper realized that the spiked Tang had faded and Utah now seemed to him a drab, ordinary slab of rock and sky poked with church steeples and Ramada Inns. He hoped to remedy that behind the wheel and so he asked to drive.

Lou tossed him the keys. "All right, speed racer, the steering's got a good bit of play. So be careful. I don't know you well enough to die in a fiery crash with you."

They drove, the thick aroma of burned cougar wafting through the vents and cling to their nose hairs as Lou lit some temple incense and stuck it in a hole on the dash. When they passed the bus of rowdy high schoolers, Lou stuck his arm out the window and gave them the finger.

As the sun began to set, Lou kept pressing his face against the carpeted motor hump, listening for vapor locks, and the whine of old belts.

"Look," said Cooper, "if you're worried, why don't we drop a can of Slick 50 in this pup and you'll be good to go."

"I'd rather pee in the tank."

"That stuff works."

"That's your opinion, but I don't wanna be at the mercy of some crooked shade-tree mechanic who'll slip Allen wrenches into the gear box and then bleed us for unnecessary repairs." He shook out a few Dexatrim and chewed them without benefit of water. "We're almost there. The van will rest and there's a creek to wash up in. It wouldn't hurt you to get wet and borrow some soap, and don't blame it on the puma. You were ripe when I first met you. Suppose we were to meet a few road honeys. What then? I'd be forced to develop stories to explain away your b.o."

Cooper stuck a finger in his armpit and smelled it—onions, wet cardboard, and rice wine. "Some women find man smell a turn-on."

"Maybe in Mexico, but not the women I truck with."

"Doesn't your friend have a shower?"

"His name's Rosenbaum and he lives with his mother, who says the shower's off-limits to guests. She's concerned about her grooming products going missing. Mess with Frau Rosenbaum and she'll lower the boom on your hippie ass. Trust me, the creek's the better deal. Plus we can bunk in the barn, which is the key to any Rosenbaum stay—low impact. We'll need to be gone at first light. I hope you're not one of those slow-to-rise types."

"No, I am not."

"Oh, and he's a thumb-sucker so if you catch him going at it try not to stare. He gets nervous and regresses."

"No problem."

"Now, how about that sunset?" He pointed at the orange ball hunkering down over the dry white mountains, tipping shadows across the tan alfalfa fields as it seeped along the northern rim.

"I'd give it a seven," said Cooper.

"Eight," Lou said. "Now take the next exit and hang a roger."

Cooper signaled and took his foot off the gas, listening as Lou told him about Rosenbaum—how he made his nut selling mail order ant farms. "We're picking up a special package. Are you okay with that?"

"You gonna tell me what it is?"

"No."

"Yeah, I'm okay with it then."

"Keep straight. I'll tell you where to turn."

Cooper hunched over the wheel, watching as the van startled the occasional mule deer off its feed and the first stars struggled to be seen in the dusk.

■

CLARE DIDN'T SPEAK to him on the drive home. She maintained the silence even as Frank fumbled with the house keys, trying to pretend he was halfway sober but only making things worse. Inside she sighed, flicked on a lamp, her eyes drifting to the unblinking answering machine—no calls. Without giving him a look or word he could read to get some idea where things stood between them, she drifted upstairs. Frank waited until he heard the shower running down the drainpipe before calling Anne, taking a minute as the connection was made to blow his nose and clear his throat.

She answered on the second ring, her voice thick with sleep and wine.

"You called?" he said.

She mumbled yes and before she could say another word he asked where she'd been, worry leaking into his voice as he kept an ear cocked, listening to the drainpipe, making sure Clare was still in the shower.

She told him that she'd been staying at her sister's for a couple of days because she'd seen someone outside the window.

"J. B.?"

"I don't know," she said. "Look, it was late and I was scared. I don't even know why I woke up and looked out the window."

"You should have called. I was worried about you."

"I figured you would be." He heard the rasp of a lighter. "It was probably nothing, some kid or a guy out walking his dog. I don't know what happened, but I just got scared and I didn't want to be here anymore and I didn't want to call anyone and have it turn out to be nothing, so I just left."

He told her that she'd done the right thing and tried to circle back to what she'd seen.

"A man. Like I said, it was dark and he left the minute I put a light on."

"Where was he?"

"Across the street, under the tree."

He thought a moment, trying to decide what, if anything, he could do. But then the water quit upstairs and he told her he had to go and that he wanted to stop by and see her the next day. She said okay and there was a second or two of uncomfortable silence before he pressed the phone to his stomach to dampen the disconnect beep. He put the receiver back in its cradle and thought that he'd simply go upstairs and tell Clare exactly what he'd been up to the past couple of weeks, leaving out the kiss, of course, and painting himself as some kind of hero for stepping in and interceding on Anne's behalf. He'd tell her he was just helping out, trying to fix something he should have fixed before. But midway up the stairs he bailed: Clare was too mad about the whole evening and he knew that if he hit her with some half-assed story he'd only sound guilty and drunk and it would only make her madder. Instead he went back downstairs to find the bottle of Nyquil. He wanted to sleep the whole thing off, wake in the morning, and start pulling himself together now that Anne was okay and accounted for.

CHAPTER TWELVE

Clare was already up when he rolled out of bed. He could hear her in the kitchen going about her breakfast routine, opening and shutting cupboard doors, the clatter of a spoon on the stovetop, the clink and jiggle of the soy sauce bottle rubbing against mustard and jam jars as she swung open the fridge door, looking for half-and-half. He rubbed his face, palmed his eye sockets, and took stock. The cold had lodged itself in his head and chest like posthole cement. Like all illnesses, this one stirred in him the idea that he somehow deserved what was happening to him, that the shakes and cluttered cold medicine thoughts that flocked him in and out of the half sleep were a fuck-you note from his neglected body. He groped for the Nyquil and drank what he figured was three tablespoons and then went into the bathroom to take a shower.

In front of the mirror he dropped his boxer shorts, peeled off his stale T-shirt, and deposited them next to the hamper before reaching in and dialing the shower controls. As he stepped into the tub he caught a glimpse of his sagging body in the mirror and quickly looked away, vowing to put things right, taper back on the vodka, and get running again before it was too late.

As he stuck his head in the stream he saw the blurry outline of Clare through the sculpted glass door. Her arm appeared over the stall, shaking a bottle of vitamin C tablets. He grunted good morning.

"Take these and stay away from me," she said. "I can't afford to get sick. I've got six showings today and a million phone calls to make."

"It's too late for vitamins," he said.

"Just take them. I'm putting them next to the towels." She continued to lecture him about taking better care of himself but he heard only bits and pieces and didn't answer. When he stepped out, groping for his towel, she'd gone to finish breakfast. He took some vitamin C, dressed, and when he clomped downstairs he found Clare already stepping out the door.

"I'd kiss you, but I don't want that cold," she said, turning around and giving him a stiff little smile. "Harvey called and said the man came by to fix the garage door."

"I'll go have a look."

"Only if you feel better."

"I'm fine."

"You don't look fine. Take a nap. I want you home and feeling better when I get back."

He saluted her, hoping she'd smile and give it right back to him. Instead she stepped out the door without looking back. He had some work to do, things to figure out.

Then he called Peck at home and told him he'd spoken with Anne, explaining how she'd been staying at her sister's. He said nothing about the man she'd seen outside the window because he knew Peck would escalate things and he didn't exactly want to be parked outside her trailer when the agents showed up.

"Still want that file?" Peck asked.

Frank said he did and arranged to pick it up tomorrow.

"Maybe we can go knock on some doors."

"This about the great Cooper hunt?"

Peck said it was and Frank agreed, just wanting to get off the phone and get over to Anne's.

More Nyquil and three Sudafed later, Frank stumbled downstairs, not feeling half bad, the medicine momentarily carbureting his heart and unstuffing his head.

Before going out to the car he took his retirement gift, the brand-new Heckler & Koch 9mm and sank a full clip. He racked the slide, chambering a round with a satisfying ching. With his legs spread he brought the weapon up, letting it float into position as his thumb slid to the safety and the sights drew down nice and clear, his finger curling around the trigger guard, ready to slip inside and make it all work. Pleased with the gun's weight and pull, he tucked it into his shoulder holster and checked his pocket for the finger bone. It was there, pressing against his thigh. He left.

He drove over to Anne's with the radio off, dimly aware that all around him people were going about their business, pumping gas, obeying traffic rules, putting shopping bags in trunks, walking dogs, calling cats, herding children into station wagons, buying things, and making small talk on street corners. His plan was to get in and get out without making any more promises. He had a job to do and that job was to make sure she was safe and that she would be safe no matter what happened. And then he didn't know what he'd do, probably humor Peck and go looking for signs of Cooper and fill the young agent with stories about the manhunt. Maybe he'd even pick up the pond girl's case again and fill his spare time trying to solve it.

Anne met him at the door, her eyes red-rimmed, a cigarette burning in her hand, and before she'd even undone the screen door lock she told him that she was leaving. "I've reserved a U-Haul and called around about schools."

"Aspen?" he said.

She nodded. "I'm really going to do it, Frank. I need to get out of here. I can't live like this anymore."

He stepped in. The air smelled like bacon grease and overripe bananas. There was mail stacked on the kitchen table, a plastic bag full of packing tape, and several empty cardboard boxes folded and leaning up against the broom closet. Her two boys sat slack-jawed on the couch watching *Scooby-Doo*. Rory looked up and waved at Frank. He waved back and then pulled Anne around the corner, out of sight.

"Now hold on a minute," he said. "I want you to tell me exactly what you saw the other night. I need to know if it's something I should report or not."

She shook her head and pointed at her sons in the other room. "Please, Frank." Her voice cracked. "I'm trying to make it like this big adventure for them. I don't want them to know."

"I understand," he said. "But he'll find you if he wants to bad enough."

"I don't need this right now."

He ignored her and parted his jacket to make sure she saw the gun. "We should have reported this like we were supposed to. I don't know what I was thinking."

"I do."

He tried hard not to blush, his hands groping for and finding the counter edge so he could lean against it as he tried to refocus. "Well, it's over. We've waited long enough and when I leave here the first thing you're going to do is make the call."

"Keep your voice down."

"Are you listening to me, Anne?"

She glared at him, veins popping in her neck. "No," she hissed. "I'm going to do what I'm going to do and if you don't like that you can leave."

But he didn't move and instead waited until she turned and met his gaze. "Can you at least show me where you saw him?" he asked.

She stubbed out the cigarette and went to the small window above the kitchen sink. She pointed. "There," she said, "next to that tree."

He followed her finger, stepping close enough that he could smell her, and for one trembling moment thought about putting a comforting hand on her shoulder, but stopped himself. She was going to

Aspen and he had to find a way to let her go without betraying the cop instincts he'd honed for more than half his life. He excused himself and went out to have a look at the spot.

Walking past her car he was jolted by the sight of his reflection in the side-view mirror. His hair looked unkempt and there were great scary bags under his eyes and he had the clumsy walk of a man deep into his middle age. He kept moving toward the bent tree, its trunk scarred from car bumpers and staples from old tag sale signs.

He could see Anne watching him from the window, her face a small pink oval behind the dusty glass as he bent over, duck-walking back and forth under the tree, his head pounding again, a light sweat breaking out across his forehead. Beside the usual trash of straw wrappers, twist-off tops, and mashed, rain-ruined circulars, he found a single cigarette butt, a Camel. He picked it up. It looked fresh and smelled as if it hadn't been out there too long, the filter still damp.

He took it inside, showed it to her, asked if J. B. smoked.

"Sometimes," she said. "But mostly it wasn't his thing."

"When he did," he said, rolling the Camel butt back and forth across the counter. "Do you remember what brand he liked?"

"Anything he could get. He wasn't particular. He only smoked when he was high or drunk, and then he usually bummed one. Is there a point to this? Because I've got better things to do than stand around looking at cigarette butts."

"What else did you see? How tall was this person? What was he wearing?"

"Frank, please, enough with the cop bit."

He put a hand up. "Okay, I know," he said. "But if he's back and that was him—"

"I'm going to Aspen. I've made up my mind and I really don't care what J. B.'s up to or where he is."

He dropped the butt into the garbage and suddenly felt foolish for having rushed over to see her and yet he couldn't bring himself to walk out and leave, even though he knew he should. Instead he asked if she had enough money.

She shook her head, reached for a dried-out sponge on the sink edge, and held it under the faucet. "But I'll get it," she said, her back turned to him as she dumped soap on the sponge and started wiping up the bacon spatter around the stove. "I'll do what I have to do."

"I hope you're not going to do anything stupid."

She threw the sponge down and glared at him. "Like what? Rob a bank?"

"I didn't say that. I just meant that you need to be careful."

"I don't need your advice."

He apologized, watching her for a minute before deciding to press on. "I really need you to report this for me. I'll leave and get out of your life as soon as you do that. It's just I can't sit around and let you ignore this. Just tell them about the phone call, that's all I'm asking, all I came over to say."

"And what good would it do? I mean, come on, Frank, you know they aren't going to let me leave if I tell them."

"Well, I . . ."

"Well what?" she snapped. "You drove all the way over here to tell me this? You promised me that you'd give me some time, that we'd see what happened."

"And you disappeared on me."

"I told you I was at my sister's."

"Maybe so, but I was wrong to make that promise," he said. "I should never have . . ." He fumbled for words. "Anne, if you don't report this I'll be forced to, and I don't want to do that. It could get messy for both of us and, like I said, it's probably nothing, but I'd sleep better knowing someone was watching over you."

"I'll think about it," she said, slapping the sponge into the sink.

He picked up the phone and tried to hand it to her, telling her he'd dial and tell her what to say. But she just stood there, hands clamped under her armpits, looking right through him, until he lowered the phone put it back in its cradle.

"I don't know what you want anymore," she said.

"I was worried."

"Yeah, you told me that already," she said in a tense whisper.

"Now, what else? Because if you came over here to save me, I don't need it. I don't really care what J. B. does. I'm done with it, and as a matter of fact, I'm done with this whole place. It can go fuck itself. I need to start something new—"

"Mom?" one of the boys said from the other room.

"It's okay, honey," she said, poking her head around the corner and putting on a smile. When she turned to face Frank again, her face had softened. "It's sweet of you to worry, but really, I'm going to be okay. I just want to get out. I want to disappear, leave all this behind, and never come back."

"You can't do that."

"Why not?"

"What if he were to come back?"

She laughed uncomfortably. "See, that's just it, exactly what I've been thinking about these last couple of days. So he comes back. What's the worst that could happen?"

Frank said, "I can show you pictures."

"It wouldn't be like that." She reached for a pack of cigarettes on top of the refrigerator. "I mean, he's probably just lonely and I don't think he'd hurt us. I'd tell him I don't have what he thinks I have and he'd leave."

"Suppose he didn't believe you."

"Maybe you could stay here with me and shoot him when he comes."

"I can't do that. I'm not even supposed to be here."

"I was joking, Frank."

"And I'm not," he said. "What are you going to do?"

"Don't worry about me, I'll deal." She lit a cigarette off the stove pilot. "I'm not going to let this stop me from doing what I should have done a long time ago."

He moved toward the door. "Well, if you're not going to make the call I'm going to have to let somebody at the Bureau know he made contact with you." He started to tell her that it was his job to notify them but stopped himself, letting the inane cartoon chatter fill the space between them. His eyes focused on a tiny blue vein just above her collarbone that beat every time she took a hit from the cigarette. "You can call me if you change your mind."

"Hold on—"

He put a hand up, silencing her. "That's all I came here to say." And with that he swung open the door and strode out to his car. She followed him, calling his name, but he ignored her and kept walking, reaching for his keys through the tangle of loose change, the finger bone, and the foil blister pack of cold medicine.

It wasn't until he was behind the wheel that he allowed himself to look up. She was standing on the cracked cement stoop staring at him mutely, the trailer framed by boiling white clouds, high-tension wires, and an oak tree surrendering its leaves to the wind.

But by the time he'd pulled out of the trailer park and managed to corral his thoughts, he was pretty sure he'd wait a bit and mull things over before making the call. He'd tell Peck about the man outside the house and the calls—the best-case scenario being that the younger agent would step in, smooth things over, and leave Frank to fade into the background. In the meantime he'd give her some time to come to it herself. He owed her at least that. He didn't want to wreck her life but he would if had to.

■

ROSENBAUM LIVED UP a rutted dirt road on a dark patch of dry land. Moon shadows suggested nearby hills or bluffs and not many trees, save a few miserable-looking cottonwoods grouped around the warped barn and a tiny wood-frame house behind which ran a creek.

"Careful you don't hit Rosenbaum," Lou said, pointing at the figure that had emerged from the darkness to swing open a steel bump gate. He was holding a Remington rimfire .22 at his side and his long brown hair fluttered with the breeze. He had troubled eyes, tattered

jeans that hung off his bony frame, and a patchy little Vandyke dribbling down his chin. Cooper pegged him for midthirties, maybe
younger.

Lou leaned out the window. "Don't shoot, Rosie."

"Just park her over there," Rosenbaum said. He stepped out of the
way and pointed to a line of stake trucks and busted American cars
piled around the barn.

They parked and Lou introduced Cooper.

"Cooper's an old hippie—you guys will have lots to talk about.
Maybe he'll pass down some of his hard-won dharma bum wisdom
to you." He reached over and fluffed a little of Rosenbaum's hair.

"Knock it off. I'm tired, Louis, and I'm not a hippie just cause I got
long hair."

Lou turned to Cooper and said, "Zero sense of humor. Rosie's all
business. He's a mail-order empire builder, isn't that right?"

Rosenbaum ignored him and pointed to the house. "You guys
hungry? We were expecting you hours ago. Mom's worried about
the food going to waste."

"I thought I smelled biscuits," Lou said. "I've been talking your
mother's cooking up to Coop here since Moab. It's been a short,
strange trip, Rosie. Sorry we're late, but we killed a puma."

"Let's not bring that up at dinner. It'll only upset her."

"Of course not," Lou said. "I know better. Besides, she loves me."

"She tolerates you."

"I don't believe that for one minute."

"Suit yourself," Rosenbaum said, heading toward the house.

They followed him down to the house and, after removing their
shoes in the mudroom, stepped into a small and brightly lit kitchen.
Rosenbaum's mother stood leaning against an old porcelain O'Keefe
& Merritt range, tea towel draped over her shoulder, drinking a can
of Kingsbury NA beer. She was a sturdy woman with a skull full of
ginger-gray hair and dark gold eyes. She was dressed plainly—tan
slacks, a faded denim shirt with pearl snaps over a white tee, and
some scuffed deck shoes with cheap gum rubber soles that made
busy squeaking sounds on the tile floor.

Lou greeted her politely and introduced Cooper, who tried not to stare but couldn't stop looking at the nonalcoholic beer clutched in her ranch-chapped hands.

"Gretel Rosenbaum," she said, making a point of giving Cooper her whole name, hoping to prompt him a little.

"I can't vouch for his table manners either," Lou said. "He's been down in Mexico—no telling what strange customs he's picked up. Don't worry, I'll keep him in line."

Cooper smiled and dusted off a little of his charm to try on Rosenbaum's mother. "It sure smells good in here, Gretel. It's been awhile since I've had home cooking."

He saw right away that using her first name like that had been a mistake because her shoulders stiffened and the Brenda Lee smile dropped from her face as she stepped closer and whacked down his bullshit charm with a look. Her eyes settled on the cougar blood spotting his dirty jeans and the tender-looking new skin on his sun-fried arm. She shook her head and shuffled back to the stove, grasping the Kingsbury again.

"You'd better sit and get started," she said, "food's getting cold."

Rosenbaum went over to the fridge and poured them all iced tea in purple aluminum tonic glasses. "We don't get many guests," he said, motioning for them to sit.

"Well, you're a touch off the beaten path. I'd say that's gotta be a factor," said Lou.

"We like it here," Gretel Rosenbaum said. "We can hear ourselves think. It gives us clarity, isn't that right, Gary?"

Her son nodded and mumbled something about peace of mind and waited for his guests to take chairs. Cooper fully expected that before he was able to dig in he'd have to hurdle some long hand-holding prayer of thanksgiving. But nothing of the sort happened. Lou picked up his fork and tucked a square of Bounty into his shirt collar as Gretel Rosenbaum rolled out the grub—fried pork chops, slaw with red onions chopped into it, applesauce, parsley potatoes, and, yes, warm biscuits with little pats of butter cut on top.

"It would have been better an hour ago," she said bitterly, fetching another can of Kingsbury NA from the fridge. "Enjoy, boys, there's a Burt Reynolds movie on the network."

She left and they chowed down. Cooper, remembering what the Dumpster pizza back in Tucson had done to his guts, took it easy, grooving on the good old American home eats as he forked biscuits in half and made little pork chop sandwiches with applesauce and slaw smashed in between.

After they'd cleaned up the kitchen, Rosenbaum took them out to the barn for a tour of his ant farm operation and to show them where they'd be bunking for the night. Cooper helped him slide back the barn door, watching as he groped around for lights and clicked them on to reveal dozens of coffin-sized Plexiglas boxes sitting on sawhorses and milk crates. Each box contained a different ant nest. Some nests looked like busy pueblos built into the sides of miniature volcanoes and others had large underground chambers full of eggs and twigs.

Rosenbaum walked down an aisle ticking off the various names: "Pyramid ants, thief ants, big-headed ants, pharaoh ants, leaf cutters, velvety tree ants, and over in this apartment I've got some crazy ants, and right here's your basic pavement ant."

"I wanna see them fire ants again," said Lou.

Rosenbaum walked them over to the far corner and showed them a box filled with play sand where hundreds of ordinary-looking red ants were busily building a Tower of Babel out of the sand and bits of leaf molt.

Lou tapped on the plastic, trying to stir them up. "These dudes don't look so bad to me. What's all the fuss about?"

"Strength in numbers," Rosenbaum said. "One bite burns, but when several hundred bite you it feels like you've been dipped in Drano." He lifted up the lid and took a stick and knocked down their mound. The ants boiled out from under the rubble, confused and angrily looking for some enemy to carry off and bite to death.

"What did you do that for?" Lou asked as the ants swarmed over their wrecked project.

"You've got to keep them busy," Rosenbaum explained. "Otherwise, if I let them establish themselves they start looking for something else to do. They keep building and building."

"You sell fire ants?" Cooper asked.

"I'm not supposed to, but I get requests and I don't ask questions." Lou looked at him and smirked.

"I meant, do you make any money off them?"

"For the common stuff I can hunt up around here I get a penny an ant, plus shipping and handling, of course," Rosenbaum said. "Now, some of the more exotic stuff I've got to wheel and deal for costs a little more. All in all I'm doing okay. I've made my hobby pay and it beats school."

"Root canals beat school," Lou said. "Hell, I'd rather buff floors than go to school. I'd rather assemble boxes and have gout. I'd rather—"

"We get the point, Lou," Rosenbaum said. "Now, should we show Coop the battle arena?"

"Hell, yes."

Rosenbaum ushered them over to a large birdcage-looking contraption built out of one-by-ones, porch screen, and Astroturf. There were tiny trap doors at the bottom and top and an empty Cool Whip tub in the center containing a stew of dirty honey and broken Nilla Wafers. Thousands of dead ants littered the edges, along with the dried-out bodies of other insects—walking sticks, locusts, yellow jackets, dung beetles, termites, centipedes, earthworms curled into hard brown question marks, capsized June bugs, wolf spiders, scorpions, silverfish, and dozens of strange bugs Cooper had never seen before.

"What is it?" asked Cooper.

"This is my insect coliseum," Rosenbaum said. "I tried to build it to scale but it didn't come out right."

Lou said, "You oughtta see some of the killer battles we've had, Coop."

"Who wins?" Cooper asked.

"Most of the time the ants overcome with teamwork, persistence, and a willingness to die for their queen," said Rosenbaum. "She's got a grip on them."

"Hey, what happened to the chariots, Rosie?"

"The carpenter ants ate the cardboard ones," said Rosenbaum. "I think I'm going to leave it just like it is."

"You'll let me know when you do the killer bees versus the fire ants."

"I'm still working out the details," Rosenbaum said.

"It's gonna be bloodier than Antietam," Lou said. "Get it?"

"Ants and bees don't bleed," said Rosenbaum. "Sure, they ooze a little Technicolor stuff, but you couldn't call it blood."

"Whatever, the point is the body count's gonna be high." He turned to Cooper. "I keep telling him he should mount some cameras and sell the footage to PBS or some shit like that."

"I don't seek publicity," said Rosenbaum. "You start sucking on that tit and it's all over."

"True, very true," said Lou.

Rosenbaum shrugged and took them over to a corner of the barn where a pair of futons sat on a raised plywood platform with a nightstand sandwiched between them. "Here you go. Don't mess with the ants—you monkey with the wrong ones and they'll kill you. Same with the thermostat. I can't have you guys messing up the room temperature. I've got a system."

Lou clicked his heels and saluted. "Yes, sir!"

After they'd hauled their bags in from the van, Rosenbaum called them over to a workbench and pointed at a small goldfish bowl filled with ants. Next to the bowl sat a bag of jumbo marshmallows, a tin of lighter fluid, and a tray of disposable syringes.

"Watch this," he said, taking a marshmallow from the bag. "These guys lost their queen."

"So they're expendable?" said Lou.

"Oh, I suppose I could let them assimilate into some other colony, but what's the fun in that."

"That's the spirit, Rosie," Lou said.

"I call this one marshmallow napalm death."

They watched as he filled the syringe with a few ccs of lighter fluid, sank the needle into the marshmallow, and injected it. Then he took a piece of thread, stuck it in the marshmallow like a wick, slicked the whole thing with a little spit, and dropped it into the fishbowl. The ants promptly swarmed the sticky obelisk.

When the marshmallow was completely upholstered with cinnamon-colored ants, Rosenbaum handed Cooper a lighter. "You can have the honors," he said, pointing at the thread dangling over the lip of the bowl.

It took several tries but Cooper finally got the thread to catch. They crowded around the fishbowl as the thread burned down the side of the glass. A few of the more alert ants tried to escape but were blown back when the flame hit the pocket of lighter fluid, the marshmallow quickly transformed into a ball of molten sugar and dying ants.

Lou hunkered over the workbench. "It's a good thing ants can't scream," he said.

Cooper felt guilty as he watched the marshmallow expand into a bright orange globe, shedding fried ant bodies and a plume of evil black smoke that smelled like torched hair and burnt bologna.

Rosenbaum clamped a board over the opening and smothered the fire. "Okay, that's enough," he said.

"Not bad," Lou shouted, "not bad at all!"

Once the smoke cleared, Cooper studied the bubbling remains of the marshmallow for survivors. But there were none and so he handed the lighter back.

"What's the matter?" Lou asked. "I mean, that was pretty fucking cool, right?"

"It was okay."

"Okay, what do you mean, okay?" Lou said, dancing around him. "Hey, Rosie, I think we have a conscientious objector here, a bleeding heart."

"Without a queen they would have run around in circles and died," Rosenbaum said. "They had nothing to live for."

Cooper said he was tired and went to have a look at the futons. Mice had been at them and there was a hard-looking spider crouched on the nightstand waiting for its supper.

When Lou came over, Cooper reminded him about the phone call he needed to make.

"Of course," Lou said. "My wallet's still smarting from that fill-up in Page. I don't believe you meant to push regular and hit ultra."

"It was a mistake," Cooper said. "Just keep a tab. I have every intention of settling the bill."

Lou huddled with Rosenbaum and after a minute Cooper was led back to the house.

Rosenbaum stood lookout for his mother as Cooper dialed directory assistance. He got Moe's number easy enough and then Moe, who came on the line with a croak, sounding half whacked on something. It took Cooper a couple of minutes to jog Moe's memory. He cupped the receiver, whispering, "Moe, it's me, Fitch, come on, you remember. Old Ain't-It-a-Bitch-Fitch, your old war buddy . . . Yeah, that's right, just like Sarge Butera . . . No, I did not like the way he called cadence." He chanted into the phone: *"M-1 tanker gonna take a little trip, mission unspoken, destination unknown, don't even know if I'm ever comin' home . . ."*

Rosenbaum motioned for Cooper to speed up the phone call. Mother was stirring in the other room.

"That's right," Cooper said to Moe, "we'll shoot the shit and then some. Ice the beer, I'm comin', buddy."

He hung up and dashed out the back door, and when he got back to the barn he was greeted by Lou, who was holding the old Wanted poster, grinning like a monk. Lou had obviously rummaged through his bags because not only was the parachute spread across the futon but the articles about the D. B. Cooper Day celebrations and Book IV were scattered across the pallets.

"Irv Cooper, my ass," Lou said.

Cooper froze, not sure if he should run or try to concoct some loopy story and deny. He quickly surmised that both options lacked charm and neither would serve any purpose. There was no place to run to, plus he figured Lou was crazy enough not to get all worked up about his criminal past. But more than that, he was tired and no longer cared.

"Here I thought you were some kind of clever mooch, stringing me along with that buried-stash story of yours," Lou crowed. "Turns out I've been sharing the road with D. B. fucking Cooper." His eyes darted back and forth between the Wanted sketch and Cooper, now longhaired and slouching toward him. "I can see the years have been rough on you and then some. Your neck's filled out, and what do you have against sunblock?"

He snatched the poster and book from him, shoving them back inside his duffle. "That's not me."

"Nice try," Lou said, "but they got them beady eyes of yours right. And there's no mistaking that brow."

"Shut up."

"Relax, Jackson, I'm not going to turn you in. I'm just having some fun. I have no love for law enforcement. Hell, I'm not even going to tell Rosenbaum, because he's liable to tell his mother, who strikes me as a police scanner junkie. You'd do better to worry about melanoma than the Feds, as far as I'm concerned. I was born to keep my mouth shut. It's a must in my line of work. Come to think of it, I'm probably a wanted man someplace."

"So you're not going to turn me in?"

Lou laughed. "What the hell for?"

"Well . . . there's the reward."

"Oh yeah. Right. My lucky day."

"What's that supposed to mean?"

"It was a long time ago, Coop. The law's moved on. All you've gotta do is turn on the boob tube to see crime's gotten more violent. But why don't we go down to the creek first and wash up. I've got a lot of questions."

"Such as?"

"Let's see," he said. "For shits and grins, tell me how you end up broke and hitching rides in Tucson after you nipped the airlines for all that money?"

"My big mouth, a girl, fear of Mexican banks, and some crafty bandits who were not above violence."

"Ouch," said Lou, tossing him a thin towel and a bar of hotel soap. "You coming?"

Lou led him across a dusty field to the creek. They walked along its rocky bank until they came to a sharp bend where the water elbowed around a long stone shelf and then bunched up into a slow gravel-bottomed pool before racing down past the dark Rosenbaum house.

"How cold is it?" Cooper asked, watching the moon and stars ripple and blink on its surface.

"It's a nut froster. You're better off jumping. You should be good at that."

They undressed on a stone ledge and plunged into the heart-arresting cold of the back eddy, their toes grabbing smooth gravel. Cooper surfaced with a whoop and quickly hit the vitals, rubbing soap over his balls, pits, face, and ass before dipping under for a rinse and crawling back to the ledge, where he toweled off.

Lou followed and they sat on the ledge, listening to the creek burble by and a coyote yipping after something in the dark. Both men listened as other coyotes joined in.

"Sounds like they got what they were after," Lou said, when the yipping suddenly stopped.

Cooper slicked back his hair. "Hoo, boy, I needed that. I feel like a new man." He peeled some more skin off his arm and rubbed the rest of the scab off the back of his skull.

"So how did it feel?" Lou said, pounding on his head, trying to dislodge some creek water from his ears.

"Cold."

"No, I meant taking all that money and jumping out of the plane?"

"That was cold too. I picked the worst day and at first it was like I was going to die, but when I landed and figured my knee wasn't too munched and I could walk, it was like I was never gonna get old, like I was some kinda secret hero and not just another hopeless asshole. A lot of that was the money and the fact that I hadn't killed myself."

"How come you never did it again?"

"I didn't want to press my luck."

"Everybody thinks you croaked," said Lou. "They had you on *In Search of . . .*, man. Spock was talking you up. I remember because my brother couldn't get enough of the Bigfoot episode and we had to watch that stupid show and be fooled every week."

"Well, I didn't die. I'm right here. I'm back."

"And nobody's gonna care."

"You don't know that."

"Trust me, nobody's gonna give three shits. Half the folks in this country can't even name their senator—what makes you think they're gonna remember you?"

"I'm not worried about the folks, it's the law I don't want to meet and greet."

"No problem," Lou said. "I do it all the time."

Cooper stood and tried to catch his reflection in the moonlit creek but saw only a shadowy tower of refracted starlight and a dark water moon where his head ought to be. He looked up and saw hundreds of bats cutting across the night sky, chasing dinner. It bothered him that birds seemed to get all the attention; the bat world seemed as rich and varied and twice as secretive. Plus they had radar, or was it sonar? He could not remember.

"Don't worry, I'll get you to Oregon," Lou said. "As long as we've still got a deal. I'm not going to gouge you. As far as I'm concerned, any dude who jumps out of a jet deserves whatever he can take."

"Actually, it's Washington I need to get to, not Oregon, but just across the river."

"So we'll go to Washington. Same difference. It's not every day you get to meet a famous criminal and revisit former glory."

Cooper stood and offered to shake hands on the deal.

"Don't worry, I'll get you there."

"I called my buddy and we're all set."

"This isn't some kind of ambush, is it? Lure a good Samaritan such as myself to some dark woods and then you and your mutant friends have some fun with me."

Cooper said it was not and they shook again, dressed, and went back to the barn, and after Lou ran out of questions they turned out the light and fell asleep listening to the ants tunneling along the walls of their Plexiglas apartments, building towers of sand that in the morning would be leveled by Rosenbaum and his stick.

■

AFTER LEAVING ANNE'S, Frank stopped by the realty office to see Clare and ask if she wanted to get some lunch. He'd left the gun in the car and missed the weight of it on his ribs but knew that it would only make for more questions and he already felt guilty enough about his recent foolishness and wanted to make it up to her. But she was out at a showing and so he chatted with Cecil about parking tickets and some graffiti Cecil had observed in the courthouse bathroom about two blind men groping an elephant. Cecil kept excusing himself to pick up the phone and answer vague questions about various listings, all the while rolling his eyes at Frank and saying, "Yes, that's right, it's pretty firm, but there might be a little wiggle room. Let me take your number." He did not take down any numbers.

Frank stood to go. "I'd better let you get back to work."

"You want me to tell her anything for you?"

Frank shook his head. "Just killing time. Haven't been by in a while, but I see not much has changed. It's busy, the phones are ringing, and the coffee still tastes like cat piss."

"What about you? Have you been keeping busy?"

Frank gave him a cagey, guy-to-guy look and said, "I've been poking around."

"A shark swims to keep alive."

"What do you mean by that?"

Cecil shook his head. He'd missed a few spots shaving and had a dab of dried cream perched behind his left ear. "Clare told me you were a little out of sorts."

"Did she?"

"She did," said Cecil. "She was worried and wanted my advice on retirement. You know, back when I retired from the school I spent a lot of time in the garage drinking."

"That's not the problem."

"I got help, Frank. There is a higher power, you know."

"I don't need AA."

"There are a lot of misconceptions about the program."

"I don't want to get into it."

Cecil tilted back in his chair and smoothed his candy-striped tie across his belly, ready for Frank to tell him he'd been drinking too much and not sleeping.

Instead Frank stood to go. The cold medicine was wearing off and he was beginning to feel like shit again. "Well, it was good seeing you, Cecil. Tell her I'll be home and have dinner ready."

After an awkward silence Cecil walked Frank past the maze of tan work cubicles and light-starved plants to the front entrance. Cecil greeted a young couple who'd obviously exhausted the stack of out-of-date magazines. The girl's hair was twisted into athletic pigtails and her equally sporty husband sat bouncing his legs and staring up at the stained ceiling tiles, slack-jawed. Ten years ago Frank would have pegged them as possible drug addicts. But now the girl, with her gaunt cheeks and soft brown eyes, reminded him of Anne.

"Market virgins," Cecil said, pointing at the young couple.

The girl sprang to her feet and forced a smile while her husband ogled the putty-colored appliance and steel hook that was Cecil's hand.

"I'll see you," said Frank, stepping out the door.

But Frank didn't go home. Instead he drove by the rental to check on the garage door repair and saw Harvey's car in the driveway, dripping transmission fluid. The grass had been mowed, the leaves raked, and even the usually errant trash can lids sat snugly in place atop their canisters. He parked and walked up the drive, past a flock of greedy sparrows crowding the bird feeder in a rush to insert their beaks and a couple of old redwood deck chairs that needed to find their way to the curb for pickup.

He saw that the door had been repaired. Three hundred and eighty-five dollars later it worked fine; even the splintered jamb had been painted over and caulked. Unable to resist the urge, he stuck his finger in the white bead of caulk and left a fingerprint, and just as he was about to sneak back to the car he turned around to find Harvey standing there, his mad scientist hair tamed, nails clipped, and smelling of talcum powder. He was, Frank thought, a monument to the look-sharp, be-sharp school of grooming

"She's back," said Harvey.

"Who's back?"

"Stephanie," he said. "And this time I think it's for good. She's ready to commit to our relationship."

"Harvey, I'm just your landlord, remember? You pay the rent on time and stick to the lease and that's all I need to know."

Harvey continued, unfazed. "She's inside. Would you like to meet her?" And before Frank could answer, he yelled, "Stephanie, come on out and meet my landlord, sweetie."

There was no answer and so Frank reluctantly followed him through the back door and into the kitchen, where two vanilla tea candles labored near an open window and a clock radio over the sink rattled out some anonymous rock tune that Frank used to know.

"Steph?" Harvey called.

A woman emerged from the bedroom dressed in sweatpants and a black lace top with billowy sleeves. She was big but moved with an unexpected grace that forced Frank to acknowledge her zaftig beauty—the thick curly hair, buttery cheeks, ample shoulders, and moist hazel eyes with lashes to spare. She greeted him with a shy dip of her head and apologized about the state of the house as Harvey hovered, grinning and adjusting his glasses.

"I'm sorry about the garage," Stephanie said. "I was in a state and I guess I wasn't thinking too clearly."

He told her it was okay.

"I'd still like to make you something," she said.

Harvey jumped between them. "Stephanie does miniature topiary." He pointed to a fake globe-shaped tree sitting in an imitation brass bucket near the door. It seemed to Frank to serve no possible function other than to vaguely remind one of a plastic scrotum.

"Really, it's okay," he said.

"What about a potpourri pie?" Stephanie asked. "Maybe your wife would like one?"

"Hey, that's a great idea, sweetie," said Harvey. "Wait till you see this lattice crust she makes out of felt. I swear they look just like the real thing."

"They smell delicious too. I'll be sure to use lots of lavender and maybe some sweet william," said Stephanie. "Cinnamon is always nice too. Do you like cinnamon?"

"She's good with her hands," Harvey chimed in. "She won an award at the craft fair last year."

"It was just a ribbon, Harv."

"A special merit ribbon."

"Whatever." Stephanie sighed, tossing her hands up. "I'd really like to make you one. It would make me feel better about breaking the garage."

There was no way out and so Frank said, "Okay."

Stephanie clapped her hands. "Which one do you want? Do you want a topiary or a potpourri pie? Or even both, if you want."

"I think maybe just the pie," said Frank. "But there's no hurry. I just came by to check if the work had been done on the garage door. Now I'd better get back."

Harvey followed him all the way to the curb like a large tomcat clumsily stalking mice. "So what do you think?" he asked.

"I think the guy did nice work on the garage door."

"No, I meant about Stephanie."

"She's a keeper."

Harvey nodded. "I'm a pretty lucky guy. I let her go and she came fluttering back to me."

"Good-bye, Harvey," said Frank. "We'll send a copy of the bill and you can pay it with the rent or break it up over a couple of months. Let us know if you want to add Stephanie to the lease."

The grin dropped from Harvey's face. "Hmmm . . . I don't know about that just yet."

"If she's going to be breaking things, I'd like to have her on there. It will protect you too."

"But it was an accident."

"And an expensive one. You might want to consider putting her on the lease."

With that, Frank tossed him a crisp good-bye salute and slid into the car.

He went home and made dinner for Clare, a quick pasta sauce—his one and only dish. She arrived late, still mad and wanting to know if he felt better. He lied and said he did, ushering her toward the table, Coltrane playing softly on the stereo even though she hated jazz and had merely learned to tolerate it after all the years.

"I used vermouth this time," he said, setting a plate down and pouring them both some wine. Clare picked at her food and was unusually quiet, leafing through an inspection report on a house she had a lowball offer on.

Later, as they stood to clear the table, he asked about her day, explaining how he'd stopped by to see her.

"Cecil gave me the message."

"Well, how was your day?"

"It wasn't all dancing," she said. Then she asked what he'd done with himself and he told her how he'd finally met Harvey's girlfriend and how the garage door had been repaired. He said nothing about how he'd gone by Anne's, because it would be too much to explain and in the end she might suspect something.

He waited and then told her he might do something with Peck.

"Something?"

He told her how Peck wanted him to go out and look for Cooper with him, trying hard not to make it sound like anything more than a stupid lark.

"Now?" Anne said. "I mean, that was a long time ago, and what do you have to do with Cooper?"

"I was there," he said. "Remember, I found that girl's body?"

She shivered with the memory and he asked her what was wrong.

"It just sounds a little weird, Frank."

"Well, I'll humor him. It'll get me out of the house. That's what you want, isn't it?"

"Not just out of the house but productively out of the house."

"It might be fun," he said, mustering a smile.

"Okay, that's enough wine for you," she said. She dumped his remaining wine into her glass. "You're looking sick again." She pointed at his eyes. "I can see it here."

"I'm fine, really."

"Instead of messing around with Peck, why don't you see about a job?"

"I will," he said.

She crinkled her nose and stared at her hands, pressing on the veins, trying to make them look younger, or maybe she was still thinking of the pond girl and how he'd come home for months after that moody, morose, and willing to talk only after he'd put down three or four beers and then only about Cooper and what kind of guy would pull a crazy-ass stunt like that.

He hugged her and she turned into it, facing him. "I'm serious," she said.

"I know you are."

She sighed, pushed him away, and said she'd finish up the dishes. But he lingered and pitched in until her mood lightened and she went into the den to watch television without him.

CHAPTER THIRTEEN

The next day Frank waited until Clare had raced off to show a three-bedroom saltbox on two acres west of town before he arranged to meet Peck and have a look at the file. He felt better but still a little stuffed up so he took some cold medicine and drank two glasses of juice. He did not want or need the thundering headache of the previous day to return and chop his day in half. Unable to sleep, he had risen, as had become his custom, to go downstairs looking for the vodka bottle. Only this time he'd remembered to cover his tracks, washing and replacing the glass, making sure he draped the dishcloth over the center of the sink exactly as Clare had left it, before making his rounds.

Next to the phone he found a note Clare had left, telling him that Walt had called. He fingered the note, sifting through the last forty-eight hours, trying to remember what he'd said to Walt, only half remembering some vague promise he'd made to tool around the river in the refurbished boat. But when he called there was no answer and so he left.

He'd resolved to let things take their course, and when Peck pulled up in his car and handed Frank the file, he told Peck to make the report—that he'd spoken to Anne several times and wanted to step back and make sure nothing bad happened.

Peck wiped road dust off his rearview. "Don't worry, I'm already on top of it. This is not a nice man. If this Blackwood's out there, I'd like to know," he said.

"Oh, he's out there."

"I mean here," said Peck.

"I hope not."

"Is there anything I should know before I go sticking my neck out? You did tell her not to mention your name, right? Not that it would be a big deal, it's just I'd like to know what she's going to say when I have someone sent over."

"I want you to do it. I mean, you did get the first call."

Peck thought a minute and then said, "Okay."

"She told me she was moving."

"Yeah?"

"Out of state."

"We'll see about that." Peck checked his watch as a logging truck shuddered to a halt at the intersection. The air tasted like exhaust and there was some kind of dark bird circling a stubbled cornfield. "Anything else I need to know about?"

Frank gave him the stare and waited until the younger agent broke it, before telling him about how she thought she'd seen somebody outside her trailer.

"And you think it was her ex-husband?"

"I don't know. She said she woke up and there was this guy standing outside under a tree."

"I'll get on this as soon as possible."

Frank nodded, part of him relieved to have the whole thing out in the open and Peck running with the ball. "She's not going to cooperate, because she doesn't want her life ruined. She didn't want me to say anything."

"What life? She lives in a trailer."

Frank restrained himself from defending her. It would only cloud the issue at hand. He needed Peck to be the one to handle the case and not some by-the-book hard-ass. "Well, that's what she thinks is going to happen," he said. "And I can't really blame her. She hasn't committed a crime."

"She doesn't have much of a choice now, does she?"

Frank shrugged. "She's a friend."

"Don't worry, that's between us. Let's just hope it's nothing. Now, do you have time for a drive later?"

"I was going to have a look at this," Frank said, shaking the case file. "But yeah, maybe. It's not like I've got anything better to do."

"Call me."

Frank said he would, watching as Peck gave him a goofy thumbs-up, circled back, and pulled into traffic.

With the car idling and his foot on the brake pedal, Frank flipped through the copied file, the details coming back to him in punchy little crime-scene summaries and eyewitness accounts, each a testament to Blackwood's criminal chops and ability to avoid capture by both law enforcement and the half-dozen bounty hunters who'd been looking to pick him up for a fee all these years. Why shouldn't he come back? And why shouldn't Frank assume that the worst could and would happen? He lingered on a mug shot of Blackwood. In it he was giving the camera a cold jailhouse stare, his jaw jutting forward like it wanted to put out the lens. Behind the photo was one of Anne. She was younger, her hair shorter. She looked better taken care of, a little eye shadow and a tan, but there was a hardness in her eyes he recognized. It was the same expression she'd flashed at him the day before when he'd told her he was going back on his promise. Under the photo there was a sentence detailing her distinguishing marks: brown hair, hazel eyes, five foot six, etc., and a spider web tattoo on her hip. He'd forgotten all about the tattoo and remembered seeing it only a few times when she'd bent to pick up some toy on the floor. Even now, just reading about it, he felt himself getting aroused as he thought about trying to see her again.

He shut the file and went over their last conversation. She'd been serious about moving to Aspen, a place where he imagined rich people sat around massive stone hearths talking about double black diamonds and single malts in bored tones as their kids, named after rivers and mountain ranges, dismantled the twigged-out knick-knacks. These people, Frank believed, were capable of farming out the dull day-to-day tasks such as housework and lawn maintenance without suffering even the slightest twinge of blue-collar guilt. She would certainly make more money and when he saw her again he'd be sure to encourage the move.

He drove by the marina and found Walt's car in the lot. The *Weaver's Beam* was gone and he imagined his father-in-law tooling up and down the river, getting the feel of the boat and practicing his sea squint. He killed an hour at the hardware store and another at the shooting range, where he fired the 9mm for the first time, staying at the benchrest until his shoulders ached and his bunchings began to pull together. Not as good as back in the day when he'd made a habit of shooting twice a week, but not bad and certainly better than the stoned black kid doing some sideways gangster bullshit with a chromed .357 in the lane next to him or the gray-haired man hunched over the bench in an old-style marine stance, squeezing out rounds on his vintage Colt. Frank picked up his casings, folded his targets, and Frisbeed them into the trash and left, the gun tucked under his arm. The heavy primer-laden air of the range had done nothing to drive Anne from his mind. He could still shoot, though, and what good that did him he did not know.

By the time he found his car he'd already decided to drive by Anne's again before going home to wait for Peck's call. He'd made up his mind to apologize for his behavior, but when he pulled down her street and saw a sedan with government plates parked behind her Taurus, he kept driving and stopped alongside the tree where Anne had seen the man. He dropped the car into park but left the motor running, trying to figure out how foolish he should feel riding over there with the freshly fired 9mm strapped to his side like he was still on the job, when the job was parked back there in front of her trailer. He found a half-evaporated bottle of NyQuil he'd stashed in the glove box. It was left over from the last cold, and when he unscrewed the

lid, blue crust fell in his lap. He sniffed and took a drink. It tasted
stronger than usual and as he pawed his tongue against the roof of his
mouth, trying to get the medicine taste off it, he eyed Anne's trailer,
wondering how Peck had managed to act so fast and why it was some
other agent's car parked outside. Had something gone wrong? Or had
Anne made the call herself? Either way, he didn't know where it left
him, except to wait and try to find out. He took comfort in the fact
that had something really gone wrong and J. B. had shown up there
would have been a helluva lot more action—local cruisers with flashing lights, a few more agents, and perhaps even a paramedic. Instead
it was just the one car, no lights, no yelling, just Frank sitting in his
idling car thinking about whether or not he still wanted to fuck Anne
or if it was enough that he'd finally tiptoed up to the line without
fouling anything up too bad. Sure, he could walk away and be back
to his normal old self in a week, but he'd still be retired, still lacking a
comfortable routine to carry him through the stack of days. Then
what?

The whole thing had made him awkward, hopeful and like some
hopped-up sixteen-year-old, recklessly out of touch with his feelings.
And maybe that's what he'd wanted all along, a taste of the other side,
and Anne with her fucked-up past and day-to-day struggles and spider web tattoo was just that. Only she'd spun it all around on him and
he had no clue how that had happened or where that left him, just
that she'd kissed him and he'd liked it even though he knew he would
never really do anything besides toss the consequences around.

An hour and a half later he saw Agent Sanitsky exit Anne's trailer
and stretch his back before getting into his car and leaving.

Frank sat tight for another twenty minutes until he was sure Sanitsky wasn't coming back. He rehearsed what he could say to her that
would get him off the hook. But he couldn't work out the details and
so he floated up to her door on a crosswind of NyQuil and nerves. He
knocked.

She answered in a pair of worn gray sweatpants that hung low on
her hips to reveal little half moons of flesh but no tattoo. It was
lower, Frank thought, as he forced himself to meet her gaze.

"That was a shitty thing to do," she said.

He looked around. The boys were gone, the ashtray was full, and the cardboard U-Haul boxes he'd glimpsed the other day stood stacked in the hallway, filled and taped shut.

"You're right, but—"

"Asshole," she hissed, her hand coming up like she wanted to smack him. He let her pace a minute, searching for her pack of cigarettes and finding only the lighter.

"I did it because I had to, because—"

She cut him off again. "I don't wanna hear the job bullshit, Frank. I mean, spare me, you're retired."

"I was going to say I did it because I cared, because I'm worried. I mean if something happened . . ." He knew it sounded all wrong and unintentionally insincere, but he couldn't bring himself to cut through all the crap and tell her what was really on his mind, how he didn't want her to leave, but that he understood, and how it was the same for the kiss the other day.

"Nothing's going to happen, Frank. Nothing except I get my life invaded all over again while everybody else is just *doing their job.*"

"You can still make the move," he told her. "It might just take a little longer."

"Please."

He apologized but didn't dare step across the floor to try to comfort her. Instead he stood there until she got a hold of herself and looked at him, ready to talk. "Okay," she said, "it's done. They know. Now, why did you come back here?"

He didn't have an answer for her and she knew it.

"Forget it," Anne said, hiking up the sweatpants and taking a deep breath. "I probably already know the answer to that one."

"So what are they going to do?"

"He said they were going to send some tech guys over to look at the phone. Oh, and he promised to keep the intrusions to a minimum, but I've heard that before."

"They say anything about a hardwire on the phone?"

She nodded. "I agreed after he explained how they would move to get a court-approved electronic something or other if I refused."

"Standard operating procedure," he said. "And did you tell him about the key or the man you saw standing outside?"

"He just wrote it down and said he'd get back to me."

"But you told him everything, right?"

"Of course I held back a few details," she said. "I didn't tell him about you, if that's what you're asking."

Frank leaned against the kitchen counter as his head began to clog again. "I was just getting to that part."

She squinted at him until he felt a blush rise in his cheeks. "Well, we're at it. See, I kept my end of the deal. And the other thing."

He struggled to say something halfway coherent but found himself momentarily light-headed. "You mean? . . ."

"I mean what happened between us the other day. The kiss."

He nodded. "That other thing."

"It's okay," she said. "It did relieve some of the tension, didn't it?"

Unable to answer, he paced into the living room and saw the couch. The afghan was twisted over one end and the shades were down. He watched the shadowy black dots of trapped flies buzzing behind them. When he turned around she was right behind him. He wanted to reach out and touch her. But he checked himself and felt stronger for it. He could do this—get back to normal, go see his daughter, look his wife in the eye, retire, get old, and maybe even go look for Cooper with Peck.

"If you want to go to Aspen, I think you should go," he said.

"I don't need your permission to move to Aspen. I just need money, which at the moment I don't have."

"I already told you I could help you with that."

"Now you're making me angry," she said, shaking a fist at him and pretending to be mad. "I don't expect you to give me money any more than I expect it to fall out of the sky."

"What I meant is that you shouldn't wait around here for this to sort itself out. Chances are J. B. won't call again and then you're

back to square one. They might even put you back under full surveillance."

"I know that." She sighed and collapsed into a fake leather arm-
chair. "Suddenly you're the one with all the answers."

"Let's hope not."

She looked up and smiled at him. "Come here, you."

Frank hesitated and finally shook his head. "No, I'd better not."

The surprise on her face at least partially confirmed for Frank that
a little of what she was doing was fucking with him, a not-so-subtle
attempt to keep him off-balance.

"I just came by to say that," he said.

"Say what?" She sat up and flicked her hair away from her face.
"You didn't say anything."

He leaned close. "What I mean is that if you want to go, I won't
say anything."

"Well, that's rich of you, Frank." She laughed.

"I mean it," he said. "You should really go."

Something in his voice spooked her because she nodded and
didn't say a word even as he turned and let himself out.

■

BY DAWN COOPER and Lou had shot through Salt Lake City and
crossed over into Idaho, where the sky stretched blue over brown
fields, aluminum grain elevators, spidery irrigation wheels, and
faded rail towns. Hawks drifted above, policing the gophers below
with their speeding shadows, and everywhere he looked Cooper saw
cattle grazing ignorantly.

Lou asked him about Mexico and Cooper told him about the camp
and the book.

"So you were looking for something?"

"Maybe," Cooper said. "I didn't have much of an agenda past getting the money."

"Did you find anything?"

"Hard to tell," he said. "Point was I got out and had some fun and it sure as hell beat working for a living. Doesn't seem like I've been gone long. I guess the time sort of got away from me."

"That doesn't sound all that bad to me."

"It wasn't."

They stopped for crullers and disappointing coffee at a Texaco, where they watched a man drain his Chevy's oil pan into a storm drain while the attendant looked on, shaking his head.

"You know," Lou said. "I think I remember something about some of your loot washing up along the Columbia."

Cooper chucked the rest of his cruller. "What are you talking about?"

"I recall reading something about it."

"Bullshit."

"No, some kid was building sand castles in the sand or something like that and he found this money that matched the serial numbers of the bills you took."

"Any reason you're telling me this now?"

Lou shrugged, his mouth full of donut paste. "I didn't want to dampen your enthusiasm. It's a long drive and it just came to me."

Cooper tried not to act rattled by the news as he pressed for more information, asking Lou exactly what paper he'd read this in.

"It wasn't the *National Enquirer*, if that's what you're asking," Lou said.

"Do you remember how much they found?"

"Not much, I don't think. The kid wanted to keep it."

He asked more questions and although Lou remained foggy on the exact details it was enough to start the dark bloom of worry growing in Cooper's gut as they trudged back to the van and hit the road.

A hundred miles later Lou asked him where he'd buried it.

"How do you know I buried it?"

"How else did it end up in a riverbank?"

"Don't worry about where I put it."

"Well, I am," Lou said. "Gas, food, and lodging are not free, Coop.

Gone are the days of free rides and charitable strangers. We live in suspicious times—"

"Okay, okay," he said. "I put it near a creek."

"Creeks flood, everybody knows that."

"I'm trying not to think about that." He changed the subject pointing at the large vented cardboard box sitting in the back of the van. "What's in the box?"

"Who knows," Lou said. "Rosenbaum's full of surprises and it's company policy not to ask too many questions, but a good guess would be ants or some other kind of bug. He said we had three days to get it there. Now, about this money."

"I don't want to talk about it."

Lou fired up the stereo and they drove.

Later they stopped at the Egg and I Diner, a small roadside establishment that smelled like cigarette smoke and Raid. The walls were festooned with oil paintings of white-tailed deer standing on sundappled ridges and nosing into glassy streams at dusk as rabbits and squirrels looked on. There were several signed head shots of celebrities Cooper didn't recognize. The menus were yellow and egg-shaped.

After ordering chicken-fried steak, Lou badgered the waitress with requests for coffee refills and fresh creamer. Cooper chose the hash and was disappointed to learn it didn't come with any eggs.

"You have to order it that way," Lou told him. "Eggs are no longer part of the deal. You go into one of these Greek places, they serve it with pepper rings."

"Pepper rings?"

"Yeah, I know."

He pushed the hash around. "You figure a place called the Egg and I . . ."

"Well, this steak tastes like deep-fried gym socks," Lou said. "Maybe we should hog and jog. I've hogged and jogged in twenty-six states and this meal's not worth the muscle to chew."

"I'm not going to do that."

"We could shout our dissatisfaction on the way out."

"And have them call the police. I don't think so."

"Suit yourself."

When the bill came, Lou grabbed it. "Okay, you don't wanna hog and jog, this one goes on your tab."

The cashier, a cheerful, chubby woman in a black T-shirt garlanded with cat hair and dried cornflakes, met them at the register humming "Momma, Don't Let Your Babies Grow Up to Be Cowboys."

Lou snapped a ten and a five down beside the register. She punched the keys with a pencil and made change the right way, handing Lou the paper and letting him put it back in his wallet before giving him the coins. He smiled and asked if she would answer a question for him.

"Yes," she said, "but I should warn you, I have a very large husband."

Lou snapped his fingers. "Lucky man."

She blushed and made busy, ragging a stubborn maple syrup spatter on the countertop.

"Do you know who D. B. Cooper is?" he asked.

"D. B. who, hon?"

"Cooper, D. B. Cooper."

Cooper froze, his hand on the steel toothpick dispenser, midroll.

"You don't mean Blake Cooper over on Ridge Road, do you?" she said. "He doesn't come in so much anymore."

A man wearing a creased feed cap looked up from the lunch counter and said, "Blake Cooper's dead, that's how come he don't come in anymore. He had a bad mole and they tried nuclear medicine but it failed."

"He wasn't much of a tipper," the cashier said. "Still, it's sad."

"No," Lou said. "I meant D. B. Cooper."

She chewed her lip and thought a minute. "No, I don't know any D. B. Cooper. What's the D. B. stand for?"

"Good question," he said, grinning over at Cooper. "I don't know either."

"I hope this isn't a joke, young man. I don't appreciate being made fun of."

"No, this is not a joke, ma'am. This here's D. B. Cooper. He hijacked a plane. Maybe you'd like him to sign a napkin or something."

"Stop it," Cooper said. "I'm splitting."

"This man's a famous criminal. He ate at your diner and did not like the hash."

With that Cooper reached out and grabbed Lou's windpipe, hoping to shut him up. In the short struggle that followed, the toothpick dispenser was knocked to the floor and they crashed into a revolving pie cooler, smashing one of the glass doors and toppling several massive VFW Softball League trophies that had been displayed on top.

The woman began pounding the service bell and yelling for someone named Marion. Cooper let go but it was too late, as the swinging doors that led to the grill parted and a heavy-set man in a bloody apron emerged brandishing a grill brick and a dripping deep fryer basket. He had thin blond hair, short yellow teeth, and narrow mean eyes that quickly took in the mess—toothpicks, bits of trophy marble, and small gold men holding bats—scattered all over the floor. "What's the commotion?" he shouted.

"These men are violent, Marion," the woman said, pointing an accusatory figure at them. "And this one's a hijacker."

"Is that so?" Marion said. "The Egg and I Diner does not want your business." He came out from behind the counter with surprising speed, ready to lay the grill brick upside their heads and pummel them with the deep fryer basket.

Cooper and Lou ran out the door and all the way to the van as Marion stood on the diner's cement stoop telling them he was calling the state troopers to have them arrested for disturbing the peace. Lou laughed and shot him the bird as they crawled inside the van and hit the road, leaving Marion to glower under the diner's happy yellow egg logo.

When they'd put a few sirenless miles between themselves and the diner, Cooper turned on Lou. "You're going to get me arrested."

"I was just trying to prove a point, that's all. I mean, you didn't have to put the kung fu grip on me."

"What point might that be?"

"That fame's delicate, fickle, and fleeting." He adjusted his glasses. "Nobody can remember your name. So you can stop worrying. Stress is a killer and, not to take anything away from your crime, but you've been forgotten, Coop. That lady had no fucking clue who you were."

"I'm not stressed and I'd appreciate it if you didn't do that again. You're now an accomplice."

"Accomplice to what?"

"Whatever they charge me with."

"You're paranoid, man. And if it came to that I'd just tell them you threatened to blow up my family."

"It may come to that."

Lou laughed. "Chill. Nobody cares what you did, and if they did they can't remember. You're old news."

"I don't know how I can relax with you running your mouth like that."

"I was just trying to illustrate a point."

"I don't need any more points illustrated. I just wanna get to Washington."

Lou apologized, but it wasn't the end of it. At a Gulf station he struck up a conversation with a doughy Methodist who was on his way to Boise to lecture the local Elks Club about tax shelters. He asked the man if he knew a D. B. Cooper.

"I'm good with faces, bad with names," the Methodist said.

The gas station proprietor hadn't heard of him either, although he did give them a free key chain shaped like a dollar sign and told a long story about his wife, who insisted on cutting his hair with a vacuum cleaner and pinking shears.

Unable to bear the thought that some freak flood had washed away the rest of his loot, Cooper convinced Lou to stop at a small library in Gooding, where they scanned headlines on microfiche and found the article. It was dated February 1980 and had a picture of fourteen-year-old Brian Ingram displaying several waterlogged twenty-dollar bills. Cooper read and reread the article as Lou shook his head and whistled, annoying a wiry reference librarian with crooked teeth who was reading *Megatrends*.

Outside, Cooper stared as a jet spat a contrail across the sky. He was pretty sure that what the kid had found was part of the smaller of the two stashes, which meant the Frigidaire had somehow been tipped into the creek or flooded out to the Columbia, as Lou had said. He was banking on the larger sum he'd sealed in the trunk of the abandoned Galaxy. If not, he'd come a long way just to swap war stories with his half-blind war buddy.

"Tough break," Lou said. "I hope you diversified."

"Fuck off."

Lou grabbed at his heart as if he'd been shot, drawing the stare of a droopy-lipped pensioner making his way up the library steps with his blue-checked slacks yanked up to his chest.

In Nyssa Lou asked a man sweeping a bank parking lot if he remembered D. B. Cooper. The man shook his head and moved away from the van, and the girl behind the counter at the Dairy Queen said no and so did two deliverymen eating parfaits at a nearby booth.

It wasn't until they stopped for dinner that a sleepy-looking trucker from Mountain Home said he remembered the name. "Jumped out of a plane, didn't he?"

"Yes, he did," said Lou, poking Cooper in the ribs.

"Well, let me tell you, there are days when I'd like to jump out of a plane and vanish. But I have a wife and kids and this job," the trucker said. "I'm all tied up."

A pimply-faced teen clutching a pair of sticky menus showed them to a booth, mumbled the specials, and took drink orders.

"See," Lou said. "You got lost a little too well. Nothing to be ashamed of. Most people can't even get off the ground with their dreams."

"I don't want to talk about this anymore. I just want to get the money," Cooper said. "You've made your point. Repeatedly. I never wanted the attention. It wasn't about that."

Lou asked him what he did want.

"To get away."

"And you did that and now you're back. What are you going to do after?"

Cooper said he didn't know.

"You should write a book."

"I have no interest in that."

"I could ghost it for you," Lou said. "I'm hell on the old word pi-ano. It could be the untold but true adventures of D. B. Cooper or something old-timey like that. I'd take a blurry photo for the jacket and throw in some bogus bit about how you're currently a produc-tive member of society living somewhere in the Midwest."

Cooper said no and even passed on a piece of coconut cream pie. He went back out to the van to consult the road map while Lou fin-ished up his coffee. Place-names came back to him as he stared at the tangled flow of roads and interstates, his finger stabbing a route north and west toward Moe's farm.

And by the time Lou strolled out of the diner, pausing to belch in front of a powder-blue Corvair and admire the last strobe of sunset pinking the hills, Cooper knew that he would need a plan if he was going to make it through without any more fuckups or detours. And that plan did not necessarily include Lou, merely the use of his van.

■

FRANK WASN'T HOME more than an hour when the phone rang. It was Peck calling from the field office.

"What's up?" Frank asked, waiting for the right moment to ask him how come Sanitsky had gotten to Anne so quick.

"So you wanna go for a drive and check out those places?"

Frank said sure.

"And there's something else."

"Yeah?"

"Meet me and I'll tell you," Peck said. "I don't wanna go into it here."

"This about Blackwood?"

There was a moment of silence on the other end.

"Just tell me."

"I would if I could," Peck whispered. "Know what I mean?"

"Okay," Frank said, deciding to hold on the questions until Peck told him what he had to tell him.

They arranged to meet at a gas station just off 205 and hung up. The phone immediately rang again, but Frank let the machine pick up as he stepped out the door, snagging his raincoat and an old baseball cap in case the weather turned to shit.

When he pulled into the gas station Peck was already waiting for him. He'd changed out of the jacket and tie and was leaning against his car dressed in tan hiking boots and a brand-new flannel shirt, the neck tags thrusting stiffly out of the neck hole.

After going inside for a cup of bad coffee, Frank asked about Anne and watched as Peck stalled, dumping a third creamer into his coffee.

"What about it?"

"I went by there and Sanitsky was already there," Frank said. "I thought you were going to take care of it."

"I did."

"Well then, what happened?"

Peck blew through the plastic vent at the coffee before answering. "When I ran it by Woodrell he insisted on putting Sanitsky on it ASAP."

Frank was puzzled why Woodrell, the special agent in charge, a man with too much crime and too few agents, would hop on an old case so quickly. "He give a reason?" he asked.

"Remember Wayne Garvey?"

Frank nodded. Garvey had been one of Blackwood's errand boys who'd been sent up for a five-year jolt, a kid, really, with a drug habit, an unpredictable temper, and soup for brains.

"Well, he got paroled last May," Peck said. "And two days ago they found him beat to death."

"Where?"

"His mother's house. Down in Blodgett."

"Blodgett?"

"East of Corvallis."

"I know where it is," Frank said.

"Woodrell's the one who made the connection."

"Does he think Blackwood was involved?"

"Well, he sent Brown and Rispoli down to check in with the local sheriff and M.E., but no, there's nothing yet. Just names in a case file, something the computer spit back at us."

"Shit."

"Look, Frank," Peck said, "it's probably nothing and you don't have to worry about the girl. I tried to step in and smooth things out, but they've already scheduled her for a hardwire and notified the local police department. They're also getting ready to put out photos of Blackwood—"

Frank squared up in front of Peck and put a grip on his shoulder to stop the list of bullshit procedural. "What else are you not telling me?"

"It's nothing."

"Well then, tell me if it's nothing."

"Okay, okay," Peck said. "It's just Woodrell said something about you and the girl."

"What do you mean?"

Peck shrugged. "It was just a little comment like he knew what was going on."

"There's nothing's going on."

It was Peck's turn to stare.

"Tell me what he said," Frank demanded.

"He just said that you'd gotten a little too close on the case before, that you'd become friends with her and that he might need to pick your brain about the situation."

"Was he talking about now?"

Peck shook his head. "Before, and I don't think he meant anything else besides you took a personal interest in Blackwood's ex,
that's all."

Frank thought a moment, trying to remember how Woodrell
might have gotten that impression. "You didn't tell him I've been
over there?"

"Of course not. Jesus, Frank, I'm on the hook as much as you
are."

He cuffed Peck on the shoulder and smiled. Now was the time to
drop it, he thought, walk away and let things take their course. Either he was fucked or he wasn't and in the end it didn't really matter what Woodrell thought or suspected about him and Anne. What
mattered was that she get out of this okay and that the Garvey thing
ended up being just some spectacularly odd-timed piece of random
violence and not connected to Blackwood at all.

They reached their cars and Frank took one last sip of his coffee
before dumping the rest into an oily mud puddle. "You'll let me
know what happens?" he asked.

"Of course," Peck told him. "But it's out of both of our hands now.
Now, we'd better hurry, it's getting late. You still want to do this with
me, right?"

There was no way he could say no, so he just nodded and followed Peck's Dodge east on 14 along the Columbia. It looked like
rain as they crossed the confluence of the Washougal and Columbia,
skipping briefly across Lady Island. Boats bobbed, cutting wakes in
the water below, as a steady pulse of cars tilted past them in the opposing lane. He tried not to think of Anne, but he couldn't stop feeling that, despite Peck's assurances to the contrary, he'd mucked
things up. He figured that the best-case scenario was that J. B. would
screw the pooch and press his luck with a traceable call and they'd
scoop him up, and that would be the end of it. Maybe then Anne
could get on with her life. About all he knew was that something had
gone awry and that he'd stumbled into some stupid midlife crisis of
his own design. So much so that he was about to go look for clues to

the whereabouts of a man who'd been gone more than a dozen years, a man who Frank now hoped had escaped to the sweet life.

Twenty minutes later he followed Peck's car down a narrow road, where it stopped along a weedy pull-off. Clouds obscured the Cascades and twisted sheets of fog crept down out of the surrounding pines, drifting across green pastures and whitewashing a nearby barn. They got out and Frank waited as Peck unfolded a series of road and topo maps across the hood of the car.

"What's the plan?" Frank asked.

Peck marked out a dozen houses and farms he wanted to check out. Some fronted small creeks; others were set off the river itself in dark pinewoods. The deeds ran back to before the skyjacking, he explained, and at least five of the men had served in the armed forces or had sons who'd been drafted. Frank couldn't remember if all this had been checked after the money had washed up, but he went along and listened to Peck, happy to have something to take his mind off Anne and the cards-on-the-table talk Clare had been waiting to bludgeon him with.

"And what are we looking for?"

"I don't know," Peck said. "I'm going on the assumption that the money could have been buried somewhere along the river or along one of these creek drainages."

"Maybe he put a big old pirate X to mark the spot or maybe he'll answer one of these doors and invite us in for coffee."

Peck ignored him. "You know, on the map it looks manageable, but . . . ," he said, pointing at the landscape, which seemed too vast a place to stumble on anything by accident, "you get out here and it's another story. I remember that from last time. You remember checking any of these?" Peck pointed at the list of names.

"Except for that Dipner I told you about, no. They were old dairy farmers."

"I told you about how the son's got the place now."

"Well, he wasn't there or I don't remember him." Frank looked around at the dense green. "At the worst, we'll get a hike in."

"We'll split them up," Peck said, handing him a copy of the map. "Meet back here in two hours."

He took a look at Peck's proposed search area and knew that it would take several such mornings of searching and knocking on doors to exhaust the list. He tried mustering some energy by telling himself that many a case had been broken or solved with thimble-fuls of sheer good luck and just such last-ditch throw-it-all-against-the-wall-and-see-what-sticks efforts.

So he drove up and down the small dirt roads checking battered aluminum mailboxes for addresses. He knocked on a few doors and tried to explain what he was looking for, but his heart wasn't in it and his story didn't make much sense. The people he did manage to catch gave him only brief answers before they shut the door in his face.

He stopped to ask directions from a man he'd spotted brush-hogging a drainage ditch and could feel the man staring at his city looks, the uncallused hands, his relatively clean clothes.

"State your business," the man demanded.

As he fumbled around for a convenient lie, the man scowled, restarted his tractor, and resumed mowing without looking back.

At a well-used access site he helped a young woman portage a ca-noe while her German shepherd ran circles around them barking at birds and crickets. He waited until she put in before hiking up the river to a flat rock pool, where he watched crippled mayflies swirl past him, riding eddies and small watery seams, as rising trout picked them off.

He hiked farther into the woods, sticking to a ridge, until his legs burned and he felt phlegm rattling inside his lungs. By the time he made it back down to his car, he was sweating, his whole body trem-bling with exertion.

He took it easy, walking along the water's edge, checking fields and banks until he was no longer sure what it was they were look-ing for. Maybe only Peck knew what that something was but more likely it was the thrill of exploring the riverbank and imagining the washout holes, undercut banks, tangled snarls of uprooted trees, and river trash deposited by recent floods to be the final resting place of D. B. Cooper or his lost stash. But his search turned up little more than a few cow bones and a dead and bloated raccoon caught in a back eddy.

As a slow drizzle began to dampen his hair and shoulders, the search seemed crazy to him and the lies he was forced to tell the cagey locals became harder and harder to sell with a straight face. Most of the folks he'd visited had run out to meet him halfway, turning him away from the house before he could get too close or else letting their dogs surround him, barking and snarling. The truth, he figured, would be not only easier but far more interesting. Telling them he was looking for a man who'd jumped out of a plane over a decade ago would be a hell of an icebreaker.

As it was, he obeyed the No Trespassing signs if they looked new and had been posted on every available stump or fence post.

When he came to Moe Dipner's overgrown farmhouse he stopped for a moment to admire the rusty sprawl of farm implements—the hay rakes and retired manure spreaders sprinkled across the front field like lawn ornaments. He had decided that this would be the last house of the day because his socks were wet and he was tired of dodging deerflies. Plus he'd banged his shin on a river stone.

So he pulled into the half-moon drive and parked next to an old Ford tractor that had once been a bright fire engine red but now was little more than a muddy beet-colored heap of metal standing guard near the stone path leading to the dilapidated house. He looked around. Hawthorne, sumac, thistle, and bright green juniper bushes had conquered the pastures. Sprung wire curled around crooked fence posts. There was a milking barn filled with moldering hay bales and brown grocery sacks stuffed with waterlogged newspaper. The barn sagged badly, its paint peeling in large white flakes, the gutters hanging off its sides like dropped straws.

Frank scanned the property for the nose of a Remington pump or the blur of an attacking dog before approaching the house. There was a small porch running along the front with a series of broken gliders, dozens of empty Boone's Farm wine bottles, and a dented milk jug that said Dipner's Dairy.

He went up and knocked on the storm door. There was no answer and so he pressed his face to the dirty glass. The inside had fared no better than the outside. Trash bags lined the foyer. Chunks of plaster had come away from the lathe and shattered across the floor, and real estate circulars and Twinkie wrappers trailed into the dark recess of the house like bread crumbs.

Upstairs, Moe heard Frank's knock but didn't get up. He couldn't, not since he'd gotten the call from Fitch and had decided to have a second celebratory bottle of strawberry wine instead of his usual one. Not only had he woken to find that he'd pissed himself but also his vision, which was cloudy on a good day, was now dim and tele-scoped. He figured it was probably some nosy Realtor or tax asses-sor—not enough person to haul himself out of bed and risk breaking his neck navigating the steps with the wicked hangover. Let them knock. It was raining and all he wanted to do was lie in bed and lis-ten to the water as it infiltrated the shingles, dripping down the ceil-ing joist, where it would eventually find its way to the plaster heave over the door frame. But the knocking continued until Moe figured he'd better see if it wasn't Fitch, arrived a day or two early.

On the porch Frank was just about to give up when he heard the slow thump of somebody coming down the stairs.

He stepped back, checked his reflection in the window, and when he turned to the door again he saw a chubby gray-haired man stand-ing there, holding a bright orange beach towel wrapped around his waist even though he was wearing tattered Dickies and a pair of milking boots that had been cut off at the ankle. By the way the man moved to open the door, Frank figured he was blind or close to it. Then he saw that the man's eyes were covered with a milky film.

"Who is it?" the man asked. He had exactly three brown teeth in his big wet mouth.

Frank told him that he was looking for a Morris Dipner.

The man straightened up, the towel dropping away to reveal a piss stain.

Moe wiped the crust from the corners of his mouth and said, "That would be me. Who wants to know?" He cleared his throat and spat something brown that arced across the porch and landed with a splat.

Without thinking, Frank answered, "Frank Marshall with the FBI." He thought about correcting himself and making up some lie. But then he caught a whiff of the alcohol and b.o. pouring out of Moe and figured the man wouldn't remember a thing.

"FBI?" Moe said. "What does the FBI want out here?"

"We're doing some background on an old case."

"What old case might that be?"

"I'd rather not say," Frank said, trying to sound both official and routine. "But I can assure you that your cooperation would be greatly appreciated."

The man said nothing and so Frank decided to barrel ahead with his questions, asking him about his service record and how long he'd been living in the house.

Moe answered his questions with a vagueness that would normally have struck Frank as suspicious. But the man groping the door frame with piss all over his pants, shirtsleeves shiny with snot, stringy unwashed hair, and all of three teeth in his mouth looked nothing like the sketch of D. B. Cooper that he'd burned into his memory.

"Oh, and one more thing, Mr. Dipner," Frank said. "Did you jump out of a plane in the service?"

"Only in boot camp," Moe said. "I'm afraid of heights, always have been."

Frank checked his watch and knew he had to get back.

"Were you over there?" Moe asked.

"Over where?"

"If you've got to ask, then you weren't there."

"Oh," Frank said. "No, I . . ."

Moe held up a hand, "I don't wanna hear it. I was lucky, the government only took my eyes."

Frank nodded, unsure what to say next.

Moe stepped across the porch. "You sure you're not a Realtor? I get them slithering around here all the time with their plats."

"No, sir, I'm not, but if you don't mind I'd like to have a look around your property."

"I could sue you for misrepresentation, you know that, don't you?"

Frank laughed. "I promise you, I'm not a Realtor."

"Go on ahead then. I've let it go pretty bad. I hope your tetanus is up-to-date, you're liable to come across some barbed wire."

Frank thanked him and stepped off into the drizzle, and when he looked back, Moe was at the edge of the porch wetting his hand where the water spilled off the eaves and rubbing it against his face and neck.

He had a quick snoop around the barn as the rain, now somewhere between a shower and a downpour, made a marvelous racket on all things metal. He spooked a rabbit and watched it carom between its choices of cover before disappearing under a collapsed shed thick with blackberry bushes. The place reeked of generational misfortune. He could guess the broad sketches easy enough, beginning with the line of rock-hard Dipner dairymen—sunup-to-sundown men who'd battled and toiled to carve a life out of their animals and land only to see the ball dropped by the prodigal son, returned home from the war with deep addictions, night sweats, and zero work ethic. It was hard to assess blame or to come to any sort of conclusion. The old men relied on backbreaking work to prop them up and give shape to the onslaught of seasons. While the son had been blessed early with the knowledge that in the end it didn't matter how early you rose to meet the milk truck or how much shit you mucked or fence you repaired—all of it was eventually a losing battle.

He came to a cinder road that snaked around the barn and looped through more overgrown pastures to a decent-sized creek, which in turn fed into the Washougal and from there to the Columbia, all the way to the ocean. Earlier he might have traced the creek over to the next property line, but he was wet and had developed a cough and so he turned and walked back to his car, where he took out the scribbled list Peck had given him and checked off Dipner's name.

On his way out, something caught Frank's eye, registering only after he'd pulled onto the main road—a flash of some shiny object hanging from a mossy fence post, just where the creek turned under a culvert and began its run to the pasture. A dozen yards later he realized that they had been dog tags, the bead chain long since fused to the wood with moss and rot, and the tags themselves a ghost of their former spit and polish after so many years and so much weather. Had the rain not gone to buckets he might have actually turned around and had a closer look. Instead he tapped the gas pedal, tires spitting mud and gravel as he went to meet Peck and report on his fruitless search.

CHAPTER FOURTEEN

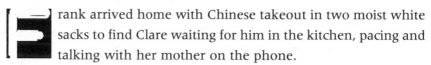rank arrived home with Chinese takeout in two moist white sacks to find Clare waiting for him in the kitchen, pacing and talking with her mother on the phone.

"Where the hell have you been?" she said, covering the receiver.

"Out," he said. He set the food down and went and got himself a beer and listened as she finished the phone call.

"The important thing is he's okay," Clare said. "Yes, he just got back." She looked at him again. "I don't know what happened but I'm going to ask him."

She slammed the phone down and turned to him with an exasperated growl.

"What's the matter?"

"My father wrecked his boat," she said. "And you . . . I left a note telling you he'd called. Didn't you get it?"

"I got it and I called him, but there was nobody home and I had things to do . . ."

"Things to do?" She rolled her eyes. "What things do you have to do?"

"Calm down," he said, putting a hand on her shoulder and feeling her stiffen.

"I'm calm and I hate when you tell me that."

"No, Clare, you're yelling at me."

"I'm not yelling. If you want to hear yelling . . ."

"Okay," he said, his hands up in surrender. "Clare, I'm sorry. I should have called and told you I was going to be late."

She shook her head at him. "Frank, none of this would have happened if you'd have been with him. You told me yourself he doesn't know what the hell he's doing on that boat."

"And I'm sorry," he said. "I mean he's okay, right?"

She took a sip of his beer and nodded. "Yes, he's okay. Now, where have you been all day?"

He told her he'd been with Peck, making it sound like that was all he'd done. And then he asked her to tell him what had happened.

She took another sip of beer. "What happened was that you were supposed to meet him and when you didn't show he took that goddamned boat of his out and ran into another boat. I don't know how bad it is, just that the Coast Guard's got him and I could have used your help tonight. I really could have used your help."

Frank winced and then pointed at the food. "I got takeout." He didn't know why he said it, because it only made her madder.

"I just want you to listen to the messages she left," she said, punching PLAY.

He tried to stop her but then thought better of it and listened to the hysterical messages Mary had left. The last one ended with "Would somebody please call me." Her voice sounded soft and a little ragged, the anger of the two previous messages given way to fear.

"I think we have to go over there," Clare said.

Frank sighed and put the food into the refrigerator, took one last sip of beer, and found his keys. He was hungry and tired, basically in no mood to deal with the scene he knew awaited him at his mother-in-law's house, nor was he up to the car ride over there with Clare because there would be no getting on her good side no matter how much he explained. And so he just drove and let her vent, telling him how she'd been down to the marina and on the phone, first with the state police and then with the Coast Guard, who seemed to view her father's accident with slight bemusement and had told her that he was much too inexperienced to attempt a run out past Cape Disappointment, especially this late in the season. Frank kept quiet and didn't tell her how he'd known all along about her father's plans to take the thirty-six-foot Grand Banks out to blue water.

Mary wasn't much better and he jumped at the chance to drive up to Kelly's Point and retrieve Walt from the Coast Guard station, leaving Clare with her mother, who for the first time he could remember was smoking.

When he arrived Walt was waiting for him, looking sheepish, small, and old. He got in and after some awkward silence gave Frank a full accounting of how his big trip had gone so wrong. "I lost my shit," he said. "I think that would be an accurate description of what happened. I thought I knew what I was doing and then one thing led to the next and I lost my shit. I mean, I panicked, cut left when I should have cut right."

"They impound the boat?"

Walt nodded. "You know, for a while I thought I was really going to do it, make it out to sea, I mean."

"What happened?"

"My trouble started when I decided to dock and call Mary and tell her what I was up to. I was feeling guilty and things were going good and I figured I owed her at least a call. I see this gas island and a marina so I go to take her in and hit some buoys and that rattled me and then I oversteer and before I know it I've bumped into this houseboat."

"Bumped or crashed?"

"Oh, I hit her pretty good," Walt said. "I don't know if you call it a crash, but I did some damage. It's going to cost me."

"Maybe you'd better soft peddle the whole thing to Mary."

"Like it's going to matter. She's gonna clip my wings, and deservedly so."

They spent the rest of the long drive back commiserating about what awaited them. But by the time Frank delivered him back home, Mary was asleep on the couch, her head in Clare's lap. *The Asphalt Jungle* was on the television, the sound turned down low. It was the end, the scene where the horses were gathering around the unlucky and dying crook.

Frank and Clare didn't get home until after three in the morning and collapsed into bed without speaking. But for the first time in weeks he made it through the night, sleeping until somebody started up a leaf blower outside the window. He shut the blinds and went downstairs, leaving Clare to sleep.

In the kitchen he called Cecil, told him of the previous night's excitement, and had him cancel Clare's appointments. Then he called Peck and asked if Brown and Rispoli had come back with anything on the Garvey murder.

"Nothing yet," Peck said. "And if I keep asking Woodrell about it he's going to know something's up. He's on me about my time and I had to tell him a little about this Cooper thing."

"What did he say?" Frank asked.

"Put it this way, he wasn't amused," Peck said. "I told him about the deeds and gave him my theory and he told me the same thing you did."

"What's that?"

"That it's a cold case and I have better things to be wasting my time on."

"You'll call me if you find out anything?"

Peck said he would and they left it at that.

He sat for a long time thinking about Anne, deciding finally that the least he could do was to help her escape to Aspen. Even if what happened to Garvey had nothing to do with Blackwood, he figured she deserved better—had always deserved better.

It wasn't until he'd sampled the cold Chinese takeout that Clare came downstairs still tired, demanding coffee and wanting to know who'd called. When he told her he'd taken care of everything, she smiled and kissed his neck. Things, it seemed, were looking up.

■

LATER THAT MORNING, as Lou gassed up the van, Cooper called Moe to let him know he was close, only to have Moe tell him how the FBI had stopped by.

"Are you fucking with me?" Cooper asked, trying hard not to just bash the phone to little plastic pieces.

"That's what he said. I couldn't see too good and he did want to have a look around."

"Son of a bitch."

"Well, he coulda been a Realtor," Moe said. "You know, they want to chop up the farm and make me rich."

Cooper pressed his head against the phone box, willing himself to think, hoping Moe was just having some paranoid fun with him. He noticed that somebody had scratched "EAT ME" under the coin slot. As Moe continued with his account, he scratched a B in front of the E.

"He said they was doing background on some old case. He left me a card."

"Tell me his name."

"You on the lam or something?" Moe asked.

"No."

"Okay then, supposing it was the Feds—who gives a shit?"

"Can you just find that card for me, buddy?"

He set the phone down and there was a racket on the other end, doors slamming, shit being knocked, and Moe cursing, cocksucker this and cocksucker that. When he came back on the line he said he'd found it but it was too wet to read because he'd left it on the front porch.

"Just save it."

Moe laughed and Cooper said he'd be there soon and hung up.

He said nothing to Lou about the phone conversation and instead checked the map again. He figured they were no more than a tankful of gas away from the farm. He started to plot a way to shake Lou. He made sure he was behind the wheel when they broke over the high desert of eastern Oregon into the riotous heart of the Cascades. The first sight of the heavily timbered hills tinted with fall and rolling on for what seemed forever brought it all back home to Cooper. He remembered how the sky seemed to press down and the rain, always the rain.

An hour north of Bend the day turned ugly. First the low scooting black clouds and then rain farther east, not exactly a storm, more like a routine soaking that would deposit snow in the higher elevations, swell the creeks, and slick the roads.

The sudden rain had forced him to scrap his previous plan of stranding Lou with his bags and a jug of water down a desolate road. What he wanted was some friendly place to make his move. He piloted the van, stealing glances at the map on the dash while Lou manned the tape deck and prattled about nothing.

He found the perfect place when they stopped for a piss and a stretch at a deserted campground. There was a small log shelter with fire warnings and trail maps, gray picnic tables, and concrete fire rings. But most importantly there were no pay phones and the road in looked little used.

Cooper kept the van running and waited until Lou had stumbled out into the relative dry of the log shelter before tossing Lou's backpack out the door and whipping the van around the gravel turnaround.

As he sped away he watched Lou shrug and toss his hands in the air before bending to retrieve his bags and drag them out of the rain. It looked to him as if Lou had been anticipating just such a sneaky move.

What happened next depended on how Lou took the note Cooper had stuffed in his backpack. The note outlined how he'd leave the van at Multnomah Falls in a day or so. He also agreed to pay what he owed as per their handshake agreement, providing he recovered the money.

He figured the plan would work only if Lou didn't run screaming to the police or FBI. On this matter Cooper went with his gut, trusting that Lou, if he didn't try to follow, would at least keep his piehole shut and honor the fraternity of shady brothers in arms. As a bonus he'd left him Book IV, figuring he'd find something of interest or at the very least have a peep at the nude sketches of Jane and the maps that he now knew ultimately led to the big nowhere down in Mexico.

And so he crossed the state line and swung the van along the winding Lewis and Clark highway, under blasted rock walls and past bent guardrails scarred with crash marks. He was thankful for the hiss of rain on the radials; it was the only thing to distract him from the creeping fear that nothing waited for him in Moe's back pasture, nothing except the sight of his fallen-down friend whiling away his days and nights in drunken paranoid reel. That or maybe this phantom FBI man, who he hoped was just a figment of Moe's cooped-up imagination. Whatever the case, he vowed not to linger. Money or no money. What happened after that, happened. He'd come too far to turn back.

■

IT WAS LATE in the afternoon when Woodrell called Frank and asked him to come by the office, saying he had something interesting to show him. So he went upstairs and told Clare where he was going. She reminded him that they were driving up to visit Lucy on Saturday and that she'd made reservations at the Hyatt.

He kissed her and went downstairs to grab his gun from the desk. Then he went out to the garage, where he found the pint of Smirnoff he kept for just such occasions. Before slipping it into his pocket, he wiped the dust off the bottle's shoulders, spun the cap open, and took a belt, letting the liquor fall into his belly. Frank wanted to be loose and ready for Woodrell. He took one more and then crunched up two breath mints and went to the car, stashing both the gun and the bottle under his folded-up rain slicker.

Woodrell was out front having a cigarette under the awning and greeted Frank after taking one last drag and tossing the butt into a nearby puddle. He suggested they get coffee. Frank played it cool and they walked up a couple of blocks to a narrow coffee shop that was cluttered with old record jacket sleeves and corny posters of monster movies. The air smelled like clove cigarettes and strong coffee and there was some sort of scratchy blues playing on the stereo. It didn't take him long to realize they were the oldest people in the place.

Frank waited until they'd taken stools and ordered coffee before asking what was up. It was still raining and he discreetly slipped another mint into his mouth, wondering if maybe he should order a muffin or something to soak up the sour booze boiling around his guts.

Woodrell took his time, shaking and dropping an Equal into his coffee and then stirring it. "You been talking to Peck, right?"

Frank nodded. "A little."

"I take it he's told you about his cockamamie D. B. Cooper theories, right?"

"Oh yeah."

"Don't worry, Frank, I'm not out to bust balls. I know you've been out sniffing around with him and it's okay. He's got lots of energy and, hell, I know he looks up to you because you helped him out and showed him the ropes back when he was just a baby face."

"I guess so." Frank shifted his coffee mug. He was starting to feel uneasy and wished Woodrell would just come out and say what he had to say and stop beating around the bush and giving him the rolling boss cop eyes.

"You have any thoughts on the matter?"

"On Cooper or Peck?"

Woodrell laughed. "Reason I ask is this." He unfolded a piece of tractor-feed paper from inside his jacket and put it on the counter between them. "It's been a crazy fucking week."

Frank read it. It was a report about a disturbance at a diner in Idaho. A man claiming to be D. B. Cooper attacked another man and did several hundred dollars' worth of damage to the place. A description of the men followed. Frank skimmed it and saw that they were driving a van.

"The attending officer recognized Cooper's name and made a few calls and found out he was still officially wanted. Funny how this shit finds its way through the system. I know it's probably nothing but it was weird, especially after I find out Peck's been slipping away and looking up where that kid found the money."

"It was probably just some drunks having a little fun."

Woodrell folded the paper up and set it next to his mug. "Same thing I thought."

They sipped their coffee and watched as a countergirl folded napkins. She had a buzz cut, thin arms, and about two dozen tiny hoop piercings in her ears and more metal around her neck.

"You didn't say anything to Peck about this, did you?"

"Not yet," Woodrell said. "He doesn't need any encouragement. He's a good agent but he shouldn't let this get in the way. As it is, he's got a full plate."

"I told him how many false leads and bad tips we got on the case back when it was hot."

"A lot—I checked," Woodrell said. "You been doing much fishing?"

He said he hadn't.

"What's a matter? You look like twice-baked shit."

"Late night," Frank said. Then he told him about his father-in-law, Walt, and the accident.

"You gotta know what you're doing out there."

"Well, he didn't," Frank said. He drained his coffee and made motions to go, looking outside, the rain still dribbling down the front window.

"Look, Frank, reason I asked to meet is this Blackwood case."

He felt his stomach flop. "Yeah?"

"Well, I don't know what Peck's told you," he started. "Hold on, maybe I oughtta back up."

"Just level with me, Chuck."

He cleared his throat and then told Frank how they knew he'd been over to see Anne. "And I want you to know that it's okay. I mean, it was your case."

"I can explain."

Woodrell swiveled around to face him. "You don't need to explain."

"No, I want to."

"Okay, but really, Frank—"

"I like her and I think she's trying to get her life started, and this stuff with her ex-husband, well, it's not what she needs."

"That's beside the point."

"Let me finish," Frank said.

Woodrell twisted his tie and told him to continue.

"She deserves better and I just don't want to see her slide back into something because of all this. I know it's not my place, but there it is," he said. "And I want you to know absolutely nothing inappropriate happened."

"I didn't think that, and even if I did, well, you're no longer with the Bureau and—"

"I wanted to help her, that's how it all started."

Woodrell reached out and put a hand on Frank's shoulder. "Frank, listen to me—you don't need to explain yourself. All I wanted to know was whether Peck's told you about this Garvey guy they found dead down in Blodgett. That's all."

"He did."

Woodrell let out a breath. "Well then, all I'm saying, and this is friend-to-friend, is that if this Garvey thing turns out like I think it's going to turn out, maybe you should try to keep away. A lot of folks haven't forgotten what Blackwood did and want to catch him pretty bad and if there's any chance of that we need the girl to cooperate."

"She will."

"I just want to be sure about that."

"Peck say something?"

Woodrell pulled out his wallet and dropped four ones on the counter. "No, he didn't." He stood to go. "You take care of yourself. Hit that lake I told you about. You won't be sorry."

Frank forced a smile and shook his hand.

As he watched him go, he still wasn't sure what exactly had happened. One thing he was certain of was that Woodrell hadn't told him everything and there was no reason he should have. He was mad at himself for going on like that, letting Woodrell know more than he needed to know. He also didn't appreciate being talked to like he was some fuckup, a complication to be brushed aside.

The countergirl came over to clear away the mugs and take the money.

"You want more?" she asked, pointing at Frank's mug. He shook his head and pushed the mug across to her and that's when he saw them. Around her neck hung two shiny dog tags and they clinked on the counter as she leaned across to grab the wire report Woodrell had left behind. Frank stared at them, remembering what he'd seen hanging over the post on the busted dairy farm.

"Hello . . . is this yours?" she said, waving the paper in front of him, breaking his gaze.

He nodded, took it from her, and watched as she straightened and tucked the tags back inside her shirt. He knew then that he didn't want to go home, nor did he want to talk to Peck about what Woodrell had just told him. He just wanted to go back to the farm and see about the dog tags he should have checked out in the first place. It would be a small time-killing task but one that his gut told him he had to accomplish. Or maybe it was the vodka, he didn't know.

Outside he flipped up his collar against the rain, and when he retrieved his keys from his pocket he found that the finger bone had wedged itself inside one of the key rings. He dislodged it and went to put it back but stopped and forced himself to take a long, hard look at it. The bone had been polished from years of tumbling alongside loose change, car keys, and the occasional bullet. After all these years it had become just another thing to carry around—a piece of something he should have let be. It had done him no good. He still knew nothing and now even Cooper and his crime had pretty much been forgotten. Without breaking stride, he dropped the bone into a sewer grate and crossed the street.

While he waited for the defroster to clear the windshield he reached under the seat, found the Smirnoff, and had another drink. The liquor pushed some color back into his face as he read the report Woodrell had showed him earlier.

Then he started driving north, getting lucky with the traffic all the way across the Columbia as he turned east into the hills and trees, hoping to get a little clarity on some things.

A LOT HAD CHANGED since Cooper had last seen the Dipner farm. Everything seemed rusted, full of rot, tilted, and tired-looking as if the whole place was just waiting for the bulldozers to come push it down and plow it under. He looked around for some sign of an ambush until he realized he didn't know what he was looking for. It was wet and getting dark and his money was out there and Moe had probably been fucking with him about the FBI guy and, if not, he figured agents had better things to do besides creep around forgotten farms. So he eased the van over the drain culvert and stopped in front of the fence post where he saw his dog tags hanging right where he'd left them thirteen years ago. It was a good sign. He got out and on closer examination saw the Kennedy half-dollar he'd wedged in a crack in the wood. It was nearly part of the post now, and after rousting a few earwigs he pried the coin out and decided to leave the dog tags. He flipped the coin into his pocket, got back in the van, and instead of pulling around to the house veered down the cinder road toward the creek, where he hoped at least some of his money waited for him. He cursed himself for having left even a penny of it, although at the time it seemed an impossible load, just the sheer weight of all those twenties enough to get him caught and sent to jail, where he figured he would not flourish or remake himself into some master criminal. But he'd escaped, and now here he was sneaking around in the rain.

Even through the rain and ground fog he could see the white nose of the Ford Galaxy parked forever beside the rising creek. He got out, goose-stepping over the snarl of baling wire, garden hose, and vines that seemed to sew the whole mess into some unified web. His clothes picked up sticktights and burrs. In the pastures where cows once grazed there were deer and they looked up from their grassy supper, trembled, and then bucked off into the fog. He turned and headed toward the line of abandoned vehicles and farm equipment until he came to the Galaxy. Broad sections of its quarter panels were still impossibly white and there was even some chrome. He cleared the trunk of the bricks, river stones, and rotten barn wood he'd piled over it, only to find that the hinges had rusted shut. He looked around and found a bent stave iron and went to work on the sucker, quiet at first and then swinging and wedging with everything he had until it popped open.

And there it was, just as he'd left it—the drywall bucket and inside the money wrapped in garbage sacks. After wiping away the jungle of spider webs and wayward vines that had found their way inside the trunk, he swung the bucket out and pressed the trash bag until he felt the square edge of bundled twenties. He allowed himself a small silent cheer and sigh of relief, before hustling the bucket back to the van, where he set it beside Rosenbaum's undelivered box.

Even though he was pretty sure the refrigerator was gone, he went back and scouted the small ridge of trash, trying to remember its exact location. He stumbled along the creek until he found the refrigerator door tangled in creek debris fifty yards downstream. It explained how the stash had washed downstream like some message in a bottle all the way to the Columbia, where it had been discovered by the kid. Or at least he thought it did. Either way, it didn't matter, because he figured that what hadn't been washed up had become fish food or maybe fluttered out to the ocean, where salt water and the surf had melted it.

"Fuck it," he said. "All's well that ends well." And with that he turned to go, starting back along the creek bank to where he'd parked the van. Just as he rounded a brush pile he saw a car nose down the cinder road. Its headlights were off and the windshield wipers revealed in brief swipes a tall, stoned-faced man stuffed behind the wheel, looking surprised to see him.

Cooper froze. He had no fucking idea what the car was doing, but he didn't like it and quickly began calculating the distance to the van. The car moved closer and he tried to play it cool and think of some story to explain what he was doing in the pasture. But nothing came. All he knew was that everything he needed was in the van and so he kept walking, the plan being to mind his own business back to the van, get in, and haul ass back to Mexico.

But before he could reach the van, the car cut him off. A man got out. He was holding the dog tags he'd found on the fence post in his left hand.

Cooper sized up the situation. The man walked like a cop—chest puffed out, legs bowed, arms swinging, riding some improbable hunch, but under all that maybe a little tired and, yes, surprised to see another person limping around the brush pile.

"Hey," Frank called out.

Cooper kept walking and got as far as the van door before Frank said, "I bet your friends call you Fitch or maybe D. B., is that it?"

Cooper expected the man to whirl into action, cuff him or pull a gun on him—the whole thing like some crazy, fucked-up bad dream.

"Cooper's fine," he said. "I never liked Fitch much."

He could see it on the man's face, first disbelief and then an awestruck acceptance of the impossible.

For a long time nothing happened, except rain and some mist sealing up both ends of the road like a curtain. Then the man stuck out his hand and said, "Frank, Frank Marshall."

They shook. He had a good, tight grip.

"I take it you're some kind of John Q. Law, am I right?"

Frank dipped his chin, rain spilling off his brow. "I was FBI, but now I'm just wet and cold. Same as you."

Cooper shook his head back and squeezed the rain from his pony-tail, nodding, not sure what his next move should be. He tried to imagine running but figured he'd lose the race and possibly even get himself shot.

"All this reminds me of another day a long time ago."

"Funny, I was just thinking the same thing," Cooper said, grinning. "How did you . . . I mean . . ."

Frank tossed his hands up. "You wouldn't believe me if I told you."

Behind them porch lights clicked on, casting soft shadows over the pasture.

"What happens now?" Cooper asked.

"I don't know, but I have a gun in my car," Frank said. "And some vodka."

"I don't think we need either of those thing," Cooper said, sliding the van door open. "Why don't we talk in here." He waited until Frank had stepped inside and taken a seat before climbing in behind him.

He slid the door shut and it was just the two of them sitting in there, the rain pinging down on the van, bucket of money behind them, and Rosenbaum's box making a strange scratching sound.

Frank wiped the rain from his face.

"Have you been looking for me?" Cooper asked.

"To tell you the truth, I thought you were dead."

"I'm not."

"And I'm not even going to ask why you did it because I was out there looking for you that day you jumped and I didn't really care that much then."

"You were?"

"Yeah, but I found something else instead."

Cooper could tell from the look on the man's face that he shouldn't ask what he'd found.

"I just want to know why you came back."

Cooper looked over his shoulder at the bucket of money.

"I met a woman and one thing led to another and she had me robbed and no way was I staying in Mexico and getting a job."

"So you stashed some of the money?"

Cooper nodded.

"Smart. Anything else you wanna tell me?"

"I guess you could say I had a pretty good run. I didn't die and I had some laughs."

"I've never been to Mexico," Frank said. "Is it nice?"

"I had a little house on the beach, a few friends. I could sleep till noon and drink beer whenever I wanted and eat sausage for dinner. The sunsets were nice and the locals weren't too bad. Yeah, I suppose I did okay for myself. I mean, it's not like I was going anywhere up here."

"What's in the box?" Frank said, pointing at Rosenbaum's box. "If that's your stash, it's making noise."

"The money's in the bucket," Cooper said. "Look, are you gonna arrest me or what?"

"That depends," he said. He was quiet then.

"Depends on what?"

He didn't answer and Cooper clicked on a dome light to get a better look at his face. "Is there something the matter? I mean, you don't look too good."

"You're the second person who's told me that."

"It's just an observation, and if you aren't going to arrest me, I'd like to know what you're doing up here."

Frank looked at him quietly a minute and then shook his head and began telling Cooper his problems, starting with the pond girl, Clare, the job and finishing up with Anne and J. B. and the kiss.

Cooper listened. It made a fractured kind of sense, but then logic had never been one of his strong suits. He had no words of wisdom or tricky little parables to relate in the hopes of solving this man's problems and he supposed that wasn't the point, but by the time Frank finished, the rain had stopped and the windows were fogged and he looked lighter, as if in the telling some solution had presented itself that did not involve arrest. "One more thing," Frank said, pointing at the T-shirt Lou had given him. "That supposed to mean something?"

Cooper looked down at the black zero, shrugged, and said, "Probably, but I borrowed it. Same with the van. I suppose it could mean anything you want it to mean."

Frank then told him about the police report of the diner disturbance and how there was this young FBI agent infatuated with the case who'd dragged him up here looking for clues.

"He gonna know about this?"

Frank shook his head. "I think it's better for him if you're still out there, at large. Now, how much money you have in that bucket?"

"Forty thousand, give or take a few thousand."

"And can you get by on that?"

"For a while. The exchange rate's in my favor. But sooner or later I'm going to have to make another move or maybe even get a job."

Frank shuffled to the back of the van and dragged the bucket up between them. "I want to see it."

Cooper looked at him, not sure what he was asking.

"The money," Frank said. "I want to see it."

Cooper told him to go ahead and have a look if he wanted. "It's just money." He made no move to stop Frank as he gently unwound the bag and peered in. "But if you're gonna rob me, I'll be forced to take the appropriate action."

Frank looked up from the bucket and smiled. "I'm not a thief, but I am gonna ask you for a donation to a worthy cause."

"What's in it for me?"

Frank grinned. "Well, we shake hands and you go get lost again and do whatever it is you've been doing."

"You mean you're gonna let me go?"

"It would be like we never even met."

"I think I'd like that."

"Well?"

"How much are you talking? I mean, I've come a long way. It hasn't been a cakewalk."

"Well, neither has my last couple of months," Frank said. "But I'd say five thousand oughta do it."

"And can I ask what you need it for?"

"I'd rather not say."

Cooper thought about it, not sure if the man was just having some fun with him, dangling a deal only to snatch it away. "Let me get this straight," he said. "I give you five thousand dollars and you let me walk?"

"That sounds about right."

"What kind of lawman are you?"

But Frank didn't answer that. Instead he set out several bricks of bills and stuck out his hand. "Do we have a deal?"

"Do I have a choice?"

"Of course you do," Frank said. "But I think it's better for the both of us if you take the deal."

Cooper nodded. They shook on it. Then Frank popped open the van door and stepped out.

"That's it?"

"It was good meeting you." And with that Frank shut the door and walked through the mud to his car, the money tucked under his jacket.

FRANK WAITED UNTIL after dark before he crept up to Anne's trailer and set the envelope inside the screen door. The envelope contained five thousand in musty twenty-dollar bills and a note that read "Go to Aspen." He was sober and tired and did not bother to look in the dark trailer windows to see her. He just left, walking along the road to where he'd parked the Buick. The moon was behind some fast-moving clouds and he could see his breath puffing away out in front of him. A dog broke silently from the shadows and trailed him for fifty yards before it peeled off after a cat. The only noise was the hum of a television from a nearby trailer and the wind stirring up dead leaves into dramatic little whorls. He did not look back or think about what might happen next. Although two weeks later Peck would shoot J. B. Blackwood dead and Frank would stop by one chilly morning to help Anne load boxes. And she would thank him and give him a hug that scared him.

But for now he drove home and found Clare waiting for him and didn't even bother telling her where he'd been. She was mad and confused and tired of his little breakdown. The look she gave him said it all.

So he lumbered into the laundry room and stepped out of his muddy and wet clothes and changed into some fresh ones and then went to sit next to his wife on the couch, with the knowledge that whatever he said or did this night or even the next would simply be inadequate. What was needed was a slow turning until he was once again just dependable, steady, and even-keeled Frank Marshall. It was just about the only way he could figure out how to make it back.

ON HIS WAY to drop off the van, Cooper pulled over and waited to see if there were any unmarked police cars or copters tailing him. There were none and so he stepped out to take a leak, his hands still shaking as he puzzled over the strange meeting with Frank.

He shook, zipped, and shivered and kicked his legs until he felt blood coming back into them. Then he opened the back door of the van and hid the drywall bucket under an old army blanket as a trac-tor trailer hissed by, its taillights blinking a warm red. He had another look at Rosenbaum's box, shaking it until he felt something stir in-side.

Curious, he found a utility knife, slit the packing tape, and pulled back the flaps to reveal a clear plastic case. Inside the case were thou-sands of teeming wine-colored ants and across the top was a piece of tape with Latin written on it. He figured it was some old fancy name for the ants and tore it off.

Then he held the box up to the dim van light and watched the ants crawl all over one another. It was hard to tell if they wanted out or if they were just enjoying the scrum, reveling in their common destiny. He watched them for a long time, the headlights of oncoming cars momentarily lighting up the box like an X-ray machine until he could see right through them to his hand holding the box on the other side. The ants looked hungry.

Cooper thought a minute. The ants were probably intended for some elaborate torture or confinement in a bug enthusiast's dank basement. He could change that—it was the least he could do. Lou would get the van and some bucks for his troubles, but the ants had a lucky turn coming.

And so he grabbed a flashlight and tucked the box under his arm, determined to set them free.

After locking the van, he walked into the woods and scrambled up a narrow game trail, dodging rotten logs and low-slung branches, until he came to a small depression surrounded by the dark outline of trees, their limbs throbbing with rain. He heard animals retreating from him through the wet underbrush and saw in the distance the dim glow of a house tucked away in the trees. His shirt was wet, his socks soaked, the air tasted like exhaust, and he couldn't stop thinking of how close he'd come with the agent back there on Moe's farm. He'd dodged something, and although he was five thousand dollars poorer, he was still at large and liked the way that sounded. The headline D. B. COOPER STILL AT LARGE AFTER ALL THESE YEARS!! ripped around his own private newsroom.

He figured that if he were the boss ant this dark and sheltered patch of woods would be as good a place as any to start over. So he knelt on a bed of pine needles and pried open the box. For a minute nothing happened. The ants seemed to shrink together, huddling as if discussing their next move.

Impatient, he shook the box and tipped it on its side, watching as they finally poured forth from their confinement. He expected them to disappear into the mulch but instead they began massing into an undulating fist-shaped pool, their shiny shell backs catching tiny bits of light.

"Go," he said. "Get out of here." He looked around, feeling foolish for talking to the ants.

He bent down and blew on them, but they wouldn't budge and

seemed to be waiting for something. He checked the box and discovered the queen lying on her back, her too-small legs grasping at
nothing but air. He shook the box gently. She slid out and landed
atop the mosh pit of antennas and outstretched legs and was quickly
carried away on the river of her subjects into the damp Pacific Northwest woods, ready for empire or slow, cold death—he did not know.

He followed their progress with the flashlight beam until they disappeared and were gone and it was just him alone in the woods,
good deed done and all that. Only then did he pick his way back
down to the van, ready to get back to Mexico and settle on some new
sandy beach, get warm and tan and anonymous again until he could
figure out the next move. Because after all the hiding and running
around looking for that elusive something, it occurred to him that
perhaps there would always be a general lack, a slackness in everything, and that life was just an elaborate shuck and jive.

But for the moment he was on the roam.

ACKNOWLEDGMENTS

Many thanks to my brutally honest agent, Sloan Harris. Also big thanks to retired FBI agent Sean McWeeney, retired FBI agent and D. B. Cooper expert Ralph Himmelsbach, Leah Stewart, Tom and Charlotte, Phil and Karen Moore, Kendra Harpster, and road friend Harlan Auer. This book would not have been possible without the generous support both financial and alcoholic of the folks at the Sewanee Writers' Conference and the Tennessee Williams Foundation—Wyatt Prunty, Cheri Peters, and Phil "Sleep 'n Eat" Stephens.